tricks

Also by Ellen Hopkins

Crank

Impulse

Burned

Glass

Identical

Fallout

Perfect

Margaret K. McElderry Books

tricks

Ellen Hopkins

Margaret K. McElderry Books
NEW YORK   LONDON   TORONTO   SYDNEY   NEW DELHI

MARGARET K. McELDERRY BOOKS

An imprint of Simon & Schuster Children's Publishing Division

1230 Avenue of the Americas, New York, New York 10020

This book is a work of fiction. Any references to historical events, real people, or real locales are used fictitiously. Other names, characters, places, and incidents are products of the author's imagination, and any resemblance to actual events or locales or persons, living or dead, is entirely coincidental.

Copyright © 2009 by Ellen Hopkins

All rights reserved, including the right of reproduction in whole or in part in any form.

MARGARET K. McELDERRY BOOKS is a trademark of Simon & Schuster, Inc.

For information about special discounts for bulk purchases, please contact Simon & Schuster Special Sales at 1-866-506-1949 or business@simonandschuster.com.

The Simon & Schuster Speakers Bureau can bring authors to your live event. For more information or to book an event, contact the Simon & Schuster Speakers Bureau at 1-866-248-3049 or visit our website at www.simonspeakers.com.

Book edited by Emma D. Dryden

Book design by Sammy Yuen Jr.

The text for this book is set in Trade Gothic Condensed 18.

Manufactured in the United States of America

10 9 8 7 6 5 4 3 2 1

The Library of Congress has cataloged the hardcover edition as follows:

Hopkins, Ellen.

Tricks / Ellen Hopkins.

p. cm.

Summary: Five troubled teenagers fall into prostitution as they search for freedom, safety, community, family, and love.

ISBN 978-1-4169-5007-3 (hc)

[1. Novels in verse. 2. Family problems—Fiction. 3. Emotional problems—Fiction. 4. Prostitution—Fiction.] I. Title.

PZ7.5.H67Tr 2009

[Fic]—dc22

2009020297

ISBN 978-1-4169-5008-0 (pbk)

ISBN 978-1-4169-9642-2 (eBook)

This book is dedicated to the fine members of law enforcement, social work, and the judiciary who truly care about young people forced to walk the streets in search of simple sustenance. With a major nod to Randy Sutton of the Las Vegas P.D., Judge William Voy, and Children of the Night.

Special thanks must also go to three amazing friends, exceptional writers Susan Hart Lindquist, Jim Averbeck, and Suzanne Morgan Williams, who push me to reach ever deeper for the very best stories I'm capable of writing. This book is better because of them. And my life is better because they are in it.

tricks

A Poem by Eden Streit
Eyes Tell Stories

But do they know how
to craft fiction? Do
they know how to spin

lies?

His eyes swear forever,
flatter with vows of only
me. But are they empty

promises?

I stare into his eyes, as
into a crystal ball, but
I cannot find forever,

only

movies of yesterday,
a sketchbook of today,
dreams of a shared

tomorrow.

His eyes whisper secrets.
But are they truths or fairy tales?
I wonder if even he

knows.

Eden
Some People

Never find the right kind of love.
You know, the kind that steals

your breath away, like diving into snowmelt.
The kind that jolts your heart,

sets it beating apace, an anxious
hiccuping of hummingbird wings.

The kind that makes every terrible
minute apart feel like hours. Days.

Some people flit from one possibility
to the next, never experiencing the incredible

connection of two people, rocked by destiny.
Never knowing what it means to love

someone else more than themselves.
More than life itself, or the promise

of something better, beyond this world.
More, even (forgive me!) than God.

Lucky me. I found the right kind
of love. With the wrong person.

Not Wrong for Me

No, not at all. Andrew is pretty much
perfect. Not gorgeous, not in a male

model kind of way, but he is really cute,
with crazy hair that sometimes hides

his eyes, dark chocolate eyes that hold
laughter, even when he's deadly serious.

He's not a hunk, but toned, and tall enough
to effortlessly tuck me under his arms,

arms that are gentle but strong from honest
ranch work, arms that make me feel

safe when they gather me in. It's the only
time I really feel wanted, and the absolute

best part of any day is when I manage
to steal cherished time with Andrew.

No, he's not even a little wrong for me
except maybe—maybe!—in the eyes

of God. But much, much worse than that,
he's completely wrong for my parents.

See, My Papa

Is a hellfire-and-brimstone-preaching
Assembly of God minister, and Mama

is his not-nearly-as-sweet-as-she-seems
right-hand woman, and by almighty God,

their daughters (that's me, Eden, and my
little sister, Eve—yeah, no pressure at all)

will toe the Pentecostal line. Sometimes
Eve and I even pretend to talk in tongues,

just to keep them believing we're heaven-
bound, despite the fact that we go to public school

(Mama's too lazy to homeschool) and come
face-to-face with the unsaved every day.

But anyway, my father and mother
maintain certain expectations when

it comes to their daughters' all-too-human
future plans and desires.

> Papa: *Our daughters will find
> husbands within their faith.*
>
> Mama: *Our daughters will not
> date until they're ready to marry.*

You Get My Dilemma

I'm definitely not ready to marry,
so I can't risk letting them know

I'm already dating, let alone dating
a guy who isn't born-again, and even

worse, doesn't believe he needs to be.
Andrew is spiritual, yes. But religious?

> *Religion is for followers,* he told
> me once. *Followers and puppets.*

> At my stricken look, he became not
> quite apologetic. *Sorry. But I don't*

> *need some money-grubbing preacher*
> *defining my relationship with God.*

At the time, I was only half in love
with Andrew and thought I needed

definitions. "What, exactly, *is* your
relationship with our Heavenly Father?"

> He gently touched my cheek, smiled.
> *First off, I don't think God is a guy.*

> *Some Old Testament–writing fart*
> *made that up to keep his old lady*

5

in line. He paused, then added, *Why
would God need a pecker, anyway?*

Yes, he enjoyed the horrified look
on my face. More laughter settled

into those amazing eyes, creasing
them at the corners. So sexy!

*Anyway, I relate to God in a very
personal way. Don't need anyone*

*to tell me how to do it better. I see
His hand everywhere—in red sunrises*

*and orange sunsets; in rain, falling
on thirsty fields; in how a newborn*

*lamb finds his mama in the herd. I thank
God for these things. And for you.*

After that, I was a lot more than
halfway in love with Andrew.

The Funny Thing Is

We actually met at a revival, where nearly
everyone was babbling in tongues,

or getting a healthy dose of Holy Spirit
healing. Andrew's sister, Mariah, had

forsaken her Roman Catholic roots
in favor of born-again believing and had

dragged her brother along that night,
hoping he'd find salvation. Instead

he found me, sitting in the very back
row, half grinning at the goings-on.

> He slid into an empty seat beside me.
> *So . . . ,* he whispered. *Come here often?*

I hadn't noticed him come in, and when
I turned to respond, my voice caught

in my throat. Andrew was the best-looking
guy to ever sit next to me,

let alone actually say something to me.
In fact, I didn't know they came that cute

in Idaho. A good ten seconds passed before
I realized he had asked a question.

"I . . . uh . . . well, yes, in fact I come here
fairly regularly. See the short guy up there?"

I pointed toward Papa, who kept the crowd
chanting and praying while the visiting evangelist

busily laid on his hands. "He's the regular
preacher and happens to be my father."

Andrew's jaw fell. He looked back and
forth, Papa to me. *You're kidding, right?*

His consternation surprised me. "No,
not kidding. Why would you think so?"

He measured me again. *It's just . . . you look
so normal, and this . . .* He shook his head.

I leaned closer to him, and for the first
time inhaled his characteristic scent—

clean and somehow green, like the alfalfa
fields I later learned he helps work for cash.

I dropped my voice very low. "Promise not
to tell, but I know just what you mean."

It Was a Defining Moment

For me, who had never dared confess
that I have questioned church dogma

for quite some time, mostly because I am
highly aware of hypocrisy and notice

it all too often among my father's flock.
I mean, how can you claim to walk

in the light of the Lord when you're
cheating on your husband or stealing

from your best friend/business partner?
Okay, I'm something of a cynic.

But there was more that evening—instant
connection, to a guy who on the surface

was very different from me. And yet,
we both knew instinctively that we needed

something from each other. Some people might
call it chemistry—two parts hydrogen,

one part oxygen, voilà! You've got water.
A steady trickle, building to a cascade.

If Andrew

Was the poser type, things would
probably be easier. I mean, if he could

pretend to accept the Lord into his heart,
on my father's strictest of terms, maybe

we could be seen together in public—not
really dating, of course. Not without a ring.

But Andrew is the most honest person
I've ever met, and deadly honest that night.

> *Did you* have *to come to this thing?*
> *It seems kind of, um . . . theatrical.*

We had slipped out the back door,
when everyone's attention turned to

some unbelievable miracle at the front
of the church. I smiled. "Theatrical.

That sums it up pretty well, I guess.
You probably couldn't see it in back, but . . ."

I glanced around dramatically, whispered,
"Brother Bradley even wears makeup!"

> Andrew laughed warmly. *So why do*
> *you come, then? Pure entertainment?*

I shrugged. "Certain expectations are
attached to the 'pastor's daughter' job

description. Easier just to meet them, or
at least pretend they don't bother you."

It was early November, and the night wore
a chill. I shivered at the nip in the air,

or at the sudden magnetic pull I felt toward
this perfect stranger. Without a second

thought, Andrew took off his leather
jacket, eased it around my shoulders.

> *Cool tonight,* he observed. *All
> the signs point to a hard winter.*

He was standing very close to me.
I sank into that earthy green aura, looked

up into his eyes. "You don't believe in
miracles, but you do believe in signs?"

> His eyes didn't stray an inch. *Who
> says I don't believe in miracles?*

> *They happen every day.* And I think
> we both knew that one just might have.

11

It Was Unfamiliar Turf

I mean, of course I'd thought guys were cute
before, and the truth is, I'd even kissed

a few. But they'd all been "kiss and run,"
and none had come sprinting back for seconds.

Probably because most of the guys here
at Boise High know who my father is.

But Andrew went to Borah High, clear
across town, and he graduated last year.

He's a freshman at Boise State, where his mom
teaches feminist theory. Yes, she and his rancher

dad make an odd couple. Love is like that.
Guess where his progressive theories came from.

That makes him nineteen, all the more reason
we have to keep our relationship discreet.

In Idaho, age of consent is eighteen,
and my parents wouldn't even think

twice about locking him up for statutory.
That horrible thought has crossed my mind

more than once in the four months since
Andrew decided to take a chance on me.

Four Months

Of him coming to church with Mariah,
both of us patiently wading through Papa's

sermons, then waiting for post-services coffee
hours to slip separately out the side doors, into

the thick stand of riverside trees for a walk.
Conversation. After a while, we held hands

as we ducked in between the old cottonwoods,
grown skeletal with autumn. We joked about

how soon we'd have to bring our own leaves
for cover. And then one day Andrew stopped.

He pleated me into his arms, burrowed his face
in my hair, inhaled. *Smells like rain,* he said.

My heart quickstepped. He wanted to kiss
me. That scared me. What if I wasn't good?

> His lips brushed my forehead, the pulse
> in my right temple. *Will I burn if I kiss you?*

I was scared, but not of burning, and I wanted
that kiss more than anything I'd ever wanted

in my life. "Probably. And I'll burn with you.
But it will be worth it." I closed my eyes.

It was cold that morning, maybe thirty
degrees. But Andrew's lips were feverish

against mine. It was the kiss in the dream
you never want to wake up from—sultry,

fueled by desire, and yet somehow innocent,
because brand-new, budding love was the heart

of our passion. Andrew lifted me gently
in his sinewy arms, spun me in small circles,

lips still welded to mine. I'd never known
such joy, and it all flowed from Andrew.

And when we finally stopped, I knew
my life had irrevocably changed.

Day by Day

I've grown to love him more and more.
Now, though I haven't dared confess

it yet, I'm forever and ever in love with
him. After I tell him (if I ever find the nerve),

I'll have to hide it from everyone. Boise,
Idaho, isn't very big. Word gets around.

Can't even tell Eve. She's awful about
keeping secrets. Good thing she goes to

middle school, where she isn't privy
to what happens here at Boise High.

I'm sixteen, a junior. A year and a half,
and I'll be free to do whatever I please.

For now, I'm sneaking off to spend
a few precious minutes with Andrew.

I duck out the exit, run down the steps,
hoping I don't trip. Last thing I need

is an emergency room visit when I'm
supposed to be in study hall. Around one

corner. Two. And there's his Tundra across
the street, idling at the curb. He spots me

and even from here, I can see his face
light up. Glance left. No one I know.

Right. Ditto. No familiar faces or cars.
I don't even wait for the corner,

but jaywalk midblock at a furious
pace, practically dive through the door

and across the seat, barely saying hello
before kissing Andrew like I might

never see him again. Maybe that's because
always, in the back of my mind, I realize

that's a distinct possibility, if we're ever
discovered kissing like this. One other

thought branded into my brain is that maybe
kissing like this will bring God's almighty wrath

crashing down all around us. I swear, God,
it's not just about the delicious electricity

coursing through my veins. It's all about love.
And you are the source of that, right? Amen.

A Poem by Seth Parnell
Possibilities

As a child, I was wary,
often felt cornered.
To escape, I regularly
stashed myself

        in the closet,

comforted by curtains
of cotton. Silk. Velour.
Avoided wool, which
encouraged my

        itching

the ever-present rashes
on my arms, legs. My skin
reacted to secrets, lies,
and taunts by wanting

        to break out.

Now I hide behind
a wall of silence, bricked
in by the crushing
desire to confess,

        but afraid of

my family's reaction.
Fearful I don't have
the strength to survive

        the fallout.

Seth
As Far Back

As I can remember,
        I have known that
        I was different. I think
        I was maybe five
when I decided that.

I was the little boy
        who liked art projects
        and ant farm tending
        better than riding bikes
or playing army rangers.

Not easy, coming from
        a long line of farmers and
        factory workers. Dad's big
        dream for his only son has
always been tool and die.

My dream is liberal arts,
        a New Agey university.
        Berkeley, maybe. Or,
        even better, San Francisco.
But that won't happen.

Not with Mom Gone

She was the one who
    supported my escape
    plan. *You reach for your*
    dreams, she said. *Factory*
work is killing us all.

Factory work may
    have jump-started it,
    but it was cancer that
    took my mom, one year
and three months ago.

At least she didn't
    have to find out about
    me. She loved me, sure,
    with all her heart. Wanted
me to be happy, with all her

heart. But when it came to
    sex, she was all Catholic
    in her thinking. Sex was
    for making babies, and only
after marriage. I'll never forget

what she said when my cousin
        Liz got pregnant. She was just
        sixteen and her boyfriend hauled
        his butt out of town, all the way
to an army base in Georgia.

        Mom got off the phone with
                Aunt Josie, clucking like a hen.
                Who would have believed
                our pretty little Liz would
        grow up to be such a whore?

        I thought that was harsh,
                and told her so. She said,
                flat out, *Getting pregnant*
                without getting married first
        makes her a whore in God's eyes.

I knew better than to argue
          with Mom, but if she felt
          that strongly about unmarried
          sex, no way could I ever let
her know about me, suffer

the disgrace that would have
          followed. Beyond Mom,
          Indiana's holier-than-thou
          conservatives hate "fags" almost
as much as those freaks in Kansas

do—the ones who picket dead
          soldiers' funerals, claiming
          their fate was God's way of
          getting back at gays. How in
the hell are the two things related?

And Anyway

If God were inclined
        to punish someone
        just for being the way
        he created them, it would
be punishment enough

to insert that innocent
        soul inside the womb
        of a native Indianan.
        These cornfields and
gravel roads are no place

for someone like me.
        Considering almost every
        guy I ever knew growing up
        is a total jock, with no plans
for the future but farming

or assembly-line work,
        it sure isn't easy to fit in
        at school, even without
        overtly jumping out of
that frigging closet.

I can't even tell Dad,
        though I've come very
        close a couple of times,
        in response to his totally
cliché homophobic views:

Bible says God made
              Adam and Eve, not Adam
              and Steve, and no damn
              bleeding-heart liberal
gonna tell me different.

Most definitely not *this*
              bleeding-heart liberal.
              Of course, Dad has no clue
              that's what I am. Or have
become. Because of *who*

I am, all the way inside,
              the biggest part of me,
              the part I need to hide.
              Wonder what he'd say
if I told him the first person

to recognize what I am
              was a priest. Father Howard
              knew. Took advantage, too.
              Maybe I'll confess it all
to Dad someday. But not

while he's still grieving
              over Mom. I am too.
              And if I lost my dad
              because of any of this, I really
don't know what I'd do.

So I Keep the Real Seth

Mostly hidden away.
        It is spring, a time of hope,
        locked in the rich loam
        we till and plant. Corn.
Maize. The main ingredient

in American ethanol,
        the fuel of the future, and
        so it fuels our dreams. It's
        a cold March day, but the sun
threatens to thaw me,

like it has started to thaw
        the ground. The big John
        Deere has little trouble
        tugging the tiller, turning
the soil, readying it for seed.

I don't mind this work.
        There's something satisfying
        about the submission, dirt
        to churning blades. Submission,
yes, and almost as ancient

as the submission of one
        beast, throat up to another.
        One human, facedown
        to another. And always,
always another, hungering.

Hunger

Drives the beast, human
      or otherwise, and it is
      the essence of humanity.
      Hunger for food. Power.
Sex. All tangled together.

It was hunger that made
      me post a personal ad
      on the Internet. Hunger
      for something I knew
I could never taste here.

Hunger that put me on
      the freeway to Louisville,
      far away enough to promise
      secrecy unattainable at home.
Hunger that gave me

the courage to knock on
      a stranger's door. Looking
      back, I realize the danger.
      But then I felt invincible.
Or maybe just starved.

I'd Dated Girls, of Course

Trying to convince
        myself the attraction
        toward guys I'd always felt
        was just a passing thing.
Satan, luring me with

the promise of a penis.
        I'd even fallen for a female.
        Janet Winkler was dream-girl
        pretty and sweeter than
just-turned apple cider.

But love and sexual desire
        don't always go hand in hand.
        Luckily, Janet wasn't looking
        to get laid, which worked out
just fine. After a while,

though, I figured / should
        be looking to get laid, like
        every other guy my age. So
        why did the thought of sex
with Janet—who I believed

I loved, even—not turn
        me on one bit? Worse, why
        did the idea of sex with her
        Neanderthal jock big brother
turn me on so completely?

Not that Leon Winkler
       is particularly special.
       Not good-looking. Definitely
       not the brightest bulb in the
socket. What he does have

going on is a fullback's
       physique. Pure muscle.
       (That includes inside his
       two-inch-thick skull.) I'd catch
myself watching his butt,

thinking it was perfect.
       Something not exactly
       hetero about that. Weird
       thing was, that didn't
bother me. Well, except for

the idea someone might
       notice how my eyes often
       fell toward the rhythm
       of his exit. I never once
lusted for Janet like that.

I tried to let her down
       easy. Gave her the ol'
       "It's not you, it's me"
       routine. But breaking up
is never an easy thing.

Not Easy for Janet

Who never saw it coming.
When I told her, she looked
as if she'd been run over
by a bulldozer. *But you
told me you love me.*

"I do love you," I said.
"But things are, well . . .
confusing right now. You
know my mom is sick. . . ."
Can't believe I used

her cancer as an excuse
to try and smooth things
over. And it worked, to
a point, anyway. At least
it gave Janet something

to hold on to. *I know, Seth.
But don't you think you
need someone to . . . ?*
The denial in my eyes
spoke clearly. She tried

another tactic, sliding
her arms around my neck,
seeking to comfort me. Then
she kissed me, and it was
a different kind of kiss

than any we'd shared
            before. Swollen with desire.
            Demanding. Lips still locked
            to mine, she murmured, *What
if I give you this . . . ?*

Her hand found my own,
            urged it along her body's
            contours, all the way to
            the place between her legs,
the one I had never asked for.

To be honest, I thought
            about doing it. What if it
            cured my confusion after all?
            In the heat of the moment,
I even got hard, especially

when Janet touched me,
            dropped onto her knees,
            lowered my zipper, started
            to do what I never suspected
she knew how to do. Yes . . .

No! Shouldn't . . . How . . . ?
            The haze in my brain
            cleared instantly, and I pushed
            her away. "No. I can't,"
was all I could say.

All Janet Could Say

Before she stalked off
        was, *Up yours! What are
        you, anyway? Gay?* Not
        really expecting a response,
she pivoted sharply, went

in search of moral support.
        So she never heard me say,
        way under my breath, "Maybe
        I *am* gay." It was time, maybe
past, to find out for sure.

But not in Perry County,
        Indiana, where if you're
        not related to someone,
        you know someone who
is. All fact here is rooted

in gossip, and gossip can
        prove deadly. Like last year,
        little Billy Caldwell told Nate
        Fisher that he saw Nate's mom
kissing some guy out back

of a tavern. Total lie, but
        that didn't help Nate's mom
        when Nate's dad went looking
        for her, with a loaded shotgun.
Caught up to her after Mass

Sunday morning, and when
          he was done, that church
          parking lot looked like a street
          in Baghdad. After, Billy felt
kind of bad. But he blamed

Nate's dad one hundred percent.
          Not Nate, who took out
          his grief on Billy's hunting
          dog. That hound isn't much
good for hunting now, not

with an eye missing. Since
          I'd really like to hang on
          to both of my eyes and all
          of my limbs, I figured I'd
better find my true self

somewhere other than Perry
          County. Best way I could
          think of was through the
          "be anyone you choose to be"
possibilities of online dating.

Granted, One Possibility

Was hooking up with a creep—
        a pervert, looking to spread
        some incurable disease to some
        poor, horny idiot. I met more
than one pervert, but I never

let them do me. Nope, horny
        or not, I wasn't an idiot. No
        homosexual yokel, anxious
        enough to get laid to let any
guy who swung the correct

direction into my jeans.
        I wanted my first real sex
        to be with the right guy. Someone
        experienced enough to teach
me, but not humiliate me.

Someone good-looking.
        Young. Educated. A good
        talker, yes, but a good listener,
        too. Someone maybe even
hoping to fall in love.

Incredibly

Unimaginably, Loren turned
       out to be all those things,
       and I found him in Louisville!
       He opened my eyes to a wider
world, introduced me to the

avant-garde—performance art,
       nude theater, alternative
       lit. He gave me a taste
       for caviar, pâté, excellent
California cabernet. After

years of fried chicken and
       Pabst Blue Ribbon, such
       adjustments could only be
       born of love. Truthfully,
love was unexpected. I've

said it before, and I'll repeat,
       I didn't fall out of the tree
       yesterday. But that first day,
       when Loren opened his door,
I took one look and fell

flat on my face. Figuratively,
       of course. I barely stumbled
       as I crossed the threshold—
       into his apartment, and into
the certainty of who I am.

A Poem by Whitney Lang
Stumbling

I only have one question,
scraping the inside of me.
Answer it, and I will

stumble

back into her shadow.
Shut my mouth, never
ask again. I've tried to
ignore it, but it won't go

away.

It haunts my dreams,
chases me through
every single day, and I

don't

have the strength to
turn around. Face it
down. So please tell me
and I swear I'll never

ask

again. It's in your
power to make it go
away. And all you have
to do is tell me

why

you love her more.

Whitney
Living in Someone's Shadow

Totally blows. Don't get
me wrong. I love my sister.
Just not as much as my mother
loves her. Doesn't matter how

hard I try, I can never quite
measure up to Kyra. I'm pretty.
She's beautiful. I'm smart.
She's a genius. I can sing

a tolerable alto. She'll solo,
lead soprano, at the Met.
Mom's own failed dreams
resurrected in Kyra.

And speaking of dreams,
mine are small. *Shortsighted,*
Mom calls them. Interior
design, maybe. Or fashion.

Kyra, however, is majoring
in International Relations.
I don't get it. What does
she want to be? A spy?

I thought things would get
better when she went off
to Vassar. Two thousand,
three hundred and fifty-six

miles away from Santa Cruz,
the pretentious California beach
town where we live. But no
amount of miles can make

her shadow disappear. It's
only longer, stretched across
the continent. Her on one side.
Me stuck fast on the other.

It's Not So Bad

When my dad's home. He's an
investment banker in the fine
old city of San Francisco.
Too far to commute every day,

so he keeps an apartment there
four nights a week, comes home
for regular three-day weekends.
Used to be regular, anyway.

My dad's my hero, and when
he's home he makes Mom stay
off my ass. I don't say words
like "ass" when he's around.

Don't want him to think I'm
a "foul-mouthed bitch," as my
mom enjoys calling me. Wonder
where I got the mouth from.

Anyway, Daddy loves me,
and if he happens to play
favorites, the dice usually roll
my way. Probably just making

up for Mom. But hey, that's
okay. One out of two ain't bad.
I just hate when they argue.
Because it's usually about me.

More and More Lately

It seems like Mom makes
a point of staying gone when
Daddy's home. She golfs. Plays
tennis. Spends hours at the gym.

Sometimes she visits a friend
in Monterey. I assume a female
friend, but wouldn't put it past Mom
to have a thing going on the side.

Pretty sure she doesn't have a bi
side, but whatever floats her lead-
bottomed boat, as long as it means
she's hanging out anywhere but here.

I love when it's just Daddy and me.
Usually it's here in SC, but once
in a while, I'll go into the city,
spend the weekend with him there.

San Francisco has to be the most
beautiful place in the world, with
its stunning old homes, stacked
like Legos on its incredibly steep

hills. There are museums. Galleries.
The symphony and the ballet.
Daddy has taught me to appreciate
all of these things, and not give

a sideways glance at SF's uglier
underbelly. Homeless people.
Panhandlers. Drug dealers, pimps,
and Tenderloin freaks, often only

a street or two removed from
the thriving business district
and the vibrant waterfront tourist
traffic. A city of enigmas.

I like enigmas. I mean, face
it. Semi-absent father. Absent-
for-the-moment sister. Totally
absent mother, not a whole lot

of affection, but plenty of time
all on my own, I'm a walking,
talking poster child for early
promiscuity. Aren't I?

Well, Not Exactly

See, between the longtime local
hype about AIDS and a real-time
example of how rotten young
mothering can make a person

(Mom was only nineteen when she
had Kyra; I followed a little over three
years later), not to mention how truly
disgusting venereal diseases

look in those movies they show
you in school, I have not been
in a hurry to let just any guy
pluck the rosebud. True love first,

I've always said, and that has
been enough to keep me a virgin.
Up until now. I mean, technically
I'm still a virgin at fifteen.

But I'm also in love, and I'm pretty
sure Lucas loves me, too. We've been
skin-on-skin. I just haven't let him
talk me into "all the way in."

That's Liable to Change

Any time. I've been holding out,
wanting to be certain that he loves
me for more than my bod. But how
can you really know that?

We've been together almost
a year. He's a senior at Kirby,
the same private college prep school
that prepped Kyra for Vassar.

She was valedictorian, of course.
I take AP classes at Empire. Less
pressure. Less having to live up
to valedictorian expectations.

Lucas and I met at a Kirby honor
choir performance last spring. Kyra
sang two solos. Lucas stood in the back
row, mostly faking the words. Once

in a while he actually belted out a few
in a deep, mellow bass. I couldn't
help but stare. And not at Kyra.
Lucas stole my attention completely.

I mean, he's freaking beautiful.
His hair falls, a lush gold cascade,
well past his shoulders. It frames
the steep angles of his face perfectly.

His eyes are green, but almost
clear, like cool emerald pools.
You want to dive deep down
into them and swim awhile.

That first night, after the sheet
music was all stored away,
I went looking for Kyra and cookies,
not necessarily in that order.

I found her, talking with Lucas.
And for not even close to the first
time in my life, the little green
monster sank its fangs into me.

Kyra wasn't interested in Lucas.
Her taste in men runs toward PhD
candidates (total geeks). But I
wasn't sure Lucas knew that.

So I took dead aim at making
darn sure he did, pushing straight
in between them. "Hey, sis," I said,
"Mom is looking for you."

That Was Mostly a Lie

But it worked. Kyra kisses
Mom's butt almost as much
as Mom kisses hers. She took
off with a simple, *Excuse me.*

I turned to Lucas. "Good
performance. You've got
a great voice. . . ." Better
eyes, but I didn't go there.

His smile revealed major bucks
in dental work. *Yeah. At least
when I can remember the words.
So . . . you're Kyra's little sister?*

The "little" made me wince.
Of course, I was only fourteen
at the time. Kyra's eighteenth
birthday was sneaking up.

Whatever. I had to play nice.
"That's me. Kyra's little sister.
But you can call me Whitney
if you want. It's shorter."

Something about the tone
of my voice tipped him off.
Ooh. Struck a nerve, huh?
Well, little sis, no worries.

He gave a long, assessing look.
You measure up okay. Besides . . .
He lowered his voice. *Just between*
you and me, your sister's a bitch.

O-M-G! No one, and I mean *no*
one, had ever told me that before.
I studied his face, trying to find
a hint of insincerity. Couldn't.

Something sparked between us.
Maybe it was as simple as him
thinking my sister was a bitch.
Sharing my opinion. Something

others rarely do. And not only
sharing it, but not being afraid to
voice such an unpopular sentiment.
"Just between you and me, I agree."

Okay, Very Likely

He saw how much I needed
to hear that, and maybe he figured
it might be a way into my panties,
and maybe it will lead to that eventually.

Maybe even soon. I'm not really sure
how or why I've held out this long,
except that protecting my virginity
is one thing I can accomplish

all on my own. Won't give it away
too cheaply. Not even to Lucas,
whose touch simply electrifies me.
That night, as the reception broke up

and we started toward our families,
our hands touched. The energy
was pure magic. He felt it too,
turned back to me immediately.

His smile was lupine. Ravenous.
I needed to get to know this guy,
and so when he said, *Uh . . . don't
suppose you'd give me your number?*

I recited it once. Repeated it.
Asked him to repeat it to me,
a feat that he managed easily.
He remembered it too.

It Kind of Surprised Me

When he called a couple of days
later. Not sure why. I guess it's
because I always set myself up
for disappointment. Not that time.

> *Hey*, he said, *it's Lucas, from
> Kirby. . . .* Like I wouldn't have
> remembered! *I was thinking about
> a day trip to Big Sur. Interested?*

Like I wouldn't have been!
But I didn't want him to know
my temp had just flared well over
one-oh-one. "Uh, maybe. When?"

> *I don't suppose you could, like,
> ditch school tomorrow?* At
> my long pause, he laughed. *Okay.
> How about Saturday, then?*

That gave me two whole days
to make up a believable excuse.
No way would Mom let me go
to Big Sur with a guy I just met.

Okay, she wouldn't have let me
go with any guy. Not that I cared.
Getting away with stuff was a well-
loved hobby. And even if it wasn't,

I would have done just about
anything to spend the day with
someone who made me feel
important. Pretty, maybe. Alive.

Believe it or not, my mom made
it easy. *I'm playing golf with Cyn
tomorrow,* she told me on Friday.
And we're doing dinner afterward.

You'll be okay here alone, right?
She barely even heard my ramble
about going over to Trish's for
the day. *Great. I'll be home late.*

Just like that, my Saturday had
opened up. And, very much like
my wandering mother, I was oh-
so-ready to go out and play.

We Played That Saturday

Lucas's silver Eclipse Spyder
seemed to maneuver those
Highway 1 curves all by itself.
Good thing, considering how

buzzed we got. Okay, it wasn't
the first time I'd smoked weed,
but I'd rarely smoked myself
so close to outer space before.

Finally Lucas pulled well off
the road, parked. *C'mon.*
I want to show you something.
He took my hand, led me along

a narrow trail to a steep rock
wall. No way could you climb
up from the front, but around back,
little ledges allowed access to the top.

Despite the residual morning mist,
the view of the crest-and-crash
Pacific literally stole my breath
away. "Insane," I managed.

We sat, lost in our buzz and the roar
of the sea, and when he slipped
his arm around my shoulder, it
felt right. No, better than right.

It felt necessary. He wanted
to kiss me, I knew that. And
I wanted to let him, but I was
afraid I'd look like an idiot.

I'd only ever kissed two other
guys, in an eighth-grade game
of Truth or Dare. Not real kisses.
Not even real practice kisses.

      Still, when he touched my face,
      it rotated easily toward his. And
      when our eyes locked, I dove into
      those emerald pools and our first

      kiss was an effortless float.
      All the love I'd ever thirsted
      for swelled, symphonic. Finally,
      too soon, he pulled away. *Wow*.

A Man of Few Words

Most definitely, but I didn't
need words then. I needed
another kiss, which he gave
me, and another. And another.

Without asking for more. Even
though by the end of that make-out
session, my body was saying, "Please,
more." And it has many times since.

A few days ago Daddy was in the city,
and Mom was off at some fashion
show. I asked Lucas to come over.
We were making out hot and heavy.

He started to unbutton my blouse.
I let him. And when he unzipped
my jeans, I helped him help me
out of them. Snared by the heat

of his kiss, I barely noticed when
he slipped out of his own Levis.
Skin urgent against skin, only
panties and boxers between us,

I was ready to shed that final thin
barrier, allow him access to the most
private part of me, when familiar faces
floated past the window. Not-quite busted!

A Poem by Ginger Cordell
Faces

I wear many faces,
some way too old
to fit the girl glued
to the back of them.

                                        I

keep my faces in a box,
stashed inside of me.
It's murky in there,
overcast with feelings I

                                        don't

allow anyone to see.
Not that anyone cares
enough to go looking.
No one wants to

                                        know

what bothers me. Too
hung up on their own
problems. Sometimes
I think I have to see

                                        the real

Ginger, so I open
the box, search inside.
But no matter how hard
I look, I can't find

                                        me.

Ginger
SOP

Standard operating procedure.
      Iris is yelling again. At the phone.
At the guy on the other end.

At what he's done to her world—
      her totally messed-up, totally self-
centered piece of the universe.

Wish she would just shut the fuck
      up. Hang up. Forget Hal or Bill
or Joe or Frank or whatever this

one's name is. I can't remember
      them all. Only a couple of names,
a face or two. A few other body

parts I'll never be able to forget.
      All because of Iris's "womanly
needs." That's what she calls

her overinflated sex drive. Why
      can't she stop thinking about
herself and act like a mom?

She could start by letting us call
            her Mom. But, no, she insists on
Iris. Says it makes her feel pretty.

Not sure she was ever really
            pretty, but if she was, too
many babies and too much

hard living has sucked her dry.
            Too much, too many. That
describes Iris pretty damn well.

Too much booze. Too many
            smokes. Way too many
pills. Speed. Downers.

Everything in between. Any-
            thing to shut off and shut
up what's left of her brain.

A Door Slams

Guess she's done on the phone.
        Done with another Mr. Wrong.
Thirty seconds, she'll be in here,

crying. Wanting me to say, "Don't
        cry, Iris. Everything will be okay."
And, you know, maybe it will.

"Okay" is all in how you look at
        things. Compared to some bum
on the street, or some starving

kid in Africa, we're okay, living
        with our grandma, who manages
to feed Iris and us six kids.

Six kids, five different fathers.
        Only Mary Ann and I share one,
not that we know one damn thing

about him, except he's an army
          lifer who gave us his face (neither
of us takes after our mother) and his

last name. Guess Iris actually
          married him. Wonder if she
ever officially unmarried him.

Yes, no, or maybe so, the other
          kids—Porter, Honey, Pepper,
and Sandy—all have different

fathers, but share the same last
          name. Belcher, just like Gram's.
Our first names come courtesy

of Iris's infatuation with ancient
          black-and-white TV reruns. Ginger
and Mary Ann were characters on

Gilligan's Island. Porter and
        Sandy were on a show about
a dolphin named Flipper. Pepper

was *Police Woman*, and Honey
        West was a private investigator,
cop, or other woman-in-danger.

Anyway, we've been at Gram's
        place in California for seven months,
eating every day, sleeping warm.

But I don't know how long it will
        last. Iris gets along with her mother
about how she gets along with her men.

Thirty Seconds Is Up

Iris doesn't bother to knock.
> She slaps against the door,
pushes her way into the room

that I share with Mary Ann, Honey,
> and Pepper. Four girls, two
beds. Luckily, only I'm here now.

> > Iris tosses herself across my bed,
> > > lands facedown against rumpled
> > blankets. *Bastard! Why are they all*

> > *such bastards?* She sobs, and her
> > > body shakes like she's got the DTs.
> > Like she'd ever suffer through detox.

I should feel sorry for her, I guess.
> But I don't. I can't. She makes
me sick. Maybe because I know

I could turn out just like her. No way
> to dig myself out of this grave for
the living. No way I've found yet.

I try to dig up a little sympathy.
> "He wasn't such a great guy
anyway, Iris." He was nasty.

But she doesn't think so. *No one's*
              p-perf-fect. I thought we
were doing just f-f-fine.

Anger punches me suddenly,
              hard, little blows to the gut.
"Maybe he found out how you

make your . . . uh . . . living.
              Not many guys will put up
with someone who screws

other guys for money. And if
              they do, then all they're after
is free booze and an easy lay."

              She jerks upright, grabs me
                            by the shoulders, shakes till
              my teeth rattle. *You little bitch.*

How dare you talk to me like
              that? You know anything
I do to get by, I do for you.

"You"

Meaning her collective offspring.
        I look into her eyes and find only
honesty there. She means every

word, hasn't even the slightest
        clue how full of shit she totally
is. I don't care. She should know.

"Some people wait tables or work
        in grocery stores, Iris. Hustling
BJs is lazy work." All on your knees.

Emotions cycle through her eyes
        like a color wheel. She wants
to hit me. Wants to hug me.

        Her hands, still attached to my
                shoulders, tremble. *I'm sorry.*
        I just don't know anything else.

        Finally her hands fall away.
                I thought maybe things would
        change with Greg. Get better.

What planet does she live on?
        "Get real! What guy wants
a woman like . . . like you?"

Smacked Down

That's how she looks, but I don't
        feel bad about it. She wants me
to mother her. Well, what mother

with half a pair of balls wouldn't say
        the same thing? (Not counting
my mother!) And I've got a full pair.

        I swear I can see smoke billowing
                from her ears. *Who made you so
stinking mean?* She spits the *s*'s.

What a fucking stupid question!
        Isn't she expecting my answer?
"Who do you fricking think?"

        She wants to say more, but at this
                exact moment, Gram comes
        into the room, carrying an armful

        of detergenty-smelling laundry.
                Her head swivels toward us.
        Uh. Am I interrupting something?

Iris shakes her head. *Nothing
        important. I need a smoke.*
She rolls off the bed. *And a beer.*

I Must Look

As pissed as I feel. Without
          a word, Gram lays the folded
clothes on the other bed.

She turns toward me slowly,
          and for maybe the hundredth
time, I wonder what has carved

such deep wrinkles into her face.
          She's only, like, fifty-three
or so, and I'm pretty sure that,

          unlike Iris, Gram used to be
                    a knockout. *You okay?*
          Her voice is pillow soft.

My eyes sting suddenly. It
          should be Iris—Mom—
asking if I'm okay. "No."

          Gram comes over, sits on
                    the edge of the bed. Up
          close, her face looks like

          earthquake-splintered stone.
                    Worn, but not worn out.
          I wish I could change things

for you. And for her, too.
        Her childhood was no
walk in the park either. Not

easy, being an army brat. And
        touching down in Barstow
wasn't exactly a reward for years

spent hauling around the U.S.
        Then, when her dad got killed . . .
well, she went starved dog wild.

Between Fort Irwin, Edwards,
        and the Marine Corps bases,
there were plenty of men willing

to be stand-ins for her fallen
        father. Only it wasn't exactly
daughterly love they were after.

Guess That Explains

How she got knocked up
          with me when she was
only sixteen. Just my age.

And maybe it explains why
          she never outgrew teendom.
Still, "Why are you taking her

side? She pisses you off too.
          Not like we can't hear you
yell at each other, you know."

                    Gram nods. *I know. I'm sorry.*
                              It's not such a big place.
                    Barely enough room to fit

                    you all in. But we'll get by.
                              Yes, I get mad at Iris. She can
                    be downright infuriating. Always

                    was a selfish girl. Never one
                              to think about others, or try
                    to spare their feelings. Not

                    mother material, not at all. Not
                              fair to any of you to pop you
                    out, then leave you to mostly fend

for yourselves. Even coyotes and
                    jackals do better by their pups.
All I'm asking is for her to get

a job. Something legit. Pay taxes,
                    stop whoring arou—She skids
to a stop, has said too much.

"It's okay. I know what she does.
            Hate what she does. She'll never
stop. Not for you. Not for any of us."

In the Next Room

Sandy starts up a fuss. Short
        nap. He'll be a little turdcake
tonight. Gram and I move at

the same time. Iris will let him
        squish around in his wet Pull-Up
until someone else changes it. I stop

Gram with a touch of my hand.
        "I'll get him. You do enough."
I kiss her cheek gently before

sliding off the bed, onto the chipped
        linoleum floor. Nothing special
about Gram's house. Except Gram.

    One second, she says, giving me
        a fierce hug. *I know things haven't*
    been easy for you kids. A regular

    parade of Iris's men, most of 'em
        bad ones, in and out of your lives.
    Not even knowing your daddies.

    Moving around, cycling through
        homes. No homes at all sometimes.
    And not because the army was giving

anyone orders. I wish I'd known
        sooner, but Iris didn't talk to me
at all for years. Anger just eats

a person up inside, and I swear
        that girl was born angry. Anyway,
that ain't no here nor there.

But now you know where I live.
        Whatever happens, I want you
to remember this is always your home.

Love, unlike any I've ever known,
        floods through me. I kiss Gram's
cheek. "I will." I want to say more,

but I'm afraid if I do I'll jinx
        myself, and the other kids too.
Speaking of them, there's Sandy

again, crying like he's dying.
        "Better go!" I dash toward
the door, and as I leave, I can

        hear Gram's quiet, *Tsk-tsk.*
                Then she whispers, *Too bad Iris*
        can't be more like her daughter.

I Don't Think

She meant me to hear it.
        But I did, and I flush,
blood warm with pleasure.

That was probably the nicest
        thing anyone has ever said
about me, if not to me directly.

I start toward the small bedroom
        that used to belong to Iris when
she was in high school. I hate

going in there, because I know
        it's where she got preggers
with me. Same bed, even. No,

I'm not guessing. One night,
        after a beer or two too many,
Iris felt the warped need to share

the whole story—how Private First
        Class Kenneth Cordell sneaked
in through the window, not once,

but enough times to make damn
        sure and knock up one Iris Ann
Belcher. Thanks so much, Daddy.

A Poem by Cody Bennett

Not Damn Sure

*Where my real daddy ran
to, if he settled down in some
Podunk town or if he fell flat
off the face of the earth.*

No clue

*who he is or why Mom
slept with him seventeen
years ago, give or take.
Maybe it was rape.*

No lie.

*Mom is pretty much
a prude. A nice prude.
and all things considered,
a really great mom.*

No complaints

*about her or how we
live. Yeah, I've got
a stepdad, but he's pretty
damn good to us.*

No reason

*to turn all emo over not
knowing my real—scratch
that—I mean biological
father. Why would I want to?*

No worries.

Cody
After Wichita

Vegas is a strange, strange city.
I mean, everything in Wichita is
ebony and ivory. Everyone knows
where everyone else stands on things
like immigration (electrify the wall)
or global warming (greenhouse . . . huh?).

But in Vegas, no one knows
one damn thing about their next-
door neighbor, even. We moved
here almost two years ago, and
the only reason I know anyone
on the block is because of school.

Even there, unless you really
push hard, you don't make
friends, and if you do, they're
liable to move away before long.
They say Vegas is a transient
city. Whole lot of truth in that.

People come. People go. Not
like Wichita, where people
mostly stay. Guess I miss
some things about Kansas.
But worrying over it won't help
anyone. Especially not me.

I Go with the Flow

Don't make waves, don't
buck the current. I clean my
room, play nice with my little
brother. Maintain a solid 3.0
GPA. Might even go on to
college. Meanwhile, I work

part time at GameStop to pay
for gas and insurance. My hair
is trimmed, my clothes are neat,
and I never wear all black,
except to funerals. You probably
wouldn't notice me walking

down the street, unless you
happen to be attracted to
"average." It's not such a bad
thing to be. When you fly
well below the radar, you get
away with a hell of a lot.

Of Course

My mom would forgive me
just about anything. Always
trying to make up for the absent
father thing. Not sure why.
My stepfather, Jack, is really
pretty cool. To her. To me.

He's an aircraft mechanic,
working a civil service job
at Nellis AFB. Mom met him
at Boeing in Wichita. She was
a receptionist there. It wasn't
exactly love at first sight, at least

not for her. She called him
"persistent." He called himself
"bit by the love bug." Okay,
that's corny, but hey, that's Jack.
I've gotten used to corny. Typical
Jack joke: *A rope orders a drink,*

> *but the bartender says, "We don't*
> *serve ropes here." The rope goes*
> *outside, ties himself up, unravels*
> *one end, goes back inside. Bartender*
> *says, "Hey, aren't you that rope?"*
> *Rope shakes his head. "Frayed knot."*

Get It?

You know, "frayed knot,"
meaning "'fraid not." Corny
as hell, like I said. But also kind
of funny. Anyway, it's easy
enough to put up with corny when
it's from-the-heart honest.

Jack is honest as a mare-sniffing
stud, which is why he gets along
with Mom. She can't stand when
people lie. Can't blame her, so I try
not to do much out-and-out lying.
"Omitting" is something else.

I do my fair share of omitting.
Despite Mom's ongoing request
to know where I'm going, who
I'll be with, and when I'll be home,
she rarely questions the bare-bones
details I usually provide.

I suppose that might change if
I ever fall into serious trouble.
But so far I've done a whole
lot of weekend partying without
getting busted, addicted, or dead.
Smarter than the average stoner.

Tonight Being Saturday Night

I plan on a little fun before
going home. First I have to
finish my shift. One hour and
counting, the door buzzer
signals a customer. Hope he
knows exactly what he wants.

Oops. I mean she, and not just
any "she," but Veronica Carino.
I haven't seen her around much
lately. Not since I broke up
with Alyssa, her best friend.
"Hey, Ronnie. What's up?"

She barely glances my way
as she starts a counterclockwise
circumnavigation. Wii. Xbox.
PlayStation. Doesn't she know
what system she has? "Can I help
you find what you're looking for?"

> Finally she reaches the counter,
> leans across, inflating the scoop
> of her tank top. *Thanks, but I think
> I found it.* She wets her lips with
> the tip of her tongue, pouts full on.
> *How come you haven't called me?*

Is This a Trick?

Something she and Alyssa cooked
up to make me look like a jerk?
Ronnie Carino has never even
batted her pretty green eyes at
me before. Let alone given me
an up-close view of those tasty-looking

tits. Something twitches
behind my zipper. Glad I'm
standing behind the counter.
"Uh . . . called you? Guess
I figured since 'Lyss and I broke
up, you'd probably be mad at me."

Ronnie takes a deep breath,
rounding the mounds I can't
quit staring at. Then she exhales
in a big sigh. *Why would I be mad
at you? You and 'Lyssa weren't
good for each other. Oil and H_2O . . .*

True enough. We argued over
everything, from music to sports.
Only one thing was really good
between us. . . . That twitch again.
"So, are you saying you want to go
out with me?" The direct approach

usually cuts straight through
the bullshit, but it can backfire.
I half expect her to laugh and tell
me I'm out of my mind. Instead
she smiles a total come-on. *Yeah.*
Why? Does that surprise you?

Can't she see the shock in my
eyes? I feel like I touched a hot
wire. "Kinda, I guess." I watch
her inhale. Exhale. Ah, why not?
One reason comes immediately
to mind. "What about Alyssa?"

> *She'll get totally pissed off. But*
> *after she thinks about it, she'll be*
> *okay . . . or maybe she won't. . . .*
> Ronnie dips even lower, giving
> me a quick nipple shot before
> drawing back and straightening.

> *Right now, I don't care what*
> *'Lyss thinks. Do you?* She waits
> for me to answer. The thought
> crosses my mind again that this
> could all be a setup. Still, I shake
> my head. *Great. How 'bout tonight?*

I Watch Ronnie Leave

Wondering what the hell just
went down. Thinking with my
dick. That's for sure. So what
is Ronnie thinking with? That
makes the dick in question
think even harder. Thank God

when the door opens next, it's
a bunch of kids. Keeping an eye
on them will help me forget
about what might happen tonight.
Ronnie and I are going to Frozen75,
the only underage club in Vegas.

I guess she's on some special list
so we won't have to wait in line
to get in. No booze inside, but
whatever. I just want to watch her
dance. We can keep the refreshments
in my car. And as for dessert . . .

Stop that! One of the kids comes
over, whining about Pokémon
Purple, and why don't we have
it, when it's right in front of his
grubby, little face. "Hang on a
sec and I'll get it for you." Brat.

The Rest of the Hour

Creeps by. *Tick-tick . . . tick.*
I'm actually happy when people
come in, asking dopey questions.
At least it keeps me from looking
at the freaking clock every ten
seconds. Why am I so anxious?

Well, yeah, there is the idea
that I just might hook up with
one very hot girl. I have to admit
I have thought about boinking
her more than once, while
taking solo care of a hard-on.

Oh yeah, the big M. I probably
do it more than I should, and
Ronnie is definite boner bait,
at least when I'm left to my
own imagination instead of
Internet porn. Viva la webcams!

Good thing Mom and Jack
aren't too nosy when it comes
to my personal web-browsing
history. One very good example
of "omission." If they asked, would
I out-and-out lie? Who wouldn't?

Now, at Least

I won't have to lie about where
I'm going tonight. I can omit
confessing the fun stuff, should
any of it actually happen. Finally
I get to clock out. Need to shower
off the customers' germs, put on

clean clothes. Girls love clean.
I'm good with giving it to them.
It's warm for late March, but then
it never gets really cool in Vegas.
The dry desert air is peppered
with exhaust and city noise.

It's a short ride home, radio
screaming, and I'm singing
to myself as I park, head up
the walk to the front door. Life
is good, and I can't help but smile
as I go inside. Mom and Jack

     are in the kitchen. Even from
     here, the tone of Mom's voice
     makes me know something's
     up. I close the distance quietly.
     Wait and see what the doctor says.
     Could be lots of things besides . . .

Doctor?

Is someone hurt? Sick? What?
I push through the door. "Lots
of things besides what?" My eyes
whip back and forth between them.
Both their faces are the color of old
paper. Almost, but not quite, white.

> Jack recovers first. *Not important,*
> *son. I've just been having some*
> *problems with indigestion. Went*
> *in for tests. Could be an ulcer.*
> *Or maybe just your mother's*
> *cookin'. Nothing to worry about.*

Then why is Mom wearing
worry in two long horizontal
lines across her forehead and
two short vertical creases just
above her nose? She's easier
to read than a comic book.

Right Now

I don't really want to read her,
at least not all the way to the last
page. So I'm relieved when she
reaches deep down for some humor.
You want to blame my cooking?
Then take me out to dinner.

The garage door slams and in
marches Cory. He's thirteen,
a skater, and thinks he's tough.
I let him maintain the fantasy.
Cory may be pushing six feet
tall, but he's a little kid inside.

We all clam up immediately,
something Cory totally misses
as he launches a verbal upchuck.
I can't believe it! They outlawed
boards at the park. Something
about liability. Damn it to hell!

Mom sucks in her breath, and Jack
jumps up from his chair. *What*
did you say, young man? You
apologize to your mother right
this minute! His face is bright
red. But he doesn't look sick.

Cory does not apologize. He stomps
into the living room, muttering
a long string of very bad curse
words. *Hmph . . . mother . . . sucker . . .*
hmph . . . have to if . . . Hey, did he
say something about me?

Jack trails him, and Mom and
I follow. We are just in time to
see Jack grab Cory by the collar.
He spins him around until they're
face-to-face. *This is still my house,*
young man. Now you apologize.

There is something mean in
Cory's eyes, something I don't
remember seeing before. But Jack
is in charge. Cory lowers his glare
to the floor. *Sorry. Now let me go.*
He tempers his tone. *Please.*

It's Almost Seven

By the time I pick up Ronnie,
who claims the front seat like
she owns "shotgun." Damn,
the girl is fine, in a short denim
skirt and skimpy lavender tank
top. Oh, Ronnie and her tanks.

> *Wave nice to my mommy,* she
> says, turning to do the same.
> Then she yells out the window,
> *Don't worry, Mom. We won't
> stay out too late. Cross my heart.*
> Now, a mean whisper. *Let's go!*

She doesn't have to ask twice.
Last thing I need is her mom
smelling the bud in my pocket.
I aim for the freeway. "You look
great." Compliments are good ice-
breakers. Ronnie is the ice queen.

> But tonight she seems almost
> thawed. Not quite warm, but
> not completely bitchy. She sniffs
> the air. *Smells like you brought
> the party.* We've never gotten high
> together. First time for everything.

By the Time

We reach Frozen75, we've def
gotten high together. This guy
I work with scores really good
bud, and he's not above dealing
a little to me. "So what do you
think about the smoke?"

> The ice queen has defrosted all
> the way to room temp. She laughs.
> *It's awesome.* Then she reaches
> over, touches my leg. *Tonight*
> *will be fun. Thanks for taking me.*
> Her hand strokes my thigh gently.

Which raises my heart rate,
which raises several questions.
Why me? Why now? Why go out
of her way for tonight? But one
of those questions will do for now.
"I . . . I have to ask. Why me?"

> Out of the corner of my eye
> (I don't dare look away from
> the road), I can see her shake
> her head. *You really don't know,*
> *do you? Cody, I've been in love*
> *with you for a very long time.*

A Poem by Eden Streit
Being in Love

Means hard questions.
Will I? Won't I? Should
I? Could I? Yes? No?

You?

Me? There is no me
without you. Is there
a you without

me?

And if we're truly one,
how will I breathe when
circumstance pries us

apart?

You are my oxygen, my
sustenance, the blood
inside my veins. When

we

touch, you are my skin,
hold all my joy inside
of you. When you go, I

wither.

Eden
Saturday Evening

Papa is officiating a wedding. Mama,
of course, went along. Few enough

excuses to get all dressed up around here.
Eve put on her Sunday best and went too.

The bride has a really cute little brother,
just about a year older than Eve.

The groom has a nice-looking brother
too, but I'm not the least bit interested.

I've got someone I'd much rather see,
so I begged off. Told them I didn't

feel very well. God is going to strike me
down for sure if I keep lying this way.

But I've got at least three hours
to spend with Andrew. There's a park

right down the street from our house.
It's a short walk on a cool night,

but by the time I reach Andrew's truck,
I'm hot all over. From the inside out.

No One Around

I slip into the Tundra unobserved.
As the interior light goes dark,

I move into Andrew's arms, accept
his gentle kiss. But we don't dare

stay here. "Let's go for a drive. Can't
believe how much I've missed you."

He grins and puts the truck in gear.
It's only been four days, you know.

I slide my hand into the warmth of his.
"And all I could think about was you."

True. Too true. In class. PE. The library.
At home. Bible study. The dinner table.

Faces. Whiteboards. Gym mats. Smudged
together. Bells. Laughter. Curses. Blurred

into white noise. Locker room armpits. Floor wax.
Gourmet cafeteria. Marker ink. All smeared

into senseless potpourri. Four days, the only
clear picture, Andrew's face. The only sound

I wanted to hear, his soft *hello*. The only scent
my nose kept sniffing for, alfalfa green.

We Drive into the Foothills

Andrew knows this area well. He turns
up a dirt road, slick with spring melt ice.

Unlikely we'll run into anyone back here.
Certainly not any old spy from Papa's church.

> Andrew parks. *Pretty tonight. Looks*
> *like you could reach out and touch*

> *the stars. Come on.* He tugs me into
> the chill March air, lifts me into the bed

> of his truck. There's a double sleeping bag
> there. We climb inside, and he slides his arm

> around my shoulder, pulls my head against
> his chest. *Nice.* He sighs. *Very, very nice.*

Suddenly we're kissing, beneath an ocean
of distant suns. Can't believe it's me here,

in this amazing place, with this amazing guy.
I want him to hold me forever, never let go.

I feel like I'm in a movie. Unrehearsed words
tumble out of my mouth. "I love you."

There

Said it. Didn't really mean to, but now
I've gone and done it. I tense, waiting

for his response. It's swift. *Oh God,*
Eden, I love you, too. How did I ever

live without you? It's like I was missing
a huge part of me. The best part of me.

Until I found you. I want . . . I want . . .
He loses his words. He never does that.

I kiss his temples. Close his eyes with
kisses. "What? What do you want?"

His eyes stay closed. I stare up into the night
as he says, *I want to be with you always,*

to share forever with you. I want to give
you more than I have to give now—security,

a comfortable life. He pauses. Considers.
Decides to finish. *I want to take from you*

what I've no right to take. Not now. Not yet.
But that doesn't make me want it less. . . .

I Get What He Means

And as much as I would like to chalk
it up to him being a guy, truth is I want

it too. At least I think I do, and only when
I'm this close to Andrew. When I am, God

forgive me, I want to know what it means
to give myself to him so completely. Want

to feel what it's like when it's absolutely
right. Not that I've felt it when it's wrong,

or felt "it" at all. But I don't want my heart
to feel wrong about my body feeling good.

I have no doubt it will feel incredible with Andrew.
"I want to too. But I'm scared. I've never . . ."

> *I know. I know you haven't, and I know*
> *you're scared. I'm scared too. You might*
>
> *not believe this, but I've never either.* He
> stops. Smiles. *Don't tell anyone, okay?*
>
> *When you're ready, when you trust me*
> *enough, I want you to be my first. My only.*

I So Want to Be

His first. His only. I so want him to be
mine. "I promise to be your first.

"Your only. If we just had a little more
time, I would be those things tonight. . . ."

> No. Not tonight. Not in the cold, hard bed
> of a pickup truck. When we do it, it will
>
> be in a warm feather bed, with soft quilts
> and pillows you fall into. I want it
>
> to be perfect. And if we don't get it right
> the first time . . . He lets me finish.

"Practice makes perfect?" We laugh
together. Easy. Meant to be. And I know

the first time someone makes love to me,
it *will* be perfect. Because it will be Andrew.

We Should Head Back

But I can't. Not quite yet. I need some
answers that will prove he means what

he says. "So why did you wait? And how
did you know the right person was me?"

>*I know all guys are supposed to be sluts
or something. But sex with just anyone*

>*never did seem exactly right to me.
Maybe it's my Catholic upbringing,*

>*or hell, who knows? Maybe I need Viagra
already.* He laughs. *Nah, that can't be*

>*the problem. When I'm with you, I don't
need a pill to want to make love to you.*

He always says the right things.
Maybe he should be a politician.

>*As for you, I suspected you might be
the right person the first night we met.*

>*You were so sure of yourself, your beliefs,
and you didn't let me sway you. I loved*

>*your self-confidence, your obvious loyalty.
Your solid sense of right and wrong.*

Okay, so maybe he's not exactly politician
material. "When did you know for sure?"

> The first time I kissed you. One kiss,
> I was totally hooked. Addicted to you.

> I could never love anyone the way I love
> you. I'd follow you across the universe.

I look up at the sky, brimming stars
and the rise of a waning moon.

"The universe is a big place. If I was lost
up there, how would you ever find me?"

> He gathers me in, kisses me gently.
> Don't you know? We're connected

> by an invisible chain. It's very long, very
> light. But also very strong. It can't rust.

> Can't break. And the only thing that can
> sever it is if you ever stop loving me.

We Drive Back into Town

Back to the park, which is deserted.
Dark, but for a single streetlight

at the far end. Andrew parks away
from it and I slide across the seat, into

his arms. One last kiss. Or two. I don't
want to stop. Don't want to go home.

"I'll never stop loving you," I whisper.
"And I want to make love with you soon."

My body aches with wanting that very
thing. "Maybe we should run away."

> *If I thought that was the right thing
> to do, I wouldn't hesitate one minute.*
>
> *But it's not. You'd never forgive yourself,
> and that would mean never forgiving me.*
>
> *Once you turn eighteen, once I graduate,
> we can go anywhere. I'll get a job. You can*
>
> *go to school. Or stay home and let me take
> care of you. Whatever makes you happy.*
>
> He kisses me one last time. *As long as
> we're together, everything will be all right.*

I Walk Home Slowly

Trying to soak up the things Andrew
said tonight. Sponge them up, absorb

them through my skin, into my flesh, so
they'll always live inside of me. I know

Andrew and I were meant to be together.
How can I prove it to my parents? How

can I make them understand that love
this real, this deep, must come from God?

I look up again at the night sky, but here,
city lights take center stage, mute

the celestial backdrop. I don't belong
here, in the city. Don't belong in my

parents' cold house. I'm a stray, called
to another place. A wild place, where

rules and expectations don't dare intrude.
A warm place, safe in Andrew's arms.

The House Is Quiet

They're still not home, and that's great
by me. I don't need questions. Don't want

to make up excuses. Have no patience
for a sister-to-sister chat session.

The clock says nine thirty, but it seems
much later. I go into my room, trade

jeans for a soft flannel nightgown,
lie on my bed in the dark, listening

to silence. Something happened tonight.
Something wonderful. Terrifying.

An awakening. This must be how Eve
(the original) felt after taking a bite

of forbidden fruit. Every nerve on fire,
every fiber of flesh alive with desire.

If Andrew was here, beside me on my
not-exactly-a-feather bed, I would give

him my virginity, give it gladly, without
a second thought. It belongs to him.

I close my eyes, return to the foothills,
to the back of the Tundra, to a double

sleeping bag. I slip inside, into the warm
envelope of goose down. And Andrew.

His voice fills my head. *I want to
take from you what I've no right to. . . .*

Oh, Andrew. I want that too. Tonight.
Right now. My body is begging to learn

what your body wants to teach it. Need
blisters up, and with it, a way to teach

myself some of what I'm dying to know.
Abstinence programs encourage it.

Mama not only discourages it, but swears
it put Mary Magdalene on the highway

to degradation. What Mama forgets is that Mary
Magdalene was the forgiveness poster child.

My Hand, Disguised

As Andrew's hand, moves lightly
down my neck, over collarbone,

breastbone. Goose bumps rise in
unusual places, and my body tingles

in a completely foreign way. Because
of Andrew. But he's not here. I pretend

he is and let "his" hands explore the rounds
of my breasts, move in tighter and tighter

orbits, and now fingers circle the hard
center nubs, raised like it's cold in here.

It's not. I'm burning up. Delirious with
raw need. My hand wants to slide lower,

to a place I know nothing about except
what they call it in books. And suddenly

it comes to me how completely inept
I'll be when Andrew and I finally

share that warm feather bed, with comfy
quilts and pillows we can fall into.

I Turn on the Light

Go to the computer, try to avoid
looking at the Calvary screen saver.

Jesus, hanging on the cross, staring
down at his poor crying mother.

Mama downloaded that, no doubt
specifically to deter the kind of

Internet exploration I have in mind.
I just have to be very careful not to surf

to the wrong kind of website. A touch
of the mouse, Golgotha dissolves

into the ether and voilà, up pops
Windows. Double-click on Explorer.

Here it comes, ready to take me where
I need to go. But where is that, exactly?

Might as well get straight to the point.
I type in, "losing your virginity."

When I Hear

The door open, the sounds of return,
I hurry to turn off the computer

before Eve catches me, breathlessly
reading stories about other girls' first

times. Some wonderful, some awful.
Some taken by force, some given

away. Some total disappointments.
Some more than they expected.

What none of them had, at least I'm
pretty sure they didn't, was Andrew.

I rush into bed, pick up a book on
the nightstand, pretend I'm reading.

> Eve breezes into the room, sighing.
> *I love weddings. You should have come.*

Her goofy grin says a lot. "So . . .
Zach asked you to dance or what?"

> *Mama wouldn't let me. But he asked.*
> She looks at me. *How did you know?*

"I'm a good guesser." And I'm guessing
she never once thought about losing it.

A Poem by Seth Parnell
Losing It

Some days I think
I'm losing my mind.
What seems so

        clear

most of the time
becomes a big question
mark. Am I really

        the way

I perceive myself, or
is the person others see
the truth of me? I wait

        for

answers, but inside
I know I have to go out
and find them. And

        answers,

like knowledge, are
not always where we
look first for them.

Seth
Worked My Farmer Butt Off

All day. Can't believe
     my dad wants to give
     me grief over going out.
     What's a Saturday
night for, anyway?

          I think you should stay
               home tonight, he says.
               Hard to get up Sunday
               morning when you're
          out late the night before.

We're at the dinner table,
     finishing off big ol' plates
     of venison sausage, biscuits,
     and mushroom gravy. A mediocre
rendition of Mom's recipe.

          Dad seconds my opinion.
               Not as good as your
               mother's, I know. I don't
               have her magic touch.
          But I do the best I can.

He does. If he left it to
        me, we'd eat nothing
        but bologna and cheese,
        with the odd pizza thrown
in for a little variety.

I save my more gourmet
        palate for when I go out
        with Loren. Not that Dad
        would understand the draw
anyway. Caviar? Fish bait,

right? And pâté? Glorified
        liverwurst. Still, in some
        circles, venison sausage
        is probably considered
quite the taste sensation.

"Dinner's great, Dad. I bet
        some of those hoity-toity
        big-city chefs would kill
        for this recipe." Probably
not. But Dad's face lights.

        Think so? Well, I wouldn't
        want 'em to kill anyone,
        but I wouldn't mind
        selling the secret formula
        for big bucks, you know?

Other Than Large Male Deer

Big bucks are something
        I'm pretty sure Dad
        gave up on having a long
        time ago, if he ever really
cared about such a thing.

I glance toward a photo
        of Mom and Dad, taken
        on their twentieth anniversary,
        before we knew she was sick.
They look content. In love,

despite years of worry,
        debt, and loss. Through
        years of struggling to make
        ends meet, they had each
other. And that was plenty.

Dad wears his age less
        gracefully now. Factory
        work and farming, a one-
        two punch. Add loneliness . . .
Guilt swells. But I have plans.

Plans

For an evening with Loren.
        Plans that require getting
        out of the house. Plans
        I would rather not outline
in detail. I hate lying to Dad,

but I can't see a way around
        it. "Tell you what. I'll do
        a little research. See if I can
        find a five-star chef with a
hankering for deer meat.

Meanwhile, I'm gonna run
        into town. Billy Clayborn's
        band is playing at Bristow
        Tavern. Thought I'd take
a listen. Maybe I'll get lucky. . . ."

I leave it hanging. Dad
        has never asked, but
        surely he's wondered
        if, at almost eighteen,
I've ever once gotten lucky.

        The comment sinks in
            like a hog in mud—
            slow but sure. Finally
            he says, *Okay then. Just*
      don't stay out real late.

I Know

He wants me to go to Mass
        with him in the morning.
        How can he go through
        the motions? I've heard
him talking to himself.

He blames God for taking
        Mom early, taking her
        first. Yet come Sunday
        morning, he's on his knees,
genuflecting. Bowing down.

Maybe he's searching.
        For Mom. For proof
        that there's something
        beyond this soil. This
earth. Maybe it's a way

to keep on belonging.
        Whatever it is, I sweeten
        the deal, mostly because
        I plan to stay out pretty late.
Scratch that. Real late.

"How about if I go
        to Mass on my way
        to Bristow? That way,
        if I do get lucky, I'll
already be absolved."

Dad Laughs Softly

Shakes his head, but says,
Okay. I guess you're old
enough to make your
own decisions about
stuff like religion and . . .

He can't bring himself
to finish. But Catholic
or not, I'm sure he wants
his son to have "normal"
sexual desires. Wonder

if he suspects otherwise.
I'm relatively sure he knows
I have no plans to fulfill my
Mass obligation tonight
or any night. I've pretty

much given up on the idea
of salvation. Catholicism
and homosexuality only
go hand in hand in the
highest church circles.

Not Much Doubt

I'm damned anyway,
        so I swing the old Chevy
        toward the freeway, Louisville,
        and Loren. My heart pumps
wildly in anticipation.

I turn up the radio, change
        the station from country to
        alternative. My Chemical
        Romance fades and the DJ
segues into a Muse rocker.

Before I met Loren, I'd never
        heard of either group. Now
        the Dixie Chicks and Rascal
        Flatts have taken a backseat
to music more relevant to me.

Muse, in fact, was playing
        the first day I let Loren
        show me what love can
        be when two people give
themselves completely

to each other. It was our
        fourth date. Up until then,
        we'd only talked. Kissed
        a little. Touched even less,
and only with our clothes on.

Loren was patient about
            the rest. *I'm not looking*
            for an easy lay, he said.
            If I wanted that, I'd
pick someone up in a bar.

He could without even
            trying. He's beautiful.
            I'm happy he doesn't do
            gay bars. "So what are
you looking for, then?"

            A friend. A partner who
            I can trust. Sex that
            is more than mutual
            masturbation. Sex that
is an outpouring of love.

Up Until

Our fourth time together,
        individual masturbation
        was the bulk of my sexual
        experience. There were
a few short chapters of "touch

me here, I'll touch you there"
        in my very slim book of
        adolescent sexual escapades,
        but nothing more. I had no
idea what to do beyond that.

When I slipped into my
        fantasies, I always had
        sex with men. But that
        day, overwhelmed as I
was with desire for Loren,

I was scared. Nothing
        had ever scared me so
        much, not even knowing
        my mom was going to die.
Does every person feel

like that their first time?
        Like what if they do it
        wrong? Or worse, what
        if they do it poorly—so
horribly their partner laughs?

Loren Didn't Laugh

There proved to be nothing
            to laugh about. Unexpectedly,
            it all came very easily.
            Like, yes, that was exactly
how it was meant to be—

me, taking control. Before we
            started, I had no clear idea
            about our roles. Who's on
            top and who's not means
nothing when you aren't

completely positive
            that you belong in either
            position. But that night,
            one kiss and need struck
with enough force to erase

all doubt, all hesitation.
            I didn't wait for Loren to
            say it was okay, didn't ask
            him to show me what to do.
Pure animal instinct led me

just where I wanted to go.
    It wasn't tender. Wasn't
    pretty. It was a raw, naked
    joining, energized from years
of dreaming about what it

could be like, or should be
    like. I gave, he took, and
    when it was over, like Adam,
    I shook at the forbidden
taste of new awareness.

    Afterward, with his head
        nested gently against my
        chest, Loren whispered,
        Are you sure you've
    never done that before?

"Never." My voice floated
    up from a deep haze of
    contentment. "But I want
    to do it again." It was a long
few minutes before I could.

Since That Day

I've grown more and
        more confident in
        the part I'm supposed
        to play. Loren is older.
More experienced. Wiser,

in many ways. He is also
        softer. Passive. Anxious
        to please me, let me have
        my way. He has become
my favorite teacher ever.

I can barely make it through
        each week, pretending to
        be the same old Seth at home,
        when a short drive will
allow the new, improved Seth

to come out and play. I am
        torn, wanting to keep
        my dad satisfied, when
        I know Loren is waiting
to satisfy me. One day soon

I'll have to decide which
        Seth I can live without.
        Until then, Improved Seth will
        have to escape when he can.
And he's escaped tonight.

By the Time

I knock on Loren's door,
        treading a maelstrom
        of love and lust, I have
        almost made up my mind
to leave Dad and home in

my wake and move to
        Louisville before
        I graduate in June.
        I know it's not long,
but I'm sick of pretending.

Loren opens the door.
        I don't wait for his greeting
        before pushing inside and
        yanking him tight up against
me. "God, I've missed you!"

        He stiffens, and I finally
           take a good look at
           the worry sculpted in
           his face. *I missed you,*
too. Come on. Sit down.

Something is definitely
        wrong. I follow him
        to the couch, afraid
        to ask what it is. What
kind of bad news do I have

to hear now? He couldn't be
        sick, could he? No. Too young.
        Too healthy. Unless . . . No!
        Stop it. Just ask. I search
his eyes. "What's wrong?"

        Nothing. He takes my hand.
                I mean, nothing major.
                Relax, Seth. It's just . . . He
                reaches toward the coffee
        table, picks up a letter.

        I got this today. He cradles
                the paper protectively, like
                he doesn't want me to know
                what's there. *You know I go to*
        school at Louisville Seminary. . . .

Uh-huh. Louisville Presbyterian
        Theological Seminary. Studying
        marriage and family therapy.
        I nod my head, but I'm
totally confused. "Yes. So?"

        A requirement for my BA
                is three months of "field
                study." They're sending
                me to a congregation in
        New York for the summer.

114

Something Thick

But tasteless rises up my
        throat, into my mouth.
        I break out in a panicky
        sweat. "Congregation?
You mean, like a priest?"

        He manages a thin smile.
            More like a minister, but
            yes. That is my calling.
            But you knew that.
        He rests a hand on my knee.

"I don't know. I guess . . ."
        Guess? What else would
        a seminarian have planned?
        But what about me? Us?
"What does that mean for us?"

        Time apart. You can't
            come with me. I'll be
            living at the church. He lets
        that sink in. *Don't worry*
        now. I don't leave until May.

Don't worry? He hacked
        me off at the knees.
        But it's only temporary.
        "You're coming back, right?"
The silence screams.

A Poem by Whitney Lang
Scream

*I whisper and you close
your eyes. I speak and
you turn away. If I
scream, will you finally*

hear

*me beg you to hold me
close to you, promise
you'll never let go? Do*

my tears

*upset you? Can you
see them fall on fallow
ground—the soil
of your heart?*

Fear

*is a better friend than
you, who feels nothing,
beneath the weight of*

my pain.

I Despise Shopping

But it's Paige's idea of heaven,
so we're going to Capitola Mall.
Mom hangs out with Paige's mom
and *encourages* our friendship.

She wouldn't, if she knew anything
at all about Paige other than that her mom
plays a mean game of tennis. But she
doesn't, so we're on our way to the mall.

> *Did you go out with Lucas last*
> *night?* Paige broke up with her last
> boyfriend a few months ago and dates
> vicariously through me. Voyeuristic ho!

I don't mind entertaining her—or
making her jealous, either. "Actually,
we spent most of the day together.
We hung out down at the Boardwalk."

> *Uh-huh. And what else?* Voyeuristic
> enough to want details beyond
> arcade games and carnival rides.
> *Have you two done the dirty yet?*

I swear, she's panting. I could
make her day—her month, even—
by inventing something juicy. But
where would that leave what's left

of my reputation? Do I care? Jeez.
My reputation might just improve
if people believed I was having
regular sex with someone

as delicious as Lucas. One thing
for sure. Whatever I tell Paige
will most definitely get around.
She's not very good at secrets.

Maybe I'll just keep her guessing.
I attempt an air of mystery. "C'mon,
Paige. You wouldn't want me
to screw and tell, would you?"

We Both Know

She would, and we both know
the way I've circumvented
her question means I'm still
a virgin. Technically, anyway.

It's the "technically" part that
has now piqued her interest.
*Okay, then. How far have you
gone? I want every single detail.*

Ah, what the hell? "We almost
did last week. In fact, we were
just about naked. . . ." I tell her
the story about not quite getting

busted, right there on my living
room couch. "You've never seen
two people get dressed so fast.
I didn't even have time to put on

my bra. Good thing Daddy dropped
his keys. Gave me time to hide it
under the cushion. Things had to
look pretty suspicious, though."

Paige giggles. *Oh, yeah. Messy
hair and smeared makeup.
Been there, done that. But what
about yesterday? Did you . . . ?*

"Nah. Everything but. Wrong
time of the month and all." Now
that was a big slice of truth. I don't
usually talk about my periods.

But Paige wants even more.
Did you, like, use your mouth?
Her eyes light up. Is she waiting
for a (ha!) blow-by-blow description?

"Why? Need instructions? 'Cause
you can get tips on the Web, you know."
I am something of an expert there,
because I checked 'em out myself.

She laughs. *Nah. That's okay.*
I think I've got it figured out.
Just wondering if you have.
Anyway, it's not rocket science.

Now I have to laugh. "Except the part
where it goes off like a rocket."
We both bust up, and now she knows
I've got it figured out too.

Capitola Mall

Isn't huge, but it's big enough.
And, it being Sunday, it's pretty
crowded. I don't mind crowds.
People watching is a fun pastime.

Paige cruises the parking lot slowly,
waiting for someone to vacate
a spot close to an entrance. "There's
probably room in the garage."

> *Probably. But you never know
> what kind of weirdo might be
> lurking in a parking garage.
> Mom says it's safer out here.*

Is there more than one kind
of weirdo? Okay, I can't let
that one slip past. "How many
kinds of weirdos are there?"

> She doesn't laugh. *Lots. And
> the worst are the ones you
> don't suspect. They're the ones
> you invite inside your front door.*

Inside the Mall

I can't help but go on a weirdo
watch. Paige is right. Potential
freaks loiter everywhere, and
they come in all shapes, sizes,

genders, and ages. "Hey, Paige.
Check that out." I point to a boy,
maybe six, staring, drop-jawed,
through the window of Victoria's

Secret. "Future weirdo, for sure."
We crack up, but when we're well
down the aisle I glance back over
my shoulder. He's still there.

Paige doesn't notice, could
care less anyway. *Let's go
to the Gap. I need some jeans.*
Her focus shift is immediate, intense.

Mind on her goal, she picks
up her pace. So much for people
watching. Faces, bodies, and packages
blur. Motion sickness threatens.

Finally, Gap in sight, she slows
a little. Enough for me to notice
a really cute guy sitting outside
the door, waiting for someone,

at least that's my guess. As we
approach, he notices us, too, and
the smile he gives me could melt
an entire iceberg in two seconds flat.

Weirdo? Maybe. I mean, he's at least
ten years older than me, and he's def
taken an interest. Do weirdos come
this hot? My guess is no, but I'm not

here to pick up a guy (yeah, Lucas,
remember him?), especially one who
could be my—what? Big brother?
Wow, it might be cool to have a big

brother hot enough to be a rock star.
No, wait. All my friends would want
me to introduce them. Then they
wouldn't be my friends any more,

because they'd be doing it with my
brother. Scratch all that. Don't want
a hot brother, or any brother at all.
Don't even want my sister, and why

the heck am I thinking all this,
anyway, just because some pervert
guy sitting outside the Gap might
or might not have checked me out?

Warped

But who's warped, him or me?
Okay, I'm pretty sure I know
the answer. Pretty sure I've gone
from appreciating some nice-looking

(hot) older guy to imagining
I have some fictional brother who
is doing unmentionable things with
my best friends. I steal a covert glance

at Paige, who is def not noticing
the guy (who is def not my brother)
at all, let alone having sex with him.
I need food. Haven't eaten today.

As Paige and I go inside, I can feel
not-brother's eyes crawling all over
my back. I nudge Paige. "Psst. Did
you see that cute guy checking us out?"

> *What guy?* She turns, and I follow
> her eyes, only to find his eyes
> locked on me. *Well, he's def*
> *checking* you *out. Talk about*
>
> *robbing the cradle, or wanting to.*
> *Like, totally tasteless. C'mon. There's*
> *a pair of skinny jeans with my*
> *name on them right over there.*

Someone Should Tell

Paige that "skinny jeans" are
most def not her best friend.
She and I are the same age,
and about the same height.

But she's got a lot more
curves. In a way, I envy that.
Paige looks more like a woman.
I, on the other hand, look like a girl.

> Skinny jeans work better for girls.
> Still, Paige manages to pour
> herself into a pair. *Do they*
> *make my butt look big?*

Well, duh. But I'm not
about to say so. Friends
don't tell friends they look
fat. Or even curvy. "Nah."

> *Cool. So what are you waiting*
> *for? Try some on. Check it out:*
> *Thirty percent off.* She stands,
> hands punctuating well-defined hips.

Debate is useless. I slip into
a pair and have to admit they
look pretty good. Oh, why not?
What's a trip to the mall for?

Shopping with Paige

Reminds me of that TV show:
TLC's *What Not to Wear.*
Paige has spent big bucks, and
what does she have to show for it?

A couple of pairs of too-tight
jeans, three blouses guaranteed
to show too much tummy and/or
cleavage, and a pair of hot pink

sneakers with soles as thick
as six hundred-page novels.
Now we're leaving Claire's,
where I'm pretty sure Paige

took advantage of a five-finger
discount. Not that she can't afford
a cheap pair of earrings. But ripping
them off gives her a total rush.

> *Hurry up,* she urges, glancing
> nervously over her shoulder
> as we hustle toward the food
> court. Talk about obvious!

Still, by the time yummy scents
of fat-laden foods entice our noses,
we see no sign of security on our
tail. Way to "borrow," Paige.

What do you want to eat? asks
Paige, sniffing the air. *Subway?*
Pizza? Hey, you know what sounds
delish? A hot dog on a stick.

The built-in joke is just too good to
pass up! "Damn, girl. You really *do*
need a boyfriend, you know?" We both
snort into gut-busting, pee-your-pants

laughter. "Oh . . . my . . . God!"
I stutter. "I have so got to pee."
I turn, ready to run. And who's
sitting at a table nearby, grinning

like an orangutan—a very hot
orangutan? The guy. The cute
not-my-brother weirdo. And he's checking
me out again. Is he, like, stalking me?

I Still Have to Pee

But before I do, I have to say
something to the hot monkey.
Ooh. That was a very bad thought.
Wonder how hot his monkey is.

Okay. Way worse thought.
What's up with me? "That guy
is over there, staring," I tell
Paige. "Let's go talk to him."

> She pulls her eyes away from
> the Hot Dog on a Stick sign.
> *What? Hey. No. That's stupid.*
> *He might get the wrong idea.*

Or exactly the right idea. "Yeah,
maybe. But don't you want to
know where he's coming from?"
I don't wait for her to answer.

> I pull myself up very tall, take
> dead aim at my stalker. Behind
> me comes the sound of Paige,
> scrambling to catch up. *Wait.*

Almost to his table, my courage
dissolves and I think seriously
about turning around, grabbing
Paige, and hauling buns out of there.

Too Late

The guy looks up, and the warmth
of his smile melts all thoughts of
running. *Hello.* One word out of his
killer mouth, I think I'm lost.

"Oh. Hey." Now what do I say?
"I . . . uh . . . just wondered if you
were looking at anything special."
Totally brilliant. Set myself up.

But he knows just what to say.
*Well, actually, yes. I was looking
at you, wasn't I? You're quite
special. But then, you know that.*

Is he saying I'm stuck-up?
Beside me, Paige chokes on
a half laugh. Guess that's what
she thinks he was saying.

He studies my face with amazing
eyes, the blue of robin eggs. *You are,
in fact, the most special young
woman I've seen in a long time.*

He so *is* a stalker. But a stalker
who knows how to make a girl feel . . .
uh . . . special. "I'm sorry, but
I don't get it. What do you want?"

His grin widens. *Now that's*
a loaded question. I want *more*
than you'll probably give me.
But I'll settle for your name.

Paige elbows me and clears
her throat, like I don't have
enough sense not to give my name
to a stranger. A totally luscious,

completely random, too-old-
for-me-to-even-consider-him,
somehow hypnotic stranger.
I find myself saying, "Whitney."

Whitney, he repeats, nodding.
The name fits you. Well, Whitney,
pleased to meet you. I'm Bryn.
Care to sit down for a few?

This Is Insane

For some stupid reason,
I really, really do want to
sit down with him for a few.
What is the big attraction?

It's not like a guy has never
put the moves on me before.
And I'm pretty sure that's what
this is, even though he's smooth.

> But Paige isn't taking the bait.
> *We were going to get something*
> *to eat, remember? And I thought*
> *you had to go*—She catches herself.

Fact is, I do have to go. Now.
"I'd like to sit, Bryn, but Pai—
uh . . . my friend is hungry.
Maybe another time?"

> His smile slips a little. But
> he says, *Of course.* Then he
> reaches into his pocket. *Here's*
> *my card. Call me sometime.*

A Poem by Ginger Cordell
Reach

They say you should
reach for the stars,
and I'd like to, but

my arms

are much too short.
They say to reach
out for hope, but I

don't

understand what hope
is. They say to reach for
goals, but I don't

know

how to define mine,
and so I won't listen.
But if you only tell me

how to

love you, I'll reach
into the depth of me
and find a way to

hold you.

Ginger
School Sucks

Don't even know why I try.
                We've moved around so
much, I've always been behind.

I'm not going to graduate without
                a hella lot of summer school
or something. And I don't plan to

spend summer vacation locked up
                in Barstow High, trying to figure
out algebra. Who needs it, anyway?

Not like I'm going to college. I'll be
                happy waitressing. Minimum
wage and tips isn't such a bad life.

Would be nice to settle into a town.
                (Not that Barstow's the one—it's
not!) Have a nice, steady job. A friend

or two. Maybe even fall in love,
                if there is such a thing, and if
I can ever get past . . . Anyway,

we've never stayed in one place
                long enough for me to make friends.
All I've had to hang with are sisters.

Actually, I've Kind of Connected

To one girl, Alex. She's in my
            creative writing class, and
she's totally goth. Black clothes,

black fingernails. Heavy black
            eyeliner, which somehow
makes her seem innocent,

like a little girl, trying too hard
            to look all grown up. There's
something about that—something

about her—that is really
            attractive to me. More than
once since I've gotten to know

her, I have thought about
            what it might be like to hold
her. I've even fantasized about

kissing her. It's major weird
            and kind of messed up, I guess.
I've never kissed anyone,

guy or girl. Been kissed,
            but it was never my idea,
and I hated it. Hated them.

I want to know what a real
            kiss is like. But why I keep
thinking about doing it with

Alex is a mystery. She has
            never even halfway come on
to me. That's cool. Who needs

complications? It's good
            enough to have a friend.
And anyway, I'm guessing

it isn't easy for her to get
            close to people. She has
had a tough life, maybe

tougher than mine. Her mom's
            doing hard time for armed
robbery, and she lives with her

loser stepdad, who's a bartender
            at some sleazy club out on
Old Highway 58. Wonder if

I should try to set him up
            with Iris. A pair of low-life
druggies. The perfect couple.

Alex and I

Are hanging out downtown,
         scoping out people, scoping
us out. I take a deep drag off

a bummed Kool, cough like a
         dweeb on the exhale. "Does
your stepdad have a girlfriend?"

                 Alex keeps watching people
                         walk by. She rarely looks you
                 in the eye. *Nah. No one special,*

                 *not since Lydia boogied on
                         down the road. Guess he has
                 fuck buddies, though. Why?*

"I dunno. It just came to me
         that maybe he and my mom
should hook up or something."

                 She doesn't miss a beat.
                         *You kidding? You don't
                 like your mom or what?*

I laugh. "Not much, actually.
         But she's easier to deal with
when she's got a man in her life."

Really? Seems to me life is a lot
          easier without getting attached
to someone. Too complicated.

"God, do you know my mom?
          But she thinks having a guy
around makes her important."

          Alex snorts. *How old is she,*
                    anyway? Sounds like she
          still plays with Barbies.

"I doubt she ever played with
          Barbies. Just a shitload of
Kens." And Sams. And Bills.

But, as much as I think Alex
          is pretty okay, I'm not about
to share too much information

about Iris and how she brings in
          cash. Besides, maybe Iris would
stop tricking for the right guy.

Maybe if the right guy came along,
          we could live a nice, normal
life. However that's defined.

I Guess Nothing Says

Moms have to be good
          people, though. I mean,
look at Britney Spears. She

might not be a complete
          whore, but she's not
exactly a shining example

of motherhood. And, just
          down the block, a woman
in baggy sweats yanks her

                    little girl along, yelling,
                              Hurry the hell up, would
                    you? The kid's bawling.

And then there's Alex's
          mom. Busted for robbing
a liquor store with a gun.

All for another fix. A few
          hours of finding a way to
forget everything. Alex included.

I hope I'm never a mom. But
          if I am, I'll make damn
sure my kids look up to me.

Speaking of Kids

I really ought to get home.
        Gram has a hair appointment
this afternoon, so unless Iris

suddenly figured out motherhood,
        Mary Ann is the only one there to
take care of the little kids until I get

home. "Better go," I tell Alex.
        "Time to play mom. How
'bout a smoke for the road?"

        She grimaces. *At least my winner*
               mother had the sense to get fixed.
        You're gonna pay me back, right?

Pay her . . . oh, for the cigs.
        "Yeah, sure. I can 'borrow'
some from Iri—uh, my mom."

Not sure why I don't want
        Alex to know I call her Iris.
Yeah, it makes her seem like

less of a mom, but Alex knows
        she's not much of a mom anyway.
Anyone with eyes could guess it.

I Walk Up the Street

Slowly, sucking nicotine into
        my lungs. Tastes like crap,
and I know if I don't stop it will

kill me. But it satisfies some
        deep call. And what the hell?
I don't want to live too damn long.

Suddenly an ambulance screams
        by. Fear punches my gut. Without
a doubt, I know exactly where

it's headed. I throw the lit Kool
        into the gutter, start to run,
choking on yellowish smoke.

I round the corner and sure as day,
        the square red truck is in front
of Gram's, warning lights spinning.

Beside it, a police cruiser blocks
        most of the street, and another
is parked farther up the road, routing

traffic away. Shit, shit, shit! I run
        faster, barely able to breathe.
Fricking cigarettes! I skid to a stop,

try to take in what I see. Two
        paramedics kneel next to Sandy.
His little body lies in the street,

unmoving. "Is he okay?" I scream,
        trying to push closer, only to be
stopped by a young police officer.

        Give them some room. The little
                boy is breathing. That's all
        we know. Are you the mother?

"No. I'm his sister. But I—I—"
        What else is there to say right
now? "Wha-what happened?"

        Hit and run. His radio scratches
                some unintelligible information.
        Hang on. I've got to take this call.

        Your, uh, sister over there saw
                the whole thing. Why don't you
        talk to her? But stay right here.

Like I would go somewhere?
        Damn me. Why wasn't I here?
Must be what he's thinking too.

Mary Ann Stands Sobbing

On the sidewalk, eyes wide
        with fear. "What happened?"
I struggle to keep my voice gentle.

      He—I—Sandy was kicking
            a ball on the lawn. Pepper
      and Honey started to fight, and . . .

      when I tried to stop them, I guess
            the ball rolled into the street
      and Sandy ran after it and . . .

      I guess a motorcycle came down
            the street and ran over him and
      just kept going and . . . and . . . I

      was right there and I didn't mean—
            Oh my God, I'm so sorry. . . . Oh
      my God, I'm so sorry. . . .

I grab her shoulders, shake hard.
        "Stop it. It's not your fault. Go
take care of the kids. They're scared."

They all stand huddled together
        on the doorstep. Mary Ann goes
over to them as another ambulance

arrives. Two ambulances for one
                person? Talk about overki—
Don't dare finish the thought.

Two new paramedics open the back
                doors of their ambulance, remove
a gurney and a backboard.

Together, the four prepare Sandy
                for a ride to the hospital. I can't
do anything but watch them

lift his still motionless form, tubes
                running into his arm and an
oxygen mask over his face, onto

the wheeled stretcher. As they load
                him into the waiting ambulance,
Officer Lemoore comes over to me.

                Your brother has internal injuries.
                            They'll need someone to give
                permission for treatment. Where

                are your parents? Can you call
                            them and tell them to come
                to Emergency right away?

143

I Tug My Eyes

Away from the ambulance,
        finally really look at the
policeman in front of me.

He must be straight out of
        the academy, not too many
years older than me. He's

good-looking, in a straight sort of
        way, with topaz gold eyes.
Eyes brimming sympathy.

"I—I'll try to get hold of my
        mom. But it will probably be
my grandmother. Is that okay?"

        He hesitates. The information
                sinks in. *Your mother would
        be best. She has custody, right?*

I nod. "But she's not always,
        uh . . ." How can I say this?
"Easy to track down."

I see. Well, do the best you can.
  If we need to, we can get a court
order, but that takes time. And . . .

He shakes his head, and his
  meaning is very clear: There
might not be a whole lot of time.

Guilt churns. I want to heave.
  "Can't I go in the ambulance?
If he wakes up, he'll be scared."

He won't wake up. He's sedated.
  Besides, you need to find your
mom. And someone needs to take

care of your brother and sisters.
  He gestures toward the crew.
You're the oldest. It's up to you.

I Am the Oldest

It was up to me to make sure
          something like this never
happened. But no, I needed to

hang out downtown, smoking
          with Alex. If Sandy doesn't
pull through, I'll make sure a hit

          and run happens. To me. The cop
                    follows me to the front door.
          I need to ask you a few questions,

          he says to Mary Ann, moving her
                    off to one side. *Tell me again*
          what happened. Can you describe . . .

I push the other kids inside.
          "I need to get hold of Gram.
Go watch TV. And don't fight."

I try to call Iris first. Her cell
          goes straight to voice mail. Big
surprise. Gram left the beauty parlor

number next to the phone. No
          surprise there, either. She's
good about communication.

Hands Shaking

I dial the number, ask to speak
        to Vivian Belcher. "Gram?"
I force my voice calm, hope

she'll respond in the same way.
        "You have to go to Emergency
right away. There was an accident. . . ."

I don't tell her everything. Don't
        have to. Enough for her to know
Sandy's life hangs by a sliver.

I poke my head into the living
        room. Porter lies on the sofa,
absorbed in Hannah Montana.

Pepper and Honey sit on the floor,
        holding each other in silent
acceptance of one another, and

maybe of the small part they,
        too, played in the afternoon's
drama. I go to tell Officer Lemoore

that I got hold of Gram. He's finished
        with Mary Ann, whose face is white
as smoke. "Let's go inside," I say.

A Poem by Cody Bennett
Smoke

You stand in front of me,
pretending to be solid,
but you are nothing
more than smoke and

                    mirrors.

You said you'd never
leave, that you would
care for us forever.
But now you claim you

                    cannot

stay, that you've been
called away. When you
go, who will I turn to
when it all crashes down?

                    Tell

me who. Then tell me
how I can believe in
anyone again, if all your
promises have been

                    lies.

Cody
Nothing's Static

If I've learned anything at
all in sixteen years, it's that
things change. What you feel
bad about one day can turn
around like that. Same goes
for the things you care about.

Three weeks ago, I kind of liked
spending time at home, goofing
off online or picking at my guitar,
or just watching TV. But now
everything feels strained
at the Bennett house. Not

really like home at all. Everyone
is strung tight. On edge.
Concerned about the future.
Something to do with Jack's
digestive system. Whatever
it is, neither he nor Mom

wants to talk about it. Silence,
thick with apprehension, hangs
over the place like a shroud.
No more dinner table banter.
No more cheerful ribbing.
No more stupid jokes.

Three Weeks Ago

I didn't have a girlfriend.
Not being partnered up
wasn't so damn bad, not
that I totally mind having
the hottest girl in my crowd
acting like she can't get

enough of me. It's just kind
of complicated because, as
I suspected, Alyssa is not
very happy about Ronnie
jumping my bones, jumping
'Lyssa's ship in the process.

The first time 'Lyssa saw us
together, I thought she'd shit
on the spot. We were sitting
together (okay, like glued
together, front to front, Ronnie
in my lap) on the grass at

> school. 'Lyssa came hauling
> around the corner, headed
> somewhere in a hurry. But
> when she saw us, she braked
> and did a double take. *Just
> what do you think you're doing?*

I'm not sure if she was talking
to Ronnie or me, but Ronnie
jumped right down her throat.
*What does it look like we're
doing, Alyssa? Having tea?*
Then she laughed. Too hard.

'Lyssa puffed out her cheeks
and her face turned red—the rotten
red of an overripe tomato. Her
hands clenched. Unclenched.
I thought we were dog meat. But
all she said was, *That's fucked up.*

Oil and water or not, Alyssa
was the first girl I ever had
real feelings for. And now
her feelings were shredded.
I felt like shit. Still do. But
not enough to tell Ronnie to

take a hike. She's freaking
beautiful, with black coffee
eyes, shiny dark hair, and legs
that go up to there. Slipping
in between them is like making
love to warm milk and honey.

We Had Sex

The very first night we went
out together, although I didn't
think it was going to happen,
what with her brother being
a bouncer (okay, security guard)
at Frozen75, something she

neglected to tell me until we
slithered up to the front of
the line. Pissed off a bunch
of people, for sure. But, just
like any club, I guess, they
have an Invited Guest line.

And if your brother's a bouncer,
you're invited. Especially if he's
a bouncer the size of a VW
Beetle. Vince Carino plays
linebacker for the UNLV Rebels,
a decent university team,

usually the second best in the state.
Never mind there are only two,
and the one from that cowtown
up north, Reno, generally comes
out on top. Not always, though,
and when Vegas wins, it's party time.

Then Again

It's pretty much always party
time in Las Vegas. They don't
call it Sin City for nothing.
Ronnie and I partied down
that first night for sure. And
we've been partying ever since.

See, Vince is not only okay with
his sister and me being together.
He encourages it. Says she needs
a guy in her life to keep her in
line. Not that I'd ever try *that*
with Ronnie. I'm a pacifist.

Vince is not. But he is a partier.
Drinks like no serious athlete
should, not that I think he's
especially serious. What I think
is, he likes knocking people down—
smashing them into the ground.

Glad he seems to like me. Booze
isn't his only bad habit, though.
Pot. Pills. Crack. Probably other
stuff, but that's all I've seen. And
that's plenty. I so do *not* want to
know too much about Vince Carino.

Vince and I Have Shared

A bottle or two, a fistful of doobs,
pipes and pipes and pipes. Tonight,
we'll pass around all three at his
regular Friday poker game. Not sure
how I reached the heart of his inner
circle so quickly. Suppose it could

be because I'm usually the one
supplying the weed. Anyway,
I know zip about poker, but it
sounds like a hell of a lot more
fun than staying home, listening
to Jack cough and Mom sigh.

Before I go, I guess I should
brush up on the rules a little.
Punch a few words into my
search engine and I come up
with . . . whoa. Way too much
information. Let's start with

the basic what hand beats what?
One pair, two pair, three of a kind.
Easy enough to remember. Straight.
Flush. Full house. Four of a kind.
Straight flush. Royal flush. Together,
do those equal a hetero queen's toilet?

Damn It, Jack

You've cursed me! *You're*
the one who's supposed to
be coming up with corny jokes.
I'm supposed to laugh at them,
whether or not they're funny.
Now I need to check up on you.

He's in the living room, adrift on
anonymous painkillers. The TV
is blaring, and his eyes are aimed
at it, but vacant. Dread shoots through
my body on a wave of adrenaline.
"Hey, Jack. How's it going?"

> He jumps a little. *Huh? Oh.*
> *Hey, Cody. What's up, son?*
> His speech is slurred, just
> barely coherent. Fucking
> meds. *Where's your mom?*
> *Is she home from work yet?*

Damn. For a minute, I really
thought he might be dead. But
why would I think that? He's
only got indigestion. Jeez, man.
Talk about jumpy. Freaking
crack is famous for that.

But I've got to admit I like
the way it makes every nerve
come alive. Just like Ronnie
said it would. She's got a tidy
little habit. I have to be careful
not to let my own toking get

so out of hand. I swear I never
had a clue she had made friends
with the pipe. Best thing about
it is what a little horndog she turns
into when she's smoking. Boo
frigging yah! Whatever I want.

Jack Coughs

Pulling my mind away from
Ronnie's superior body, back
into the present, toward the sofa.
I go sit next to Jack. Boy, is his
face pale. "Mom's not home
yet. Can I bring you something?"

He turns toward me, eyes wet
with tears. (Tears?) *No, Cody,*
I'm okay. Where are you off
to tonight anyway? Got a hot date?
Before I can answer, a door slams.
Must be Cory. He's the only one

who comes into the house like
that. Sure enough, he stomps
into the room, grinning like a goat.
Damn, even from here he smells
like a brewery. *Hey! What's up?*
Why you look sho—so serious?

Jack takes it in. Turns to me.
He's messed up, huh? I could
say no, and Jack might even go
for it. But Cory's way too young
to start down this ol' road. I nod.
You been drinking, Cory boy?

Cory's face flushes, from beer
and defiance. *So what? Cody
drinks all the time. You never
sh—say nothing to him!* Fingers
knotting and unknotting, he
waits for someone's next move.

If he's expecting me to deny
it, he's drunker than he looks.
I don't want the situation to
get out of hand. I'll try humor.
"'Never say nothing' is a double
negative. What you said means—"

Suddenly Cory wobbles.
Weaves. Drops face-first to
the floor. *Holy shit,* says Jack,
trying to get up, and wobbling
almost as bad as Cory before
he took his literal nosedive.

I nudge Jack back down on
the overstuffed cushion. "No
worries. Other than a lump or
two, I'm guessing he'll be fine
once he sleeps it off. I'll get him
to bed." Like when he was little.

I Pick Him Up

Off the floor, haul him to his
room, thinking about when we
were younger, before Jack came
along. I took my big-brother job
seriously then, and often helped
Mom feed him, bathe him, put

him to bed. Déjà vu! Except this
time he smells like cheap brew.
Thirteen! How did he even get
hold of the stuff? Ripped it off,
no doubt. But from where? Or
who? Damn it all, Cory! I tuck

a light blanket around him, go
to check on Jack. He's snoring,
pushed down into a painkiller
pit. I pull up the foot of the La-Z-
Boy, cover him with Mom's
favorite afghan. She'll be home

soon. Think I'll make my escape
now. Things could get ugly—or
at least complicated—when everyone wakes up and accusations get
kicked back and forth. I don't want
to play explanation dodgeball.

It's a Short Drive

To Vince's apartment, not far
from the UNLV campus. But since
it's Friday evening, just past six,
the freeway looks like a boulder
field. I opt for surface streets,
which aren't a whole lot better.

Which gives me way too much
time to think about what's going
on with Cory. I've been watching
the anger build up inside him, and
I know it's because things feel
fragile in our once rock solid home.

I wasn't much older than he is
the first time I sucked a few down.
But I drank those Coronas for fun.
I think Cory wanted to swallow his
fear and it took a couple too many
brews to make that happen.

Ah, here we go. Magenta Springs.
Why does that remind me of blood?
It's a pretty nice place, at least from
the outside. I park in a visitor's space
behind a tall stucco wall. My beater
car is probably safe. What about me?

The Game Hasn't Started Yet

Four or five guys are drinking.
Smoking. Snorting something
off the glass-topped coffee table.
They barely notice me join the party,
and that makes me a little nervous.
Vince is setting up the card table.

> He, at least, sees me come in. *Hey.*
> *Help me out here. You brought*
> *some of that good green, didn't you?*
> As I suspected, the key to my invite.
> When I nod, he surprises me. *Cool.*
> *I'll throw some extra chips your way.*

When he actually does, I'm even
more surprised. Six of us belly up
to the table, and I light a big fat one.
I buy in for fifty, and he slides me
sixty in chips. The dope is worth
more, but I didn't expect anything,

so I figure I'm ahead. "Thanks."
The poker-for-beginners rules
said to watch the other players,
learn how they "tell." In other
words, read their body language.
Three might as well tell for real.

You can see what they've got in
their eyes. But Vince and some guy
called Fly (pretty sure I don't want
to know why) are damn good at bluffing.
I keep my bets low. One pair ain't going
to beat much, and that's all I'm dealt

for several hands. I bluff a couple of
times, to make 'em think I know
the game. Down thirty, the deal goes
to Fly. I turn my cards over one at
a time. Ten. Eight. Ten. One pair.
Here we go again. King. Ten.

Holy crap. I swallow the rush. Can't
tell 'em I've got three of a kind. Ante up.
Don't bet too much. Ask for two cards
without smiling. One dude folds.
Another bets five. Vince calls, raises
ten. I flip one card. It's a three. Fuck.

Bet comes to me as I flip the last card.
Ten. Four of a kind? Calm. Stay calm.
I raise Vince twenty. Fly folds. Vince
looks into my eyes, but I give nothing
away. He calls, shows two pairs.
I win! For once in my life, I win!

I Leave Vince's

Two hundred dollars richer.
I'm walking on water, oh yeah,
and the rush is effing amazing.
Only one thing could make
this night better. I dial Ronnie's
number. "Hey. It's me. You

up for some fun?" I knew her
answer before I asked the question,
and she doesn't live far. When
I get there, it's too late to knock
on the door, so I go to her window.
It's the only one with a light in it.

My head is Tilt-A-Whirling with
substance abuse, but more because
of finishing off the evening as
a winner. I won at poker. And I'm
about to win at something even
better. Ronnie comes to the glass,

opens it, lets me inside. Her room
smells of roses, and she has nothing
on but a thigh-length shirt. She puts
a finger to her lips, but there's no
need for words once we fall together
into her bed. Night slips away.

A Poem by Eden Streit
Once

I thought fairy tales were
lies or worse, promises
spoken, yet meant to be
broken. Intent is all.

                                          Why

do grown-ups feel
the need to make up
a story, only to later
confess that it was a

                                          lie?

Why look for a prince
when frogs are much
more common? Why
reach for a dream

                                          when

you're at ease within
your nightmares? Why
scramble to disguise
what your personal

                                          truth is

when reality not only
hurts less in the long
run, but is most often

                                          the easier path?

Eden
Spring Break

And for once, it actually feels like spring
in Idaho. For most of my life, spring break

was called Easter vacation. Daddy about had
a meltdown when the school board caved

in and changed it. *What's this country
coming to when the Spring Bunny delivers*

spring eggs to children? As if he ever gave
two cents about bunnies and egg hunts. Not

in *his* church. Not on the holiest day of the year,
and Easter Sunday remains that for Christians

near and far. For the family of Pastor Streit,
it is even more, because at Papa's church,

it's an all-out celebration of the Resurrection,
and, dressed up in our Easter bonnets, we sit

front and center. I've never really minded
that before. But today, I'd much rather hang out

in back, pretending not to notice the good-looking
reformed Catholic sitting nearby.

Papa Has Noticed

Andrew, of course. No way would he miss
a possible convert wandering into his hallowed

sanctuary. Once or twice he's made the effort
to engage Andrew in conversation and Andrew,

bless his heart, does his best to respond
positively. No dunking yet (and Papa is quite

likely the reincarnation of John the Baptist
himself!), but he is cordial almost to the point

of brownnosing. Almost. And speaking of
nosing, Mama's ever-observant gaze is harder

to avoid. She must have seen something,
because two Sundays ago, she went fishing:

> That McCarran boy is a fine-looking
> young man, don't you think, Eden?

If Papa is John the Baptist (again), Mama
is the Inquisition incarnate. I tried not

to gulp, struggled to meet her eye. "Who?
Him?" I pretended to study his face

for the first time. "Well, now that you mention
it . . ." Then I almost blew it, almost smiled.

My mouth twitched. Mama pounced,
all lioness to my poor little gazelle.

> *Appearances can be deceptive.* Her hand
> settled on my shoulder. *Why, if I had tumbled*

> *for every handsome boy who looked my way,*
> *I shudder to think where I might be today!*

I bit hard on my lip, excused myself
to go to the bathroom, barely making it

through the door before shuddering
myself—with uncontainable laughter.

Needless to Say

Andrew and I have been completely
discreet at church since then. And today,

no way to flirt even a little, it's going to be
really tough. But you know, just seeing

Andrew at all makes any day special.
He's already there, with his sister

and mother, when we arrive. Mariah
smiles and waves. She is four years

older than Andrew, but the two are tight.
So tight, in fact, that he has confessed

our secret to her. So tight that, despite a little
righteous worry, she has chosen not only

> to keep quiet about our relationship, but
> also to nurture it. She comes over now.

> *Happy Easter,* she says to Papa before stroking
> Mama. *Lovely dress. That color is wonderful*

> *on you!* She takes my arm. *May I borrow Eden?*
> *I'd like to introduce her to my mother.*

> *Andrew and I are hoping to get her to church*
> *more than two or three times a year.*

If Mama is surprised that Mariah
and I are acquainted, she hides it well.

*Of course. Eden, you know where
to find us. See you in a few minutes.*

Mariah steers me toward love. Andrew wears
it like skin, so obvious it makes me blush.

His mother's face, so like his, lights as she
takes my hand in hers. Her voice is soft,

and still she forces it low. *Hello, Eden. I hope
you don't mind that I tagged along today,*

but I simply had to meet you. She draws me
a little bit away from anyone likely to overhear.

Then she looks me in the eye. *I've never
seen Andrew so happy. Thank you for that.*

My reply comes easily. "There is no
one like Andrew. Thank *you* for *that.*"

Old Mrs. Beatty

Launches a spirited "Old Rugged Cross"
on the aging organ, and I must fall back

into the role of perfect preacher's daughter.
I take my expected place in front, but find

every opportunity to glance behind me,
even as I hear the well-known story

of a love greater than any human love
could ever be. So sayeth Papa. Again.

Three rows back sits the greatest love
I'll ever know, and my heart promises

that our love was sparked, as all love is,
by God's love. So why—WHY—is it wrong?

Rephrase. Why—WHY—does my own
family think it's wrong when his doesn't?

Three rows back sits the one true love
of my life, surrounded by his own

family's love. A family that accepts me
for who I am, to him. A family I long to

be part of. And if that means leaving
my family behind, maybe I have to go.

As Soon as the Thought

Crosses my mind, I backtrack. Can't
go. Not yet. He's not ready for me.

And I am only sixteen. Sixteen.
Immersed in the Easter story. Thinking

about loving Andrew, about giving him
the ultimate gift—my virginity. This week.

Not that he knows it. But it's spring break.
Lots of girls give it away on spring break, right?

So it's normal. And, despite sitting in the front
row while my papa preaches about resurrection—

including ways to avoid it—I want to be normal.
Not "normal" as defined by abnormal people.

My people. My parents. I never considered
them (and so never considered me) abnormal

until I met Andrew. But it's completely clear
now. And the best way I can think of to become

completely normal is by becoming a woman.
All I need is the opportunity. Eve, help me.

Ironically

It is Eve (not the original) who sets it up.
See, my sister has asthma. Talking major.

And like I said, it is spring, also in a major
way. We had snow over the winter, an early

melt. Rain to follow. And that means wild
flowers. Early bloom of sage. Beautiful.

Obnoxious to someone who can't tolerate
pollen. Especially someone young. Someone

like Eve. It is Tuesday. Spring break. Eve
wakes, wheezing. Papa is off somewhere,

leaving Mama to rush my little sister
to Emergency. She calls just before noon.

> *They want to keep her for observation.*
> *I have to stay with her. You'll be okay?*

"I'm fine, Mama. You do what you need
to. If I'm not here, I'll be at the library.

I have to research a history paper." Guilt
wants to well as I hang up. I force it

back down, call Andrew, knowing
it's wrong. Wondering if I'm damned.

In the Back of My Mind

I'm thinking he'll take me to a hotel, all the while
stressing about how we'll get away with it.

Spies, remember? But when he picks me up,
we head out of town, and it occurs to me

that I never confessed what I had in mind
for the afternoon. "Where are we going?"

> He pulls me very close to him, right
> up against his very warm body. *Home.*

> *My parents went to Elko for a few days.*
> *Not exactly a world-class destination,*

> *but for them it's a second honeymoon.*
> *You and I will go to Hawaii, okay?*

He always says the right thing. "Okay.
But I'm allergic to pineapple." I'm not,

at least, not that I know for sure. But
they say humor steadies the nerves.

Nervous?

Let's see. Why wouldn't I be? My mom
and sister are at the ER, which is the only

reason I'm here. What if Mama calls and
I'm not home? Will she buy the library thing?

And what if something is really wrong
with Eve? Should I be *there*? Or here?

Andrew's parents are likely a few hundred
miles away. But are they really? And are

they discussing the likelihood of what is
going on *here*? Are they talking about me?

And even if they're not, and everything else
is on the up-and-up, am I seriously considering

doing that stuff I read on the Net the other
night? I answered all those "Are you really

ready" questions and came away with
a definite "Yes." But am I really, really?

Andrew answers the question for me,
though I'm sure he has no idea that's what

he's doing. *I can't wait to show you the ranch.*
Someday it will be your home too. No hint

of hesitation. He's not only saying his home
is mine, he's telling me his life is mine.

We turn down a long gravel driveway,
the smell of spring sharp through the windows.

Cattle graze in one field, horses in another.
I know nothing about either animal except

what I've seen on TV. But that will change
with time. Time with Andrew. One day,

not far in the future, we'll have plenty of time
together. Something powerful rises up inside me.

Home

Andrew parks the Tundra and we are home.
A bluetick pup lifts her head from the porch,

and when she sees Andrew, sprints to greet
him, tail stub wagging. I know how she feels.

Andrew bends to scratch her behind an ear.
Here now, little Sheila. Say hello to my Eden.

And now she is my puppy too. She licks
my hand, telling me so, and I cannot believe

that any of this is real. Where is my familiar
home? Where is Boise? I never want to return

to either. I slide my arms up around Andrew's
neck. "I love you. More than anything in

this world." And, for a swift-passing moment,
the thought crosses my mind that I love him

more than anything in *any* world. Torn, always
torn, I throw out a silent entreaty to whatever

might exist beyond this world: "If love like this
is wrong, Lord, go ahead and damn me."

I Feel Zero

Trepidation as Andrew takes my hand,
encourages me through the front door.

I hold my breath, not sure why. I feel
like a bride on her wedding night, despite

the nag inside my head who insists:
Not married. Not right. Not married . . .

"Shut up!" I will her, silently. Because,
despite the lack of white gown and cake,

dripping frosting flowers, I know what will
happen soon means Andrew and I are forever

one. Sheila, puppy of honor, follows us
inside. She's probably not nearly as impressed

as I am. The decor is simple. Real. Wood.
Leather. Antiques, refinished, as if the people

who own them care about their history.
And, of course, they do. "Oh, Andrew.

It's all so perfect. I love it!" And I do.
"But not nearly as much as I love you."

We're kissing. We've never kissed exactly
like this, because we've never felt this easy

with each other. No one here. No one
to see. Only Andrew and me.

(Sheila doesn't care. Doesn't count,
because she only wants what Andrew

and I do. Love.) We could talk, I guess.
But there's nothing, really, to say beyond

I love you, and we've already said that.
Andrew stops kissing me, and his eyes

ask what he's afraid to, and my eyes answer
in the same way, so he takes my hand, leads

me down the hall to the bedroom that I would
have picked as his without analyzing. It has

a big feather bed, with massive quilts and
pillows I have to fall into. With Andrew.

I Thought It Would Be

So easy. That loving him as much as I do would
conquer any hint of fear. But when he kisses

me, I'm shaking, and there are tears
in my eyes. *We don't have to,* he whispers.

"I know. I want to. I'm just . . ." Unsure.
I'm completely unsure about my body.

What if he hates it? But now he touches
me. His hands are tentative, and I remember

that this is new for him, too. *Is this
okay?* he asks. *Tell me what you like.*

He kisses me as he picks me up, lays
me gently on the bed. A slow, mutual

exploration begins. As we learn together,
the fear falls away, and sheer exhilaration—

like standing on the very edge of a cliff,
with the wind in your face—replaces it.

He likes my body, and I love his, and there
are only a few seconds of pain, before waves

of pleasure. Wave after swelling wave of
everything right. Wave after wave of love.

A Poem by Seth Parnell
Nothing's Right

Not when you know
someone you love
must leave too soon.

The thought of

losing a friend stings.
The pain of losing
a parent revisits you.
The insanity of

losing someone

who has become
your very heart slices
you right in two.

You can't

eat. Can't sleep. Can't
concentrate on simple
things. All you do
is wonder how you'll

live without

the necessary beat
inside your chest.
The weight of dread

takes your breath away.

Seth
Three Weeks

Until Loren leaves me.
            One month until my life
            falls into limbo. I never
            knew limbo was meant
to be experienced on earth.

I'm halfway there already.
            I fake my way through
            every day, eating, drinking,
            staring off into the classroom
void, with finals fast approaching.

I don't care about school,
            about getting into some
            highbrow university.
            Don't care about the price
of seed or serious lack of rain.

Will I care about any of
        that when he's gone?
        Maybe it will be easier,
        not sneaking off to see
him every stinking chance

I get. Not trying with
        every ounce of what's
        inside me to make him
        damn well remember
me every minute he's away.

I'd Be Lying

If I said things haven't changed
            between us already. It's like
            we've erected a tall wall
            of silence, and neither of us
will break down and be first

to try and scale the stupid
            thing. We used to talk for
            hours, discuss issues, confess
            latent secrets. We used to
have fun. Used to go out.

Now when he opens the door,
            I don't even say hello, just
            push my way through,
            barely close it behind me
before pulling him off down

the hall to the bedroom.
            We have changed there,
            too. Especially me. I take
            control from the start,
don't ask, only demand.

I want to hurt him, like
            he will hurt me when he
            goes off to minister. I only
            have one way to do that.
And I'm doing it now.

He Accepts

Every jolt of punishment
        without a word or even
        a sigh. When I can't give
        any more, when the act
is finished, I stand back,

        waiting. Expecting anger.
                Tears. Anything but his
                soft, *Don't you know how
                sorry I am that I have*
        to go? I love you, Seth.

And the tears that finally
        come are mine. "Jesus,
        Loren. Why did I have to
        meet you at all? What do
I do when you leave?

"Go back to school, back to
        farming? Back to the old
        me, who was never me
        at all?" I look at him, find
his eyes, but no answers.

He comes over to me,
		slides his arms up
		around my neck, kisses
		the kind of kiss that makes
me want more. A lot more.

Just when I think I'm ready
		for more, he stops me.
		Let's clean up and go out
		for a while. I'm starving.
How about some Italian?

As I start to say no, my
		belly rumbles a good one.
		I haven't eaten a darn thing
		since morning Cheerios.
"Sure, why the hell not?"

Probably a good idea
		to get out of this place
		before I start to cry again.
		Sometimes, top crust
or not, I feel like a total girl.

Despite That

And despite being an hour
        from home, I don't want
        to look like a girl when
        Loren and I go out, not
even in this neighborhood,

where many of the people
        I see could easily be identified
        as "gay." Not even knowing
        most everyone here *is* gay.
Who knows who might be

cruising this place for
        a date or just for kicks?
        Hetero couples wander
        the sidewalks. Looking
for a threesome? Or just

to be somewhere safe, where
        one half of the couple won't
        ask the other, *What the* HELL
        are you looking at? Somewhere
safe? Is there such a place?

Loren Leads the Way

Weaving us in and out
       of the Bohemians
       crowding the sidewalk.
       It's nice to be out with
him. But it also makes me

sad. We used to do this
       more when we first got
       together. Restaurants.
       Theater. Long walks,
talking about life in general.

Then it all became about
       sex. More sex. Better
       sex. Unusual sex. Like
       most couples, I guess.
Is that what I'm really

afraid of losing? Not
       connection or affection,
       not the growth caused
       by absorbing love? If
so, what have I become?

I Can't Help

But think about that as
        Pietro escorts us to
        our favorite table, one
        we haven't asked for in
too many weeks, a fact he

        reminds us of. *Why have*
            you stayed away so
            long, misters? I was
            beginning to think you
    maybe got bad fish last time.

    Loren always orders the
        fresh fish. He responds,
        Now you know we've never
        gotten so much as a single
    bad mouthful here, Pietro.

    The broad Italian smiles.
        Well then, we have on
        the menu fresh sea bass
        tonight. . . . He goes on to
    describe the specials in detail.

I'll stick with my usual
    mushroom raviolis.
    I lost Pietro after sea bass,
    wondering if, without Loren,
I'll ever eat here again.

I Guess I Might

If I ever happen to come
        to Louisville again, once
        Loren's gone. The food
        is delicious. If the place
was in a different part of

town, I might even bring
        Dad along, see if he could
        interest Pietro in his supersecret
        recipe for venison
sausage, biscuits, and gravy.

        The thought makes me smile,
            and that makes Loren smile
            too. *What?* he says, the corners
            of his mouth still curled in
        that oh-so-familiar way.

It's hard to put him and Dad
        in the same place, even if
        that place is inside my head.
        "Nothing." Under the table,
Loren's hand finds my thigh.

        So, he says, *I thought*
            we might go out for
            a little while after we
            finish dessert. There's
        a club not far from here. . . .

His touch is doing strange
        things to me. At least, they
        feel awfully strange in a
        restaurant. "A club? You
mean . . . ? You're not serious."

        Completely serious. Tonight
                they even let underage guys
                inside, as long as they have
                a sponsor. I figured I could
        sponsor you. How about it?

Right now, my body wants
        him to do more than "sponsor"
        me. But I have to admit, I'm
        a little curious. "I thought
you didn't like gay bars."

        I don't. Not alone. But I'm
                not alone tonight, am I?
                He spies Pietro, bringing
                our tiramisu, and his hand
        falls away. Leaves me cold.

Cold Becomes Clammy

As Loren and I make our
        way past Mr. ID Checker
        at the door to Fringe. He
        looks at Loren's license,
nods, barely glances at mine.

I shake my head. "What was
        that? He didn't give a damn
        about how old I am. And just
        why do you have to show ID
to prove you're underage?"

        Loren grins. *You're supposed*
                to be eighteen to get in.
                But you're right, he doesn't
                really care. Kentucky
        is notoriously lax on

        such things. It hasn't been
                all that long since they
                raised the drinking age
                to twenty-one, and they
        don't very often bust bars

        for serving to minors.
                Still, I wouldn't stand
                right in front of the guy,
                sipping bourbon. He
        might decide to get nasty.

Fringe

Is a lot different than I
        thought it would be.
        I expected sleazy, but it
        borders on upscale, all dark
wood and brass and suede.

It's not that late, as bar
        scenes go, so the place
        isn't too crowded. Still,
        maybe fifty or sixty guys
are drinking, laughing,

and hitting on other guys,
        if they're not coupled up
        already. Loren and I find
        cushy chairs in the back,
and he goes to order drinks.

I use the opportunity to
        check out the river of faces.
        Many are average. You
        wouldn't look twice at
them on the street. A few

you wouldn't want to look
        at. Okay, they're not very
        attractive, and when they
        openly stare at me, it
creeps me out completely.

There are also some beautiful
        men here. Most of them are
        younger, yet a fair number
        gravitate toward much older
guys. I don't think it's all about

love. I watch a decent-looking
        middle-aged man, sandy
        haired and very well dressed,
        head off to the men's room.
Within three minutes, his young

companion flirts obnoxiously.
        Glad he didn't pick me to flirt
        with. When the older guy
        returns, he is not pleased.
He slams his fist on the table,

grabs his designer overcoat,
        and stomps toward the door,
        followed by the younger guy.
        If I beat up a table, would
Loren follow me out the door?

Would He Decide to Stay

If I tried coercion instead
        of a simple plea? What if
        I threatened his family?
        Like I could, considering
I don't know who—or where—

they are. He's never shared
        that information with me, nor
        told me where he went to school,
        or how (or if) he outed himself.
That's a lot not to tell me.

He returns now with two
        sugar-rimmed glasses,
        filled with amber liquid
        and some sort of green
leaves. *Mint juleps,* he says.

Froufrou drinks? I take a big
        swallow, fight to not choke.
        "H-holy crap. What's in
        these things?" Whatever
it is burns going down.

        He can't help but laugh.
            Bourbon. A little sugar
            syrup, some mint leaves,
            but other than that,
        bourbon. Sip, don't gulp.

I'm Doing a Fair Job

Of sipping, not gulping,
        when one of the most
        incredible-looking men I've ever seen
        shakes his butt by. My mouth
must have dropped open,

        because Loren turns to see
            what I'm staring at. *My, my.*
            He is *a fine work of art, isn't*
            he? We watch the guy cozy
up to a what might be less

than affectionately termed
        "old faggot." Within five
        seconds, the ancient dude is
        buying the fine work of art
a drink. "What's up with that?"

        Oh hon, haven't you ever
            heard the term "sugar
            daddy"? Lots of young
            guys go looking for easy
        drinks, easy meals, maybe

        even a place to stay. When
            you look like him—he
            points toward Pretty Boy,
            then he turns and his eyes
scan my face—*or you,*

it isn't hard at all to find
  someone who'll take
  care of you. Sometimes
  they'll set you up in your
own place, or move you

into theirs. Sometimes
  you live like a movie
  star, even. The price
  tag is regular sex.
He waits for my reaction.

"Regular sex, with someone
  like that?" I take a deep
  drink of minty bourbon,
  actually enjoy the burn.
"I could never do that!"

Loren shakes his head.
  Never say never, dear.
  You might be surprised at
  what you can do, should
circumstances dictate.

A Poem by Whitney Lang
Circumstances

Create our conception,
how we live, what kind
of person we manage

to grow

into. Another day,
a different hour, take
a left and not a

right,

you'd wind up a whole
different being. Knowing
if that would be better

requires

a realm of experience
only decades can build.
Roses? Lilies? Moonlight?

Sunlight?

Which do I prefer? Ask
me again in thirty
or forty years.

The Best Thing

About my mom being such
a bitch is not worrying
about trying to make her
proud of me. Smoke it

up, drink it up, and if
I happen to get caught,
well, wouldn't it just slay
her if the news got around?

Kyra, too. Oh, she'd pretend
that her concern was all
about me, rather than her
precious reputation,

but that would be total
toad crap. "Total toad
crap." TTC. Hey, I like
that. TTC, my new spew.

Kyra's Home

From Vassar. Normal
college geeks go to places
like Florida or Mexico
for spring break. Not Kyra.

She comes home to spend
time with Mom, who actually
rescheduled a tennis game
to take her into the city.

> *I sooooo need some new*
> *clothes, Kyra fished.*
> *The styles back east are*
> *sooooo not me, you know?*

Like jeans aren't the same
beyond the Mississippi.
Like you can't find angora
in Manhattan! TTC, for sure.

> *Mom swallowed the bait.*
> *We'll run up to Sacramento*
> *Street. There's a new boutique*
> *I've been dying to check out.*

> *Then maybe Daddy can take*
> *time to have lunch with us. New*
> *York seafood can't possibly*
> *compare to San Francisco's.*

Sounds fun, said Kyra. *Give
Daddy a call and see if he can
make it. I'll go take a shower.
Unless you want it first. . . .*

Directed at me. "No, no.
Go ahead. I'm not planning
on going anywhere special
today, just hanging out here."

Mom just shook her head, but
Kyra sputtered, *You're not
coming? But you have to! It will
be so much more fun with you.*

Like they really wanted me
to come. Talk about TTC!
"No, you guys go. I don't feel
so great today, anyway."

Kyra might have argued
more, but Mom decided,
*You should stay home then.
Last thing I need is a bug.*

Last Thing

Any of us needs is Mom
with a bug. She's bitchy
enough totally healthy.
Weird, but I can't remember

the last time she was sick.
Too freaking mean, I guess.
She probably scares the bugs
away. Anyway, Kyra and

she continued their mutual
butt-kiss fest all the way out
the door. I have to admit
I half wanted to change

my mind and go with them.
If I believed they really
wanted my company, I just
might have. Instead, knowing

I'll have the place to myself
most of the day, I called Lucas
as soon as the door slammed
behind Butt Kissers One and Two.

After the Last Fiasco

Lucas was just a bit hesitant.
Are you sure*? Man, last time*
was a way close call. I definitely
don't need that kind of trouble.

What a wuss! But that's not
what I said. What I said was,
"They won't be home until
three at the absolute earliest.

Come over right now. Please?"
Then I made my voice all
breathy, hoping that was sexy.
"I really, really need to see you."

Need to see him, to melt like candle
wax against his heat. Need his heat.
Any heat. Need to feel warmed,
wanted. For a change.

But I didn't say any of that,
either. No use letting him know
I'm needy. Anyway, it worked.
He should be here any minute.

I Did Shower

Even borrowed some of Kyra's
way expensive ginger-scented
shampoo and lotion. No wonder
she always smells so good!

The last time I went to the mall
with Paige, one of the few
investments I made was in
a sapphire blue satin nightshirt

with matching bikini panties.
Good thing my cute stalker,
Bryn, didn't see me buy
this outfit. He would have

followed me home for sure.
I still have his card in my purse.
Not sure what for. Anyway,
all dressed down in sapphire

satin, damp hair, and smooth
skin perfumed with ginger,
I feel sexier than I ever have
before. Could I really *be* sexy?

Lucas Makes Me Wait

Almost two hours. It's closing
in on noon by the time he decides
to grace me with his presence.
I've chewed three fingernails

clear down to the quick,
yanked several strands of hair
out of my head. Not great
ways to deal with nerves,

and I know it when I'm doing
them, but can't seem to stop
myself, especially just sitting
in limbo next to the window.

By the time his Eclipse streaks
into view, I'm totally in need
of fake nails and my scalp
pulses pain. And I'm pissed.

But when I open the door,
see Lucas standing there, in
all his tanned hotness, anger
morphs back into neediness.

>He checks me out, gives a low
>whistle. *You should dress like
>that more often. Nylons and heels,
>you'd be just about perfect.*

The pout that pops up is not
manufactured. "What do you
mean, 'just about'? Not the right
thing to say to someone you

kept waiting for two hours."
I let him in anyway, and he
rewards me with one of his
luscious kisses. Def perfect.

Too soon, he pulls away.
*Sorry I'm late. But I wanted
to pick up a little something
to make the afternoon interesting.*

He reaches into his jacket
pocket, pulls out a small metal
can. Inside is a miniature baggie,
a razor blade, and a short length

of drinking straw. *All we need
is something to chop this up on.
Something glass, like a mirror
or maybe a picture.*

I'm not sure what's in the bag,
let alone if I want to try it.
So why do I jump to my feet
to go find something glass?

What's in the Baggie

Is a half-dollar-sized chunk
of something yellowish white.
It sparkles in the sunlight.
Lucas slices off a thin section

> and tells me, *Cocaine, clean*
> *as you can find anywhere.*
> *My brother knows the importer.*
> *Wait until you try it.*

I don't want to admit the idea
scares me. Weed is one thing.
Cocaine is another. I've seen
it waste people. Seen it waste

entire families, in fact, when
one parent or the other (or both)
invests everything they have
into staying buzzed on coke.

> Lucas keeps chopping, but my
> silence alerts him. *You've done*
> *coke before, right? No? Oh,*
> *baby, you're gonna love it.*

> *You're totally gonna fly.*
> *Don't worry.* He grins like
> a leprechaun. *You're safe*
> *flying with me. Mostly, anyway.*

I Watch Lucas

Suck two long, thin, sparkly
yellowish lines up his nose.
Then he hands the picture to me.
Not too hard or you'll sneeze.

I inhale gently, one line up
the right nostril, the other
up the left. Immediately,
both sides of my nose go

cold and numb. Now, just like
that, my heart is racing and
the hairs on my arms rise,
sending little chills throughout

my entire body. OMG. No
wonder people like this drug.
I look at Lucas, who's watching
me carefully. "More, please."

He laughs. *Careful now.*
A little of this goes a long
way. But he indulges me,
and himself, with two more.

Every nerve jumps to attention.
I can't feel my mouth or nose,
but other parts of my body
are begging to be touched.

Lucas indulges them, too,
with his hands and his mouth.
I love how he kisses, love how
his fingers move over my body.

Everything is hard. Everything
is warm. No, cold. No, warm.
I've never felt so alive. Never
felt so in love. I glance at the clock.

Not even one. We have plenty
of time. But I don't want to
do it here on the couch. "Let's
go to my bedroom, okay?"

I Don't Have to Ask Twice

Lucas scoops me up into
his toned arms, carries me
down the hall, like a groom
clutching his bride. The thought

makes me blush, and I have
no clue why. I rest my head
against his chest for the entire
ten-second journey. Then

he lays me gently on the bed,
unbuttons my shirt, peels
back the blue satin, stares
at what he has uncovered.

I am totally exposed, totally
flying high, and yet I do, in
fact, feel safe with Lucas,
even as he lowers himself

over me. Every ounce of me
wants what he's about to do,
and yet for just an instant,
regret stings and I say, "Wait."

> He pauses. *What? You*
> *don't want me to stop,*
> *do you? Because I don't*
> *think I can. I need you. See?*

He lowers my hand to feel
his need, and my heart screams,
"Hurry!" Still, my brain whispers,
"You can never take this back."

I look up into Lucas's eyes.
"I don't want you to stop.
But please don't go too fast.
I'm afraid . . ." Afraid it will

> hurt. Afraid it will change me.
> Afraid . . . afraid . . . the word
> thumps in time with my heartbeat,
> even as Lucas soothes, *I'll go easy.*

And he does. And I'm ready.
And it does feel good, despite
the pain, because it also hurts.
And then, it's just over.

Still Buzzed

And yet also drained, we lie
together for a while. I don't
know if it was good for Lucas
or not. I want to ask, but I don't

want to ask because if I do and
he says no, it will leave a scar.
I don't even know if it was good
for me, because I'm not sure

what "good sex" is. Your first time
probably isn't so good, right?
Because I didn't exactly feel
fireworks. Maybe I was too

numb. Doesn't matter. What's
done is done, and I love Lucas
even more now because he is
my first. My ear rests against

his chest. I listen to the promise
of his heart, and suddenly
my mouth is moving and what
spills from it is, "I love you."

I Wait for Him

To tell me he loves me, too.
After several seconds, I notice
I've been holding my breath.
I grab air as he rolls out of bed.

*It's getting late. Don't want
to get busted.* He stands, looks
down, at himself and the bed.
But not at me. Why won't he

look at me? *We'd better clean
up. And you might want
to wash your sheets. You're
not on your period, are you?*

"No, not for . . ." Now I notice
how the front of him is splashed
red, and the crimson stain
flowering on my bed. My face

burns. "It's not my period."
How could he not know that
the first time can make a girl bleed?
Or did he maybe not believe . . . ?

A Poem by Ginger Cordell
Bleed

Open a vein, feel
the rush, exodus,

delicious.

Don't be afraid,
there's no pain
in the letting,

delectable.

Watch the red
flow, let it go,

drip,

make it slow,

drip.

If you've done
it right, you won't
wake from the night's
indescribably peaceful

dream.

You Would Think

The possibility of losing
        a child would be a wake-up
call. Not for Iris. No way.

Sandy is still in a coma,
        wandering around some-
where deep inside his brain.

The doctors don't know
        if he's going to make it.
They say we should pray.

Gram's done a whole lot
        of praying. She's the one
who sits by his side, day

after day. Iris says it's too
        hard to see her little boy
that way. She's only been

to the hospital two or three
        times. Makes Gram mad.
Makes me mad too. Iris

doesn't give two squirts
        who she pisses off. All
she cares about is herself.

It's Been a Month

A month of worry, of guilt,
        of my having to play the role
of "Mom" even more, because

Gram isn't there to help
        me do it. A month of
Mary Ann, withdrawing

into a silent, blank-eyed
        world where accidents
don't happen, especially

not on her watch. I try to
        help, but she isn't ready
to quit blaming herself.

A month of mounting bills—
        doctor bills, ambulance bills,
hospital bills—that Gram

        is determined somehow
                to pay. *Where there's a will,
        there has to be a way.*

            A month of Iris diving
                deeper and deeper into
            bottomless bottles of numb.

She Has a New Boyfriend

A big-boned truck-driving
        son of a bitch, with eyes
like a crow's—black, dead.

I've seen eyes like those
        before, on another of
Iris's badass lays, one

I can't forget. I do my best
        never to think of him, what
he did. Try never to remember

that place in my childhood,
        but sometimes it pops into
view despite all my efforts

to keep it hidden. I was almost
        ten, and we lived in Pahrump,
the butthole of Nevada. Iris

worked at a cathouse, making
        money her usual way, only
without walking the streets.

Walt was a miner, and though
        he was a regular paying
customer at Mimi's, he had

an appetite for younger
           meat. Iris was younger then
too, but even at twenty-six,

she was way too old for Walt.
           Still, he paid for her, then he
followed her home. She let

him move in for a while.
           I remember his sour sweat,
coming in after working backhoe.

I remember how he touched
           Iris, and how she didn't
care that her kids could see.

           I remember his Marlboro breath
                   falling all down around me when
           he said, *Let me show you something.*

On Another Day

It wouldn't have happened,
        couldn't have happened.
Too many witnesses around.

But for some odd reason,
        that particular afternoon,
Iris had taken the other kids

        to play in the park. *You stay
               and start dinner*, she said.
        We won't be gone very long.

I didn't mind. I was too old
        for swings, and I've always
liked spending time by myself.

But it wasn't more than ten
        minutes before Walt came
through the door. He didn't

        ask where Iris was, or why
               the house was so quiet.
        He didn't say one word.

I opened a can of refried
        beans, spooned them into
a pot. I had no real reason

to be afraid. So why did my
        hands shake? I kept my back
to him but could feel his eyes,

        carving into me. Finally,
                he started toward the living
        room. *Bring me a beer, sweets.*

        I dug one from the fridge.
                But he wasn't on the couch,
        as expected. *Back here,* he called

from Iris's room. He was already
        out of his jeans. I didn't know
much then, but I knew there was

something very wrong about
        that. Still, I took him the beer,
holding my breath against his

        stench. He grabbed my hand,
                jerked me hard against him.
        Let me show you something.

I tried to run, but he was faster.
        Tried to fight. He was stronger.
Tried to scream. He choked my cries.

When He Finished

(Thank God it didn't take long),
　　　　he rolled off me with a grunt.
Reached for his beer. Slammed it.

Ripped and pried, swallowed
　　　　up by the shame of what that
meant, I crawled into the bathroom

to scrub away the evidence.
　　　　Not that I'd dare tell anyone.
Not when he followed me,

　　　　　　stood in the doorway, watching
　　　　　　　　me, finally said, *Tell a soul,*
　　　　I'll do your sister, too. He knew

that was a bigger threat than
　　　　saying he'd hurt Iris or some
other TV kind of shit. Because

I knew he *would* come back
　　　　for Mary Ann. She was only
eight. If he did this to her, she'd

die for sure. It had almost
　　　　killed me. I'll probably
always link sex with pain.

All That Comes Back

Like a sucker punch, mirrored
       now in Harry's corpse-cold
eyes, moving all over my body—

climbing up, shimmying back
       down. I hate them. Hate him,
because he's no different from Walt.

       Iris doesn't notice, or maybe
          doesn't mind. She's always
     saying, *You be nice to Harry.*

     We want to keep him happy.
          She's bold about bringing
    Harry around, bold because

Gram is mostly at the hospital.
       Her path has only crossed
Harry's a couple of times,

and when that happens, their
       dislike for each other hangs
thick in the air like smog.

Iris pretends that it doesn't.
       Iris is good at pretending.
She breathes make-believe.

Not Sure

If Harry is tuned in to
       how Iris earns her booze
and pill money. Don't think

so, though. She has always
       tried to keep pleasure and
business in two different boxes.

Ugh. Bad double meaning
       there. A sick sort of laugh
escapes and Iris, who is at

       this very moment sitting
              across the room from me,
       asks, *What's so funny?*

Which makes me bust up
       even more. All I can do
is snort, "Nuh . . . nothing."

       Harry, who is sitting next
              to Iris, slurping a Keystone,
       butts in. *Then why the hell*

are you laughing? Those crow
            eyes take even bolder liberties
with my body, and there's

            something in his voice—
                        something far beyond mean.
            Something approaching

            sadistic. *People don't just up*
                        and laugh for no damn
            reason, do they, little girl?

Anger firecrackers. I want
            to yell. Instead I keep my
voice very low. "I don't know

who in the fuck you think
            you are, but you're nothing
to me. I don't answer to you."

            Fists knotting, Harry jumps
                        to his feet. Iris reacts by
            jumping to hers. *W-wait,*

            baby. No need to get mad.
                        The words puff from her
            mouth. *She's just a dumb kid.*

A Nuclear Bomb

Goes off inside my skull—
        a white-hot mushroom
cloud of rage. "Yeah, well,

at least I'm not a whore! Wait.
        'Whore' is too good a word
for you and what you do.

'Hooker' works much better."
        I hesitate just long enough to
gain some satisfaction from

the look on Iris's face. Then
        I escape out the front door
before the shit smacks the fan.

It's May, and Mojave heat
        practically knocks me off
my feet, but I run. Run from

Iris, from her crow. He'd pick
        my bones clean, and I know it.
Run from Gram's house, not

home without her in it. Run
        from shadow into overbearing
sunlight. Run toward town.

I wish I could keep running.
        Farther. Forever. Wish
nothing could turn me back.

I run all the way to Alex's house.
        By the time I get there, sweat
streams from every pore, washing

        away hurt and anger. Luckily,
                when I pound on the door,
        it is Alex who answers. *Hey.*

        She steps back, and I fall into
                cool darkness. It's like diving
        deep. *What happened?* she asks.

We are alone in the place,
        and that is good, because
for some stupid reason, I tell

her the entire story, including
        the stuff about Walt. Words
keep spilling out of my mouth

as if a faucet broke. When I
        finally stop, I'm crying.
And Alex is holding me.

No One Has Ever

Held me like this before,
            strong but kind. Gentle,
even. Fact is, I'm surprised

I'm letting her hold me.
            My MO is to withdraw.
But this feels good, and that

makes me cry harder. What
            have I missed? "I'm sorry.
You didn't need to hear all that."

            Alex brushes the hair from my
                        forehead, mindless of sweat.
            It's okay. I understand. Men

            are dogs for the most part.
                        Scratch that. Dogs are kind
            of cute, and they only come on

            strong when the bitch is
                        in heat. She goes quiet,
            lets me finish feeling sorry

for myself. Finally I go quiet
            too. I look up, wanting to
thank her. She smiles. Kisses me.

It's a Soft Kiss

On the mouth, sensual,
        and it's exactly the way
I imagined it might be.

Her lips are smoothed
        by a sheen of raspberry
ice, and they make no demands

beyond this sweet three
        seconds of connection.
Iris's men dissolve, salt

        in rainwater. There is no
                more, no "let's have sex,"
        which leaves me both content

        and confused. *I think you
                need a drink,* she says.
        As she goes into the kitchen,

a new fantasy springs
        to life. "Have you ever
thought about running

away?" I call after her.
        She returns with a couple
of Cokes, spiked heavily

with what I think is rum.
All the time. No one would
even miss me. What about you?

"I'd go right now, but who
would take care of the kids?
And anyway, where would I go?"

We sip our drinks in silence.
The afternoon slips by, hazy
with alcohol. Finally I glance

at the clock. Almost six. I don't
want to go, but someone has to
make dinner. When I get home,

Iris is on the phone. She turns,
smiling. *Sandy will be okay.*
They'll release him in a few days.

A Poem by Cody Bennett
Release

I'm not the religious
type. Mom goes to church
but I mostly ignore it.

                                        Not sure

if there is a God or why
some all-powerful being
would give half a damn

                                        about

the likes of me. Lately,
though, I've tossed out
a prayer or two, thrown
them like fastballs at

                                        heaven,

if there is such a thing.
I'm afraid they only
bounced back to

                                        Earth, or

spun out into space,
unheard. Either way,
guess I'll give it another
try. Why not? What the

                                        hell

have I got to lose?

Falling Apart

That's how everything feels,
like it's dissolving one molecule
at a time. I'm scared. Damn it,
I hate to admit it, but my gut churns
night and day. I can barely eat.
Only booze goes down and stays.

Mom is at church right now.
Church, of all places! We haven't
been regular churchgoers since
we left Wichita. Now she's not only
religious. Apparently she's Catholic,
and asking for intervention. Praying

for a miracle. Some sort of Hail Mary
sign that Jack will make it home
again, happy, healthy, and maybe
a little wiser about indigestion and
what that can mean. That persistent
bellyache? Turned out Tums

weren't going to fix it. No wonder
I can't eat. Too much information
about what causes stomach cancer
and what happens when it metastasizes,
infiltrating blood and cells to infect
the esophagus, pancreas, and who

knows what else. It's just about
enough to make me choose a liquid
diet. Water. Bottled. (Tap water can
be carcinogenic.) V8 (low sodium—
salt is a factor in stomach cancer)
for your veggies. A little bouillon

(takes care of the protein requirement,
right?) watered down with vodka.
And for dessert, stiff megashots
of gin. Hey, someone besides Cory
should drink it. He's developed
a tidy habit and isn't real good

at hiding it. But Mom and Jack
can't turn him around. They barely
notice him. Or me. More important
shit on their minds. Like praying
for miracles. Like staying alive
just one more fucking day.

So Cory Drinks

Way too much. Pickling his brain,
and much too young to end up relish.
But how can I say anything when I
drink? And more. I smoke. Snort.
Pop pills. Anything to keep from
thinking about death, come knocking.

When Cory and I finish off Jack's
dwindling booze stash, scoring more
won't be a problem. Vinnie will happily
buy. At least as long as I keep bringing
bud to the Friday night games.
I've become a regular, and I've learned

to play poker, not that I always
win. Not even. I've dropped a dime
or two. But the rush that comes
when I do win is worth every penny
down the drain. Gambling is like
snorting cocaine. Up. Down. Up.

And, despite knowing you have to
crash sometime, all you can think
about when you're doing it is the high.
I've dropped two hun in a single night.
That sucked. But once I won almost six.
Oh, yeah! Put me clear through the roof.

A New Rush

I've just tapped into is online
gaming. Roulette. Blackjack.
Poker. More. I've learned how
to play games I never even knew
existed. It's fun. Really fun. In
fact, it's a total, amazing rush,

and you don't even have to leave
home to get it. All you need
is a computer and a way to deposit
some cash in your own Internet
casino account. And hey, I've got
a bank card. Not a whole lot in my

personal checking, but that's about
to change. All I need is one big win.
And what's really insane is the casino
gives you a cash bonus to sign up. I put
in five hundred; they threw in three.
I'm ahead already. Well, was ahead.

I've gone through the bonus and a little
more. But that's the nature of gambling.
Win some. Lose some. Just have to
stay on top of things. Walk if it isn't
your night. Tonight I'm almost even.
All I need is one hand, the right hand. . . .

Shit!

Okay, that wasn't the right hand.
At least I only had twenty riding.
Maybe I should switch to roulette.
My brain isn't working so well right
now. Not sharp enough for poker.
Roll the ball, watch it go round

       and round. Come on, twenty-seven!
       Just as the traitorous ball drops
       into thirty-four, my cell phone rings.
       My face flushes hot, like a little kid
       caught dipping his fingers in the frosting.
       But it's just Ronnie. *Hey. What's up?*

"Uh . . . not much. What's up with
you?" She wants me to come get her,
and as she waits for my response,
I can picture her face, all pouty
with impatience. Pretty face. Better
body, all sleek and tan and . . .

Ah, what the hell? I'm not making
much progress here tonight. "Sure,
babe. Give me a few." Why not?
Would be good to get out of the house,
and boning Ronnie is the one thing that
can take my mind off everything else.

First Things First

Just one more spin of the ball.
Come on, twenty-seven, come on,
twenty-seven. Sixteen? Shit!
Stop. Ronnie's waiting, something
she's not real damn good at.
Besides, Lady Luck doesn't seem

to have joined me tonight. Bitch.
One more. Ten on twenty-seven.
Odds are better if you play the same
number. Yeah, I know I could play
columns or colors, but what's the fun
of winning even money or two to one

when thirty-five to one puts you over
the top? Come on . . . Twenty-seven!
Fuck yeah! There it is! Maybe you
just gotta call ol' Lady Luck names.
Three-fifty in the bank and I'm going
after the finest little piece of pie

in Vegas. In a minute. I'm playing
on casino bucks now, and I'm on
a roll. Think I'll try a hand or two
of blackjack. Another swallow
of gin to keep the courage flowing.
Oh yeah, it's definitely this boy's night.

Damn Lucky Dealer

So much for three of the three-fifty
I won earlier. Blackjack
isn't my game tonight, that's for
sure. I need to learn the finer points,
like when to double down. Ah, hell.
The phone again. What time is it?

> Almost ten? Where did the last
> two hours go, and what does this
> do to my odds of getting laid?
> Ronnie's pissed, I'm guessing.
> She is. *I thought you were coming*
> *over. I've got school tomorrow.*

Quick! Make something up. "Sorry.
I . . . uh . . . Cory came in all messed
up. I had to help Mom get him to bed."
I'll probably burn for lies like that,
but I think it worked, so I sign off,
delete all incriminating history.

> The extra-long pause means she thinks
> I might be bullshitting her. But finally
> she gives in. What else can she do?
> She so wants me! *Come over anyway.*
> *My parents are in bed. I'll sneak*
> *you in through the window.*

Her House

Is fairly close to mine. Good
thing. Hanging out in my room,
I didn't notice how buzzed I was.
I'm definitely feeling it now,
though. It's hard to drive a straight
line. Thank God I can take side

streets. If I actually had to talk to
a cop, he'd haul my ass in, no
doubt. Gonna be hard enough trying
to say a few coherent words to
Ronnie. Even this late at night,
it's really warm—probably pushing

eighty. I drive with the windows
down, letting air movement fight
brain blur. Every street in Vegas
is well lit, and everywhere you
look at night, bursts of neon
color the obnoxious skyline.

I cruise slowly, tripping on a tall
turquoise tower, how it seems
to weave in and out of the breeze-ruffled
palm trees lining the street.
Suddenly, something—someone?—
dashes into the road right in front

of me. I punch the brakes, honk
the horn, barely manage to miss
the dimwad, who skids to a halt
on the far side of the street.
Then he turns back toward
my car. What? Who? Cory!

He rips around to the passenger
door, jerks it open, jumps inside.
Go! I shake my head, try to make
some sense of what just went down.
Did I almost run over my brother?
Fucking hurry up, okay?

The Tone of His Voice

Is enough to make me comply.
I punch the gas pedal, no tangible
clue why, almost overwhelmed
by the smell of cheap booze clinging
to my little brother. "What the hell
is going on, Cory?" As the question

> sputters from my mouth, I get
> a sickly feeling I don't want to hear
> the answer. But hey, he's not exactly
> dying to give me an answer. *Nothing.*
> *Not a goddamn thing.* So why
> are his hands shaking? And how

is it obvious, in the murky half-light
inside the car, that his face is
approximately the color of dirty cotton?
Whatever. He'll tell me when he feels
like it—or maybe he won't. I'm not
the type to pry. As I turn the corner,

I hear his small, tortured exhale as
he scrunches down in the seat. A patrol
car comes cruising up the block toward
us, spotlight sweeping sidewalks,
yards. Looking for Cory, no doubt.
What has the dumb shit done?

I Try Not to Think

About that as I fight a sudden
explosion of fear. I'm driving in
a straight line, under the limit, at
least the speed limit. As for blood
alcohol, there is a very good
possibility that I'm well over

the .08. And should this cop decide
to pull me over, just in case he
really ought to take a look (and hey,
apparently he should!), exactly
what charges might I have to face,
for no more reason than having

a certain passenger in my car?
Whatever Cory has done, I want
to wring the little prick's neck.
"What the hell did you do, Cory?"
My hands are slick with sweat
against the sticky steering wheel.

I keep glancing in my rearview
mirror, sure I'm minutes away
from a trip to juvie. But the cop
keeps driving up the block, likely
positive in his little pea brain that
whoever he's looking for is on foot.

Or maybe he's just too lazy
to worry about possibilities
(and viable possibilities at that),
driving by in the other direction.
Speaking of driving by, I just
motored on past Ronnie's.

The house was dark, except
for a light in a single window.
A bedroom window, where
I have no doubt a gorgeous,
well-built girl sits waiting to
do me, after she's finished

bitching me out completely.
Major butt kissing in order,
if I happen to actually make it
home without becoming a suspect
in a . . . what? What the fuck?
Suddenly my head is clear.

I turn another corner. Drive away
from home. Stay under the limit.
Find a deserted street, pull right up
against the sidewalk. "If you don't
tell me exactly what's going on, I'll
knock your bony ass to the curb."

His Answer

Is a couple minutes coming, like
he's considering making up a lie.
Finally his shoulders sag. It will
be the truth. *I kinda broke into*
a house. They had an alarm.
He doesn't look at me, just stares

out the window, into the night,
the same night I'm staring into.
"What do you mean, 'kinda'?
You can't 'kinda' break into
a house. You did or you didn't."
Jeez, I sound just like Jack, at

least just like Jack before . . .
Now I get to play dad to Cory,
not that it's a role I want, or
do very well. Still, I can't just
sit here and say okay to burglary.
Anyway, "Kinda or not . . . why?"

Zero hesitation. *Why the fuck*
not? Jesus, Cody, do you live
on a different planet? We need
the stinking money! Jack's never
going back to work. You know that.
Don't you hear Mom jabbering

about too many bills, not enough
insurance and such? What do you
think's gonna happen to her
when he kicks the freaking bucket?
What's gonna happen to . . . us?
He stutters. Breaks. Tries to buck

up. But suddenly, like fragile glass
stressed beyond redemption,
he simply shatters. *Fuck it!*
Cory's giant sobs fill the front
seat with booze-infused exhales.
He probably wants to cry like a man—

alone within his pain. This may
be the wrong thing to do. But as
I watch him, my own fear hiccups
to the surface. I pull my tough,
break-and-enter little brother
into my arms, and we cry together.

Headlights Turn the Corner

Flooding us with halogen blue
light. Cop? No, but it comes to
me that we probably look like
gay dudes making out or something.
Cory must think so too, because
he jerks like he's been shocked.

> *Sorry. That was totally lame.*
> *Let's go before we get arrested.*
> He withdraws across the seat, gaze
> again drawn to the neon-spiked
> night. Too bad Jack isn't here,
> ready with some witty remark

to make everything okay. Too
bad Jack isn't here, period. "No
worries. But don't ever do anything
like that again. Shit, Cory, if you
get busted, you'll just make things
worse. We'll be okay. I promise."

I start toward home, chewing on
how I could have promised such
an unlikely thing. Now I've got to
find a way to keep my word.
One way comes to mind. All
I need is a little investment capital.

A Poem by Eden Streit
Need

Need is a curious thing.
Until you plant the seed,
nurture it, encourage its

awakening,

you're not even sure
it's there. But once it
germinates, nudges up,

breaking ground,

you can no longer deny
it has always lain dormant
inside you. And now,

blossoming

with every kiss, every
touch of his hand, this
new kind of need is

growing,

sprouting shoots,
tendrils of desire
threading you,

consuming you.

Eden
Six Months

Since Andrew and I first started seeing
each other. Almost a month since

we took our relationship all the way,
clear over the top, dropping me eye-deep

into a bottomless pit of obsession.
That's pretty much how it feels.

Like I'm in so deep I'll never climb out,
not that I want to. So okay. I'm obsessed.

Whether or not God will forgive me remains
to be seen. But I have absolutely no clue

how I could un-obsess myself if Andrew
ever decided he didn't want me in his life.

So far, though, Andrew seems every
bit as obsessed with me as I am with him.

We have learned a lot about each other.
How to touch. Where to kiss. When to let go.

Before this month, I didn't really believe
I was his first. But I was. Am. I have taught

him as much as he has taught me, all
through mutual experimentation. Mad

sex scientists, that's us. There have been
clumsy moments, yes. But they are rare. Few.

The worst was when it suddenly came to us
that, swept downstream by a flood of desire,

we hadn't used protection the first time.
But either I'm sterile or the timing was right,

because three days later I started my period.
We've been careful ever since. I wish

I could go on the pill, but I know for certain
if I showed my face at Planned Parenthood,

word would get back to my parents. A trip
to the pharmacy would yield the same result.

Meaning birth control—condoms, not the best,
but better than nothing—is up to Andrew.

With or Without Condoms

(Because after all, we don't have to have
sex *every* time we see each other, do we?)

I'm hoping to see Andrew today. Saturday,
so no school, and I'm done with my chores.

I've just got to come up with the right little
white lie. Or big black lie. Whatever.

Mama seems kind of suspicious lately.
I think what they say about being in love

is true—some inner glow becomes obvious
to everyone around you, even those

you most want to keep solidly in the dark.
"So, Mama. Shania and I are doing

an English project on *The Lord of
the Rings.* She invited me over to work

on it. Would that be okay?" Shania
is, like, my only friend. I've known

her since she moved here in second grade
and her family joined Papa's church.

Once in a while we do stuff together,
and the English project is for real.

If I really go over there before meeting
Andrew, it will be a big white lie.

Mom is busy paying bills. She barely
glances my way. That's good, because

when she says, *Um. Guess so,* I can
actually feel the love flicker ignite.

I hurry out the door before she changes
her mind. The day is warm and scented

with spring blooms. Shania is watering
the yard when I get there. "Hey, girl."

A fair amount of surprise fills her eyes.
Eden. What are you doing here?

"Mama let me escape for a while. Just
thought I'd drop by and say hi. Why?"

She shakes her head. *It's just that . . .
well, lately . . . I haven't seen you much.*

Guilt nibbles. "I know. I'm sorry. I guess
I've been kind of distracted." By Andrew.

Can't Tell Her That Part

Or can I? Should I? It would feel good
to confess something this special.

Shania saves me the trouble. *By your
boyfriend?* Does she know? Or is she

guessing? "I suppose you could call
him that." I'm not telling everything.

Really? A big grin crinkles her eyes.
So okay, she's guessing. Good thing.

But now that the cat has halfway escaped
from the bag, she wants to know all.

*Come inside and tell me more.
Who is he? Is he cute? How old*

is he? Does he go to our school?
She grills me all the way through

the front door. "Hang on a sec.
I'll tell you all about him. . . ."

Well, not all. "But first, I need to
make a call. Can I use your phone?"

An Hour Later

I say good-bye to Shania, who
is slightly wiser about Andrew.

I didn't tell her he happens to be the very
cute guy who sits in the back at church

most Sundays, or that he is picking me
up just down the block in a few minutes.

As I start walking, I can, in fact, see
the Tundra, patiently lurking curbside.

       The obsession thing quickens my pace,
       but behind me I hear Shania's *Bye*.

I turn to wave, and see curiosity has
drawn her all the way to the sidewalk.

But Andrew is parked facing away from
her. I hurry on past the Tundra, motion

discreetly for him to follow me around
the corner. Out of Shania's sight, I fling

open the door, slide across the seat, and kiss
Andrew like I haven't seen him in days.

Mostly because I haven't. Every filament
of me shimmers. "We have got to stop

meeting like this, you know." Then
I add, "Almost forgot. I love you."

He rewards me with that beautiful
smile. *And I love you. Where to?*

I shrug. "Anywhere. But not too far.
I should probably be home by four."

Gotcha. He starts the Tundra, and
as he pulls away from the curb,

a little white car slows its approach.
I can't help but notice the driver—

Shania's sister, Caitlyn. And she most
definitely notices me. Her expression

is an interesting mixture—one part
curiosity, one part disbelief, one

part . . . jealousy? Is this trouble? I know
I should probably have Andrew turn

straight around, drop me off near the house.
But he's so close. And he smells so good.

I need to be with him more than anything.
And if this is trouble, it already is.

A Quarter to Four

Andrew drops me off around the corner
from home. It has been an amazing

afternoon, filled with love and making love.
He kisses me. *See you soon. Very soon.*

Ten to four, I walk in the door. Mama
and Papa are sitting there, waiting for me.

Nine to four, I know I'm most definitely
in trouble. Likely the major kind. "Hi?"

Mama pounces first. *Where have you
been? And who have you been with?*

Then she assesses my semi-disheveled
state. *And what have you been doing?*

Guilt flushes my face, burns my ears.
But I'm going to play stupid anyway.

"I told you before I left I was going to
Shania's." Stop there. See what happens.

Papa shadows Mama as she stands, takes
a step in my direction, fists clenching.

*You know very well what I'm talking
about. You were with that McCarran boy.*

Five to Four

My life is over. At least the slender
wedge of it that holds happiness.

Denial is ridiculous. Still, the words
pop out of my mouth, "Says who?"

> I already know the answer. It is Papa
> who gives it. *Caitlyn Curry. Your mother*
>
> *called to ask you to pick up some butter
> on your way home. Caitlyn said you had*
>
> *already left. And that she saw you in
> a truck with the young man. Now I want*
>
> *to know why you were with him. And why
> you lied.* His face is redder than mine.

Deception impossible, defiance
flares. "I was with Andrew because

I'm in love with him. And why
I lied should be pretty damn obvious."

> At the very intentional curse word,
> Mama gasps. Papa pushes her behind
>
> him, advances. *You apologize to your
> mother this instant, you little trollop.*

Trollop? Who uses that word for real?
Laughter dribbles from my mouth.

And I stand my ground. "But I'm not
sorry, Papa. I'm tired of you and Mama

treating me like a little girl. I'm old enough
to fall in love. Why won't you let me?"

Mama's turn. Her voice drips
icicles. *I believe you're confusing*

love and desire. Do you really think
that man is in love with you? What

he wants . . . Once again, her eyes travel
over me, trying to look under my clothes

to the sin she intuits beneath them.
He wants your innocence. I will not

let you succumb to temptation. She is
past Papa, hands moving toward me.

They fall. I don't dare try to defend
myself. I've been here before. Tears

sting my eyes. From the pain of her blows.
And from the heartbreak tomorrow holds.

Heartbroken

Face bruised, eyes swollen almost
shut from crying, no way can I go

to church today. Mama would stay,
to keep an eye on me, but it happens

to be Mother's Day. All the ladies will
turn out in their best dresses, to be celebrated.

> *Don't you dare take one step out*
> *of this house, Mama warns. If you*
>
> *do, I'll know, I promise you that.*
> *I'll take care of Mr. McCarran, too.*

As soon as the car is out of sight,
I rush to the phone. Thank God

> Andrew is still home. *Hey. I was just*
> *heading out the door. Everything okay?*

The whole ugly tale comes gushing
out, and I can't believe I dare to beg,

"Hurry and come pick me up. Please!"
It may be a very long time before I get

to see him again. I need to see him today.
Right away. Even looking the way I do.

Twenty Minutes Later

I am in Andrew's arms, crying softly
against his chest. He lets me whimper

> for a few minutes, then pushes me
> gently away and says, *Look at me.*

> *Let me see what she did.* His hands
> are kind as they soothe the bruises,

> trace the contours of my face. But
> his eyes smolder, hot with anger.

> *How could anyone do something
> like that to their child?* he demands.

"It doesn't matter. All that matters
is how we can see each other now.

Without you, my life is meaningless.
Without you, I have nothing to live for."

> *Don't say that! And don't mean that.
> You have everything to live for. We'll*

> *figure something out. I promise.* He
> tugs me back into his arms. *I promise.*

I Want to Stay

Knotted to Andrew forever, warm
and safe, and loved. But he insists

> I am home before my parents get
> back from church. *Don't give her*
>
> *a reason to hurt you. Please, Eden.*
> *It's my fault she did this to you.*

I start to argue, but he won't let me,
and he won't let me stay any longer.

> One last quick kiss and he urges, *Just go.*
> *If she catches you, who knows how long*
>
> *it will be before we can see each other*
> *again? I love you. Now go on.*

He's right, of course, and I hurry. But
when I turn the corner, I can see

our car in the driveway. My stomach
lurches, like I'm in an elevator and

the cable snaps. I fall to my knees
and vomit until there's nothing left

but cramps. I wobble to my feet,
up the sidewalk, and in the front door.

Mama Is Waiting

Sitting on a straight-backed chair,
facing the door. *You were with him*

just now, weren't you? She already
knows the answer. Why try to lie?

The truth is doubtless magnified by
the tear storm in my eyes. "Yes."

I expect the same chaotic anger
she threw at me yesterday. She stands,

and my muscles clench. But she stays
remarkably calm as she approaches.

*I knew it when he didn't show up
at church today. I'm not sure why*

*it took me so long to realize what
the two of you were up to sitting*

back there. . . . Her jaw goes tight,
and her left hand reaches for me.

I wince, but she simply slides her
arm around my shoulder, guides me

toward the kitchen. *We need to talk.
I'll make some tea.* She pushes me

into a chair. My stomach churns acid
as I watch her put two cups of water

into the microwave, reach for teabags
and sugar. Silence overwhelms the room

until she puts the steaming cups onto
the table. *Get the cream, please.*

I go to the refrigerator, take the cream
from its reserved spot on the top shelf.

Mama pours a little in each cup, hands
me the carton, which I return to its place.

Wordlessly she hands me a cup, takes
a sip of her own, gestures for me

to do the same. The tea is sickeningly
sweet, but I don't dare not drink it.

Finally she says, *There can only be one
explanation for such total disobedience.*

Head spinning, I wait for her to finish.
You are obviously possessed by demons.

A Poem by Seth Parnell
Demons

I never believed
in demons or monsters
lurking under my bed.
But lately I've started to

                      wonder

if evil hasn't in fact
infiltrated this world,
slithering streets and
sidewalks, wearing

                      what-

ever disguise suits its
immediate purpose.
When a choirboy
is molested, is it by

                      the devil

in a priest costume?
Or does Satan play
a more clever game
to get what he

                      wants?

To win the contest,
accomplish his goals,
might the prince of hatred
mask himself as love?

I Never Realized

What a bogus holiday Mother's
           Day is until I didn't have
           a mother anymore. No one
           to send flowers to. No one
to cook a special breakfast for.

The ironic thing is, my mom
           used to call Mother's Day
           a "Hallmark holiday." You
           know, something invented
to buy pricey greeting cards for.

           I know how much my men
                love me, she said more
                than once. *I sure don't need*
                a three-dollar card or candy
           to prove that there fact to me.

Regardless, Dad and I
           always sprang for some
           silly card, with glittery
           roses, spring greenery,
and flowery sentiment.

Maybe Hallmark should invent
          some new holidays, like Dead
          Mother's Day. They could tweak
          their old motto: *When you* still
care enough to send the very best.

Only where would you send it to?
          Better yet, how about Breaking
          Up Day? They could invent a new
          motto: *A cheerful good-bye when*
you don't give a damn anymore.

No Card

To ease the pain of Loren
        leaving today. Part of me
        doesn't want to see him.
        I'm not much good at
good-byes. But the bigger

part wants to hold him one
        last time. Wants to haul
        him off into the bedroom,
        make love to him, convince
him he can never go away.

Dread simmers in my gut.
        Approaching Loren's door,
        it works itself into a full boil.
        I reach for the bell, change
my mind, let myself in with

the spare key Loren gave me.
        "Hello?" Even as the word
        slips past my lips, I know
        he's not here. He rented
the apartment furnished.

Couch. Coffee table. Easy
        chair. Nothing missing.
        Nothing except Loren.
        His absence overwhelms
the room. "Loren?" I say it,

knowing it's useless, follow
           the silence into the bedroom.
           The closet and bureau drawers
           are empty. The only trace
of Loren is a hint of his cologne.

           That, and a note left on
                 the bed, beside rumpled
                 memories: *Dearest Seth,*
                 I'm sorry to have left you
           this way, but I couldn't say

           good-bye face-to-face. Total
                 coward, I know. Rent is paid
                 through the end of the month.
                 Go ahead and use the place
           until then, if you want. I'll

           write you once I'm settled, okay?
                 I wish I could see you graduate.
                 It's such a big day—the start
                 of the rest of your life. Enjoy!
           I love you very much. Loren.

I Haven't Cried

Since Mom died. I mean, after
                something like that, what's
                left to cry about, right?
                But I let myself cry now.
Loss is loss. Doesn't take

death to create it. My legs give
                way. I slide to the floor next
                to the bed, rest my head
                against the bare mattress.
I can smell him there, smell

us there. I reread the note.
                Phrases jump out at me:
                . . . see you graduate . . . rest
                of your life . . . love you . . .
Suddenly, certainly, it hits me.

Loren won't cheer for me
                when I get my diploma.
                He isn't including himself
                in the rest of my life. He
isn't coming back. Ever.

Why didn't I get that sooner?
         All the hurt I've been holding
         dissipates, like a ghost in sun-
         light. Something dark replaces
it—a black tidal wave of anger.

How could Loren dare say
         he loves me? You can't
         walk away from someone
         you love, leave them
drowning in your desertion.

If love has no more meaning
         than that, you can keep it.
         I don't want it now or ever
         again. Don't want to hear
the word or wear its scars.

I'll go back to the farm,
         to fields rich with hope.
         Go back to my books, prep
         for finals. I'll celebrate leaving
high school. And then what?

Suddenly I'm Thirsty

And not for water or soda.
>What's calling is a stiff
>shot of good ol' Kentucky
>bourbon. Maybe Loren

left a little behind. I go to

the kitchen, half-hopeful.
>But the cupboards, like
>the closet, are not only
>empty but spotless. That's

Loren, okay. OCD clean.

Hell, I need to get out of
>here anyway. I'll go down-
>town, find a way into Fringe.
>I remember Loren saying,

All you need is a sponsor.

So I'll go find a sponsor.
>Some old Viagra-stiff
>queen, hopeful that buying
>a drink means buying a lay.

They were thick as flies

last time Loren and I went
>to Fringe. And hey, if I find
>one, he can think whatever
>he likes. Wanting and getting

are two different things.

Sunday, Late Afternoon

The sidewalks aren't especially
        crowded. I don't want to look
        like I'm anxious for a date, so
        I hang out a half block from
Fringe, trying to find the balls

to go up to some strange, lone,
        obviously gay older dude
        and ask if he'd like to sponsor
        me past the familiar bouncer
at Fringe's front door. And what

will that guy think? And why
        do I care about that anyway?
        Just as I'm sure I should give
        up on this idea, an attractive
man, maybe fifty, gives me

exactly the right kind of smile—
        interested but also hesitant,
        as if he's not positive why
        I'm checking him out. Yes,
I think this one might just do.

The Smile

I return leaves zero room for
       misinterpretation. Where
       did I learn to be such
       a flirt? This is a whole new
side of the not-so-static me.

Wonder if it's business as
       usual for the guy, who
       on further inspection may
       be a few years beyond fifty.
Still, he's not bad-looking,

very well dressed. Familiar.
       I've seen him before. Here?
       I can barely make out his face. . . .
       Yes, here. Oh, I remember.
The guy who stormed off,

leaving the younger guy to
       follow him out the door.
       He's a regular, then. He'll
       know what I mean. I smile,
and he takes that in stride,

doesn't flinch or look away.
        I'll take that as an invitation.
        I walk right up to him,
            hoping he likes the straight-
forward approach. "Hi. I'm Seth.

I was hoping to get into Fringe."
        His eyes, an odd, almost clear
        blue, travel my body, starting
        around thigh level. Finally
they lock onto my own eyes.

        Pleased to meet you, Seth.
            I'm Carl. And I happen
            to be heading there myself.
            I imagine you're in need
        of an escort. Care to join me?

Escort?

Seems to me I'm the one
              escorting him, at least in
              the classic sense of the word.
              I guess he's using it in place
of "sponsor." Sounds less

like Alcoholics Anonymous,
              but more like Rent-a-Guy.
              Whatever. I've got my
              ticket inside. "Thanks, Carl.
I appreciate the invitation."

I fall in a step or two behind
              him, note how well his pricey
              clothing fits his slender body.
              The security dude waves us
right through the door, not even

checking IDs. He recognizes
              both of us, and if he's surprised
              I'm with someone other than
              Loren, he hides it really well.
What I want now is whiskey.

Carl reads my mind, or maybe
　　　　　it's written all over my face.
　　　　　The first drink is on me.
　　　　　What's your pleasure?
Kentucky permeates his accent.

"I'll have a mint julep, please."
　　　　　In memory of Loren. Bastard!
　　　　　I can't believe he'd leave
　　　　　without saying good-bye.
One drink will not be enough.

　　　　　Carl gives me a funny look
　　　　　　　　but goes to the bar and returns
　　　　　　　　with two frosty, mint-trimmed
　　　　　　　　glasses. He takes a long swallow.
　　　　　Oh my, that is good, but not

　　　　　for a novice drinker. Tell me
　　　　　　　　who introduced you to this
　　　　　　　　li'l libation. If it's a long
　　　　　　　　story, so much the better.
He settles back into his chair.

I sip my julep, fight the sudden
            blitz of memory. The second
            swallow is bigger. The minty
            burn clears my throat, trickles
down the esophagus, into my

rumbling belly. A little voice
            warns, "Could be trouble."
            I tell it to shut up, look at
            Carl to see if he might have
heard it. Or at least intuited it.

He wears a patient smile. Oh,
            yes. He asked for the story.
            I don't want to talk about
            Loren. But what the hell?
I'm drinking in his honor.

"I actually had my first one
           of these right here, with my . . ."
           The word sticks in my craw.
           A gulp of bourbon clears
it, raises a nice, warm buzz.

Suddenly I want to talk, and
           before I know it, I have
           vomited the whole tale,
           going all the way back
to Janet and how I lusted

after her football-player
           brother, forward past
           Mom and Dead Mother's
           Day, to Loren's promises.
Betrayal. Ultimate desertion.

Carl Listens

Without comment, except
a nod every now and again.
When I finally slow to a stop,
he raises one finger, gets up
and goes to the bar. He comes

back with two more drinks
and a bowl of snack mix.
*Thought you could use both
of these.* He watches me dive
into the pair before saying,

*One thing I've learned in one
or two years on this planet
is to put myself first. Love
is a fine thing while it lasts,
but rarely is it permanent.*

*We don't know each other
at all, but if I might offer
a word of advice, gleaned
from many relationships?*
He waits for a response,

and when I offer a nod, he says,
*In lieu of love, lust will do nicely.
Now why don't I buy us dinner?*
I start to say no, and he hurries
to add, *No strings attached.*

Two Hours

Four courses of French cuisine
        and two bottles of wine later,
        my stomach is churning with rich food,
        my head buzzing with alcohol.
Carl and I exit the restaurant

and I look for my truck. Where
        did I leave the damn thing?
        "Uh, th-thanks s-sho much for
        a great evening. I have to go.
It's-sh a long drive home."

        Carl assesses my obvious
            condition. *I can't let you*
            behind the wheel like that.
            You can stay the night at my
place. *No worries. It's clean.*

"Uh . . . I d-don't . . ." The words
        blur. I can't drive like this.
        "Okay." It's a short walk
        to Carl's tenth-floor apartment.
Once inside, I call Dad, make up

a lie about staying the night
        with some girl I met at a party.
        He sounds relieved, but whether
        that's because he can tell I'm drunk
or because of the "girl," I don't know.

That accomplished, I take
          a long look around. The place
          is beautifully decorated. Tall
          windows overlook the city.
Someday I'll live like this.

          I have to pee. Again Carl
                    reads my mind. *The guest
                    bathroom is right there. Oh,
                    you'll find new toothbrushes
          in the medicine cabinet.*

Sounds like a plan. Between
          garlic, shallots, whiskey,
          and wine, my mouth could
          use a good scrub. I take full
advantage of the guest bathroom.

          When I come out, smelling
                    of mouthwash and expensive
                    lavender soap, Carl is in red silk
                    pajamas. He hands me a matching
          pair. *Unless you sleep naked?*

His message is clear, in his words
          and in his eyes. I have the choice—
          leather sofa or feather mattress.
          I remember how he said, *Lust
will do*, and follow him to his bed.

A Poem by Whitney Lang
Follow Me

That's what he said.
Follow me, and find
the meaning of love
in my bed.

              I followed,

found sheets cold
as death. Neither of us
could warm them,
not me, not

              him.

Not a maelstrom
of body heat so intense
it felt like fever. After,
we slept, chilled.

              He tossed

and turned, lost
in some obnoxious
dream. And when we
woke, he ordered

              me away.

So Basically

Life sucks even more than it
did before. I mean, everything's
the same on the Mom and Kyra
front. Kyra went back to Vassar,

along with two suitcases stuffed
with trendy new boutique clothes.
Mom went back to tennis and
whatever else she does at her club.

Dad went back to the city, where
he seems to stay for longer and longer
periods. He and Mom barely speak,
even on those rare occasions when

they happen to be in the same room.
Nothing much new there. What's
new is no Lucas, and it has nothing
to do with his graduation, fast

approaching. He tells me he has to
study for finals, but we both know
that's bull. He'll ace them, like he
aces every test, stoned to the nth

degree or not. He's brilliant.
Beautiful. And def avoiding me.
Near as I can tell, it started right
after I gave him my virginity.

Since that day, he doesn't return
my phone calls, and if I happen to
catch him, he always has an excuse
for why he can't see me. Did I do

something wrong? He won't even
tell me that much. Only a couple
of weeks until school's out, plus
summer vacation. Then he's off

to college in San Diego. Not so far,
but far enough I won't see him often.
I want to share this time with him,
burn him into memory so I can

find him there when I need him. How
can he be so selfish as to take that
away from me? One thing for sure.
I'm going to find a way to ask him.

The Way Practically Falls

Into my lap. It's the Friday after
Mother's Day. (Still musing over
how my mom got mad because
I didn't give her a card. Some bullshit

sentimental tripe about what a great
mother she is? What's her doctor
prescribing, and can I get some?)
I'm sitting on the grass at lunch,

not eating as usual, when a shadow
falls over me, drawing my attention.
"What's up, Skylar?" She's never
been a friend. What does she want?

> *Not much*, she says. *Just wondering
> if you're going to the party tonight.*
> She stands, left hand perched on
> an all too obvious hipbone.

I may not eat much, but I bet
she throws up what she *does* eat.
Not that I care. "Party? What
party?" I haven't heard a thing.

> She smiles, and something in
> *how* she smiles activates my radar.
> *There's a party at Lucas's house.
> You* did *know about it, didn't you?*

282

Obviously, she's pretty sure I didn't.
But I can't possibly admit it to her.
"Oh. That party. Um, I haven't
decided if I'm going yet."

> *Really?* Her smile grows wider.
> *Does that mean you and Lucas*
> *aren't a thing anymore?* She looks
> like a coyote eyeing a jackrabbit.

Anger—and a fair bit of confusion—
throbs in my temples. What does she
know? "How is my relationship with
Lucas any of your business?"

> Her eyes go marble cold. *Guess*
> *it isn't, if there* is *a relationship.*
> *I heard you two broke up is all.*
> *If I made a mistake, I'm sorry.*

Off she goes, clearly knowing
something I don't. But what?
And how does she know it? Looks
like I'm going to a party tonight.

I Talk Paige

Into driving me. Mom's not home
when she picks me up, so I leave
a note: *Gone to a movie with Paige.*
More like a soap opera, probably.

I have no real idea what's going
to happen, but I've got a feeling
it may not be pretty. I've been
over and over Skylar's remarks,

and I can only conclude that Lucas
said something to somebody that
somehow got back around to Skylar.
Well, fine. If he's having a party,

makes sense he'll be there. And if
he's there, he won't be able to
ignore me. I'll see to that, though
I will try playing "nice" first.

I don't feel nice right now. I feel
angry. Ignored. About the same
way I feel around Mom and Kyra.
Suffering from "Nothing Syndrome."

Lucas Was Supposed to Be

The antidote to that illness.
Instead he has become another
symptom. What is wrong with
me? Why aren't I worth loving?

I say none of this to Paige, of course.
She's thrilled to be going to a party
with real, live guys and probable
substance abuse. Why spoil her fairy tale?

"Hang a left." We turn into Lucas's
neighborhood. Holy crud. This isn't
a party. This is a major sometime-
tonight-a-neighbor-will-call-the-cops

freaking bash. And he didn't
invite me? My earlier irritation
blossoms into full-bodied anger.
"Hurry up, would you?"

> *Where am I going to park?* whines
> Paige, cruising slowly past a mega-line
> of cars. *Looks like the whole
> darn town is here!* She turns

the corner and finally spies an empty
slot next to the curb. *Always good
to get a little exercise before getting
buzzed, right?* She giggles.

Usually I can handle Paige's goofball
laugh. But not tonight. Not right now.
Still, I'm not going to snap. I'll save
that for Lucas. Because suddenly,

without a doubt, I know I've been
dumped. But why? Why? A wave
of tears swells, hot and salty.
"Come on. I think I need a drink."

There's Plenty to Drink

People leak out of Lucas's house,
onto the porch and lawn. Some
I recognize. Others I don't, but
they all pretty much have one

thing in common—sixteen-ounce
red plastic party cups. "Let's go
find the alcohol." I don't wait
for Paige's response, just push

through the crowd, into the house.
I've only been here twice before,
and both times it was a lot emptier.
The alcohol seems to be in the kitchen,

at least that's where most of the noise
is. I work my way through the human
knot, stopping twice to take a hit
off lit blunts. By the time I reach

the kitchen, I've got a nice little
pot buzz going on, something to
mellow the fog of anger. At least
until I walk through the door.

to find Lucas, zipper to zipper
with Skylar. No. How can that
be? Oh! My! God! That whore
was effing taunting me!

Not Only That

But she wanted me to come tonight,
wanted me to see them together.
I played right into it too. Well,
if she wants me in her face,

I'm all the way there. I stomp right
up to them, push between them.
"Excuse the hell out of me!"
Directed at Lucas, who is totally

blown away by my being here,
and not just at the party, but right
here, pressed up against him.
"Thanks for the heads-up."

Directed over my shoulder at
Skylar, who backs out of my way,
grinning like Hannibal Lecter
in *Silence of the Lambs.*

Lucas gives me the stupidest
huh? look ever. "What?" I spit.
"Didn't expect me? Well, FYI, your—
your—friend, there, invited me."

Now he looks confused. *Friend—*
who—what—what do you want,
Whitney? He glances back and forth
between Skylar and me, unsure

of what I'll do next. I'll make it easy,
not that he deserves it. "All I want
is to talk to you. I think you owe
me at least that much, don't you?"

Uh, yeah . . . sure . . . He dares turn
toward Skylar, as if asking for her
permission. He never treated me
with such respect. Tears threaten.

No. Won't cry. I make my voice
hard. "I'm sure she doesn't mind,
do you, Skylar?" She shakes her head,
and I dismiss her. "Good. Lucas,

I'll meet you in your bedroom,
okay?" He exits the kitchen without
looking at either of us. I start to
follow, change my mind.

First I Pour

A hefty shot (okay, more like four)
of Cuervo Gold. No need to bother
with salt or limes, no worries
about tequila burn going down.

It feels good. Great. May make me sick
tomorrow, but it's stoking the courage
I'm in desperate need of. Another stiff
pour and I head for Lucas's bedroom,

feeling tequila heat creep back up
from my belly, all the way to my face.
My ears are ringing too. Hope I can
remember the way to his bedroom.

Both times I was here before, that's
exactly where we ended up. Nothing
major happened then, but now I wish
it would have. At least if it's over

between us, and it's def looking that
way. But why? I still don't get what
happened. All I did was finally say
okay. All I did was say, "I love you."

Lucas Is Sitting on the Bed

Wearing a completely unexpected
expression—pity. Can that be right?
What the hell? A deep swallow
of Cuervo sandpapers my throat.

I go over to Lucas, drop down on
my knees, rest my hands on his legs,
look up into his eyes, "Lucas, will
you please tell me what's going on?"

> He doesn't answer right away, and
> for some stupid reason, that makes
> me think there's hope for us. But
> when he finally speaks, his voice

> is ice. *When you first told me you*
> *were a virgin, I didn't believe you.*
> *Not a lot of those around, you know?*
> *But when I figured out you were telling*

> *the truth, I totally wanted to pop your*
> *cherry. You were my first virgin, and*
> *you'll probably be my last. Because . . .*
> *sorry, but virgin sex really isn't very good.*

I jerk my hands off his legs, wobble
to my feet. "F-fuck you! I c-c-can't
believe tha'sh all I meant to you." One
more gulp and I repeat, "Fuck you!"

291

I Stumble Out the Door

Go in search of Paige. I have to
get the hell out of here! My heart
knocks in my chest. My face is on
fire—with booze and embarrassment.

How could I have believed he loved
me? How could I have given my love
to such an asshole? "Paige?" Did I just
yell that? Everyone is staring. Maybe

that's because tears cascade down my
face, which is probably streaked black
with mascara. "Has anyone seen Paige?"
Someone points toward the living room,

where my dear friend Paige has hooked
up with some guy I sort of recognize
from school. They're making out like . . .
like they're really into each other.

She looks at me, clearly torn between
wanting to help me and preferring to stay
right where she is. "Never mind," I say.
"I'll find another ride home." On my

way to the front door, I pass Skylar,
staring at me with—fuck that!—pity.
"Hope you're not a virgin. Oh, wait.
Forgot who I'm talking to."

Now What?

I go outside, sit on the sidewalk, will
myself not to get sick. Can't call Mom
to pick me up, not here. Don't know if
I've got enough cash for a taxi home.

I reach into my purse, find my wallet.
When I open it, a business card falls
out. *Perfect Poses Photography.*
Wha . . . ? At the bottom is a name.

Bryn Dawson. Bryn? Oh yeah,
hot monkey, the guy from the mall.
I remember his face, the way his eyes
looked at me. Don't suppose he . . .

Nah, Friday night, he's out somewhere,
with some hot female orangutan.
So why does my hand reach
for my cell phone, and why do my

fingers dial his number? One ring . . .
This is stupid. And now he'll have my
number. Two rings . . . Hang up, stupid.
I can just imagine Paige, asking me

what the hey I'm thinking. Three rings . . .
See? He's so out with someone else.
And why would you think, even if he
wasn't, that he'd even remember you?

Must Be Fate

Because someone, I'm assuming him,
answers on the fourth ring. "Bryn?
This is Whitney. You probably don't
remember me, but we met at the mall

and you gave me your card. . . ."
Definitely must be fate, because he
does remember me. I break down
into an inebriated crying binge.

He'll hang up now for sure. But
when I tell him, "Sh-shorry to bug
you, but something bad just happened
and I really need a ride. . . ."

He barely hesitates before he answers,
No problem, Whitney. Always happy
to help a damsel in distress. Give me
twenty minutes. And directions.

A Poem by Ginger Cordell
Directions

Why doesn't life come
with them? "Go straight
until you hit sixteen, take a

                                        right,

then proceed slowly
until you're positive
it's okay to hang a

                                        left

toward where you belong."
I guess in someone else's world,
parents are road maps,
who tell you

                              which way

is the correct direction
to travel. But without
a map, how

                                        do I

know the best route?
Without guidance,
how do I know
which way to

                                        go?

Ginger
School Totally Blew Today

First I got back my history final,
        with a big, fat D on top, despite
all the studying I did. I completely

effed up in that class, and to cop
        the credit, which is a requirement
for graduation, I'll have to do

summer school. Then our Nazi
        PE teacher started yelling at
the back of the pack running laps

        to *Move your lazy buns.* Damn,
                it's like over ninety out there in
        the sun. Still, I probably shouldn't

have yelled back, "Why don't you
        get *your* fat ass out here and run
with us? See how fast *you* can go."

The bitch wrote me up. Detention
        at least. Maybe suspension. To
top it all off, this guy I thought

I kind of liked called me an *emo*
        freak because I put blue streaks in
my hair. Yep. School definitely blew.

I Take My Time

Walking home, puffing on
        a bummed Kool. Don't
care much for menthols, but

I need nicotine to calm my
        nerves. Iris won't really
care if I get suspended. But

Gram will be *so disappointed*
        in me. She'll be spending
a lot more time at home once

they finally release Sandy,
        today or tomorrow. Guess
they have to do a couple more

tests to find out just how bad
        his brain damage is. Right now,
he's learning to talk all over again.

The house is quiet when I open
        the door, quiet except for the TV.
Where are the kids? Something's off.

I can feel it in my bones. "Iris?"
        No answer. But something—
someone?—moves, and suddenly

the TV goes silent. The hair on
          the back of my neck rises.
Little waves of panic churn in

my gut. Ridiculous, right? No
          murderer would be sitting
there watching TV. "Harry?"

          But the face that appears in
                    the doorway doesn't belong
          to Harry. *You must be Ginger.*

          Iris has told me so much about
                    you. Hey, I like your hair. Rad.
          The last word sounds weird,

          spoken by the guy, who is maybe
                    forty-five and built like a bull.
          Did Iris dump Harry for this guy?

Not like it would be anything
          new. "Uh, right. Where is Iris,
anyway?" I need another cigarette.

          She and Harry took the kids
                    for ice cream. Say, would
          you mind getting me a beer?

Déjà Vu Strikes

Lightning. Without a doubt
        I know I need to play my
cards just right. I want to yell,

"Get the fuck away from me."
        But every instinct screeches
for me to answer carefully.

"Uh, sure." I go to the fridge,
        reach in for a Keystone.
The guy is right behind me,

        beer breath hot on my neck.
                Iris didn't lie. You really
        are a knockout. His arms wrap

around me, and his rough hands
        go straight to my boobs. I try
to knock them away but am no

        match for his strength. *You like*
                it rough? 'Cause I'm just the guy
        to give it that way. No extra charge.

The words burn into my ear. "What?
        What the fuck did you say?" A sudden
burst of will pushes him back, away.

I turn to face him. He advances,
            a thin line of spit leaking from
his mouth to his chin. I stare at

            evil. *I said, no extra charge.*
                        Already paid two hundred
            dollars for a good time with you.

            Might as well make it very good.
                        He's on me, yanking my hair,
            pushing me to my knees. He flips

            me over. *You're even prettier*
                        from behind, know that? I hear
            his zipper lower. It is the loudest

sound ever. "Don't," I try, but it
            sticks, pasted to disgust, lodged in
my throat. Useless to plead. Useless

            to fight. He yanks down my shorts
                        in a single swift motion. He is on
            me. In me. Humiliating me in every

            possible way, right here on
                        the kitchen floor. As promised,
            he is rough. Biting. Pounding.

Shredding. Ripping. "Please?"
        The word bounces off him, ping-pongs
weakly in my ears. Trying

to fight him only fuels him.
        For a fleeting second, I think
maybe someone will come

through the door to save me.
        And then, despite everything
that's happening to me, I laugh

        out loud. Save me? What did
                he say? *I already paid for
        a good time with you.* I've been

sold. And just who would
        sell me? The answer is all
too obvious: Iris. My mother.

And as he finishes, all sticky
        and stinking and revolting,
something else suddenly

becomes crystal clear. This day
        was exactly like that other day.
If this guy paid Iris, so did Walt.

When He's Gone

I use wet paper towels to clean
        the mess on the linoleum. Under
the sink, I find the Pine-Sol,

carry it to the shower. It stings,
        which means it's working.
I scrub my body over and over,

washing away all evidence of this
        afternoon. On TV, they want you
to call the cops. Tell. But what do

I say? "Hey. My mom took money
        to let some guy rape me." Who'd
believe that? I go to my room,

stuff clothes into my backpack.
        I'm gone. Where? No clue, but
this will never happen again. I feel

bad, leaving Gram to deal with Iris.
        But she's strong. And with Sandy
home, she'll be here, too. The others

will be safe. I'll write her a letter,
        tell her what she has to know so
she'll never let her guard down.

The Door Slams Behind Me

I stand on the step for a few
          seconds, confused about what
to do next. Can't pause long.

They'll be home soon. Not like
          ice cream takes forever. Only
longer than rape. Fuck! My eyes

burn, and not from the sun, sitting
          smack on the western hills. I stare
into it, and for one mega-brilliant

instant, all I can see is a stab
          of light. My feet start walking
toward it. Where else is there to go?

Throbbing with pain, inside
          and out, I find myself on Alex's
street. Should say good-bye.

          She opens the door. *Damn,*
                    man. You smell like toilet
          cleaner. What happened?

Alex lets me in and I sink
          into cool dark solace, repeat
the tale of Ginger, paid for.

I Love Alex

Love the way she lets me spew,
        contributing zero commentary,
until I'm obviously finished.

        When I am, what she says is,
                And I thought my *mother was*
        queen of the fucking wack jobs.

        So what are you going to do?
                She listens as I outline my
        non-plan for running away:

        Take off and see where I end up.
                Finally she shakes her head.
        Stupid idea. You can't just run

        off without some idea of where
                you're going and how you'll
        get there. The thing is, after we

        talked about it last time, I started
                thinking about the best way to
        leave this stinking shit hole.

Does that mean she wants to go
        too? "Really?" I hope she came
up with something good. "And . . . ?"

Remember I told you about my
            dad's old girlfriend, Lydia?
Well, she lives in Henderson.

She told me to come visit any time.
            We'll stay with her until we can
find a way to get a place of our own.

She has thought this through!
            A place of our own? Still . . . "Are
you sure you want to go too?"

            Hell yeah, girl. You can't go
                alone. Besides, there's nothing
            for me here. Adventure calls!

            I checked it out and the bus
                to Vegas costs thirty-five bucks.
            No big deal, right? Any way

            you could come up with maybe
                fifty? I've got a little stashed.
            Enough for smokes and Cokes.

Where could I get fifty bucks?
            The answer smacks me in the face.
She owes me a lot more than that.

I Leave My Stuff

Go on home. No cops, no alarms.
            No one missed me at all. Not
even Gram, who's fixing dinner.

In fact, everything seems so normal
            it almost makes me wonder if I
imagined what happened earlier.

I go over to Gram, give her
            a hug. "Something smells
good. We've sure missed your

cooking around here! Where
            is everybody? Is Sandy home?"
If he is, how can I possibly go?

            Gram keeps stirring her chili.
                        *No. The tests they ran tired
            the little guy out. They're keeping*

            *him one more day, to be sure
                        he'll be okay.* Worry weights her
            sigh. *He'll be just fine, though.*

Guilt chews at me until a sudden
            whiff of Pine-Sol reminds me
why I'm here. "Where's Iris?"

Gram shakes her head. *She and
her . . . her friend went out.
I doubt we'll see her tonight.*

Perfect. She won't miss it until
morning, earliest. By then I'll be
all the way to Vegas. Now I need

a way back out of here. "Hey,
Gram. I was invited to spend
the night with my friend, Al—"

Probably should make up
a name. "Alicia. We're going to
study for finals. Is that okay?"

*Sure thing, hon. I'm glad
you're finally making
some friends.* Her smile

initiates a new round of guilt.
Especially considering that not
long after I'm gone, she'll find

out I already messed up on my
finals. Oh, well. By then she'll
have given up on me anyway.

The Kids

Are in the living room, watching
        the boob tube. They don't see
me slip down the hall, and that's best.

I go into Iris's room. Top dresser
        drawer, beneath her underwear—
yech!—there's a navy blue sock,

where she stashes her cash.
        I watched her do it once when
she was too drunk to realize

I was standing right there. Sure
        enough, it's here, stuffed with sex
money. I count out two hundred,

which doesn't include whatever
        Walt paid her. Screw it. I take
the whole wad—four hundred

sixty-nine dollars. In its place,
        I leave a note: *Not even close
to what you owe me. I hate you.*

"Bye, Gram," I call, eyes stinging.
        I ease out the door, into velvet
night, chasing a glimpse of freedom.

When I Come Through the Door

Alex is packed and waiting,
   rocking softly side to side
in a nerve-fueled rhythm.

Wow. I've never seen her
   look so worried. "Are you
sure you want to do this?"

   Her odd movement stills
      and she looks at me with
   shimmering eyes. *I've wanted*

   to run forever, but I was
      scared to run alone. I never
   told you the truth about Paul.

   he's not my stepdad. Mom
      and him never got married.
   When they sent her away,

   he let me stay with him,
      but only if I . . . you know.
   I have nothing here, or

   anywhere, except for what
      I have with you. Let's go
   before he gets home, okay?

The Half-Empty Bus

Idles, preparing for departure.
        The diesel fumes are strong,
but the seats are comfy. No one

cares about Alex and me
        in back, sipping rum from
a water bottle. Before long,

I feel zero fear. Zero pain.
        I flip up the armrest between
us, slip my hand into hers.

Heedless of any prying eyes,
        she kisses me, and I kiss back,
inhaling her intoxicating scent.

My heart dances. My body,
        abused so viciously just
hours ago, at last knows joy.

As the bus begins to roll,
        my lips spill words unspoken
until now. "I love you, Alex."

        I love you too. Now let's get
                the flying fuck out of here.
        Together we break free.

A Poem by Cody Bennett

Flying

Is that what it's like
when you die? Do you
slip out of your skin, go

soaring

up into a butterscotch
sky? Do you surf waves
of light? How far?

How high?

I hope that's what it's
like, but I'm afraid
it's a lot more like

falling

with no net to catch
you, and no way
of knowing

how hard

you will hit or where
you'll stop. Will you touch
down back on Earth, or

will you land

in the nightmare
you always feared
you'd never wake up from?

Cody
Funerals Suck

This isn't the first one I've had
to go to. There were a couple in
Wichita. But this is the first one
that mattered. Old people are
supposed to die. Jack wasn't old,
and he sure wasn't ready to die.

It's a blistering day, and we're
standing here graveside, dressed
all in black. Fuck you, Jack. How
could you leave us? You swore
you'd take care of us. And now
you're nothing but pickled flesh,

broken promises. Mom is a mess,
although she pretends she's okay
and looks steadier than Cory, who
is completely tattered. The two brace
each other, trying to stop shaking
as the minister drones on about

> *Going home to his heavenly father.*
> Funny, but none of us really thought
> much about heaven until the last
> few weeks. Is there such a place,
> and is Jack already there? Is there
> a chance in hell someday I'll join him?

If Funerals Suck

Wakes are worse. I don't even
know who half these people
are, laughing and drinking and
scarfing the food they brought
so Mom wouldn't have to worry
about cooking for a day or two.

They should just go and leave
the food. Better yet, run to
the grocery store and fill up
the fridge. It's almost empty.
The only thing emptier is my
chest—where my heart used to be.

The doorbell rings. I open it
to find Ronnie, a total knockout
despite how ashen her face looks.
Is all that pale meant for me?
Hey, you. Her voice is soft. So
is the hand that touches my cheek.

*How are you doing? Sorry
I missed the service. I meant
to come, but I overslept and . . .*
She shakes her head. *The truth
is, cemeteries scare me to death.*
The last word makes her flinch.

"Hey, it's okay. I'm not big on
them either." I take her hand,
pull her through the door. No
one else has even noticed her
presence. Good. "Let's go
to my room, okay?" I want

to hold her, want to make love
to her. Need to feel something
warm and alive. Need to fill
that empty space inside. I lead
her to my disheveled bedroom.
"Sorry it's so messy," I whisper,

pulling her into me. "God, you
smell good." Like baked apples.
Not like flowers. Don't want to
smell those. They remind me
of death. Ronnie rises on her tiptoes,
lifts her slick, honey-sweet lips

to meet mine. It's the sweetest
kiss ever, but it soon becomes
more. I lock the door, guide her
to my bed, and for maybe the very
first time, sex is more than getting
off. This time, sex feels like love.

For the First Time

I stop myself before Big Bang,
look down into Ronnie's violet blue
eyes. "I love you." And at this
moment, I do. And at the words,
surprise (or maybe disbelief)
contorts her pretty face. "What?"

> *Nothing.* She smiles. *It's just . . .*
> *wow.* She undulates seductively,
> the rise and fall of her body like
> salty waves beneath my own.
> Another first, this time no faking
> climbing higher and higher, until

> she finishes with an amazing
> gush and tears of satisfaction.
> *I love you, too,* she exhales softly.
> We lie, tangled together, unmoving,
> unspeaking. And we both know
> this is what sex should be.

All Awesome Things

Must come to an end, damn it
to hell. Ronnie and I are slipping
toward sleep, still intertwined,
when the doorknob rattles. *Cody?*
It's Cory. Good thing I locked it.
Are you in there? Can I come in?

Ronnie starts to scramble.
I hold her tight, put a finger
to my lips. "Shh." Then I say
toward the door, "Just a minute,
okay?" I've never had a girl
in here. He probably thinks

I'm taking care of business,
solo. I really don't want to let
Ronnie go. All the hurt will
come flooding back. But Cory
is waiting. I kiss Ronnie's face,
her neck, lick the shimmer

of sweat from the deep fold
between her breasts. She sighs,
and that makes me want more.
But Cory again bumps the door.
I rest my chin on her belly,
look into her eyes. "Thank you."

We Throw on Clothes

But dressed or undressed,
it's obvious what we've been
doing in here. When I open
the door, Cory is pretty much
amazed. *Oh. Uh . . . sorry. I, uh,
didn't know you . . .*

His face is the approximate
shade of an unripe plum.
Ronnie and I both have to
grin. "No problem, bro. Oh,
this is Ronnie. We've been
going out for a while now."

Cory has no patience for my
method of dealing with grief.
His voice, curt, slices the air.
*Yeah, well, people are starting
to leave. Mom's looking for you.*
He pivots sharply, leaves the room.

I start to apologize, but Ronnie
stops me, stroking my lips with
soft fingertips. *It's okay. He's
hurting. And your mom needs
you right now. I should go.* Her
kiss is a bittersweet good-bye.

One by One

Everyone leaves. Mom stands
at the door, looking worn. Torn.
Emptied. She has managed the day
so far without breaking down.
But now she dissolves. I go to her,
put my arm around her shoulder,

steer her to the sofa. "Sit down.
I'll get you a drink." Something
strong, to help her sleep. She hasn't
slept much since the day Jack up
and left us. Mom isn't much of
a drinker. I pour her three fingers.

She accepts the brandy without
protest. Sips it slowly, stares out
the window. Finally she says,
I never believed this day would
come. Some stupid part of me kept
insisting the doctors were wrong.

Oh God, I miss him so much already.
What am I going to do without him?
She swallows the last of her drink
in a giant gulp, throws her face
into her hands and sobs. I want to
help. But I have no answers.

I take her glass, go to refill it.
She deserves a good drunk, and
so do I. As I pour, Cory comes
in, checks out the brandy bottle
with covetous eyes. Oh, why not?
Mom won't care today. We sit

on opposite sides of our mother,
downing alcohol that cannot warm
the death chill infiltrating us, inside
and out. Soon the silence becomes
overwhelming, and Cory turns on
the TV. Doesn't matter what's on.

The three of us get drunk together,
semi-listening to the announcer
on *Sports Central*, droning on about
Jet Fuel, the unlikely winner of both
the Kentucky Derby and Preakness,
his even unlikelier odds of winning

the Belmont Stakes, and so the Triple
Crown. When Mom starts to nod
off, I help her to her feet, down
the hall to her room, gentle her onto
her bed. "I love you, Mom. Don't
worry. Everything will be all right."

Why Do I Keep Saying That?

Will everything be all right? How
the hell would I know? Fuck this!
Jack, if you weren't already dead,
I swear I'd . . . I'd . . . My legs
give and I don't fight, sinking
to the floor beside the bed Mom

and Jack shared for so many years.
She snores softly, and I hope she
isn't trapped in some disturbing
dream. I look around the room,
still so full of Jack. His clothes
drape the chair beside the window.

His shoes form a straight line just
inside the closet. The scent of Brut
deodorant lingers, as does a vague
hint of medicines, sweated despite
antiperspirant. Pictures of him and
Mom hang on the walls, and one of

my favorite family photos—camping
at Lake Mead—sits front and center
on the dresser, beside his belt and
wallet. Where are you now, Jack,
having left all this behind? Are you
whole? Is any of you left here?

Also on the Dresser

Is a stack of mail. From here,
I can see much of it is unopened.
I get up, go sort through it. Bills.
Power. Water. Trash. Mortgage.
Hospital. Doctor. American Express.
And there will be more coming.

Funeral home. Cemetery. Jesus!
Insurance won't take care of it all.
Neither will Jack's pension. I've got
a paycheck coming, but that barely
covers my own expenses. Stop!
Can't think about this now. Not today.

One day, at least, to mourn. One
day to try and forget about death.
Mom's totally gone. I need to get
high. Wacked. Out-of-my-brain
fried. No need for Mom to see
bills first thing when she wakes up.

I scoop everything off the dresser,
into an empty shoe box lying on
the floor. Jack wore new shoes
to his funeral. A big, fat joint is
calling my name. And after that,
I need to hear Ronnie's voice.

Bud and Booze

May not exactly cure what ails
ya, but partner 'em up and they'll
definitely make you forget it for
a while. I turn on my computer,
and the first thing that pops up
on my Yahoo page is news headlines.

And there, again, is Jet Fuel.
They're laying odds against him.
Which makes me wonder . . . Yeah,
oh yeah, there it is—an online Sportsbook
and yes, they are most definitely
taking bets on the Belmont, as well

as just about every professional
sporting event out there, from soccer
matches to major league baseball.
Why didn't I think of it before?
If there's one thing I know about,
it's baseball. Been a Kansas City

fan since I could spit, and the Royals
are looking good this year. I want
in on this action. First I need to set
up an account. Let's see. All I need
is a credit card and something to
prove I'm eighteen, which I won't be

for over a year. But where there's
a will—and I've definitely got
that—there's a way. It comes to me
suddenly that the way just walked
into my room in a shoe box, along
with a pile of bills. Jack's wallet

has three credit cards in it, along
with his driver's license. This may
be a gamble, but I'm betting they
won't be checking to see whether
or not Jack Bennett is dead or alive.
Not as long as the cards are good.

I sort through the stack, locate
the AmEx and two Visa bills,
check available credit. Damn right,
more than I thought. Cool. In less
than five minutes, I've got an
account set up and a hundred

smackeroos riding on tonight's
Royals game. When they win,
I'll pay the electric bill and buy
some groceries. Meanwhile,
I'll polish off this roach.
And I'll give Ronnie a call.

The Pot Buzz

Should make me feel better,
but all it does is combine
with the alcohol to make
loneliness hit like a freight
train. Mom's asleep, Cory's
out somewhere, doing who

knows what god-awful things.
Jack's dead. Dead. The word
repeats itself over and over.
Dead. Damn, man. Dead.
I need to hear Ronnie's
voice. She answers her phone

on the first ring. *I thought
you might call. Are you okay?*
She knows I'm not, but waits
for me to tell her so. *Do you
want me to come over? Vinnie's
here. He'll give me a ride.*

"Oh God, Ronnie, yes. I need
you." I do, and it feels awful
and wonderful, all smooshed
together. We'll make love, and
I'll forget about the Royals.
Forget about Jack. Forget . . . Dead.

Stinking Royals

Can't believe they lost last night,
and to the stupid Mariners to boot.
Oh, well. That means they have to
win today, so I'll lay down two
hundred. And while I'm at it, I'll
put fifty on St. Louis. Why shove

all my eggs into one flimsy carton?
Mom never even missed Jack's
wallet or the bills. She woke up,
fighting a hangover headache.
Me, being a hangover expert,
I convinced her to try a little hair

o' the dog. Cory didn't feel much
better. You'd think his tolerance
would be taller built by now.
The two of them are napping.
Good. I can't stand seeing so
much pain in two pairs of eyes.

Speaking of two pairs, just won
sixty bucks at poker. Almost made
up for the hundred I dropped
yesterday. My luck is coming
around. Just in time. Because
beyond major league baseball,

I'm planning on laying a major league
bundle on Jet Fuel. The odds on him
just keep growing longer and longer.
I'll wait a couple of days, see how
long they'll go. But right now,
a thousand-dollar bet on the win

could net almost twenty big ones.
Twenty thou would pay an awful
lot of bills. And now I need money
for my insurance. Between Jack
and Ronnie and spending a lot
of time in front of my computer,

I lost my job. Not that I care. Jobs
like GameStop are a dime a dozen.
And anyway, I've got bigger plans
than spending my days directing snot-
nosed kids to Pokémon Purple. High
finance is in my immediate future.

A Poem by Eden Streit
My Future

Is meaningless now,
flavorless as an icicle
melting, drip by

                     drip

to puddle and freeze
again upon shadowed
ground. They say to

                     drop

the pretense, as if
confessing my heart
was a game of charades.

                     Tears

such as these could
only be born of soul-
ripping sorrow. They

                     fall,

in relentless procession,
summer rain upon
parched playa,

                     relentless.

Eden
Demon Possessed

Apparently, that's the real definition of falling
in love—Satan implanted some evil angel

inside me to steer me away from God's family.
And it isn't only Mama and Papa who think

so. Or claim to, in the name of the Almighty.
Almighty dollar, that is. Samuel Ruenhaven—

who *strongly prefers* being called Father—
graduated seminary the same time as Papa.

But Father's path led him to the stark sand
of northeastern Nevada, where he settled

a sizeable chunk of desert he dubbed Tears
of Zion. Oh, it's a very special place,

where Father and his "disciples" rehabilitate
incorrigible youth. Exorcise demons.

I've been here almost a month. Mama delivered
me personally, after slipping enough Lunesta

into my tea to knock me out for eleven hours.
When I finally woke up, we were bumping along

hundreds of miles from home. It will never
be "home" again for me. I hate it. Hate Mama

worse. When she saw me conscious that day,
head thumping from a narcotic hangover, almost

immediately she started in quoting Old Testament
scripture. That was the extent of our one-sided

"conversation." She never said another word
to me. I tuned her out, concentrated on trying

to connect psychically with Andrew, who
could have had no idea what happened to me.

I didn't know the details then myself. Couldn't
have guessed where we were headed. Even

when we pulled through the Tears of Zion gates,
I had no clue what was coming. I began to suspect

it wasn't good when Father waddled out to greet
Mama. She offered a hand, free of emotion,

and her plea was simple: *Do whatever
it takes to bring my daughter to her senses.*

Father's Methods

Are likewise uncomplicated. You can sum
them up in a single word: Deprivation.

No food for the first three days. Water only.
Flushing poisons, he claimed. *Cleansing*

body before examining soul. Since then,
an unvaried daily thousand-calorie diet—

oatmeal, thin soups, flat bread. Minimal sleep,
even now. *The subconscious is Satan's*

classroom. The worst thing is the isolation.
I rarely see anyone but Father and his disciples—

creepy guys who always dress in bleached white
jeans, matching T-shirts. And the sad, sick thing

is I'm almost glad to see them. I know that's
the point. But I don't know how to fight it.

I spend every day alone, silence squeezing
me until I think I'll go totally crazy. Insanity

might, in fact, be better. I'm supposed to be
reconsidering my choices. But all I do is pace

the perimeters of this featureless room, thinking
about Andrew. And how completely I love him.

Is He Thinking

About me? Wondering where I am?
Where is he? Home? Looking for me?

Or has Mama decided to have him arrested?
I have no answers. Can't process clearly.

My brain feels like day-old mush. Unstirred.
Undisturbed. Left for scavengers. And speaking

of bone pickers, the cloying scent of rabbit
brush precedes Jerome through the door.

As Father's believers go, Jerome is the least
offensive. Not that he's good-looking.

He's short, partly because he carries himself
as if his shoulders are weighted with iron.

What hair he has left is thin, reddish. It reminds
me of an alcoholic's morning eyes. His nose

is shaped like a toucan's bill, and the watery orbs
just above it look at me with a mixture

> of sympathy and . . . lust? He places a tray
> on the splintered table. *Eat hearty.*

"Right. Lukewarm oatmeal. Mmm." Unlike
some of the other disciples, Jerome allows

me a fair amount of sarcasm. *Lukewarm*
is better than cold. And . . . He glances around

the room, as if some voyeur stands in the corner,
watching. Then he takes something from the tray.

Look what I brought you. Promise you
won't tell? He holds out a napkin, unfolds

it slowly, revealing three beautiful strawberries.
First crop. Delicious. And just for you.

Their sweet red perfume permeates
the room's stale air. My mouth waters.

I start to reach for them, reconsider,
snatch my hand quickly away. "Why me?"

He creeps toward me, baiting, pallid
tongue circling his mouth suggestively.

Because I like you. He puts a berry
to my lips. *And because you're beautiful.*

Instinctively I suck the fruit onto my tongue,
crush it against the roof of my mouth, go weak

at the intense rush of pleasure. "Thank you." It
comes out a whisper. "I promise not to tell."

Jerome Isn't Quite Finished

He takes my hand, caresses it gently before
placing the other two berries on my palm.

If you're really good at keeping secrets . . .
His eyes bore into mine. Something feral

pacing there. *We could have a little fun.*
If you be good to me, I'll be really good

to you. Strawberries are just the beginning.
Cheese. Meat. Chocolate. Maybe even some

shampoo to use instead of that vile soap.
He touches my hair. *I bet it's pretty*

when it's clean. I bet it smells like rain.
Here now. What did I say? Don't cry.

A recollection clutches my throat,
chokes. It's Andrew's voice, surfacing

                              like a creature, dead and bloated,
                              from deep sea. *Smells like rain.*

Pain throbs. No, not pain, not even
agony. Something there is no word for.

Something I can't fight. Can't fight. Can't.
All I can think to do is say, "S-sorry."

My head spins. My legs go numb.
Jerome catches me as I collapse, and my tears

soak into his bleached white shirt. *Okay,
baby*, he soothes. *Go ahead and cry*.

I should jerk away, out of his arms, but
his gentle rock cradles my loneliness.

There is nurturing here, and it comes to me,
with a whoosh like sudden wind, that there just

might be a way out after all. And that way
could very well begin and end with Jerome.

So When He Kisses

The top of my head, I stay perfectly
still against him. And when his hands

begin a slow journey over the landscape
of my body, I grit my teeth. Do not

protest. Will not complain. Forgive
me, Andrew. Please understand.

It's my only way back to you. But
I won't give him everything.

I go as far as to let him open my blouse,
touch beneath my bra. Now he kisses

down my neck, to the skin he has just
exposed. Drawn tight up against him,

I feel him grown hard against my thigh.
Now it's he who shakes. Shivers

with hunger, and just like that, I am
in control. I push him away, but tenderly,

like a mother convincing the infant
at her breast that he's had enough.

I make my voice light. "That's all
you get for three strawberries."

He is pliable. Clay. He smiles, clearly into
the game this has unmistakably become.

*Fair enough. Father would probably miss
me now anyway. Just one question . . .*

He helps himself to a final taste.
What will you give me for ice cream?

I back away, closing buttons. Reach
down deep for the "inner whore"

Father claims all women harbor inside.
I smile. "Häagen-Dazs or store brand?"

The Door Locks

Behind Jerome, who promised
to *see what I can do* about Cherry

Garcia. Dirtied, I drop to the floor, tuck
my back into a corner, as if walls could

protect me. Lord, please forgive this
sin. What I've done. What I may do,

though I'm not exactly sure what that
might be. All I know is I have to escape

this place, run far, far away. From here.
From home. Toward what, I don't know,

except somehow, some way, that "what"
must bring me closer to Andrew. I'm tired.

Hungry. I glance at the bowl on the table,
oatmeal grown granite cold inside it.

I want pancakes. An omelet with sausage.
I want the key to this unbarred cell.

Jerome has perhaps offered it, if I will
only reach for it. I close my eyes. Think

of Mary Magdalene. What was her prison?
And how far did she go to get the key?

Some Biblical Scholars

Believe Magdalene wasn't really
a prostitute at all, but the woman

most loved by Jesus. A few even
think they might have been married.

Papa preaches that she was a whore,
reformed by the love of Christ. No sex

involved in the reformation. Mama echoes
this tale. But Mama thinks I'm a whore

too. A laugh bubbles up, bounces off
the barren walls. What incredible irony.

Sorry, Mama. Making love with Andrew
didn't make me a whore. But sending me

here might very well do exactly that.
I have nothing to lose. You've already

stolen everything important. Made me
an outcast. Tossed me into this wilderness

prison. And now the question becomes:
How far will *I* go to get the key?

To Know That

I need to find out what Father has in store
for me. We meet every afternoon except

on Sunday (no work on the Sabbath),
for "prayerful counseling." So far,

it's the only time I'm allowed out of my
room, into the sunlight, the sage-tainted air.

There are two long, low buildings, with
rows of doors just like mine. I'm not

the only one here. Once in a while, I see
other kids, working alone in the garden

or shoveling manure from the chicken
coops. Punishment? My guess is reward.

There are smaller cottages, too—staff
residences, I'm sure. A large house looms

in the distance. Father's, no doubt. Wonder
if there's a Mrs. Father. Probably not.

The chapel is large, with rows of chairs,
so I imagine there are Sunday services

that I'm still not holy enough to attend.
Don't know if there are classrooms

somewhere, or if any of us juvenile
delinquents are allowed schooling

other than what's taught in the Bible.
It's the only book I have in my room,

and I have to admit with no TV or other
distractions, I've read more Old Testament

here than ever before. Today as I walk,
escorted, to the chapel, the compound

looks deserted. How many of us are there,
biding our time in solitary, entertaining

ourselves with Leviticus? Do those further
on their way toward rehabilitation interact?

How many will actually be rehabilitated?
What exactly does that mean, and how is it

accomplished? How does someone leave
this place? No harm in asking, is there?

A Dozen Questions

Fill my head as I enter the chapel.
Father's office is tucked in back

> of the altar. He is working at his
> computer but turns and stands

> as we enter. *Welcome, Eden. Brother
> Stephen, you may leave us.* He motions

for me to sit before launching into
a long-winded entreaty to the Lord

to deliver wisdom. To me, obviously.
Father already knows everything.

I keep that to myself, of course.
In fact, I say nothing as he "counsels"

> me on how I might return to the Path
> Toward Salvation. Finally he finishes

> and actually gives me the opening I need.
> *Do you have any questions for me?*

I pretend thoughtfulness for a second.
"I've had lots and lots of time to think,

and I really believe you've opened
my eyes to my sinful ways. I was just

wondering what I have to do to prove
that to you so I can go back home."

He smiles. But it is a cheetah's smile.
Do you really believe I'm so foolish?

I find no hint of contrition in you.
What I see before me is a liar. Still,

you're not stupid. So you must understand
that your behavior reflects on your parents.

They don't want you to come home, do
not want your tarnish on their sterling

community standing, or for you to influence
your sister to repeat your mistakes.

You will be here for the foreseeable future.
Shall we decide to make the best of it?

Of course. I should have known. "Thank you,"
I say, meaning it. Because he just gave me

permission to do what it is I need to do. I am
completely resolute to leave this place. Soon.

A Poem by Seth Parnell
What I Need

Is something intangible,
and so, unattainable
because it is ever

changing.

Neither can what I want
be defined. To someone
standing on the

outside

perimeters of my life,
I might look one
hundred percent

the same.

But if they had
the ability to split
me open, look deep

inside,

they would know
the mask that
appears to be

my face

is painted over
the real me, smoke
and mirrors,

an illusion.

Seth
Graduation Came and Went

Whoopee. Finally free
　　　　of educational necessity.
　　　　No more pencils, no more
　　　　books. No more Janet
Winkler's dirty looks.

I've got to stop drinking.
　　　　But not right now. What
　　　　else is there to do around
　　　　here? Funny, but not so long
ago, I swore I'd be off to college.

Now I really don't care
　　　　about moving on. What
　　　　was I thinking? I'll never
　　　　go on to school. What for?
My destiny was decided

for me by the circumstances
　　　　of my birth. Hick boy from
　　　　Indiana. What am I going to
　　　　do? Turn into a rock star?
Or maybe run for president?

Yeah, I Know

The state of Indiana has
        produced one of each. But
        neither was gay. So hurray.
        It's farming for me. Oh well.
At least this little piece of

enlightenment has brought
        me closer to Dad. No more
        long afternoons in Kentucky,
        though I do sneak off and
meet Carl every now and again.

Not for love, but for lust.
        As older guys go, he's not
        so bad in the sack. And
        besides, he's incredibly
generous with the same

sort of perks I got from
        Loren. Gourmet dinners.
        Theater and concerts.
        Art house movies. Only
with Carl, the maître d's

know him by name, and sit
        us at view tables. He's got
        off-Broadway season tickets,
        not to mention box seats
at Churchill Downs. I'm not

a big gambler, and know
        squat about horse racing.
        But Carl knows enough
        for both of us. And it is
his money we wager.

Beyond any rush at the rare
        win, I love the atmosphere.
        Rich people, outfitted in
        elegance, sipping mint juleps
and inhaling the extravagant

potpourri of leather, grass
        hay, and Thoroughbred
        manure. It's a sensual
        experience, highlighted by
Carl's commanding presence.

He hasn't made me forget
        Loren, or soothed the sting
        of desertion, but he has made
        me realize that I don't have
to live my life in isolation.

Thinking of Loren

Makes me want liquor.
        Dad isn't much of a drinker,
        but there's usually beer
        in the fridge, and the afternoon
is hot for June. A cold brew

sounds pretty damn fine.
        I'm done tending garden
        for the day. Carrying gray
        water by the bucketful.
Looking up into the sharp

blue sky, no sign of rain.
        We can grow vegetables
        this way, but the corn looks
        mighty thirsty. We could lose
the whole crop, if God

doesn't cooperate. Weird,
        but not a hundred miles
        from here in Illinois, they're
        drowning under monstrous
thundershowers. Just goes

to show the randomness
        of the Almighty's hand.
        Hey, Ma, if you're up there,
        could you put in a good word
for the farm you left behind?

I Go into the Cool

Of the house. "Dad?" He has
       drawn the shades, flipped
       the small window air con on.
       The faux breeze it has raised
blows gently over the sweat

on my face. Aaaaah! Soap
       and water attack the grime
       on my hands, and now it's
       Miller time! I reach into
the fridge, find a frosty can,

       pop the top, take a long
              swallow. A voice falls
              over my shoulder like
              a shadow. *Who the hell
are* you? Iron hands—

Dad's hands—grab hold
       of my shoulders, spin
       me around to face him.
       The look in his eyes
is a blend of disbelief and

revulsion. He knows.
       But, "How?" He points
       to the kitchen table, to
       the envelope and pages
lying spread across it.

I gather Loren's letter, glance
        at the words, talking
        about his church, his new
        home, his congregation.
Talking about missing me,

wishing there was a way
        we could be together. It's not
        pornographic, but there is
        enough detail so Dad can
have no doubt what it means.

        I saw a New York postmark.
                Thought maybe it was from
                a college or something.
                My God, Seth. How could
        you? How long have you . . . ?

A vortex of emotions—anger,
        relief, fear—roil together,
        geyser from my mouth,
        "I've been gay—can you
even say the word gay?—

since I was born, Dad.
        This"—I wave the letter
        in front of his face—"is
        who I am. Who I've always
been. I can't change that."

I'd Give Anything

Not to cry. To prove, no
        matter my sexual lean,
        that I am every inch a man.
        But tears overflow my eyes,
stream down my face.

        The only good thing is,
                Dad's crying too. And
                he's definitely straight.
                But he says, *No, no, no.*
        You can't be . . . He can't

        say the word, after all.
                Thank God your mother
                didn't find out about this
                before she . . . It would
        have killed her. Sooner . . .

"No, Dad! How can you
        say that? Mom would
        have been all right with
        it. She loved me. Just like
I am. Even if I am gay."

        He goes silent. Shrinks
                somehow, like a corpse
                too long in the sun. *She*
                would not have accepted this.
        And neither can I. Not ever.

"Please, Dad." I reach out
        for him but he recoils, as if
        "gay" was something you
        could catch. Time. It will take
time. That's all. "Please?"

        He shakes his head. Hard.
                Homosexuality is a sin, an
                abomination in the eyes of
                God. Just the thought of you . . .
        His eyes go flat, drained

        of love for me. Temporary,
                right? *I kept hoping you'd*
                find the right girl, bring her
                home. Get married. Have kids.
        But not some—some man!

        Not in my house. Not in my
                face. Oh my God. What if
                you have AIDS? Or some
                other sick homo disease?
        He slows. Catches his breath.

        Considers some moments
                before he says, *You have*
                to go. Pack your stuff and get
                the hell out of here. He turns
        his back to me. And I know

there is nothing I can say
        to make him change his
        mind. Still, I have to try.
        I swallow the mounting
hysteria. Keep my voice

low. "I'd say I was sorry,
        but I can't apologize for
        being who I am. I didn't ask
        to be gay. I was born this way,
and if you think it's been easy,

living a lie and knowing
        this day might come,
        you'd be wrong. I'm still
        the same person I was before
you found out. Still your s—"

His head starts moving back
        and forth before I can finish
        the word. "Okay, then. But
        where will I go? I have no job,
no money. How will I live?"

        Still facing away from me,
                he reaches for his wallet.
                Extracts two twenties. Tosses
                them to the floor. *Best I can do.*
        You'll figure something out.

Time

It will take time for him to
        accept this. Right? I *am* still
        his son. No way he can quit
        being my father. Quit loving
me. Not because of this. Right?

Loren's letter is still in my
        hand. I fold it carefully,
        slide it into my back pocket,
        along with the forty dollars
I retrieve from the linoleum.

My room is still my room.
        Isn't it? This has always been
        my haven. My sanctuary. How
        do I leave it, especially knowing
it may no longer be mine to

return to? Because I am who
        I am? I don't understand.
        Nothing is different. Not one
        damn thing, except there's
no reason to hide anymore.

I am not an abomination.
        In fact, I could easily argue
        that God wanted me this
        way. Dad will come around.
All it will take is time. Right?

Meanwhile, I've Been Banished

Damn you, Loren. This is
          all your fault, and you're
          not even around to give
          me a place to stay. I put
in a call to Carl. He's not

home, but I leave a brief
          message, asking if I can
          spend a day or two at his
          place. Hopefully he'll say
okay. Not sure what else to do.

On my way out of town,
          I stop by the cemetery.
          Might be a while before
          I can get back for a visit.
"Hey, Mom. How're things

Up There, anyway?" I kneel
          beside her grave, yank
          the weeds that have grown
          around her headstone. "Guess
you know what's going on

here. I'd appreciate it if you
          could maybe send a message
          Dad's way. A little intercession?
          You're not mad at me, are you?
I mean because of . . ." A fresh

storm of tears erupts.
        "You still love me, right?"
        A little breeze picks up
        suddenly, lifts my hair like
fingers. I'll take that as a sign.

I sit in the cool grass, as close
        to Mom as I can get, at least
        for now. I take Loren's letter
        from my pocket, begin to read,
dunking myself in loneliness.

                Dearest Seth, he begins. No
                        wonder Dad kept reading.
                        Sorry I haven't written
                        sooner. You probably think
                I've forgotten you. Never!

                Your touch, your taste,
                        your scent, are etched
                        in my brain forever. . . .
                        Why did he write these
                things to me now? Every

                sentence brings the pain
                        of missing him so alive.
                        I read until the letter ends:
                        Our time together will always
                remain a treasured memory.

Ba-bump!

Not that I didn't already
       suspect his leaving meant
       he was dumping me for
       good. But to have it put
so succinctly, long distance,

is a two-fisted gut punch.
       And to have a Dear John
       letter be the one to bring
       me so completely down
is more like chopping me

in two, midsection. Why
       write at all? Just to make
       damn sure I knew that he
       was never coming back?
A low throb begins in my

temples, and my eyes glaze
       red with anger. That son
       of a bitch! If he were here,
       I'd rearrange his face.
Not that I'm one hundred

percent sure how you go
       about doing such a thing.
       It's a whole new, horrible
       thought for me. Hell, maybe
I'm a *real* man after all.

I Contemplate the Meaning

Of "real man" all the way
        to Louisville. I cruise
        slowly—I have nothing
        to hurry for—and by
the time I reach the city

limits, I've decided if
        being a real man means
        smashing someone
        in the face or turning
your back on a person

because of their sexuality,
        I'll just stay a girl. Guess
        my dad is a real man
        because he's decided
I'm not. Oh damn well.

I arrive at Carl's door,
        determined not to break
        down. But the minute
        I see his face, hear his
mellow-voiced welcome,

it all comes pouring from
        my mouth. What is it about
        Carl and confessions? He
        fixes strong drinks, listens
patiently. Finally he touches

my cheek gently. *I'm sorry.*
I never dared come out
to my parents. They both
went to their graves without
knowing. I've regretted that.

He thinks for a minute.
Finally he says, *I have so*
enjoyed your company.
You have been a balm for
this lonely old man. You may

stay for now, and I'd ask
you to stay longer, but
only yesterday I received
news that my company
has landed a big contract

in Las Vegas. I have to move
to Nevada as soon as I can
put it together on this end.
I'll be there at least a year,
maybe many more, with luck.

Vegas. Hot. Dry. Fifteen hundred
miles away, give or take. Forty
bucks won't cover a ticket. But
maybe I can convince Carl
I'm worth buying a ticket for.

A Poem by Whitney Lang
Worth

*How much would you pay
to stay alive? I mean,
if you could somehow
get the money?*

                                        What

*is your life worth?
Ten thousand? A mil?
How do you measure
something like that?*

                                        Is

*your life more dear
than a homeless person's?
Or a mercenary's—who
kills innocents for money?*

                                        My life

*might seem valuable
to a kidnapper or a life
insurance agent.
But what, really, is it*

                                        worth?

Screw Lucas

Who needs the a-hole anyway?
I hope he and Skylar are totally
miserable together. And, no
doubt, they totally are. But

even if they're totally in love,
I am too, and with someone
so much better than Lucas
could ever pretend to be.

On a scale of one to ten, Lucas
might rate an eight point five.
Bryn is an eleven—classically
handsome, so smart it's almost

scary. Yes, he's a few years
older, but nothing wrong
with maturity. He knows what
he wants, where he's going.

And unlike Lucas, who is a
world-class bullshitter, Bryn, I know
in my heart, would never lie
to me. I trust him with my life.

That Night After Lucas's Party

Just as he promised, it took
twenty minutes (okay, maybe
twenty-five) for Bryn to collect
me, buzzed and brokenhearted.

While I waited, several people,
some of whom I've known
for years, walked on by me
without a word, despite

the steady rivulets of tears
ruining my makeup, streaking
my face. Too much drama,
I guess. And yet, here came

this complete stranger, in his
midnight blue BMW. He pulled
over, double-parked, came around
to open the passenger door for me.

*Come on, sweetheart. Everything
will be okay.* He settled me
into the seat, buckled me in,
as if I were a little child. *Where to?*

I shrugged. "I don't care,
as long as it's away from here."
Away from there. Away from
him. Away from friends,

not really friends at all,
if it meant you or some guy.
I stared out the window,
watching the procession

of streetlights, begging myself
not to get sick. "Thank you
for coming to get me. I didn't
know who else to call."

> *Really?* Already driving slowly,
> he took his foot completely off
> the gas pedal. *What about your*
> *parents? Or, uh, your boyfriend?*

I snorted. "My dad is hardly
ever home. And all my mom
cares about is my sister. And
as for my boyfriend . . ."

I wasn't sure how much to say.
But whatever. "That party was
at my *ex*-boyfriend's house."
There. Complete confession.

        Well, not quite complete. Bryn
        called me on the rest. *Ex, huh?*
        Then why were you at his party?
        Want to tell me what happened?

"Can we go somewhere and talk?
I know I shouldn't ask. I'm sure you
have better things to do." I could hardly
believe it when he said, *Not really.*

We Drove Down to the Beach

By the time we parked, got out,
and walked a little way, barefoot
in the cool, damp sand near the water's
edge, I had mostly sobered up.

I sat, combing the sand with my
toes, as I told him pretty much
everything about my pitiful life.
When I talked about Kyra and Mom,

> he kept nodding. Turns out he,
> his brother, and father have a similar
> relationship. *Like Dad, Shane is
> a high-priced criminal attorney.*

> *And me? Well, I'm just a lowly
> photographer. Never mind
> that I've shot most of the top
> modeling talent in this country.*

Which explained the company name
on his business card: *Perfect Poses.*
"So what are you doing in Santa
Cruz? Why not L.A. or New York?"

> He exhaled deeply. *My dad lives
> in Los Angeles. But my mom
> hated the city. She lived here . . .
> until she died a few weeks ago.*

"Oh wow. I'm so sorry. I hope
I didn't . . ." I couldn't finish.
I had sure stuck my big ol'
foot in my even bigger mouth.

*No. It's okay. I came here
to help settle the estate. She left
her house to me. So I really don't
know many people here yet.*

Which explained why he wasn't
busy that night. In need of a subject
change, I moved on to Lucas. "Not
everyone here is worth knowing. . . ."

I told the whole virgin thing. When
I finished, he responded with a hand,
placed gently on my knee. *What an
idiot. Does he not recognize*

*what a gift you gave him, what
an amazing opportunity you are?
You've lost not a thing, lovely
lady. You've lost not one thing.*

Okay, His Syntax

Can be a bit elevated. Overeducated,
maybe, like having a PhD in poetry,
which should come from the heart,
not from some cardboard rulebook.

But hey, nobody's perfect. And Bryn
comes just about as close as a guy
can come. Since that night, we've
seen each other almost every day.

It hasn't been that long—only
a couple of weeks. But day by
day, I tumble deeper and deeper
in love with him. Yeah, it was fast.

Can falling in love be too fast?
I don't think so, and neither
does Bryn. Best of all, he isn't
afraid to tell me he loves me.

The First Time He Told Me

Was the same time as our first
kiss. It was only a few days
after we started seeing each other.
He said he wanted to wait,

thinking I wasn't quite ready for
someone new. *I wanted you
to be sure. Rebound things can
be incredible letdowns. So stop*

*me if you don't want to hear
this, okay? I don't know how you
feel about love at first sight,
but that day in the mall, I knew*

*right away that you were unique,
a girl who stood out in the crowd.
And when I saw you sitting there
on the curb, crying over someone*

*who didn't deserve your broken
heart, I wanted to make everything
right again for you. I've never
fallen for anyone so fast!*

We were at our favorite beach
hideaway, listening to the symphony
of the waves as the sun set,
tangerine, on the horizon.

Bryn pulled me into his lap,
leaned his forehead against mine,
kissed me softly. *This is so odd
for me, Whitney. I've photographed*

*many beautiful girls. Had flings
with a few. But I never felt for any
of them what I already feel for you,
and we barely know each other.*

*You are more than a pretty face.
You are beautiful inside, and that
beauty radiates, shines like a star.
I know it's wrong—I am a few*

*years older than you—but you have
filled an empty place inside me.*
He turned to look me in the eye.
I love you, Whitney. I really do.

Then he kissed me, and though
I found hunger there, I also found
the love that he professed. And now
I experience that love every day.

We Haven't Made Love Yet

He says he wants me to be very,
very sure I want to, because
he treasures me for more than just
my body. I'm pretty sure I'm ready,

> but that isn't quite "very, very sure."
> Still, maybe today will be the day.
> Yes or no, first he's going to take
> some pics of me. *I want to show you*

> *just how beautiful you are,* he said.
> Then he took me shopping for what
> he wants me to wear—a long, flowing
> skirt and gauzy off-the-shoulder blouse.

> Both white. *A celebration of virginity,*
> was his explanation. *We'll send*
> *a couple to your old boyfriend.*
> He meant that last part too.

It's an incredible day—seventy
degrees, nonintrusive breeze.
Just enough to rile your hair,
carry scents of summer blossoms.

I feel pretty, all decked out in white,
with just enough makeup to enhance
my features, not make them obvious,
as per Bryn's request. Virginal.

We'll Do the Shoot

Where else? At the beach.
But down the coast, away
from town. As we S-curve
along serpentine Highway 101,

I can't help but think about
Lucas and our first time together.
Driving this same stretch of road.
Getting high. "You don't happen

to have any pot, do you?" Bryn
has never offered to get high
with me. Come to think of it,
we've never even discussed it.

>He doesn't slow down. *Afraid not.*
>*I haven't smoked marijuana in years.*
>*I do have some Valium, if you're*
>*a little nervous. In there.* He points

at the center console. Valium?
Why not? "I'm not exactly
nervous. But a good buzz never
hurt anyone, right?" I pop one,

wait for it to kick in, watching
the ocean's heave. By the time
we reach Bryn's chosen location,
I'm feeling pretty darn fine.

We walk down the deserted
beach until he finds a nice stretch
of undisturbed sand. *This will do.*
He unpacks his gear, then checks

me out, all up and down. *Take
off the bra and panties, okay?
We want a glimpse—a hint—
of what's under all that white.*

I do as instructed, allow Bryn
to position me exactly the way
he wants. He sits me, skirt tucked
provocatively between my bent

legs, and when he goes to move
my arms, his hand brushes against
the fabric covering my breasts.
My nipples go hard immediately.

Lovely, he says, assessing.
Exactly what I'm after. Then
he kisses me sweetly. *Exactly
what I'm after.* He makes me

feel like a real model—beautiful,
every man's desire. When he's
finished with his camera, he lays
me back on a thick blanket.

You are exceptionally lovely,
he says, brushing sand from
my hair. He settles beside me,
props himself on one elbow.

Bryn's free hand begins a slow
exploration of my body, over
the sheer fabric, tracing each
curve. *You don't mind, do you?*

Eyes closed to the lowering
sun, brain suspended on a Valium
cloud, I sigh, lift my head. "Kiss
me." He does, and then he lowers

his mouth to other, much more
intimate places. So this is making
love! Well, not quite. I want to know
the rest. "Make love to me."

You're sure? he asks, but there
can be no doubt I'm very, very
sure. Bryn guides me to a place
Lucas has no idea exists.

Okay, It's Kind of Disturbing

That, immediately after learning
the meaning of "orgasm," I think
of Lucas. Maybe it's because
I need to know, "Was that okay?"

> *Oh, darling.* Bryn kisses across
> my face. *That was more than
> okay. That was extraordinary.
> With just a little practice,*
>
> *you will become perfection.
> And I so want to be . . .
> want to be your coach. But . . .*
> He rolls away from me—déjà

vu of the most terrible kind.
I jerk upright, reach out for him.
"What? What did I do?" Oh my God,
he's not going to dump me too?

> *Nothing, baby.* He accepts my hand
> against his cheek. *It's just that
> I got a call this morning, from
> an agency in Vegas. They want me*
>
> *to shoot a beauty pageant, plus
> some pre-event studio work. I'll be
> gone for several weeks. Oh, sunshine,
> I am sure going to miss you!*

My Summer

Just grew a whole lot darker.
"Oh." It is barely audible, but
even if I could make words come
out, I wouldn't know what to say.

> He takes my hand, kisses
> my fingertips. *I probably*
> *shouldn't have . . . you know.*
> *But I couldn't help myself.*

> *You looked like an angel.*
> *And now I want you more*
> *than ever. If only you could . . .*
> He shakes his head. *Never mind.*

"What?" What he suggests
thrills me. Scares me. Tempts
me. And, finally, "I'm not sure
how I could pull it off."

> *I know. I didn't really think*
> *you could. But it would be*
> *like a dream to spend every day*
> *with you.* He pulls me to my feet,

> and we wander up the beach
> toward the car, his invitation
> echoing inside my head: *Come*
> *with me. . . . Come with me.*

Mom's Home

When Bryn drops me off. She takes
one look at me—how I'm dressed,
the state of my hair and makeup—
goes off on a rant. *Where in the hell*

have you been? And with whom?
I never gave you permission to go
anywhere. She catches her breath.
You do remember "permission"?

Suddenly she cares? "You do
remember that you actually have
to hang around the house long
enough to *give* permission?"

Rant becomes rave. *You shut*
the hell up. And you'd better
understand that you may not
leave this house for any reason.

I want to scream. But silence
is the better course of action.
"Whatever." I go to my room,
flop down on my bed. Where—

and why—did she find this sudden
case of maternal instinct? I consider
my next move carefully. Call Bryn.
"Okay. I'll go. Pick me up at ten."

A Poem by Ginger Cordell
Move Carefully

Who knows what lurks
beneath that beautiful
rock you want to turn

over?

I once thought
I wanted to live
on a mountain. But

how high

before the altitude
would take its toll?
Now I want to dive

under

deep water. But can
I hold my breath,
stand the pressure?

How low

can I go, and will
Fate keep the sharks
far away, or

will Destiny

in fact send some
hideous sea creature
to catch me in its jaws,

drag me down?

Ginger
They Call Vegas

Sin City, like calling it what it is
        somehow legitimizes the name.
Las Vegas *is* Sin City. Whole lot

of sinning going on, from fancy
        high-rise casino rooms to sleazy
well-off-the-strip motel dives.

People come here specifically
        to sin. But I wonder whether
it's really true that "what happens

in Vegas stays in Vegas."
        People stain themselves here.
I bet, no matter how hard they

scrub themselves after sinning,
        when they go home, a certain
amount of stain remains visible.

Then, I guess, it's up to the spouse
        or significant other to recognize
the meaning of that dark splotch

ghosting beneath the bleach.
        Most of 'em probably don't want
to look. Don't want to know.

The Reason

I know so damn much about
        the sinning is I have pretty well
been pushed into causing some

of it. As sin goes, at least so
        far, my own participation
has remained fairly mild.

See, when Alex and I first hit
        town, like a few weeks ago,
Lydia seemed okay with giving

        us a place to crash. Alex called
                her from the bus station. *Hey,*
        girl. You said to look you up if

        I ever made it to Vegas. Well,
                me and a friend just got here.
        Could you come pick us up?

It was early morning, and
        Lydia was not real happy
about having to pull herself

out of bed. We waited a couple
        of hours, sipping coffee, until
she finally showed, took us back

to her small tract house south
        of the city in a burb called
Henderson. She keeps her place

neat, with pretty flowers in trim
        beds, giving the impression
she wants to give—legitimate.

See, for a while Lydia worked
        as a stripper in a fairly nice
club near the Stratosphere.

      I made pretty good money.
             Most of it went to the house,
      which took a big cut for keeping

      the girls safe. I did all the work,
              they reaped sixty percent of
      the bennies. Hard to swallow.

So Lydia got smart, started her
        own business—Have Ur Cake
Escorts. Now she takes a cut from

      the girls (and guys) whose "dates"
             she sets up. *I still strip for fun*
      once in a while. All on my own terms.

Her Neighbors

Are completely clueless
        about her means of support.
They think she's a showgirl.

The ultimate Vegas dream.
        Anyway, she let Alex and me
move into her spare bedroom.

        But not for free. *You can stay*
            for a week gratis. After that,
        I'd appreciate a little rent.

        She never asked why we were
            there, although she did mention
        Alex's dad. *How's he doing?*

        Alex shrugged. *Same ol',*
            you know? But if he happens
        to call, I don't want to talk to him.

Far as I know, he never did,
        and Lydia let the subject
drop. Alex and I looked for

under-the-table jobs, but they're
        hard to find, unless you're good
with pulling weeds for five

bucks an hour. A week came.
       A week went by. Two. Plus
a couple of days. Finally Lydia

            said something. *Okay, here's*
                    the deal. Both of you are pretty
            girls. Great bods, with that fresh

            look guys (especially old ones)
                  appreciate. You could make
            boatloads taking off your clothes.

            The clubs are careful about
                  underage girls, but work for
            me, no one will check your IDs.

My first reaction was no way
       would I ever let evil old pervs
see me naked. That's when Lydia

            mentioned how much money
                  we could make. *Easily five*
            hundred a night. And that's no

            touching allowed. Bachelor
                  parties alone could make
            the two of you very comfortable.

What She Forgot

To mention was that her cut
          for setting us up in the exotic
dancing business was one-third

the hourly rate. Tips are ours
          to earn and keep. And hey,
considering Lydia handles all

Have Ur Cake calls, screenings,
          and advertisement, she's
worth every penny. As per her

          well-advised counsel, Alex and I
                    work exclusively as a team.
          Sooner or later, Lydia said,

          you'll have to deal with a jerk
                    who won't want to hear "no
          touching allowed," if you decide

          to stick to that. With two of you,
                    you've got a fighting chance,
          or at the very least, a witness.

So far, though we've had many
          requests for more, and a few
grumbles when we say no way,

the men have all honored
        the "look but don't touch"
rule. Our two-for-one fee

is three hundred an hour
        (a bargain!) plus tips for
straight dancing. Private

lap dances are twenty dollars
        per song. Girl-on-girl action
adds another hundred to the tab.

Besides Lydia, we give a cut
        to our regular taxi drivers,
who keep us off their meters.

They're cool and weren't hard
        to hook up with. Pretty much
everyone in Vegas is a scammer.

As for the actual stripping,
        Lydia gave us some pointers.
Turns out I'm a better dancer

than Alex. Her boobs are bigger,
        though, and really beautiful.
I swear I never knew I leaned

toward girls until I met Alex.
Guess I never let myself lean any
way at all. Didn't dare get close

to anyone, male or female.
But Alex and I are tight. I love
her heart. Her brains. Her body.

The men we perform for like
when we dance with each other,
breast-to-breast or belly-to-ass,

tan skin against pale, ebony hair
on blue-streaked blond, fingers
touching hidden places we won't

let "clients" touch. Powerful!
That's how I feel, seeing how
helpless we make them. I so enjoy

reducing them to masturbation.
It's like they are masturbating
for me, and I can control when

they come by how I move
my body, what I let them see.
It's a game I win every time.

Another Few Weeks

We'll have saved enough
        to get our own place. Maybe
a nice little townhouse closer

to downtown, where most
        of the action is. Tonight
we've got a bachelor party.

Great gigs. Tips are good.
        And when there's a crowd
in the room, the dicks mostly

stay hidden. I'm standing
        by the window, keeping
watch for the cab, when Alex

        comes into the room, wearing
                a yummy short leather skirt.
        Just got a ten o'clock. We should

        be finished with the boys before
                nine. Younger guys tend to get
started early. The best man booked

us for seven, and they should all
        be well on their way to passing
out before we even get there.

Which is why we collect our
        basic fee up front. Don't want
to get caught with our fingers

in some drunk guy's wallet.
        Of course, we do hope they
stay awake long enough to

reward our girl-girl routine.
        We knock on the condo door
at seven on the dot. The guy

        who answers is pretty cute.
            Hello, girls. Come right in.
        Can I get you ladies something

        to drink? We decline and he
            escorts us inside, where a half
        dozen guys are ogling cable porn.

While I ask Best Man for cash
        up front—six hundred, split
seven ways—Alex flirts. *Okay,*

boys, where's the groom? We
        want to treat him right! Where did
she learn that shtick? *Stripping*

for Dummies? Hah. Anyway,
        once the cash is safely tucked
away, Alex outlines the rules:

Absolutely no touching, or we
        leave immediately. One lap dance
is included, for the groom only.

If any of the rest of you are into
        that, it will cost extra. Tips are
encouraged! Any questions?

                One rat-looking dude pulls
                        his eyes from the TV screen
                action. *How much for head?*

A couple other guys laugh
        nervously, but Alex has
it covered. *You'll have to ask*

your buddies. We don't do head,
        except on each other, and that
will cost an extra hundred.

No surprise that Ratman
        reaches into his pocket
for a Benjamin Franklin.

Seven Fifty, Minus Commission

Toward a place of our own,
        Alex and I bid adieu to groom,
Best Man, et al. Poor bride.

                We're giggling as we get into
                        Leonard's cab. *What's so
                funny, girls? Care to share?*

        Alex hands over a fifty. *No
                offense, Len my dear, but
        men are just so disgusting.*

        *I mean, really. Would you dare
                beat off in front of your best
        friends?* We crack up again.

                Lenny looks into his rear-
                        view mirror, grins. *Only if
                you two were dancing for us.*

It's a short drive to our next
        appointment, in a not very nice
part of town. Lenny promises

                to stay available, *Just in case
                        you need a quick ride out
                of here. Be careful, okay?*

Hey, says Alex, *no worries.*
                    But if we don't call you in an
hour, it's okay to come looking.

She gives him a twenty for
                    caring and off we go. Unlike
Best Man, this guy is a pug,

short, wrinkled, and bug-eyed.
                    He doesn't talk as we handle
the business stuff, but he does

pay extra up front for a three-song
                    lap dance. I glance at
Alex, who nods, meaning

she'll do it for him. She knows
                    I never could. After a little
girl-on-girl rubbing, she goes

to take care of it. He sits
                    very still in his chair, staring
as she strips free of her bra.

Suddenly his hands are all
                    over her. "Hey. Cut it out.
Absolutely no touching allowed."

No good. Alex's eyes go just
            a little wild. *Okay, man, we're
out of here.* She tries, but

            the creep snakes his arms
                        around her waist, squeezes
            like a hungry boa constrictor.

            *All I want is a hand job. Give
                        it to me, I'll let you go. You,
            over there, play with yourself.*

            So much for control. Good
                        thing it doesn't take long. He
            finishes with a loud, *Aaaagh!*

He does let go of Alex, who
            wipes her hand on his shirt.
We grab our clothes, throw

ourselves out the door, mostly
            naked. Yank on what we can
at a dead run. Suddenly Alex

            starts to laugh. She holds up
                        a wad of bills. *Stupid shit
            just gave us a really big tip.*

Later, After Several Shots

Of whiskey (Lydia buys
            it for us, as long as we
drink it post-business only),

Alex and I go to bed.
            Fresh from the shower,
her skin is warm and apple-

            scented. I reach for her,
                        but she turns over, away
            from me. *Not now. I'm tired.*

Lately this happens more
            and more. When sex
is your job, it gets harder

and harder to let it be
            about love. "Please, Alex.
Can't I at least hold you?"

She sighs gently, backs up
            against me, into my arms.
Before long, she trumpets

Jim Beam–fueled snores.
            Wish I could laugh about
it. Wish she was really here.

A Poem by Cody Bennett
Might as Well Laugh

Crying is for babies,
little kids. Old people
who somehow can't

remember

the way to the toilet,
so have to rely on
Depends. Once,

when

I just couldn't hold
it anymore, I peed
my pants in the car.

Life

totally sucked until Jack
stopped and Mom got me
some clean ones. Cory

made

major fun of me for days!
Please, God, when I get
old, let me have enough

sense

to find my way to
the toilet!

So Lady Luck

Ain't no lady. She's a total bitch,
not to mention a tease. I mean
one minute she smiles, and dice
roll your way. Then she turns
right around and hands you snake
eyes. Three times in a fricking row.

Lately she hasn't even half-ass
grinned at me. Don't know what
it is, but I can't win an effing bet
to save my neck. Not even a little
one, and at the moment, I'm not
so sure I could even manage that.

The Belmont fucked me good.
I scraped together the thousand,
knew in my heart of hearts that
jerk-off Jet Fuel was gonna take
the Triple Crown, despite what
the so-called experts had to say.

That damn horse laid back just
a little from the start. I knew
the jockey was saving something
for the home stretch. Damn, my
heart got to thumping in my chest.
Thought it might give clean out,

especially when they turned
into that final straightaway,
and Jet Fuel found his stride.
I was jumping up and down.
Screaming, "Go, you sucka, go!"
He went. Finish line in sight,

he took the lead by a nose.
A neck. Then, from the back
of the pack, here came Girly
Girl, a stinking filly, no less.
I swear, once Jet Fuel took a look
at her ass, he was done racing.

Didn't place. Didn't show.
Hauled his butt across the line
in fourth. Girly Girl, a true long
shot, paid out forty to one. At
least the experts weren't right
about her, either. But Jet Fuel,

damn the nag, broke my bank
account. I should have known
to bet the filly. Girls always win,
always get their way. Except
when their boyfriends are
freaking penniless losers.

Saturday Is Ronnie's Birthday

I wish I could get her something
special, or at least take her out
to dinner somewhere really nice.
But I'm completely broke. Can't
lay my hands on a dime, thanks
to one too many bad bets. All

I need is one good wager to make
things right. But I don't have seed
money for even the smallest bet.
I suppose I could go stand on a street
corner, panhandle a buck or two.
            The sign could say: DADDY DIED.
            PLEASE HELP ME FEED MY FAMILY.

So far, we're still eating. But
Mom's bank account is definitely
dwindling. She's out right now,
looking for a job. I should be
doing that too, instead of combing
through Jack's clothing, hunting

spare bills, or at least change. One
little bet could make it all right.
Food. Bills. Insurance. Oh yeah,
and bud. I've pretty much had to go
cold turkey on that, and a good damn
buzz would make everything easier.

I've Scrounged

Four dollars, give or take, when
Mom comes slamming through
the garage door. Better exit her closet!
I tuck the cash into a pocket, head
toward the kitchen. She's at the sink,
faucet running, and over the top

of the water splash against stainless
steel, I can hear her crying. I don't
want to scare her, so I make a lot
of noise, stomping across the floor.
Her shoulders droop, so I know
she's heard me. "What's wrong?"

> She keeps her back toward me,
> keeps on scrubbing her hands.
> Only when I touch her does she
> speak. *I don't know what I was
> thinking. How can someone like
> me find work in Las Vegas?*
>
> *The only places that will hire
> a person my age are Wal-Mart
> and McDonald's, and even then
> I have to compete with young
> people. It's like once you turn
> fifty, you become disposable.*

I reach around her, turn off
the faucet. Then I spin her gently
around to face me. "You are not
disposable. Don't ever say that
again. Cory and I need you more
than ever. . . ." Especially Cory,

who needs an intact parent to turn
him around before there's no more
turning. But I can't say that. She's
got more than enough on her mind.
What I say, despite Mom's tears,
is, "Please try not to worry."

> Don't worry? We're going to lose
> the house! The foreclosure notice
> will arrive any day. We'll be out on
> the street. . . . Her body shudders,
> and she slumps into my arms.
> I carry her to the sofa. She's light

as weathered bones, and her skin
looks like old paper. "Mom? Mom!"
At my voice, she comes out of her trance.
> I'm okay, she mumbles. Jack's pension
> will come through. We can always
> rent a little place. We'll be just fine.

That Phrase Again

More and more, I'm starting
to believe we won't be "just
fine" after all. But I can't let
Mom know I feel that way.
"Yes, we will. You rest now."
She closes her eyes, and I sit

beside her for a few minutes,
holding her hand and brushing
obstinate wisps of hair back off
her face. Foreclosure. The word
has been in the news a lot lately,
especially here in Vegas. But

I had no idea it would ever
threaten us directly. Mom sinks
into troubled sleep. I have to do
something. But what? A job like
GameStop won't pay the mortgage.
Neither will Wal-Mart. So what?

Quick cash-shortage fixes
are plentiful in Vegas. Payday
loans won't work, since I'm
currently not getting paid.
Credit card advances are out,
considering every card in

the household is currently maxed.
(Thanks mostly to me.) One solution
remains. I go into my room, look
around. Not the computer. Not yet.
TV? Check. Stereo? Check.
And in the corner sits one more

dream I'll never attain anyway—
my guitar. I carry TV, tunes, and
instrument to my car, head toward
the far end of the strip, where pawnshops
are plentiful. I choose the one
that claims, "We Pay Top Dollar."

The little puke behind the counter
is not impressed by my twenty-
inch flat panel television, nor
my pricey Bose Wave Music
System. *Fifty bucks for both.*
Neither will he give me much

for my amazing Martin guitar.
Forty. But beggars have no
power to negotiate. The dude
thinks this stuff is hot, anyway.
As I'm filling out the paperwork,
he spies the ten-dollar gold piece

(a gift from Jack), hanging on
a gold rope chain (a gift from
Mom) around my neck. *You
interested in a loan against those?*
He eyes them covetously as
I run my fingers over the chain.

Fuck it. They're just things,
right? Still, I can picture Jack,
three Christmases ago, when
he handed me the little present,
wrapped in shiny purple foil.
He was so proud! I haven't

taken it off since that day.
But now I ask, "How much?"
The pissant wants to see them
closer, and after a quick inspection
offers one-fifty. "Two hundred,"
I counter, not expecting him

to say okay. But he does. I walk
out of Superduper Pawn not
quite three hundred dollars richer.
It weights my conscience heavily.
Now the question becomes,
what do I do with the money?

It Won't Cover

Even a quarter of the mortgage
payment. It might pay last month's
power bill, but that's about it.
I can't forget Ronnie's birthday.
Twenty will cover supermarket
flowers and a card. Wait.

My insurance is due. Can't let
that lapse, or the state of Nevada
will slap me with a hefty fine.
Shit. Shit. Shit. Three hundred
bucks is nothing! Maybe I should
turn around, go back for my stuff.

It's evening, thank God, a desert
breeze lifting to fight the almost
unbearable summer heat. As I go
to my car, the streetlights pop on.
They like to keep the sidewalks lit
here in Sin City, especially in

the seamier parts of town, where
crimes are nightly events. Some
are serious—robberies, gang
shootings. Others don't bother
me much. Prostitution, for instance.
A quick glance reveals five or six

working girls, a transgender and
a straight-up guy. Okay, maybe
not so straight. The driver of
the car that stops to make a deal
with him is definitely a dude.
Hey, whatever dings their dongs.

As for the girls, one is kind of
cute. She's young. Doesn't look
all used up, like the other ones.
Actually, the he/she might be
the prettiest one of all. Funny
what the right outfit and makeup

can do for a guy. The next car
to pull over, looking for tail,
chooses him/her. Wonder if
the guy knows for sure what kind
of tail lurks under those Frederick's
of Hollywood panties! Suuurprise!

Speaking of Frederick's, maybe
I'll forget about the flowers,
get Ronnie something pretty from
there. Something I can appreciate
too. Damn, now look what I've done.
I need Ronnie to ding *my* dong.

Frederick Has a Secret Too

And that is, his lingerie sure ain't
cheap. I dropped fifty without
even trying. Oh well. Ronnie will
be happy, and so will I. That leaves
me two forty, minus sales tax on
a red velvet panty/bra set and the price

of a power drink. Insurance. Gas,
at four bucks a gallon. Fuck it! I'm
broke again. Think, Cody, think.
Okay. If I fill the tank halfway,
I'll probably have twenty left for
a small bet somewhere. But where?

Sports haven't been real good to
me lately. Casino betting has always
been better. If I could parlay the twenty
into fifty, I could play poker at
Vince's tomorrow night. I always
walk away from there with serious

cash. Well, more often than not.
Now if I could just figure out a way
to score, I'd be sitting pretty, or at
least not quite so ugly. Wonder how
long the grace period is for my car
insurance. Better look into that.

First Things First

No need to worry about poker
if I don't have a stake, and twenty
won't cut it. Vince's games
have become so popular, he
made it a fifty-dollar buy-in.
I pump eight gallons into my tank,

head on home. I check the mail
on my way past the box. No
foreclosure notices, but plenty
of other bills, including American
Express and B of A Visa. I'll worry
about how to pay those another

day. Inside, Mom has moved
into her bedroom. The door
is closed, and behind it, it's coma
quiet. Cory's door is also closed.
I poke my head in, but he isn't
here. Didn't think he would be.

Not sure how he spends his time.
Pretty sure I don't want to know.
Even Mom doesn't really question
why he's out so late every night,
what time he makes it home.
What he's doing when he's gone.

I go into my room, turn on
the 'puter, navigate to one
of my favorite sites. The account
is empty. But I happen to have
one last card from Jack's wallet.
It's his ATM card, which draws

from Mom's bank account.
I've hesitated to use it because
I had no way to replace any cash
I took out of it. Now, a few bucks
in my pocket, I'll make a deposit
first thing in the morning.

A hundred should be plenty.
Ten-dollar blackjack bets are
pretty safe, and wins can add
up quickly. Hand number one:
draw. Nothing lost anyway.
Hand number two: I bust. Shit!

But I win the next two hands,
ka-ching, ka-ching. I knew
my luck would turn around
eventually. Ka-ching! So okay,
maybe a little larger bet. Let's go
twenty this time. Dealer holds

on sixteen. I've got fourteen. All
I need is seven or less. Come on!
No! Not nine! Damn, damn, damn.
It's okay. The Lady is still with me.
I can feel her, smiling. Big bet?
Small bet? Big bet? You bet!

I lay down thirty. It's my hand
and I know it. Deal to me: nineteen.
I hold. Hold my breath. Just as
the dealer draws twenty—fuck!—
the telephone rings. Who the hell
could it be, this time of night?

Caller ID

Informs me it's the "Las Vegas
Police Department." My throat
goes dry and my heart drops
into my gut. Cory! Little fucker
better not be dead. "H-hello?
Uh, no, this is his brother.

Hang on. I'll get my mother."
I start to call her, but she
materializes at my side, almost
as if she expected this call.
She takes the phone from my
hand, listens to Sergeant Givens

> without saying more than a few
> words. When she hangs up,
> she looks at me with watery eyes,
> shakes her head. *They arrested
> Cory. He assaulted a woman
> during a robbery attempt.*

A Poem by Eden Streit
Assaulted

By a glimpse of light,
I am reminded
how precious is

freedom.

Swallowed by darkness,
emptied of tears,
the song of the desert

calls

to me and I know
to find a way beyond
these plywood walls,

I must

become someone
I don't want to know.
I hope the real me will

follow.

And I pray the Lord
understands my reasons.
Forgives.

Escape from Tears of Zion

Does not come easy. Jerome is, in fact,
maneuverable, and the key to the lock.

He comes to me late at night, tells me
to do things I've never even imagined.

Things I should have saved for Andrew.
The first time will stay with me, a scar

on my heart. The door opened and though
I knew what that meant, I couldn't believe

that this supposed man of God would draw
back the sheet, pull up my shift and stand,

        staring. *Forgive me*, he whispered, and
        he meant that, even as he stripped,

lowered his ghostly white nakedness over
me. I swallowed the building scream.

Opened my legs. Wept as he plunged inside.
Choked on his Listerine-flavored tongue,

wielded like a weapon. His kiss was, in fact,
harder to accept. Sex is sex. A kiss means love.

After he left, I cried and cried, called into
the night, "Andrew, where are you?"

No answer came then. Or yet. The next
morning Jerome brought a hot biscuit,

with butter and honey. Nothing ever,
ever, has tasted so good. He came back

that night. Afterward, I cried and cried,
screamed into the night, "Andrew, save

me." But he didn't. Hasn't yet. The next
morning Jerome brought a perfect peach.

And so it has gone. I have my shampoo,
unscented so Father won't notice,

but at least my hair feels clean. Really
clean. I even got my Cherry Garcia.

Another small plus: Jerome always uses
a condom. That little detail has saved

more than a badly timed pregnancy.
It has probably saved my sanity.

Almost worse than the thought of having
his baby is the nightmare idea of his "leftovers."

After a Few Weeks

The straight sex has become routine.
Something I can shut myself off from.

> But now Jerome wants other things.
> *Let me watch you touch yourself.*

> Creepy things. *Did you know guys
> like to use vibrators too? Like this.*

> Downright disgusting things. *Your
> period? I like the taste of blood.*

How I wish I could say no. But even
if I thought he'd leave me alone,

saying yes is how I have convinced
him to make Father believe I am fit

for small freedoms. Like working
in the yard, pulling weeds and picking

vegetables. Out here, beyond the confines
of my room, I understand there is no way

to leave the place on foot. I can see
forever across the playa, and the road

is a straight, stretched wound. I can tell
cars are coming long before they arrive,

by dust mushrooms sprouting into the hot
blue Nevada sky. Hot? Working outside,

even midmorning, sweat pools in my armpits
and beads my skin, attracting bugs and dirt.

But anything is better than slow suffocation
in the tomb of my room. I observe people

come and go. Memorize schedules. Learn
where cars are parked, some left unlocked.

Ironically, Jerome is one of the worst
about leaving his keys under the floor mat.

I file that fact away. Plan A has gone awry.
Maybe it will come in handy with Plan B.

Plan A

Was to do whatever it took to get Jerome
to call Andrew, tell him where to find me.

But a major flaw in that strategy surfaced.
Oh, I have played on Jerome's sympathy.

Talked about home. Church. Papa. Told him
Mama is crazy, something he understands.

Jerome inherited his own "not rightness"
from the XX chromosome side of his family.

> *My mother used to lock my brother and me
> in the closet,* he told me. *Then she'd sit*
>
> *outside the door and listen. If she heard
> us praying to Jesus, she'd let us out.*

Even Mama isn't that bad. But our conversation
did reveal some mutual rocky ground. And keeping

him talking meant less time for other stuff.
Then yesterday I asked if he'd ever fallen in love.

> He blushed but said nothing for several
> seconds. Finally he confessed, *With you.*

Talk About Knocking

The squall out of my sails. In love with me?
Looks like loneliness works both ways

here at Tears of Zion. Jerome will not help
me reconnect with Andrew. Neither will he

leave my door unlocked so I can slip away
into the desert night (Plan B). Unless . . .

What would he do if I asked him to run
away with me? Does he *really* believe

he loves me? Would he desert Tears of Zion
and Father? Is this a job or true devotion?

Could I convince him? Could I make him
believe I'm in love with him, too? Could I

live with myself afterward? Could I ever
be forgiven for such painful deception?

>As I sit here, alone, questioning, phrases
>tumble into my head: *You'll be here*

>*for the foreseeable future. . . . Make*
>*the best of it. . . . Guys like vibrators too.*

Plan C begins to formulate. Yes, it's wrong.
But not as wrong as everything else.

Plan C

Means courting Jerome's affection,
pretending to enjoy his deviant sex.

Tonight that means letting him call me
"Mommy" as he sits on my lap and "nurses."

I stroke his hair as a mother would, dig deep
inside for the words, "Mommy loves you, Jerome."

> That excites him, as I guessed it would.
> *I love you, too, Mommy. See how much?*

Oh, Andrew. Even if you do find me, how
can you ever love me again after this?

I hold stubbornly to the dream that he will,
as Jerome turns his belly to "Mommy's."

Love or no, Jerome wants to punish Mommy.
The sex is rough, but it doesn't hurt nearly

as bad as the pretense. And it's even faster
than usual. When he finishes, I lay my head

on his knobby chest. "Too bad you have to go.
It would be nice to sleep together all night."

> Jerome's chin lifts and falls against my hair.
> *Uh-huh. That surely would be nice.*

I roll on top of him, look up into his eyes.
"What if we . . ." Soft kiss. "Never mind."

He shivers. Is much too easy. I feel
almost evil when he whispers, *What?*

I sit up, slide the naked place between my legs
over his skin. "We could leave. Together."

He shakes his head. His body stiffens.
No. I couldn't do that. It would be wrong.

"No more wrong than this." I lean forward,
cup my breasts, rub them over his face.

Confusion seeps into his eyes, and like it
or not, his muscles relax. All but one.

I rock back gently, invite him inside. "I'd be
all yours and take such good care of you."

The second time takes longer, but when
he's finally done, he says, *I'll think about it.*

After he leaves, I lie in an aura of hope.
Say a little prayer to Mary Magdalene.

Hope Begins to Fade

After two days. I haven't seen Jerome
even once. Did I scare him away?

I'm pretty sure he didn't say anything
to Father, who doesn't act strangely

at all during our regular sessions.
In fact, today he is almost friendly.

> *Brother Jerome tells me you've worked
> hard in the garden,* he says. *Is that right?*

What kind of game is this? Better play
along, whatever the rules. "Yes, Father."

> *Good. Hard work deserves a reward.
> Starting Sunday, you may attend*

> *the regular worship service. If that
> goes well, we can talk about school.*

Worship? School? No more isolation?
Is this some kind of a trick? Did Jerome

confess everything to Father after all?
I have no idea what to believe anymore.

One thing I know. It's wiser to say too
little than too much. "Thank you, Father."

Brother Stephen

Walks me back to my room. A girl,
a bit younger than me, rakes gravel

outside the chapel door. She looks up
as we pass and I smile at her, which only

makes her drop her eyes to the ground
again. But not before I see the fear

floating in them. Is she new here, then?
Or has she been here longer? Long enough,

perhaps, to know which is the greater
punishment—isolation or supervised

communion. The short exchange leaves
me uneasy. I wish I could talk to her.

But that won't happen. Stephen herds
me forward. *Hurry up, would you?*

"Why? Somewhere you have to be?"
A hard shove lets me know in no uncertain

terms that my sarcasm is not appreciated.
Except by what little is left of Eden.

Thank the Good Lord

The piece that remains is the one that can
find a streak of humor, however dark,

in almost anything. Otherwise, I would
have gone completely crackers by now.

Otherwise, *they* would have already won.
I'm not conceding yet, and I never will,

unless Andrew is out of my life forever.
Why did I think that? He's looking for me.

(Unless my parents had him locked up.)
Waiting for me. (Unless he believes

our separation was for the best.) Loving
me. (Unless he finds out what I've done.)

A wave of depression sweeps over me,
washes me into an icy black sea. I'm treading

       water, poorly, when the door opens.
       Why are you lying there in the dark?

It's Jerome. The smell of chicken broth
tells me he's brought my dinner.

He flips on the light, and I jump up to greet
him, kiss him on the cheek. "I'm so happy

to see you. Where have you been?
I thought for sure you were mad at me."

He sets down the tray. *Now, why would
you think a thing like that? I had a couple*

of days off is all. He reaches out, strokes
my hair. *So pretty. When we go, I'll buy*

*you shampoo that smells like roses.
You like the scent of roses, don't you?*

When we go? Chills charge through me.
"Of course, Jerome. Roses are my favorite."

*Good. I thought so. I have to go now,
but I'll be back later. We'll talk then.*

When He Returns

He outlines his plan. *We'll leave*
tomorrow night, when everyone's asleep.

By the time somebody misses you,
we'll be halfway to Salt Lake City.

Salt Lake City? Well, we can't go
back to Boise. Still, "Why go there?"

He shrugs. *My brother lives there.*
I can work for him under the table

until you turn eighteen. After that,
we're free to go wherever we want.

He has really thought this through.
So, "Why can't we leave tonight?"

No hurry, is there? I'm too tired
to drive very far tonight. Besides . . .

He lifts my arms, pulls my shift up
over my head. *I'm in need of your*

special brand of lovin'. Help me
out? He nudges me toward the bed.

As He Pokes

And pinches, I concentrate on ways
to *not* reach Salt Lake City. Afterward,

he takes me in his arms, like in some awful
romantic movie. Only in the movies,

the couple would really be in love, though
they might not know it yet. Despite everything

before, and what Jerome has hinted will come
soon, I have to fight not to resist him.

       It's a losing battle. My body tenses.
       He can't help but notice. *What's wrong?*

I drop my voice to a whisper. "Nothing.
It's just . . . I'm excited. And scared."

       *Don't be scared. Everything will work
       out fine. I promise.* He kisses me

and I draw from the deepest well of dark
deception to kiss him back like I mean it.

When the Door Closes

Behind him, I clean myself, as I do every
time he leaves, with soap and cold water

from the wash basin. The air in the room
is thick with heat and the smell of sweaty

sex, a smell I never knew existed until
just a few weeks ago. At first it made

me gag, but it has become something
I simply accept, because I have no other

choice. When all choice is taken from
you, life becomes a game of survival.

I lay the towel on the bed, lie on top
of it, so I don't have to touch the sheet.

Will I carry that habit with me if and when
I leave this place? Will Jerome really take

me out of here? What then? I have no
answers, but I do know I can't end up

in Salt Lake City. Wherever I go—Los
Angeles, maybe, or Reno or Las Vegas—

my only goal is to reconnect with Andrew.
And pray this nightmare ends with a red sunrise.

A Poem by Seth Parnell
Vegas

This city is a neon-
scaled hydra,
bellying across hot

                    Mojave

sand. Cobra
heads, venomous, in
disguise pretend

                    beauty,

lure you with hypnotic
eyes, copper
promises, and the

                    bare

skin of gods intent
on mortal souls. Walk
cautiously, beware the

                    brazen

slither of concrete
beneath your feet.
Do not listen to the

                    arid

hiss of progress.

Seth
Before We Came

To Las Vegas, I had an inkling
         that Carl had money.
         But I had no idea exactly
         how much until he invited
me to relocate here with him.

Truth is, I didn't really
         expect him to agree
         to bring me along. In fact,
         I wasn't totally convinced
that I wanted to come.

The night my dad kicked
         me out, I was in turmoil.
         Where to go? What to do
         next? I had no clue. Carl
was my only solid ground,

and when he said he was
         moving, the earth quaked.
         The blood rushed away
         from my face. Carl reached
for me, as a father would.

Someone's Gay Father

I propped myself against
     him. "I don't know what
     to do. I can't go home. Have
     no home. No money. No job.
Sorry. Not your problem."

     He thought silently for what
          seemed a long while. Finally,
          he led me to the sofa, sat
          next to me. *I've never told*
you about Simon, he said.

He lived with me until a few
     weeks before you and I met.
     He was what some call
     "kept." And I kept him.
It was a mutually beneficial

relationship. He enjoyed
     my hospitality. I enjoyed
     his company, and he looked
     good on my arm, at least
until he grew bored with it.

A trophy—that's what the guy
        I first saw with Carl at
        Fringe was. Carl let the idea
        filter through my confusion.
I wasn't looking for another.

But if you would consider it,
        I'd think about taking you
        along. He kissed me, led
        me to bed. *Come on. Show*
me how much you want to go.

He asked me to do dark,
        obscene things. Things
        I'd never done before.
        And he wanted me to do
them without protection.

Feels better this way.
        And it's okay. I'm safe.
        I promise. You have to
        trust me. He was right.
I had no one else to trust.

A Few Days Later

I climbed on board a jet
        for the very first time. Sat
        in first class, where drinks
        are served before the plane's
wheels ever leave the tarmac.

Less than four hours later,
        we touched down sixteen
        hundred miles to the west,
        and a billion light-years
from everything I've ever

known. We disembarked
        the silver bird in Sin City,
        where trophy boyfriends
        are almost as common as
trophy wives. Carl likes me

on his arm. I'm not sure
        how I feel about being
        someone's prize, but it's
        better than being homeless,
that much I know. Neither

am I exactly sure how I feel
        about the world—at least
        my newest little corner of it—
        knowing I'm gay. I don't feel
judged. But I do feel exposed.

Culture Shock

Barely describes what
       it's like, coming from
       the wild land of Indiana to
       the wild life of Las Vegas.
This city defines insanity.

Not that I've traveled much,
       or at all really, but I can't
       imagine many other places
       so built on extravagance.
Or so reliant on human greed.

Casinos line the glitzy strip,
       masquerading as Venetian
       canals, Egyptian pyramids,
       Manhattan skyscrapers.
Their exteriors boast fountains,

pirate ships, giant lions with
       gaping mouth doorways,
       roller coasters. And almost
       everywhere you look—
billboards and signboards,

on taxicab roofs and
       giant-screen TVs on outdoor
       walls and indoor ceilings—
       you simply cannot escape
the sight of near-naked bodies.

Skin, Skin

Everywhere skin. Instead
       of Sin City, they should
       call this place Skin City.
       Female skin. Male skin.
Something-in-between skin.

They (meaning Skin City
       marketing geniuses)
       aren't choosy about gender,
       as long as the skin is flawless.
Bronze. Young. Beautiful.

I'm not griping. I like skin
       as much as the next guy.
       Maybe the real problem is,
       except for the first few days
here with Carl, I've pretty much

been left all alone to set up
       our luxury condominium
       in an upscale fringe suburb
       of the city. There's a lake
out here, and two golf courses.

All seem totally out of place
       in this hot-as-snot stretch
       of desert sand. One hundred
       twelve degrees in the shade?
Who says there isn't a hell?

If Vegas Is Hell

The devil himself probably
　　　　lives here at Lake Las Vegas.
　　　　He'd only settle for the best,
　　　　right? Everything here is that,
from the boutique shopping

to the pristine marina, to
　　　　manicured waterfront
　　　　greens. It's beautiful, if hot.
　　　　Perfect, with one small
blemish: Here, I'm not Seth.

I'm Seth, who's Carl's.
　　　　Maybe that's not so bad.
　　　　I don't know what to think
　　　　anymore. Lots of people
would envy my life with Carl.

I eat well. Drink well. Dress
　　　　well. And don't have to work
　　　　for any of that, unless you
　　　　count the sex. All I have to do
is keep the place picked up

(a housekeeper handles the real
　　　　dirty stuff), keep myself fit
　　　　(the workout facilities are
　　　　excellent), and look pretty.
Hey, man. I'm a movie star!

One Big Problem

Is boredom. Back home
            I was never bored. Too
            much work to do. And
            when I was done, I could
go into town, hang out

with friends, play pool or
            dance or spread gossip.
            But here, I have no car,
            wouldn't know where to
drive it if I did. I can only

work out so much. Lying
            by the pool is a sure
            path to skin cancer. TV
            is a brain-sucking machine.
I need someone to talk to

when Carl is busy playing
            Mr. Real Estate Developer.
            So I've started spending too
            much time online, making
virtual friends. Fantasy

connections are better
            than no outside contact
            at all. I even found a chat
            room called Men Kept
by Men. My kind of room.

Sure, There Are Posers

Guys who only wish
            they were kept. And
            guys who wish someone
            would want to be kept
by them. Fishermen.

Then there are the guys
            who pretend they want
            to know all about you,
            and about five minutes
into the conversation,

they ask if you'll talk dirty
            to them, preferably on
            the phone. Masturbators.
            Every now and then, you
come across married guys

who want to meet for real,
            with or without their wives,
            usually the former. Cheap
            thrill seekers. I haven't
played in the flesh, but I don't

mind getting someone off
            telling dirty stories. There's
            a certain sick kind of power
            in that. I bet I've even
made a priest or two come.

Which Brings Me Back

To Father Howard. I guess
        the first time he gave me
        a hug, I was about twelve,
        and an altar boy, steeped
in Catholic tradition. I was

        preparing the altar for Mass
                when he called to me from
                the vestry. *Seth, come here
                and help me a minute, please.*
        It was a stifling summer

afternoon, and the loud
        hum of the air conditioner
        fought heavy rock music,
        streaming from the radio.
Father Howard was a twenty-

        first-century priest. *What do you
                think of these colors?* He held
                up some squares in turquoise
                hues. *I want to paint the office
        and just can't seem to decide.*

I went closer, studied
          the samples carefully.
          Finally I pointed to "Cool
          Caribbean." Father Howard
smiled. *I like that one too.*

Cool Caribbean it is, then.
          Thank you, Seth. As I turned
          to leave, his arms coiled
          around me. *You're very*
special to me, you know.

It was the first time a man
          had ever hugged me in such
          an intimate way. I liked it,
          twisted around to hug
him back. "Thanks, Father."

That was it. That time. I left,
          feeling very special. It never
          occurred to me that it might
          be wrong for a man of God
to embrace a boy in such a way.

Or Where

That first hug might lead.
  The next time we were
  alone together, Father Howard
  was bolder. His hug lasted
longer, and he massaged

  my shoulders. *You are such
    a good-looking boy,* he said.
    I bet the girls think so too.
    He paused, but when I didn't
  respond, he tried, *Other boys?*

My eyes went wide. I started
  to deny, but the adolescent
  tugs I'd felt had all been
  toward boys. I couldn't lie
to a priest. I stared at the floor.

  He tilted my chin, so I had
    to look in his eyes. *It's okay,
    Seth. You're beautiful, just
    the way God made you.*
  His lips, warm and soft,

brushed across my forehead.
  I was scared. Thrilled. Amazed
  at his acceptance of sin, born
  inside of me. Father Howard
left things there. That time.

The Next Time

Hugging segued to touching.
        Not too much. But enough.
        Later, there would be more
        touching. Mutual touching.
But always gentle. Always

with deep affection. We never
        had out-and-out (meaning in
        and out) sex. And though I'd heard
        about pedophile priests, for
some reason, I never thought

Father Howard might be one.
        Not then, anyway. Not until
        years later, when I read about
        him losing his collar because
of another boy. In another town.

The picture became rainwater
        clear. I wasn't special at all.
        I was just one of the first
        of many. I felt betrayed.
Used. White-hot pissed off.

But ultimately my emotions
        cooled. Iced over. I could
        have said no, and Father
        Howard would have backed
off. But I didn't. And while

he most definitely took
            advantage of my youthful
            ignorance, he also made me
            believe that being drawn
to men didn't automatically

condemn me to hell. After
            Father Howard changed
            parishes, I moved on too—
            to girls in general and Janet
Winkler in particular. I'll always

feel bad about hurting her,
            but I can't be what I'm not.
            Bringing me back to what I am—
            gay, and being provided for
by someone I like but don't love.

Making Me

According to this guy Chad,
        a regular chatter in Men Kept
        by Men, *A whore, and not*
        a whole lot more. No worries,
    mate. I'm a whore too.

Turns out Chad's keeper
        imported him all the way
        from Sydney, Down Under.
        But wherever he's from,
his assessment must be wrong.

Okay, I don't love Carl. But
        millions of people have lived
        together without being in love.
        I type, "How is this different
from a marriage of convenience?"

        Chad's fingers are quick:
            Did you sign anything to
            make the arrangement legal?
            If your man drops dead,
        what will happen to you?

Carl won't die any time soon.
        Right? I mean, he's not *that*
        old. Right? Okay. Valid point.
        One I should probably consider
sooner rather than later. Right?

A Poem by Whitney Lang
Sooner or Later

Someone

you could not have
ever dreamed of
appears like a rainbow
bridging clouds, and

steals

your breath away.
Someone beautiful,
inside and out,
grabs hold of

your

hand, guides you
along a rarely traveled
road, to a place
where your broken

heart

can be mended, piece
by beating piece.
The cost, gratefully
afforded, is only

your love.

Whitney
Free

That's what I am now. Free
of Mom, of Kyra's shadow.
Free of friction and the pain
of a shattered heart. I'm healed.

I'm also blown away by Vegas.
What a crazy city! I bet this
is what all those Saudi sheiks
wish their desert looked like.

Of course, on any given day,
there are probably a half-dozen
Middle Eastern moneybags
living it up here in Sin City.

This is where they come to get
away from Allah's watchful eye.
'Cause Vegas would scare the living
crap out of any deity worth his salt.

It's hot as hell and downright
filthy. Not like dusty dirty,
although when the wind blows
hard from the west, it's that, too.

Vegas is the kind of dirty every
mother worries about. What would
my mom say if she knew this is where
I ended up when I left that night?

Nothing, probably. I bet she's happy
I'm gone. One less irritation carving
wrinkles. Daddy must be worried
sick. It's been almost two months,

and I haven't let him know I'm okay.
Eventually I will. I'm more than
okay, actually. I'm great, because
I'm with Bryn, who loves me

more than anything. Who wants to
be with me always. Who needs me.
That's something all new—being
needed. Treasured. Protected.

> *I'll never let anyone hurt you,*
> Bryn promised. *You are my angel.*
> I've never been anyone's angel,
> either. Bryn has given me wings.

We're Staying

In a weekly motel—small, but mostly
clean and air-conditioned. And it's only
until Bryn has time to find us something
nicer. He's been working almost

every day, photographing wannabe
beauty pageant queens. I don't like
him ogling gorgeous girls for hours
at a time, but he comes home to me.

He photographs me, too. Lately,
the pics have all been naked.
*Such a beautiful body deserves
to be seen,* he says. *We could make*

*some extra money, too. To get
an even better place. More like
what you're used to. I want
only the very best for you.*

I don't mind posing without
clothes. Some of the finest art
ever was paintings of nudes.
Bryn makes me feel pretty,

and I like how that looks in photos.
At first it was kind of weird,
thinking about total strangers
seeing me that way, but it's not

so bad, really. And hey, maybe
Mom will come across one of them.
That would be awesome. Stupid cow
would probably be jealous.

Bryn called a little while ago.
I'm on my way home, and I've
got a little surprise for you.
Hope you're up for some fun.

Fun? Like what? He must have
gotten paid, which is good. I was
starting to worry a little about
how we were going to eat.

I guess inheriting his mom's house
was more about spending money
than making money, at least until
he can sell it. Not easy right now.

Because of the housing slump.
And because going back to Santa
Cruz would probably not be wise.
But he said we'd be fine, and we will.

Bryn Blows In

Like a breeze off the ocean,
lifting me with his presence.
Then his arms lift me for real,
spin me around and around.

> *Hey, baby.* He kisses me, infuses
> me with happiness. *What a day.*
> *Sorry I'm late.* The clock says
> it's eight eighteen. He *is* late.

> He carries me to the couch, sits
> me down. *Are you ready for my*
> *surprise? Two surprises, actually.*
> He reaches into a pocket for the first.

Guess it's not a dinner out.
Nope. Not even close. It's a dope-
sized plastic bag with some brown
substance inside. "What's that?"

> But I suspect his response:
> *Smack. One of the girls turned*
> *me on to a little. Thought*
> *you might like to share a taste.*

Heroin. I've never even thought
about trying it. "I don't know. . . .
That shit is scary as hell." Way
past meth, which is scary enough.

Bryn's Reaction

Is swift, completely unexpected.
*Oh, I see. You can do cocaine
with your other boyfriends, but
you won't try this for me?*

Holy Pete! He's never snapped
at me like that before. I've never
even heard him raise his voice.
My first instinct is to bark back,

but I don't want to fight with Bryn.
"I—I'm sorry. I just . . . didn't . . .
Uh . . ." Why am I apologizing?
"It's just, heroin is so addictive, and . . ."

He softens immediately. *No, hon.
Not if you only do a little, once
in a while. And the places it will
take you! I want to see you there.*

OMG. I can't believe I'm saying
okay to heroin. But I am. Except,
"No needles! No way will I shoot
up anything." I wait for his reaction.

*No problem. We'll just chase
the dragon, okay?* He means heated
tinfoil and a rolled-up bill to grab
the smoke, draw it up my nose.

I've seen people at parties do
meth the same way. Even before
Bryn creases the foil into a deep
V, my heart starts racing. Fear

is exhilarating, all on its own.
I watch him drop a pinhead of H
into the makeshift bowl, and goose
bumps cover my arms. I have no

idea what to expect when the smoke
lifts into the dollar bill "straw." Ugh.
It tastes like rotten ketchup. Bitter
and harsh in my throat. I start to choke.

Bryn's warning is rough: *Don't
you dare cough it out!* He checks
out my eyes. Looking for pupil
dilation, no doubt. It takes a while.

*If you shoot up, you feel the effects
instantaneously. Smoking it might
take ten or fifteen minutes. Patience.
Meanwhile, I have another surprise.*

It takes all of ten minutes before
I begin to feel kind of tingly. Euphoric.
Like everything in my life just fell
into place. The sensation is gentle,

not at all like the overwhelming
buzz I thought it would be. I can
handle this. What's all the hype
about, anyway? Bryn has finished

setting up the second surprise—
a webcam, hooked up to his
laptop. *I thought it would be fun
to put ourselves in the movies.*

America's Sexiest Home Videos.
Come here. Let's get nasty.
The tone of his voice lets me know
disagreeing is not an option.

But I don't want to disagree.
Every nerve in my body screams
to make love with Bryn, who responds
by taking "nasty" to a whole new level.

It is only afterward, floating
on a sensual fog, in an uneasy state
of half sleep, that it comes to me:
Bryn didn't join in the dragon chase.

A Week After

My first sweet-bitter taste of smack,
Bryn has talked me into indulging
again four or five times. I don't
want to get hooked, and I'm sure

I won't, as long as all I do is smoke
a little every now and again. I have to
admit I like the way it makes me
feel—like I'm on top of the world.

> Bryn never indulges. *I can't
> get it up if I do, and I want this
> to be all about you.* So why does
> he keep asking me to do things

> that seem mostly all about him?
> Things like performing dirty
> acts on pay-per-view webcam?
> *It won't be forever, I promise.*

> *Just long enough to save up
> some serious bank. I've got my
> eye on a really nice place. It's
> pricey, but you're so worth it.*

When I'm high, I don't mind.
But when I touch back down,
I start to worry. Is this the same
Bryn who valued my almost-virginity?

I Also Worry

About him spending more
and more time away from me.
Talking more and more about
"the girls," and I'm starting to

wonder if the girls he's talking
about are really pageant hopefuls.
If he's getting paid to photograph
models, he's not getting paid well.

Our money seems to come in spurts,
and some of that seems to be from
the webcam spurting going on.
He doesn't want me to work, though,

> except for private webcam spurting.
> *Some guys like to watch girls*
> *getting off all by themselves.*
> *Make it look good for the camera.*

I was never into touching myself,
but it isn't so bad, especially when
I'm high. Besides the occasional
H, Bryn supplies me with bud—

mediocre seeded Mexican—
and prescription downers. Not sure
where he gets them, and I really
don't care. As long as I'm buzzed,

the things he asks of me are easy
to do, and hey, anything's better
than wasting away in Santa Cruz.
God, if I were there, I'd be starting

my junior year of high school.
High school is so not me anymore.
Wonder what Paige is doing.
Wonder if she hooked up

with that guy after that night at
Lucas's party. Shit! Why did I have to
think about him? Wonder if he likes
it in San Diego. Wonder . . . stop

it. Fuck. Where the hell's my stash?
I locate it under the coffee table. Two
tokes of half-ass pot, a bigger question
hovers: Where the hell is Whitney?

It's Almost Midnight

When Bryn comes in. He's not
alone. The guy he's with is Latino,
I think. Olive-skinned. Dark-haired.
Okay-looking. Dressed well.

Bryn comes over, kisses me.
Hey, babe. This is my buddy,
Oscar. He nods toward the stash
box, sitting on the coffee table.

Oscar's been very good to us,
if you get my meaning. Now
I want you to return the favor
and be very, very nice to Oscar.

Very nice? Does he mean what
I think he means? Play hostess.
"Uh, nice to meet you, Oscar.
Can I get you something to drink?"

Maybe after. Oscar comes over,
touches my face. *You're right,*
Bryn. She's very pretty. Tight
little body, too. Yes, she'll do.

His hands slide over my front,
reach up under my blouse.
The skin of his fingers, seeking
my nipples, is calloused. Cold.

"No, wait. I can't. You're not
serious . . . Bryn?" He can't want
me to do this! I jerk away from
Oscar, turn to Bryn. Search his eyes.

They are deadly serious, and so
is Bryn when he says, *Yes, you
can. And if you love me, you will.
You do love me, don't you?*

"Of course I love you! But this
isn't . . ." Isn't right, is what I want
to say. But what *is* right, anymore?
Is this really what loving him means?

Bryn's hands press down on
my shoulders. *Do this for me,
Whitney. Do this for us.* He kisses
me. But it is the kiss of a stranger.

I Beg for a Buzz First

Pot won't do. It has to be
smack, and three long pulls
of the acrid smoke barely take
me to the place I need to be.

> Oscar watches. Waits impatiently
> for the H to kick in. *You should
> use a needle. Smoking the Lady
> is a waste of good dope.*

Fear-queasy, I stumble down
the hall, into the bedroom.
Oscar follows, shedding clothes.
His body is lean, muscular.

Another time, another place,
I might find him attractive,
but attraction is about choice.
I have no choice here but to

take off my own clothes, lie on
the bed, wait for him to come,
and do whatever it is he has paid
to do. I hate you, Bryn. I hate you.

Within Seconds

I hate Oscar, too. He breathes
beer, sweats onion, and there is no
love, no kindness, nothing but
greed to his sex. He grabs my wrists,

holds them over my head so I can't
move when he bites my neck,
and lower. I'll wear his teeth marks
for days. "Stop. You're hurting me."

*You think that hurts? You ain't
seen nothing yet.* His teeth close
even harder and his hand squeezes
my arms like a vise and now

his knees force my legs apart
and there is no pleasure to what
he does down there. Only pain.
Bruising pain. I give myself to

the morphine shroud, denying
the pounding between my thighs.
Something makes me look toward
the door. Bryn stands there, staring.

A Poem by Ginger Cordell
Staring

Into the midnight sky,
starlight defeated by
the scream of neon,

truth

is hard to discern.
Does it sparkle?
Does it burn? If
a weightless moment

transcends

the gravity of time,
what proof is there
of its existence?
Does it infuse

every

tick of the clock,
each blink of an eye?
Which is harder to
bear—reality, or a

lie?

Our Own Place

Wasn't easy to come by. Most
       landlords prefer their tenants
to be over eighteen. We finally

found a weekly where the lady
       in the office didn't look too hard
at our application. The four weeks

up front probably helped with that.
       The room at Lydia's was nicer.
But the drive into the city got old.

At least, that's what we told Lydia
       when we said we were moving out.
In reality, living with her was getting

       old. She could be a real bitch,
            and she was pushing us to do
       stuff besides strip. *You could make*

       a lot more if you'd treat a few
            of your clients to a little touchy-
       feely. Not all of them, of course.

       Just think about it. Getting
            paid for something most
       people give away? No-brainer.

She Pushed Hard Enough

That Alex has actually considered
          doing it. *It's not such a big deal,*
as long as they use condoms.

The thing is, Lydia wouldn't have
          to know. I could do it on the side,
and not give her a cut. We could

save up enough money to blow
          this city. Go somewhere pretty,
like Portland or San Francisco.

When she talks like that, it makes
          me think about Iris. How turning
tricks has used her up. How she

tried to let it use *me* up. Why
          couldn't I have a real mother?
Why did she have kids at all?

Iris used to talk about moving
          somewhere else—somewhere
exciting, like New York City.

Oh yeah, I can just picture
          Iris in Manhattan. Cruising
Central Park. Hustling johns.

When I Think About Iris

I can't help but think about
        Gram. She must be worried
about me. I should probably

try to send word that I'm okay.
        Alive, anyway, "okay" being
a relative term. But how can

I let her know without giving
        away where I am? Letters have
postmarks and phones can be

traced. I just hope she's taking
        care of the kids. Keeping them
safe from Iris. Most of 'em are

back in school. Except Sandy.
        He's still too little. Hope he's all
healed up, chasing balls

around again. Just not in
        the street. Oh God, why did
I have to think about them?

A Mack truck of guilt crashes
        into me. How can I be home-
sick, when I don't have a home?

I Start to Pace

North and south, across
        the grease-stained beige
carpet. Guess the last tenant

kept his moped in the living
        room. The carpet was steam-
cleaned when he moved, but some

black marks can't be excised.
        Alex went to the store about
an hour ago. I would have

gone along, but my period
        this month is major. I'm close
to bleeding out, I think, and

I've downed enough ibuprofen
        to kill a horse. But I've still
got cramps. Maybe that bastard

who raped me made me pregnant
        and God was gracious enough
to let me miscarry. Whatever

the problem is, it has definitely
        put the brakes on shedding
my clothes for strangers.

Which Means a Couple of Things

One, Alex is the only one
          working, so our income
is cut in half right now. Plus,

she's going out by herself,
          which scares the crap out
of me. I know she can take

care of herself and all, but
          still . . . Ah, can't think
about the downside of that.

If anything bad ever happened
          to Alex, I'd go crazy. Except
for Gram, Alex is the only good

thing I've ever had in my life.
          She lifts me, like a double shot
of espresso. I wish she were here

right now, to lift me out of this
          black pit of boredom. My indoor
hike carries me past the bathroom,

where the laundry basket
          overflows dirty clothes. Might
as well wash them as keep

walking by 'em, I guess.
        I gather them up, grab some
detergent, and shovel quarters

into my pockets. The laundry
        room is downstairs and in
the other building somewhere.

This will be my first trip there.
        Jeez, man. For almost October,
it's still hotter than hell. Maybe

ninety in the shade. By the time
        I locate the short bank of washers,
I am dripping sweat. Lovely!

Hopefully, the person pulling
        her own clothes from the dryer
won't get close enough to smell me.

Her Back Is Toward Me

And just in case my ripeness
        doesn't precede me, I say,
"Hello," so she knows I'm here.

She jumps about three feet.
        "Sorry. Didn't mean to
sneak up on you." When she

turns, I can see she's a little
        younger than me. Wow,
her posture made me think

        something different. *It's okay,*
                she says. Guess I was off in
        Never-Never Land. Don't use

        that washer. . . . She points.
                Someone's pen exploded
        in it. There's ink all over.

"Thanks." As I put my dirties
        into the other two washers,
she starts to fold her clothes.

I can't help but stare. The girl
        would be beautiful, except for
the dark circles under her eyes.

She reminds me of those
        models—what do they call
them? Oh, yeah. Heroin chic.

I know squat about heroin,
        but my guess is she's using
something. Or it's using her.

        Eventually she notices me
                observing her and jumps on
        defense. *Something wrong?*

"Oh, no. Sorry. You just, uh . . .
        remind me of my sister. I haven't
seen her in a long time."

Not totally true (Mary Ann
        resembles her only slightly),
but it works. The girl exhales

        (was she holding her breath?),
                and her shoulders relax. *Oh. Okay.*
        I haven't seen my sister in a while

        either. Not that she cares,
                I'm sure. Well, I'd better go.
        See you. Poof. She's gone.

The Clothes Are Still Spinning

So I take a minute to duck
       out the door, watch where
the girl goes. Not sure why.

Her room is kitty-corner from
       ours, across the parking lot
and on the ground floor. Wonder

who she lives with. Guy?
       Girl? Relative? She can't be
out on her own, can she?

What is up with me? Why do
       I care who she lives with?
Shit, I really am bored, aren't I?

Bored and bleeding. Sounds
       like the name of a book:
Bored and Bleeding in Vegas.

Okay, Alex, you'd better get
       home soon, or I'll turn into
a bored, bleeding, babbling loon.

Early Evening

And Alex still isn't back yet.
        Where the hell is she? I call
her cell, but the canned voice

that answers informs me that
        she's unavailable, meaning
she's out of prepaid minutes.

Guess I'll have to be patient.
        I fold the clothes, put them
away. Treat myself to a Lean

Pocket. Turn on the aged TV.
        Half listen to *Jeopardy!* while
I go to the window, hoping

to catch a glimpse of Alex,
        coming up the sidewalk.
I don't see her, but I do see

heroin chic going into her room,
        about six paces in front of a guy.
He's older. Balding. Her father?

My guess is no way, or if he
        does happen to be her father,
it's a definite case of incest.

Is Every Girl

In this nasty, stinking city
       turning tricks? Young,
old, at least as old as you

can get without dying
       of some incurable sex
disease? I swear, I will never

do that, never sink as low
       as my mother. My pretty
heroin chic neighbor.

My beautiful best friend,
       who I love so much it hurts.
And I swear, as soon as

I can, I will find a way out
       of this place. Will Alex come?
Or have I lost her to the night?

She Stumbles In

Around nine. Worry turns to
          relief. Then I take another
look at her—hair mussed,

makeup smeared, clothes
          wrinkled and buttons undone.
Relief explodes into anger.

"Where the fuck have you
          been?" I sound like a crow.
"You scared me shitless."

          Alex remains placid. *Been
                    taking care of business
          is all. Someone's got to.*

It's more than a little bit
          obvious that the day's
"business" included more

than stripping. The smell
          of sweat and sex hangs
in the air, a storm cloud.

"Alex, what have you done?
          You're not turning tricks
like some hooker, are you?"

A strong memory of Iris
          stumbling in after dark,
perfumed in sex, surfaces,

swims into blurry view.
          Goddamn it, no! "Please,
Alex, tell me you didn't."

          But she doesn't deny. Won't
                    say I'm wrong. *It's okay,*
          Gin. . . . It's not so bad, really.

          I mean, the sex isn't good,
                    but it's fast, and all things
          considered, the pay scale

          isn't bad. Fifty bucks for
                    under ten minutes' work?
          Three hundred an hour!

          Shit, girl, that's attorney
                    wages, and you don't have
          to go to school—

"Stop it! We don't need money
          that bad. I'll get off the rag
and we'll go back to stripping.

"Lydia can have her cut. We
            were doing okay like that,
weren't we?" We were, damn it!

            Finally Alex deflates just
                    a little. *Sit down. Please?*
            There's stuff you don't know.

Like how she knew all about
            Lydia's escort service before
we ever got here. Like how Lydia

never invited her to "come stay
            any time." Like how when we
talked about running away, Alex

called Lydia and set the whole
            thing up. Like how Lydia
promised to keep her mouth

shut, as long as Alex went
            to work for her. Like how
Alex's not-stepdad *did* call,

looking for her. But Lydia
            denied knowing a thing.
So Alex owes her, big-time.

Alex Goes to Shower

But not before promising
                again, *It will just be for*
a little while—just until

we can save up enough
                to blow this freaking city.
I love you, Gin. Stay cool.

I love her, too. And I can't
                stand the idea of her being
with a bunch of stinking, nasty

men. If I could bring myself
                to do it too, we could save
up even faster. But I don't think

I could. I'd be no better than
                Iris. Would I? Did she ever
think, *Just for a little while?*

The room still wears evidence
                of Alex's recent encounters.
I go to open the window. Notice

Ms. Heroin going through
                her door again. Followed by
another guy. Not her father, either.

A Poem by Cody Bennett
Door

I once heard an old
saying about things
going all to hell.
It went, "When

a door

closes, somewhere
a window opens."
If so, when a train

slams

into a Volkswagen,
does a BMW materialize
down the tracks? If you
remember your undies

in your

dreams, do you wake
up naked? Okay,
maybe the logic fails.
But hey, let's

face

it. Logic doesn't really
apply to old sayings,
either. Does it?

Cody
Logic?

What's that? If it ever applied
to my life, my choices, those years
(days?) have vanished from memory.
I am spinning. Spiraling. Clinging to
the eye of the tornado. If I give up,
give in to the mad desire to just

let go, I know I'll die. But death,
close by, might be preferable
to this dizzying ride. How did I get
here? How did things go so wrong,
so fast? Left? Right? Whichever way
I choose, one thing is very clear—

I can never turn around, never
go back. Twisters only move in one
direction—full speed ahead.
Like Dorothy Gale, I ran from safe
haven, searching, despite the storm
gathering strength behind me.

The Chiefs Kick Off

In about an hour. Still time to place
a small bet. I log on, check out the point
spread. Awesome! So, okay, maybe
a little larger bet. I can pay Lydia back
later. Fuckers better step up to the line
of scrimmage and play fricking ball!

       Guess I'll call Ronnie, if only to hear
       her voice. My cell phone blinks—
       did she call me? But when I retrieve
       the message, it's Misty, grating my ear.
       Hey, cutie. How about a double
       date? And can you bring smoke?

Misty is the skank who hooked
me up with Lydia. Okay, maybe
I shouldn't look at it that way.
She did me a favor, or at least
we both thought so at the time.
Her boyfriend plays poker

with Vince. One night he was
way too buzzed to drive home,
so he called Misty. I had pretty
much lost my shirt that night,
and when she showed up, I was
looking miserable. Chris still

had a sleeve or two left of his
shirt, and while he was busy
losing those, I invited Misty
to smoke some bud. We got to
talking, and the more we smoked,
the more I confessed, which made

her open up to me. *Yeah, money
sucks, but you can't live without
it. I'm paying my way through
UNLV with a little sex-on-the-side.*
She let that sink in, and it took too
long. *You know . . . escorting?*

"You mean you get paid to . . . ?"
I studied her closer. She looked
like a college student. Nothing
more. Certainly not a whore,
especially not the type I see hawking
their wares from the sidewalk.

*Yeah, and it's not so bad, really.
I mean, if you're going to have sex
anyway, why not earn a little extra
cash, you know?* She took a big drag.
Held it a long while, as if it helped
her think. *I won't trick forever.*

I had never once in my life thought
about having sex for money. Could
finding enough cash to help myself
out of debt be *that* easy? I asked for
details, and when she mentioned
working for an established escort

service, it almost sounded legit.
"Do any guys work there?" My
stupid little brain glommed onto
a picture of lonely middle-aged
women paying for an evening
of companionship, plus some fun.

> *A couple*, she said. *Lydia calls*
> *them her "boys," but I think they're,*
> *like, in their twenties. Why?*
> She winked. *You interested in*
> *a little paid action? I can introduce*
> *you to Lydia if you want.*

"Let me think about it." Wow.
Sex for money. I still hadn't
considered the possibility of it
meaning having sex with men
when I asked, "Oh. One thing.
How much does it pay, anyway?"

Her Answer

Surprised me. Thrilled me. Who
knew you could make a hundred
bucks an hour (after the service's
cut) for screwing? I thought it over
for at least a day, and even made
a written list of pros and cons.

Pro: Work one hour, get paid more
than eight hours at GameStop.
Con: What if the old babe was really
disgusting and wanted, like, oral?
Pro: My insurance had already
Lapsed, and I had no way to pay it.

Con: If Mom ever even suspected,
she'd flip her fricking wig!
Pro: If Mom ever found out about
the credit cards, she'd lose all faith in me.
Con: People who have sex for money
might end up with some awful disease.

Pro: With enough cash to place the right
bet, I could win enough to fix everything.
Con: What if having sex on the side
meant I couldn't get it up for Ronnie?
Pro: I didn't have many choices left.

Result: I picked up the phone, called Misty.

She Introduced Me

To Lydia, who outlined the rules
and regulations, not knowing
I still had women in mind. When
I finally mentioned that, her smile
slipped a little. But only for a second.
You're envisioning American

*Gigolo. Sorry, but that kind of
escorting is rare. Something you
see in the movies, really. Generally,
when I get calls for young men,
it's older men doing the calling.
You ever been with a man?*

"A man? No!" What? Did I look
gay or something? Sex with men?
Not even a hundred bucks an hour
was worth that. At least, not then.
"So every one of your 'boys' is gay?
Because I'm, like, totally straight."

Lydia shrugged. *No one is one
hundred percent hetero. We are
all bi to varying degrees. It all
comes down to necessity.* Turned
out the statement was accurate. Took
about a week to see things her way.

Sometimes Misty and I

Do have "two-fers" with confused
guys. But not today. "Sorry," I tell her.
"I've already got a client lined up."
In fact, I'd better go. I hang up, pop
a Valium, "borrowed" from a bottle
in Ronnie's medicine cabinet. Fuck.

Stealing pills. I suck. But I'm glad
I have something to push away
the pain, stash it in a compartment
of my brain I don't visit very often.
I cruise slowly, noticing cars
prowling for street-corner hustlers.

Twenty bucks for a backseat blowjob?
At least I haven't sunk that low. Yet.
No! That will not become my future.
Then again, if someone would have told
me two months ago I'd be selling myself
to men, I'd have said they were full

of shit. Necessity is a motherfucker.
And if they would have said I might
even like it, I'd have kicked their ass.
The first time I offered myself up, turned
myself into meat, I ran to the bathroom,
heaved. That guy laughed and laughed.

Lydia said it would get easier.
The first time is always the worst.
Just remember you can always
say no, if something doesn't seem
kosher. Somehow I doubt many
rabbis would bless "Cody meat."

But Lydia was right. The second
time wasn't as bad. At least I managed
to make it through without losing
my breakfast. Every time after was easier
still, except for the guys who needed
a shower. B.O. is a definite bitch.

Once in a while I get really lucky,
when a dude decides he'd rather talk
than screw. They're paying me for
my time. If they want to complain
about their significant others, hey,
I'll listen for a buck fifty up front.

But I don't have to like any of it.
Shouldn't like any of it, and getting
off is just plain crazy. I do this because
I have to. Not because I want to. I need
a good, healthy dose of Ronnie. Only
what if she doesn't turn me on now?

I Pull into Valet

At the Riviera, not the nicest casino
in town, but not the sleaziest, either.
Not that it matters. What I'm going
to do is more than sleazy. It's sick.
But I'll leave with enough money,
even after Lydia's cut, to give Mom

a hundred toward the bills. And,
depending on how generous the guy
feels after, I just might have enough
left over to place a small bet on
the Chiefs. If those bastards do right
by me, I could maybe skip a date

or two. "Date." Why don't I just call
it what it is—a trick. I'm turning tricks.
Can I really have sunk so low?
I'm having sex with men—often married
guys, trying to figure out why
they're attracted to boys—for cash.

I'm not gay! Before a few weeks ago,
I had never even checked a guy out,
let alone thought about doing one.
So why isn't it harder? Why am I
heading into the elevator, going up
eight floors, to room 822?

Two Quiet Knocks

Nothing. Two more, louder. Footsteps
toward the door. It opens. "Dan?"
The guy nods, steps aside to let
me in. The room is obsessively neat,
and a familiar scent perfumes the air.
Gingerbread? Like Ronnie's shampoo.

Dan is fortyish, short crewcut
graying slightly at the edges.
He wears no shirt, and his muscles
are tanned. Toned. Jesus. He could
be an underwear model. Why does
he need to pay for it? Whatever.

As long as he has the cash. "So, Dan.
What can I do for you?" I know the drill.
Lydia coached me in the art of paid
seduction: *Strike the deal up front. Never
give them more than they pay for.
Collect before you start. No COD.*

No cash on delivery, because after
you're finished, they might say you
didn't deliver. I've done this for
a month now, and so far, not one
has made that claim. Customer
satisfaction guaranteed. God!

Dan Has Done This Before

You can take me around the world.
He reaches for his wallet. *One fifty,*
right? He tries to sweeten the pot. *Dan*
will pay extra to go without a sleeve.
He talks about himself in the third
person? No wonder he pays for it.

No condom? It's not the first time
I've had the request. I'd kill for
the extra cash, but I'm not taking
a chance on AIDS. "Sorry. No can
do. Cover up, I'll take care of you."
I pull my T-shirt over my head, watch

him strip off his jeans. His waist
is narrow, his hips straight. Beautiful.
Stop it! What's wrong with me? He's
down to his skivvies. I should have
charged more. He's built like a fucking
bull. "Holy crap, dude, I don't know. . . ."

What's wrong, kid? Never done
it with a real man before? His voice
falls, cold and heavy as hail. *You want*
me wrapped? Do it for me! He pushes
me to my knees, comes around in front
of me. My heart thuds in my chest.

I open the foil pouch, remove
the thin latex protection. *You ever
seen a ramrod like Dan's?* I shake
my head as I roll the condom down
over it. *No, of course you haven't.
Let's see just how good you are.*

I close my eyes, fight not to gag at
the taste of lubricant, not to choke
on his thrusts against my throat.
I think about Cory, locked up
in juvie until a judge decides
he's been "rehabilitated."

Dan decides he's done with Europe.
He pulls me to my feet, moves behind
me, drapes my back with his chest.
His muscles are thick cables, but his skin
is smooth and cool as snake skin. *Check it out.
The little boy likes that.* He reaches down

between my thighs. *Look how hard he is.*
No! How could something so messed
up turn me on? Whatever he does, I won't . . .
His lips brush the back of my neck
and, still folding me into him, he moves
me toward the bed, urges me facedown.

The sheets smell of bleach. I picture
Mom, waiting tables at Denny's. Jack's
life insurance put off the foreclosure.
But not forever. And those fucking
bills just keep piling up. Her meager
tips won't pay them. Something has to.

> Down go my boxers. *Oh my. What*
> *a sweet little bottom.* Dan's hands,
> moving over my skin, are soft,
> and when he lowers himself over me,
> a cloud of cloves and apple sinks
> around me. Reminds me of . . . Ronnie.
>
> God I love her. She is my spark
> of sanity. My light against the darkness,
> closing in. She knows things are bad,
> but not *how* bad. If she even suspected . . .
> this. What I'm doing. What I've already
> done, she'd never speak to me again.
>
> *Dan is in for a real treat, isn't he?*
> He presses up against me. I brace
> and he pauses. *Do you think it will hurt?*
> *Let's see.* He pushes, but only a little.
> A test. *Oh yes, I'm afraid it might.*
> *And after Dan, nothing else will do.*

I Bite Down

On a strange metal taste—a metal
taste of emotions. An odd blend of fear
and . . . excitement. For some fucked-up
reason, I'm excited. I can't want
this! Adrenaline firecrackers through
my body. Blood pulses in my temples.

>*You make Dan happy now, hear?*
>Pain! Oh my God! Nothing
>has ever hurt like this. I tense, beg
>him to stop. But he doesn't stop.
>Doesn't slow. Can't take it. Can't.
>Through the rhythmic pain, apple.

Pressure. Pressure, deep. Oh!
Nothing has ever felt so good.
Exquisite. Exquisite. No! I won't.
No matter what, I won't. This isn't me.
I'm only here for Mom. Cory. I won't!
But I do. And when I do, it's over the top.

I Leave, Emptied

And when I get home, the house
is emptied too. Emptied of life.
Emptied of love. Emptied of . . . us.
I suppose Mom might find another man,
but he can never be Jack. And Cory?
He's already harder. A stranger.

If there's anything left of my brother,
I don't know where it is. I hate to visit
him because when I look into his eyes,
all I find is death. He's a walking,
talking, breathing corpse. Lockup
will only make that worse.

I go into the bathroom, turn the shower
as hot as my skin can stand it. Scrub.
But the universe doesn't hold near
enough soap to wash this filth away.
The slippery lather does what it often
does to me. But when I touch it, I hear,

The little boy likes that, doesn't he?
Scrub harder. I keep at it until the spray
goes cold, shrinking every body part
and raising rows of goose bumps. Can
I ever feel decent about a shower again?
Can I ever feel okay about me?

A Poem by Eden Streit
Shrinking

Do you know how it
feels to be shrinking?
Withering away into

            nothing

more than a memory?
You need to put one foot
in front of the other,

            but

running in place
is all you can do.
How do you overcome

            pain

when it's something
you breathe, a blast
of hot exhaust

            in your

face, something turned
you must eat, or starve?
How do you search for

            tomorrow

when you're mired
in an endless today?

They Say Freedom Isn't Free

I agree. My bid for freedom from Tears
of Zion has already cost me dearly.

I don't know what will happen to me
if Jerome keeps his promise, unlocks

my door tonight, steals me away from
Father's house of rehabilitation.

I have no clue where I'll end up. Maybe
right back here (please, God, no). The one

thing I'm sure of is, should I leave this
place, I will not touch down in Salt Lake

City. Will not set up housekeeping with
Jerome. I will find a way to escape him, too.

I sit in the dark, heart racing as seconds . . .
minutes . . . hours creep by. Did he change

his mind? Did someone change it for him?
The air in the room grows heavy. I sink

into it. Can't find breath. I start to drown. . . .
Suddenly I wake up. A key is turning

in the lock. Jerome came for me after all.
He pulls me to my feet. *Ready?* he whispers.

The compound is dark, everyone asleep.
We sprint across a cushion of sand

to Jerome's Malibu, slip inside. It is old,
but tuned, and starts easily. Still, the engine

sounds very loud from where I sit, looking
for lights to blink on. Not a one. Nothing

but a billow of dust, lifting into the night
sky. Night! It's been weeks since I've seen

the stars. A voice drifts from not-so-distant
memory: *Pretty tonight. Looks like you*

could reach out and touch the stars. I close
my eyes, transported to a sleeping bag

in the bed of a Tundra. Andrew is warm
beside me. *I want what I've no right to take. . . .*

Tears fall freely as Jerome turns south on
Highway 93 toward Wells. He doesn't notice,

so I let them fall. By the time we reach I-80,
the stars are nothing but blurry streaks.

Old Malibus

Aren't exactly fuel efficient. As we roll
into Wells, Jerome slows down, checks

> the gauge. *Better gas up. There's a truck
> stop ahead. Hungry? It's a long way to SLC.*

"A little," I fudge. I've barely eaten a bite in
two days. "Thirsty, too. Any chance of a Coke?"

> *What'll you give me for it?* He snickers
> at the old joke. Only he isn't joking.

He pulls up at the pumps, opens the glove
box, reaches for his wallet. And there, on

a folded road map, is his cell phone. A buzz
like a high power line vibrates in my ears.

> Jerome doesn't seem to notice. He gets
> out of the car, puts his keys in their usual

> resting place on the front floorboard.
> *Do you have to use the bathroom?*

I shake my head. "Not until *after* the Coke."
When he goes inside, I grab the phone.

One eye on the door, I dial Andrew's cell.
This AT&T customer is not accepting incoming

calls. No! Quick. Dial his home. *The number*
you are calling is no longer in service.

Andrew! Where are you? No time to worry
about it now. Not if I want to get away

this side of Salt Lake City. I need to buy
some time. The keys . . . I reach down,

locate them, toss them under the backseat,
just as he comes out the door, goodies

in hand. I have maybe five minutes.
As Jerome starts toward the island, I jump

out of the car. "Decided I should pee after
all," I say, passing him on the sidewalk.

Nerves ping-pong in my stomach. I feel
like I'm going to vomit. But I don't, and

he doesn't seem fazed at all. Over my
shoulder, I watch him go to the car, open

the door. As he leans inside, I duck
around the corner of the building.

It's quiet this time of day, and in the steel
blue of just-before-dawning, a row of semis

waits silently for their drivers to wake. I dash
across the short span of asphalt to the far side

of the trucks. Maybe there's somewhere
to hide behind them. No! Nothing but desert,

stretching all the way to the freeway. What
now? He'll come looking any second!

I run down the row, hoping for . . . ? Can I
hide in one of them? Don't think so. If I try

to open one of the back doors, it's sure to make
a racket. About three-quarters of the way

down the line, I pass a travel trailer, attached
to a big crew cab. Something about it calls to me.

If the owners are asleep in the trailer, maybe
I could slip inside the truck? Could the doors

be unlocked? As quietly as I can, I pull up
on the rear passenger handle. Holy mother!

It opens. I climb up, shut the door,
skooch down on the floor, close my eyes.

He must be looking for me by now.
When he finds me, what will he do?

But It Isn't Jerome

Who finds me. It's the owner of the fifth
wheel. It is light when he opens the door

> to let his border collie inside. *What the—*
> *What the hell are you doing in my truck?*

I'm afraid to get up off the floor.
"I'm sorry . . . I didn't mean . . ."

Come on! Think! Something sort of
close to the truth pops out of my mouth.

"It's just that my boyfriend and I got into
an awful fight. I was afraid he'd hurt me,

so I hid in here. . . ." I must have fooled
the dog, anyway. She licks my face.

> The man, who's maybe sixty, looks
> dubious at first. But something about

> my expression makes him go on the alert.
> *Think he's still here? What's he look like?*

Thank you, God. "Short. Thin. He drives
a blue Malibu. I'm really scared."

> *You stay right here with Trinket. I'll take*
> *a look around.* He shuts the door.

Relief firecrackers through me in tiny
bursts. I'm stiff. Tired. But maybe okay.

It isn't long before the guy returns.
No sign of a blue Malibu. Where you

headed, young lady? He gives me a once-
over, but if my industrial outfit makes

him wonder, he doesn't say a word.
Think fast, Eden. "We were going to

Salt Lake City. But I want to go home.
And my boyfriend has all our money."

He takes every word in perfect stride.
Okay. And just where is home?

South on 93? Keep going, and end up
in "Vegas." I hold my breath, hoping.

Can't take you all the way there.
But I can get you as far as Ely.

I finally feel safe enough to scoot up
onto the seat. "That would be great.

I can call Andr—uh, my brother to come
get me." And pray he answers this time.

At Fifty MPH

The trip from Wells to Ely takes close
to three hours. I stay scrunched down

in my seat for a long while. Wes notices
without comment. Finally he says,

> *I think you're okay now. Been checking*
> *the mirror. Haven't seen anything blue.*

I straighten a bit. Trinket squirms and yips,
as if happy to see me relax. "Good girl."

> Wes smiles. *You like dogs, I see.*
> *Have any at home, waiting for you?*

I almost say no, that my parents are
much more into God than dogs, or any

of his creatures that don't tithe heavily.
But then I think of Andrew. The ranch.

And, "Sheila. She's a bluetick hound,
just a pup." We talk dogs for some time,

then ranching. Wes has a big ranch,
with Angus and Quarter Horses.

"Andrew . . . uh . . . my brother works . . .
uh, worked on a ranch for a while."

Did he, now? Speaking of your brother,
do you want to give him a call?

We'll be in Ely before you know it.
We should have cell service now.

"I'd like to, but I left my phone in
my boyfriend's car." His phone, actually.

Wes points to the center console.
Use mine. It's right in there.

I dial the well-known numbers,
with the same results as before.

The number you have called . . . Where
could he be? Still, I know Wes and I must

part ways soon. And I suspect he'll worry
if I don't get hold of someone. I pretend

Andrew answers. "Hey. Um, something kind
of bad happened. Can you come get me?"

Where Is Andrew?

What's up with the phones? Is he okay?
What about his parents? Where are *they*?

It's all I can think about. Wes keeps
right on talking, and I try my best

to find answers to his many questions.
But most of them probably don't make

much sense. Suddenly Trinket stands up
in the backseat, whines a little, wags

> her stumpy tail. *We're getting close
> to home and she can smell it,* explains

> Wes. *The turnoff's south of town,
> so I can get you a little closer. There's*

> *a nice truck stop out that way. You'd
> be safe enough there until your brother*

> *comes, I reckon. Most truckers I know
> won't let your boyfriend mess with you.*

Sooner rather than later we turn
off the straight two-lane blacktop.

Wes decides to fill up before heading
on home. I leave his company

rather reluctantly, and before I walk
away, I go around and give him a hug.

"Thank you so much. I don't know
what I would have done. . . ."

He blushes a furious rhubarb color.
Ah. It was nothing but common

*decency. But tell you what you can
do for me in return. . . .*

Yeah, right. Figures. I can guess what
he wants in return. But whatever.

I owe him big-time. And it's nothing
I haven't already done. "What?"

*Choose your next man more
carefully. You deserve better.*

Oh my God. How could I think . . . ?
My own face flushes, red hot, and

my throat knots as my eyes fill.
"I will," I manage. "I promise."

Eyes Burning

I start away, completely awed by
the kindness of this perfect stranger.

Wes stops me. *Wait one second.*
I turn back. In his hand is a twenty.

You must be hungry. Have some lunch
while you wait for your brother.

I could protest, but I *am* hungry.
Starving, actually. I kiss him on

the cheek. "You're the absolute best!"
He drives away and I go inside.

The smell of greasy food almost
overwhelms me. It's been so long!

"Double cheeseburger, fries, and
a chocolate shake," I tell the waitress,

feeling a lot like Pavlov's slobbering
dog. After I eat, I have to get out of here.

Jerome must be looking for me, and even
a half-wit could guess I came this way.

Vegas. Why not? All I need is a ride.
And there are plenty of truckers to ask.

It Takes Three Tries

The first says he's not going to Vegas.
The second one just says, *Fuck off.*

The third, a beefy guy with bad teeth,
looks me up and down. *You running away?*

I had an hour at lunch to figure out
a good story. I use it now. "Not exactly.

He flashes his rotten smile. *Not exactly?*
What, exactly, does that mean?

"See, my parents split up, and my mom
moved me to Elko so she could live

with her boyfriend. I hate that bastard. He . . .
he . . . you know." I look down, acting

all embarrassed. "Anyway, I just want to
go home to my dad's. He lives in Vegas."

Old story, kid. But what the hell?
I'm going that way. Hop in the cab.

We climb into opposite sides of the semi.
The trucker swallows some sort of pill,

starts the engine, and as he turns onto
the highway, I say a little prayer of thanks

for my rescue. But we don't get all that far
before rescue becomes something else.

> *Don't suppose you have any money?*
> asks rotten mouth. Considering

> I'm wearing nothing but a light blue,
> pocket-free shift, and carrying not

> a thing, the answer should be obvious.
> *Diesel's getting awfully expensive.*

"Sorry. No. Stupid me, I forgot
my backpack. Wish I could help."

> *Well, there are other ways a girl*
> *can help out a guy. You know?*

Mr. So-not-nice trucker issues an ultimatum:
Oral sex or a very long walk to Vegas.

Stupid me. But it's not really anything
new. At least I don't have to kiss him.

He Drops Me Off

At a diesel stop on the outskirts of the city.
I don't say thank you. I paid my way.

It's dirty here and surrounded by desert.
Not pretty pinion-studded playa like up north,

or back in Boise. But plain yellowed sand
defiled by houses. Lots and lots of houses.

From here, I can see giant casinos, all different
shapes and sizes. Motels. Chapels. Strip malls.

Traffic clogs a maze of streets and freeways.
Honking. Puffing exhaust. Military jets scream

across the cloudless sky, and commercial
aircraft come and go in regular procession.

It's all ugly. Stinking. A sinkhole of unrealized
dreams, forfeited faith. A girl could get lost here.

A Poem by Seth Parnell
Dreams Forfeited

Diffused by distance,
him a thousand miles
away. Still you feel his

                                        pain.

It's as if you can tune
into him with a psychic
antenna, catch some unique
sonar that carries his

                                        cries

across great distances.
It stops you cold
in your plodding tracks

                                        and you

wonder where he is.
Could he be just
outside? You put your
ear to the door and

                                        listen,

crazy with want,
knowing the front
step is vacant.

Seth
Any Farm Boy

Half worth his beans and
　　　　butter would tell you weight
　　　　lifting and cardio training
　　　　are all about ego. A hard day's
work on the back forty gives

you both, and a crop to boot.
　　　　But Carl insists I stay in
　　　　shape. Guess chubby guys
　　　　stand on the low rung of
the trophy boyfriend ladder.

　　　　Truth be told, he was pissy
　　　　　　　about how he put it to me.
　　　　　　　You know what happens to
　　　　　　　muscle when you quit working
　　　　it, *right? I'm not into fat boys.*

　　　　It would be in your best
　　　　　　　interest to invest a little
　　　　　　　time at the gym. It was not
　　　　　　　a suggestion. It was an
　　　　ultimatum. One major thing

I've learned about Carl is,
            business or pleasure,
            it's his way or no way
            at all. While I can respect
that on a certain level, when

it's in my face, it's not easy
            to take. He is one hundred
            percent about control. Not
            sure why I didn't see it
sooner. Not looking, I guess.

The strange thing is, I'm not
            the least bit flabby, let alone
            fat. So why? Preventative
            maintenance? Whatever. I have
nothing better to do, anyway.

So Here I Am, Midmorning

Jogging six miles per on
            a treadmill. Going nowhere
            and doing way too much
            thinking about what I've
allowed myself to become—

powerless. Even at home,
            the only time my dad
            dismissed me completely,
            no argument allowed, was
the night he kicked me out.

Remembering him, revisiting
            the farm, stirs up a cloud
            of homesickness. Loneliness.
            I am alone in this place,
despite nightly company.

I don't belong here. I know
            that. But I don't belong
            anywhere else, either.
            And that is at the heart
of the black depression

pressing down on me,
            flattening me. I have
            no place. No home. Sex,
            but no real affection. I am
kept, but not cherished.

I Am Swimming in Sweat

When an amazing-looking
        guy decides to share the gym.
        The way he assesses me
        leaves little doubt that he's
not into girls. Maybe working

out isn't such a bad idea after
        all. He offers a ten-thousand-dollar
        smile, then sets his gym
        bag down on a chair. I can't
help but stare when he strips

off his shirt, revealing buffed
        pecs and a six-pack I'd kill
        for. The guy is a high-priced
        Thoroughbred. And I'm
definitely not talking mares.

He goes straight to weights,
        choosing some machine
        I have no clue how to use.
        When he looks my way,
I'm still staring like an idiot.

        He grins. *What? Did I flash*
                you or something? Hope
                it wasn't offensive. Most guys
                seem to like it well enough.
        He pauses. Gives me time

to formulate some inane answer.
　　　　I slow the tread to cooldown
　　　　speed, try to quit huffing.
　　　　"I . . . uh . . . sorry . . . didn't
mean t-to stare . . ." Huff, huff.

"I just started"—huff, huff—
　　　　"working out and"—huff—
　　　　"I know this is dumb, but"—
　　　　huff—"I don't know how to
use all the machines." Heart rate

slowing, I catch my breath
　　　　and finish, huffless, "I thought
　　　　I'd watch you and learn how
　　　　to do it. Uh, use the machine,
I mean." Okay, *that* was inane.

　　　　He finds it amusing. *Oh, I see.*
　　　　　　　　Well, I use the machines all
　　　　　　　　the time. Happy to give you
　　　　　　　　some pointers, if you want.
　　　　The name's Jared, by the way.

"Seth." I stop the motorized
　　　　roadway. "I'd appreciate
　　　　anything you can give me . . .
　　　　I mean tips. . . ." Shit!
I'm sabotaging myself!

Hang On

Just why did I think that?
           Sabotaging what, exactly?
           I'm not shopping for
           companionship. Am I?
"Tell me to shut up, okay?"

           Jared laughs. *Shut up,*
                      Seth. He gestures for me
                      to come over to the machines.
                      So what are you most
           interested in working?

Now we both laugh at
           the unintended (?) double
           entendre. "Well . . . other than
           that, I want one of those."
I point to his amazing stomach.

           Don't blame you. Okay,
                      you can use the ab crunch
                      and the assisted pull-up. But,
                      so you know, diet is huge too.
           This is all about protein, my man.

"No problem. I can handle
           meat. . . ." (!!) Once again,
           I give his body an approving
           assessment. "And just so *you*
know, I'm not afraid of hard work."

He nods. *Most farm boys
        aren't.* At my perplexed
        look, he adds, *It's your accent.
        Very Midwest, with a touch
of the South. Kentucky? Missouri?*

Oh man. It shows? "Indiana,"
        I admit. "I never realized
        we had accents, though,
        especially not with 'a touch
of the South.'" Really weird.

        *Not sure why it works
                that way, but it does.
                Nothing to worry about,
                though. I find it kind of
        appealing. Come here.*

I'm a kid again, called to
        the front of the classroom,
        not knowing what for.
        Will he—shiver—touch me?
But no, all he does is show me

how to properly use the ab
        crunch machine. Still, he
        stays close, and the entire time
        I'm burning gut flab, a word
floats in my head—beginning.

511

All Worked Out

Tired, sore, I start toward
>   the townhouse to shower.
>   As I leave, I venture,
>   casually as I can, "Hope to
see you around again soon."

>   Jared is toweling off
>   his own sweat polish,
>   and I'm struck again
>   by the beauty of his body.
>   *Hot tub tonight at nine?*

I hesitate. I never go out
>   when Carl's home. Still,
>   he wouldn't object,
>   would he? Long as I omit
the Jared part. "I'll sure try."

>   He gives me a wry grin.
>   Could he know why
>   I live here? *If I don't see*
>   *you tonight, I'll run into*
>   *you here, I'm sure. Later.*

I follow him out the door,
>   watch his sure gait along
>   the walkway, tugged, steel
>   toward magnet. It's odd,
really. Usually I'm attracted

to softer men, with the major
exception of Leon Winkler.
And wouldn't his football
jock butt shudder to know
exactly *how* I looked at it?

Don't know why I'm
thinking about any of this
now anyway. I'm pretty
much committed to Carl,
who should be home soon,

expecting me showered
and shaved, all smooth
and scented with Armani
Black Code, his favorite
fragrance. Expensive taste,

not a bad thing. He'll also
want dinner started. High-
end meat or seafood. Steamed
vegetables. Fresh bread.
Never the same meal twice

in any given month. Good
thing Dad taught me how
to cook. Hmm. Wonder
how Carl would feel about
venison sausage and gravy.

Venison Is Not Easy to Find

In Vegas, so I'm working on
            seafood Newberg (recipe
            care of one of Carl's large
            collection of cookbooks)
when he finally arrives.

He is not alone. Neither
            is he sober as he trips
            through the door, laughing,
            accompanied by a friend.
Acquaintance? I have no

idea. This is the first time
            he's ever brought anyone
            home. The guy is maybe
            forty-five, and everything
about him, from the square

                        cut of his bangs to the way
                                    he wears his extreme
                                    jewelry, screams "queen."
                                    When he squeaks, *Hello there,*
                        he leaves zero doubt about it.

            Carl comes over and gives
                        me an ostentatious gin-
                        flavored kiss. *Something
                        smells good, and I'm not*
            talking about in the kitchen.

He kisses me again, which
        is weird. For all the sex
        we've shared, a kiss from
        Carl is relatively rare.
I almost don't know how

        to respond. Finally he draws
            back. *Oh, how rude of me.*
            Come say hello to my friend,
            Brett. Brett, meet Seth,
        my uh . . . paramour.

        Carl takes my hand, leads
            me to the sofa, where
            Brett has made himself
            extremely comfortable.
        Pretty boy, Brett says. *Very.*

My nerves lift on sharpened
        edge, like when you go
        hunting and suddenly feel
        hunted. I force my voice low.
"Good to meet you, Brett."

        Now, now. Let's not be
            so formal. He laughs,
            and it isn't a pleasant laugh.
            Any paramour of Carl's
        is a paramour of mine, right?

Before I Can Answer

He is all over me. Hands.
        Mouth. Ugh. Tequila.
        I push him away. "Wait
        just one fucking second. . . ."
I step back, look at Carl,

        but he's into the game.
        Refereeing, in fact.
        No need to be rude to
        our guest. He's here by
invitation. Understand?

"Invi—" Carl wants me
        to be with this creep?
        What happened to our
        "exclusive relationship"?
"No, I don't understand."

        With fine diamond clarity,
        Carl explains, *I enjoy*
        a bit of variety from time
        to time. I expect your whole-
hearted participation.

        He pushes me, and not
        gently, toward Brett.
        Now apologize to my
        friend as I hope you
would apologize to me.

He Does Not Mean

With words. And he doesn't
        exactly mean solo. They
        move in unison, and I am
        sandwiched between them,
Carl behind me, moving

sensuously, while Brett dares
        kiss me again. I hold my
        breath against the assault
        of gin at my back, tequila
in my face. A strange tongue

in my mouth. Now Brett
        rests his chin on my shoulder,
        and he and Carl are kissing.
        It's a cobra dance, and despite
what it means, I am charmed.

Seduced by sensual motion.
        Behind me and in front
        of me, both men grow hard,
        and for some horrifying reason,
I respond in like manner.

I Have Never Considered

Three-way sex. How would . . . ?
        Oh. No way will I let one
        of them take me like *that*.
        Like Loren, Carl has always
played the feminine role.

But unlike with Loren (who
        insisted on using condoms),
        with Carl (who refused to),
        I set limits—"Carl, you know
the rule." My rule: hands or

        mouths only. He stops
            kissing Brett, but neither
            man quits moving, writhing
            like mating hooded serpents.
        We're playing by my rules,

        remember? But don't worry.
            I only expect you to give.
            For now. From somewhere,
            he extracts a condom, hands
        it to me, keys to the kingdom.

Don't rush, he orders,
    and don't you dare
    close your eyes. I want
    to see how much you like
it. He moves in front of me,

strips Brett from the waist
    down, pushes him onto
    his hands and knees. Then
    he drops his own trousers.
Come on, he urges, positioning

himself inches from Brett's face.
    Shaking, I move behind Brett,
    grab his shoulders. Carl's hands
    cover mine. Brett moans as I . . .
Oh my God! I am damned.

But I don't stop and I don't
    rush. Carl's eyes never once
    leave mine. Finally I beg
    his permission. "Now? Please?"
He nods and I do. We all do.

A Poem by Whitney Lang
Don't Stop

Don't look behind you.
Something is chasing
you, and if you slow

down,

it will catch you. Run!
Faster! Through alleys.
Tunnels. Underground.

Down there

in that dark place,
fear is your friend
for complacency kills

down where

instinct is survival.
Reach. Find your wings.
Fly away from the

monsters,

hard on your heels.
Don't stop. Only
then can they win.

Run!

Fighting "Night Time"

Pretty name for the hideous pukes
and soaking sweats of withdrawal.
I understand I have to go through it.
Die if I don't. Maybe die if I do.

I don't want to die. Do I? Fuck,
what if it's better than living half in,
half out of this world? Goddamn Bryn!
Bastard turned me into a zombie.

So why do I sit here, crying to see
him? Why do I love him so much?
He cheats. Lies. Lied about everything,
from start to now. I know it. Don't care.

I want to be with him. Want to make
love with him. Even though that means
waiting my turn. He has other girls.
Other zombies. Killing time in cheap

rooms like this one. Sometimes he comes,
rewards them like he rewards me,
with junk and beautiful sex. Sometimes
other men come. That sex is never

beautiful. It is selfish. Needful.
Fueled by sick desire to get off. Get
even. Get over someone who has
hurt them by symbolically impaling

someone else. So Bryn's zombie girls
stay stoned. Out of our heads
messed up. Eyes closed, we can
be anywhere. Italy. France. Australia.

Jupiter. Hell. Doesn't matter, as long
as we're not *here*. As long as we can
pretend we're still pretty. As long as we
can make believe Bryn still loves us, too.

I'm Not Stupid

I know I'm addicted. Damn it all,
despite the many promises I made
to myself, I mainline now. A needle
in the vein delivers Nirvana

so quickly! And in those first few
minutes, when all the pain is lifted,
I see what Bryn saw in me that first
day at the mall—naïveté. I was stupid.

He knew it. I was crazy hungry
to fall in love. He saw it in my eyes.
And then, when I called him, stinging
at rejection, he so had me. He is very

good at what he does. Recruiting
girls, feeding them a steady diet
of lies and drugs, then starving them
until they submit to his demands.

He is a pimp, plain and simple.
A fucking gorgeous, sweet pimp,
who I'd do anything for. Including
advertising my body: For Sale. Cheap.

He'll come to me soon. I need the Lady
bad and he knows it. Can't send me
out on the streets like this. It isn't pretty.
Probably couldn't even give myself away.

When Bryn's Key

Finally turns in the lock, I'm huddled
in a corner, covered in goose bumps,
shivering through the sweat. At
least I'm all puked out. He takes

one look, nods. *Poor baby. Don't
worry. Daddy has presents for his
beautiful little girl.* He comes over,
sits beside me. Pulls a dime bag

from his pocket like it's made of gold.
Clean rigs, too. *Let Daddy fix it
for you.* He cooks up a perfect spoon,
loads it, plunges it between my toes.

Bryn gives me wings. The sting
is luscious, the awful rush all I need.
No, not all. I need Bryn. And he's here,
all mine right now. His lap is warm,

inviting. I climb into it, slip my arms
around his neck. *Thank you. Better now.*
Oh, so much better. Soaring. Up here
in the clouds, the air is dry. I kiss him,

suck his tongue into my mouth, seeking
moisture. It curls over my own tongue,
sensuous as smoke. Time slows.
Make it stop! Make it stop with me,

here in Bryn's arms. I want him.
Want him to take me higher. Want sex
as it was meant to be, as only Bryn can
ever give it to me. "Make love to me."

He pushes me to the floor. My head
spins, dizzy with anticipation. My brain
screams, kiss me! Kiss all those special
places, just like you used to. I know

he will, but . . . But what? Why
is he stopping? He reaches into
a back pocket. What is that?
A rubber? No. We don't need that.

I'm on the pill. It was one of the first
things we did when we got to Vegas.
"N-no." Is there mud in my mouth?
I can barely cough out, "Why?"

> He stops fiddling with the wrapper,
> but doesn't answer right away. Finally
> he says, *Never know what kind of gift
> one of your customers might have left.*

What? My face flushes, hot from
the skag, hotter still with an overdose
of anger. Always, with no exceptions,
"My *customers* use condoms."

I Try to Push Him Away

But even if I were perfectly
straight, my stick-figure body
would be no match for his toned
physique. And I'm not straight.

My vision is blurred, like looking
through a fishbowl, and my muscles
feel like steel cables—much too heavy
to drag around. And the weirdest

thing about all that is how great
it feels. I'll nod soon, and that's when
the pain vanishes. So hell, he can screw
me, if that's all it means to him.

He boosts himself up over me.
Tries to look down into my eyes.
But I stare at the wall. Will myself
to go limp. Familiar one-act play.

That's it, he soothes. *No need
to waste a perfectly good boner.*
In. Out. In. Out. I close my eyes.
Float. Pretend I'm with a john.

When I Surface

From my lake of dreams, Bryn
is gone. He left a note: *Stashed
the bag and fixings in the usual
place. Same price. Tomorrow.*

How have I fallen so low? I knew
about junk, even told Bryn no way.
Then I let him talk me into it. Love
is more than blind. It's brain-dead.

My brain screeches, *Fix! Fix!
Quick, before I make you heave.
Quick, before I give you the runs.
Quick, before I start remembering.*

Remembering I once had another
life. Hated it then. Might still hate
it now. But more than I hate this?
Hate what I've become? No matter.

This is all I've got. I cook up a spoon.
Oh yes. That's good. So good.
Clock. Where are you, clock?
There you are. Evening already?

The boys are out, scamming
for play. Shower. Hurry. Night's
tick-tocking away. And I've got
bills. *Same price. Tomorrow.*

Skin Tight Men's Club

Is hopping tonight. Boys go in.
Stay a while, watching pole dancers
and cocktail waitresses, shaking
their boobs for tips. Boys come out,

horny as hell. Some go home
to beat off or bug their wives.
Some look for girls like me,
loitering in the shadows where,

> hopefully, cops cruising beats
> won't notice them. Bryn taught
> me the ropes. *Act interested,*
> *but don't push. The girls who*

> *get busted are in-your-face.*
> *Dress sexy, but leave some up*
> *to the imagination. Sexy schoolgirl*
> *That's the look you want.*

> *Ask what they want up front,*
> *and collect before you take*
> *'em home. Wouldn't want to*
> *do all that work for nothing,*

> *and believe me, plenty of guys*
> *got nothing, especially if they*
> *overspent inside. And if some*
> *dude seems hinky, say no.*

I've said no a couple of times.
It wasn't because they were fat
or bald, but because of what I saw
in their eyes. More accurately,

what I didn't see in their eyes:
life. Sharks, that's what they were.
Dead cold scary. No way was I
chancing a swim with them.

Most johns are more mackerel
than great white. Cold slimy bait
fish, quick to jump into the net,
especially when what they're

jumping in after still looks fresh.
Don't know how long that can
last. Hooking uses you up fast.
Figure in hyping, I'll look thirty

before I turn seventeen. I turn
sixteen day after tomorrow,
not that one single person in
the world gives half a damn.

Why Did I Have to Go

And think about that? Damn!
If I were still in Santa Cruz, I'd be
planning my Sweet Sixteen party.
Daddy would insist. We'd have it

at the club, and we'd have a band,
and Paige would be there and maybe
even Kyra. . . . Oh my God. What
have I done? Daddy must think . . .

What? I'm dead? Mom hopes I am.
But not . . . Daddy. I'm sorry. Shit!
I sit down hard. Sidewalk cement bites
into my butt, which is naked beneath

a short denim skirt. My head tilts
against my knees, and my eyes trickle
tears. Heavy. My head is so heavy.
The H wants to take me away

and I want to go. Away. Far. Where
nothing hurts. Nothing . . . Eyes on
me. Are there eyes? Don't look. Have to.
To know . . . Who? Can't lift my head.

Roll it sideways. *Are you all right?*
The eyes are talking. No. Not eyes.
Lips. Stupid. Eyes can't talk.
Do you want me to call 911?

"N-no thanks. I'm o-o-k-kay."
So okay I can't even say okay.
For some messed-up reason,
I start to hiccup. "Ju—" *Hick.*

"Just think—" *Hick.* "Thinking
about my b—" *Hick.* "Buh-birthday."
Hick. Hick. Hick. Somehow
I manage to focus my eyes.

>   The guy isn't pretty, but his
>   expression is kind enough. Maybe
>   even concerned. *Are you sure
>   you're okay? You been drinking?*

Can you get this screwed up
from alcohol? Looney Tunes laughter—
hick-hick—spits from my mouth.
"Sorry. No, don't drink much."

>   Now I can see the wolf in his eyes.
>   No surprise. Even nice enough
>   guys go on the prowl. *Okay. What
>   do you do that's fun, then?*

I Swear Until This Moment

I never even noticed his hand
creeping up my leg, ever closer
to my semi-exposed crotch.
Eyes can be deceptive when

they talk. I crack up again.
This time, at least, the hiccups
seem to have disappeared. But
I'm starting to ache for a rig.

Bryn's words settle through
the fog. *Leave something to
the imagination.* I give the guy
a quick feel before pushing

his hand away. "Oh, I for sure
know how to have fun." Game on.
Wait. Bryn again. *Ask if he works
vice.* "You a cop or what?"

He grins. *Or what. I'm not even
from around here.* He stands, pulls
me to my feet, steadies my wobble.
Live close? I'll walk you home.

It Isn't Far

Just eight blocks. The guy chit-
chats the whole time. Something
about Omaha. Cornhuskers? He
played for them? Bets on them?

Oh yeah. Sportsbook. Won five
big ones. (How big? Hundreds?
Bigger?) I can't concentrate on
what he's saying. All I can think

about is a syringe full of magic.
How fast can I do this guy?
We swing into the parking lot,
cut across to Building Two.

Key. I need the key. It's in my
purse somewhere. Too much crap
in here. Like, why do I carry it,
anyway? Just to irritate myself?

We reach the apartment and I hear
Bryn again. *Look around before
you open the door.* I do. A car
is parking a few spaces down.

And going up the stairs of the other
building is that girl I see sometimes,
mostly in the laundry room. Copacetic.
Cool word. Where did it come from?

I unlock the door, start to turn the knob,
when more words fall into my brain.
Business before pleasure. I turn.
The guy is so close, we're almost

attached. I give him a little shove
backward. "Before we go in, we
should talk about what you want
and how much that will cost you."

> *Cost? You want me to pay for it?*
> He pushes me inside. *I don't pay*
> *for sex. Even if I did, I wouldn't*
> *pay for you, you junkie bitch.*

He is all predator now, and on me.
Scream! But his hand is already over
my mouth. I shake my head, look
into his eyes. This wolf has mayhem

> on his mind. He takes me down.
> So okay. Give it to him. I go limp.
> *No!* he screams. *Fight, you goddamn*
> *whore! Fight, or I'll kill you.*

No fight left in me. Fuck me. Kill
me. Don't care. He wants both.
His penis stabs me, his hands lock
around my throat. Air. No air. Black . . .

Air!

My lungs grab it suddenly. I float
up into gray light, roll onto my side,
vomit. Only nothing comes out.
Noise. Someone's screaming.

> *Get the fuck out of here, you son*
> *of a bitch. I'm calling the cops*
> *right now, so you'd better run.*
> *Come back, I'll kick your ass.*

My throat throbs. The wolf! I sit up.
Too fast. My head is a merry-go-round.
Down. The carpet stinks. Saved.
I'm saved. Bryn! He does loves me.

Watches over me. "Bryn? Where
are you?" Footsteps across the stinky
carpet. Not Bryn's. Too soft.
Someone leans over me. The girl

> from the laundry room. *Just lie still.*
> *I think you'll be okay. He's hurting,*
> *though. I hit him with a book.*
> *Good thing you read big ones.*

> She smiles. Sad. She's sad. *Should*
> *I call the cops? Didn't think so.*
> *I'll stay with you for a while if you*
> *want. I'm Ginger, by the way.*

A Poem by Ginger Cordell
I'll Stay

Right or wrong,
I'll stay until
you tell me I have to

leave.

Until you can look
into my eyes, swear
you no longer love

me.

It would be a bitter
cup of broken-
promise tea, but

I'll

swallow it if you say
I must. If I go, sad
sweet dreams will

follow

me, weighting my days,
strangling my nights.
Sad, sweet dreams of

you.

Ginger
Sadness

Encircles me, a black halo.
            It's this city, this dried-up
desert well, sucking hope

like sand. People come here,
            hoping. Hoping to get rich.
Hoping to get laid. Not many

go home richer than when
            they arrived. Easier to get
laid, as long as they have

a few bucks in their pockets.
            Then there are the people
who move here with big

dreams. They dream of stand-up
            comedy, of playing rock and
roll. They dream of dancing lead

in some steamy casino show.
            If they're talented and lucky,
they might end up in a chorus

line or drumming with a bar
            band. But lots of them wind
up just like me, selling pieces

of themselves. Pieces they can
            never have back. There's this
girl who works for Lydia.

            Her name is Misty. *I won't do
                        this forever, she swears. *Just
            until I get my degree. Then*

            the world is my apple pie. . . .
                        Okay, metaphor isn't her best
            thing. And neither is school.

If she gets her degree, it will
            be because she slept with
the right teacher. Or three.

Every time I run into Misty,
            a little more of her is gone.
I can see it in her eyes.

When you sell your body, you
            also sell what's inside. Piece
by piece, you sell your soul.

Now Here's This Girl

Who almost lost everything.
         She let her guard down. Plain
and simple. If I hadn't been

doing my usual nosy thing,
         checking out the neighbors,
she'd probably be lying here

waiting for her pimp to call
         the coroner. Yes, I know who
her pimp is. He's the only guy

who comes around almost
         every day. Collecting money
and delivering sustenance—

food, trinkets, and substances.
         Heroin. I was right about that.
I watch her now, plunging

         a syringe full of hot amber
             liquid. Her head rolls side-
ways and she fixes me with

         sleepy golden eyes. *Want
             some? I don't have a whole
lot, but I kind of owe you one.*

"No thanks. Not my thing."
        Her body visibly relaxes as
relief pumps through her veins.

Suddenly she clutches her
        stomach, runs into the bathroom.
"You all right?" I yell at the door.

        She exits seconds later, pale
                but smiling. A very bad smell
        of voided body waste trails her.

        Doesn't embarrass her at all.
                Sometimes the Lady makes
        you sick. But it's good sick.

        There's room on the couch,
                and a vacant chair, but she sits
        on the floor, as if afraid of falling.

        Now she rocks herself. Forward.
                Back. Forward. Back. *Thank you*
        for . . . wait. How did you know?

"I dunno. Guess he just looked
        like bad news. Then he started
yelling crazy shit. I usually

mind my own business. . . ."
Yeah, right. "But my 'little
voice' was screaming. Good

thing you never shut your door.
Even better, he was too busy
trying to choke you to notice."

Her hands rise protectively
toward her neck. *I thought
I was on my way to hell for*

sure. She strokes the raised
scarlet finger marks gently.
Hurts like a mother. Is it ugly?

I have to say, "Pretty ugly.
You might have to take a few
days off. Most guys won't want . . ."

Too familiar. Then again,
I just watched her shoot up.
I repeat, "Take a few days off."

I Expect Surprise

That I know how she makes
            her money. Or anger at me,
because I've been such a snoop,

or at herself, because she's
            made it so obvious. I get neither.
Nothing but silent acceptance.

Is it the heroin? Or is it just
            her? Probably both. I want to
ask where she came from. What

kind of parents she has, if she
            has any at all. How she hooked
up with her so-called boyfriend.

That's, no doubt, what he calls
            himself. Want to ask, though
I know the answer, if he's the one

who started her on the junk.
            Her head sways forward
as the drug carries her toward

Dreamville. She'll be totally out
            of it soon. I'll ask something
easy. "What's your name?"

At the sound of my voice,
her head jerks up. *Oh. It's you.*
You tell me your name first.

Wow. She's pretty out of it
already. "I told you before.
It's Ginger, remember?"

She giggles like a little kid.
A stoned little kid. *Oh, yeah.*
Hey, Ginger. I'm Whitney.

Somewhere in her sudden
animation, I catch a glimpse
of Whitney, the way I imagine

she used to be before . . . him.
She nods again and I hurry,
"Are you still in love with him?"

Yo-yoing in and out of now,
she is coherent enough to know
who I mean. *Bryn is everything.*

It's the Last Thing She Says

Before dropping all the way
        into whatever dark narcotic
place the junk pushes her toward.

I swear I'll never venture there.
        Lately I don't even feel like
drinking much. All it does

is make me stupid and sick.
        It doesn't make me forget.
In fact, sometimes, the drunker

I get, the more I remember.
        I remember the kids, how
annoying and entertaining

        they could be. Do they miss me?
            Have they even asked, *Where
is Ginger? Why did she go?*

I remember Barstow, the armpit
        town where I first made a friend,
first got decent grades. Ms. Felton

        even told me once, *You're an
            excellent writer. You should
think about it as a career.*

Writer? Me? And what am
       I doing instead? I remember
Sandy, a ball in the street,

     and Mary Ann's face, scrunched
             with pain. *I'm sorry. I should*
     have . . . Only the blame belonged

to me. Which always brings
       me back to my very favorite
memories, all centered around

Gram, deceptively petite, while
       so driven. Tireless. Completely
devoted to a pack of kids she owed

absolutely zero devotion. All
       because of her giant capacity
to love. Does she hate me

now for taking the easy way out?
       Would she ask me to come home
if she could? Did she mean it when

     she said, *You know where I live.*
          No matter what, I want you to
     remember this is always your home.

Tempting as It Might Be

To get back on the bus, see
        if she would welcome me,
uglier memories intrude on

that sweet little daydream.
        Since the revelation about
Iris sicking her snarling dogs

on me, other faces—other
        mutts—materialize when
I least want to recognize them,

often just as I sink into an
        alcohol-fueled stupor, praying
it will let me sleep, dreamless.

I was so young the first time,
        I didn't know what it meant,
only that nothing had ever hurt

so bad. Walt tore me up and I bled
        and bled and when I screamed,
nobody came. And he laughed.

That's it, little baby. Scream
               for your daddy. Only he wasn't
my daddy at all. My daddy was

a brave soldier, fighting far away.
               Iris told me so. I still believed
the stuff she told me then. When

               I told her about the man, not
                              my daddy, she said, *He was*
only making you into a real girl.

I didn't understand. But I made
               myself believe her. I was a real
girl now. But what was I before?

Walt Was the First

There were others. Nameless.
      Faceless. I figured out how to
close off my brain when they did

it to me, to withdraw into a dark
      little room inside my head, where
I couldn't see them. Couldn't smell

their sweat, their stagnant breath.
      Couldn't taste the tobacco coating
their tongues, or the beer tainting

the spit they left in my mouth.
      Couldn't feel what was down
between my legs. But now they

revisit me. Is it because of what
      I'm doing? Because of these
nameless, faceless men watching

me? Even without them touching
      me, I feel dirty about what I do.
Alex does even filthier things

but says it all washes off with soap.
      I don't believe that. I think it all
leaves stains. Indelible stains.

I Wait for Her Now

Wondering where she is, what
　　　　she has done today, if she'll come
home. Lydia called. We've got

a bachelor party at ten. It's nine
　　　　fifteen already, and no sign of
Alex. I tried her cell. Went straight

to voice mail. The battery must be
　　　　gone. If she doesn't show, I'll have
to go alone. Won't be the first time,

and she knows how scared I am
　　　　to work by myself. I still love her,
but I feel her slipping away, bit

by bit, every day. Finally the door
　　　　opens. She's a total mess—makeup
smeared, hair like a rat's nest, clothes

dirty and torn. I rush to her side,
　　　　"What happened? Are you okay?"
I try to hug her, but she shoves me

　　　　away. *Don't touch me.* Tears spill
　　　　　　　from her eyes, tracking mascara
　　　　down her cheeks. She sinks down

on the sofa, puts her face into
        her hands. *Bastard screwed me,*
then robbed me. Took everything.

Again I try to hold her. This time
        she doesn't pull away, but she is
like sandstone. Hard on the surface,

crumbling beneath. "It's okay.
        We'll be okay." Then, an after-
thought, "How much did he get?"

        Her head sags against my chest,
                wetting my shirt with tears, snot.
        Not sure. Four or five hundred.

Anger flares suddenly, but not
        because of the money. Because
of what we've become. "We've got

a goddamn bachelor party,
        clear across town. We'll barely
make it if we leave right now."

        She looks up at me with ringtail
                eyes. *I can't . . . please. I'm gonna*
be sick. She runs to the bathroom.

I follow, put an ear to the door,
        hear the definite sound of puke
splash. "Okay," I call. "I'll take

this one by myself. But when I get
        back, we have to talk." For once,
I'm not afraid to do the gig alone.

The whole cab ride over, I think
        about what it is I want to say.
I arrive at a few minutes after ten.

The guys are young, not much
        older than me. Good. They won't
ask for many extras. I handle

the business end, promise a lap
        dance to the groom, who looks
excited and scared at the same time.

And for the entire hour I'm taking
        off my clothes, shimmying and
writhing and faking "sexy," my mind

is on one thing. I don't know
        how, where, or even with whom.
Just know I have to get out of here.

A Poem by Cody Bennett

Don't Know

Who I am anymore.
I was sure once, not long
ago. Knew where I came
from, and where I was

going

to. Now I don't have
a clue who puts on
my shoes in the morning,
nor what direction he's

going

when he closes the door
behind him. He looks a lot
like me. But his flame has
been extinguished, buried

too far

beneath his soil to find
air enough to smolder.
It is no more than a vague
memory, all oxygen

gone.

Cody
How Do I Find Myself Here?

Not even a year since everything
started a snowball roll toward hell.
It's a place I'm starting to know well,
a place I deserve. I mean, I couldn't
stop Cory from fucking up. He was
set on it. And Jack wasn't my fault.

I didn't make him get cancer, did my
best for him when he did. Hear that,
Jack? I wanted to help you! Couldn't.
I'm not God. What happened is between
him and you. Can't you do anything
up there to help me out down here?

Okay, maybe I'm not worthy
of your intervention. Maybe you're
just plain grossed out. Pissed off.
But if you help me, you'll help
Mom, too. She can't make it on
her own. Damn it, you promised!

And dude, if I can't worm my way
out of this crazy place, I'll have to
consider that medicine chest, still full
of pain meds and sleeping pills. Mom
would only miss me so long. The rest
of the world wouldn't miss me at all.

That Includes Ronnie

Oh, she claims she misses me now.
I only see her at school, and I'm not
there a whole hell of a lot. I should
be, of course. Just started junior year.
If I really want college, really want
more, I need to focus not only on

attendance, but on getting good
grades. Impossible. Too much
going on. Too much going down.
Hard enough, just surviving.
Trying not to think about Cory.
Not to think about Lydia, etc.

I get to class late, or not at all.
Can't find interest in any of my
classes. English? I talk good enough.
Math? Let me give you a point
spread. History? Want to hear
mine? Chemistry? Girls or men?

And Ronnie? She pleads for attention.
*Can't you please come over, spend
a little time with me? C'mon, Cody.
I miss you so much. Remember . . .*
Then she'll try to convince me,
bringing up one of those special

(God, yes, they *were* special)
times we spent in bed. Oh, I do
miss holding her close. The satin
of her hair. The luscious full curves
of her body. But sex means something
different now. I can't tell her that.

So I lie. Tell her I have to work. (For
a temp service, so she can't track
me down any certain place.) Tell
her I have to drive Mom somewhere.
(Usually to visit Cory.) Tell her
I'm just too freaking tired. (No lie.)

Sooner or later, she'll get sick
of the excuses and find another
guy. I only hope it's someone
who deserves the perfect girl.
Not an addict. Not a boy whore.
Not a fucking loser like me.

The Only Thing

I've won at lately is a few games
of chance. A hand or ten of poker.
And the Chiefs have been on a roll.
I've tried to keep the bets reasonable,
but the problem with winning is,
once you've got a bigger bankroll,

you want to make bigger bets. Got
a whopper riding this week. Enough
to let me skip a couple of "dates,"
if my luck holds. I have been smart
enough to pay my car insurance
for six months, help Mom with

the power and phone. She thinks
I'm working at a temp service too.
Since they place you in jobs
temporarily, according to different
businesses' need, it provides
the perfect excuse for sometimes

having money, sometimes not.
For being away from home odd
hours. And, since those jobs tend
to be manual labor, Mom doesn't ask
why I so often plunge straight into
the shower after coming through the door.

On a Positive Note

I've managed to make small credit
card payments. Not enough to pay
down the principal, but enough
to cover the interest, anyway. Only
one problem. As had to happen,
I couldn't keep intercepting the bills.

> Mom called me into the kitchen. *Cody,*
> *what are all these charges to Int-Gam,*
> *Inc.?* She stood there, hands on hips,
> waiting for my confession. How
> could I tell her "Int-Gam, Inc."
> was Internet Gaming Incorporated,

and that I had been using the cards
for months, losing money hand over
fist? "I'm not sure, Mom," I lied,
looking her straight in the eye.
"But just so you know, I found
those credit cards in Cory's things."

I can't believe what a liar I've become,
and lying about Cory was a way low
blow. But she bought it. Why not?
Her youngest son is a criminal.
Not much of a stretch to think
that he might also be a thief.

Credit Cards

No longer being an option, sports bets
will have to be laid down through
local bookies. Vince knows one or
two. And there's always poker.
Hey, I've got a stake—a few hun
saved up. Anyway, I've got spending

cash, thanks to Lydia. Mostly it's
from men. Thank God, I haven't had
too many experiences similar to the one
with crew-cut Dan. I can't seem to excise
that night completely from my head.
I've questioned a lot of things about

myself before. The gambling. Booze.
Drugs. Lying. But, despite sleeping
with men for money, I've never
questioned my sexuality. That's
the core of any man, any person.
How can I be unsure of that, especially

considering the pain and humiliation?
Maybe Lydia was right, and we all
swing both ways to some degree. *It's
all according to necessity,* she said.
Does that mean if every woman
disappeared, I'd actively crave men?

Not Craving Any

Of the guys at Vince's tonight.
I glance from face to face, chest
to chest. Nope. Not a single twitch.
Maybe there's hope for me after all.
Now if Lady Luck will just decide
to climb into my lap, hang out.

> *Hey*, says Vince. *Anyone bring
> smoke?* He looks straight at me,
> not expecting me to say yes. It's
> been weeks since I had enough
> cash to score. My connection had
> almost given up on me too.

I surprised him, and I surprise
Vince now. "Actually, yeah, I do."
I hand over a couple of big blunts,
light another, pass it on. Only way
to convince Vince to introduce me
to his bookie friends is with generosity.

Meanwhile, it's poker. The key
to winning this game is properly
assessing the competition. I know
most of the guys at the table—Vince,
best player here, a regular bluff master,
not afraid to lay down a major bet.

Justin is an elementary school janitor.
Can't afford to bet big. Never ups the ante.
Sitting down is Shaun, UNR freshman,
innocent-looking, but knows how to bet.
Finally, there's Misty's boyfriend,
Chris. He's a total jerk, and wasted.

A fair bit of coke has been passed
around, but I'm guessing he's been
smoking ice. Maybe even crashing,
despite the cola. His mood is mean.
Fucking deal already, would
you? Haven't got all night.

Vince stares him down, trying
to decide, no doubt, if he's going
to have to deal with Chris some
way other than nicely. He starts
with nice. *Take it easy, man.*
Where you have to be, anyway?

Chris grabs the cards, now in
a pile in front of him. He sorts
them one way, then another, shoots
eyeball arrows around the table as if
we're all just waiting to give our
hands away. *Got a date with Misty.*

Fact Is

I've got a date with Misty. Well,
not with her, exactly. We both have
a date with some sexually confused
out-of-towner. Three-ways aren't
quite so bad. Misty isn't the brightest
girl. But she's got a killer bod to focus

on. It's okay to be turned on by that.
The evening's little snort party will
help me out too. In fact, we might
even have fun. But, far as I know,
Chris isn't coming along. "You sure
you're hooking up with Misty tonight?"

> The table falls silent. Not even
> a minimal buzz as Chris gives me
> an odd look. *That's what I said.*
> *Why? You know something*
> *I don't?* He throws three cards
> on the table. Waits for more.

And also for my answer. "Uh.
It's just I thought she had to work
tonight. You know. For Lydia."
I draw two cards. Dig way down
for composure. Lady Luck is definitely
rock 'n' rolling with me. Full house.

Chris doesn't respond. For some
reason, that bothers me a lot. I look
over at him and he's staring at me,
head tipped as if listening to something no one else can hear. Little
voices in his head? Schizo, too?

It's all lost on Vince, who draws
last. One card . . . C'mon, Lady,
don't trade partners now! His face
gives nothing away. But when
he bets, we all gulp in breaths.
He tosses some chips. *A hundred.*

Justin folds. Shaun considers quite
a while, finally calls. Chris swears
softly, breaks out in a sweat, trying
to figure out if Vince is bluffing,
decides he must be. He calls. I call.
We show our cards. My full house

wins the pot! Six-fifty! Oh, yeah.
Lady and I are doing a full-on mosh
now. One thing I've managed
to learn, "Thanks so much, gentlemen,
but it's time for me to go." It *is* time,
in fact. My date is in twenty minutes.

Hot Damn

I am feeling good. I stop at the bank,
make two deposits. Into my account.
Into Mom's account. Not much, but
enough to help out a little. I'd cancel
my three-way, but I promised I'd do
it. Lydia is expecting me to. And so

is Misty. Who I really want to see
right now is Ronnie. First time in
a long time I'm feeling the need
for a long, healthy roll in the hay.
I give her a call, half expecting
her to be out with somebody else.

> But she answers immediately.
> *Hello?* Oh God! The sound of
> her husky voice lifts me even
> higher. *Uh, hello? Is somebody
> there?* When I let her know it's
> me, she is standoffish at first.

"You can be mad at me. I deserve
it. But Ronnie, I swear, I'm so sorry
for pushing you away lately. Things
have been . . . uh, bad. We can talk
about that later. I get off in an hour
and a half. I know that's pretty late. . . ."

Zero hesitation. *No! Come over.*
I'll stay up, however long it takes
you to get here. She pauses, and I
can imagine her voice growing
thick in her throat. *Goddamn you,*
Cody, she sputters. *What took so long?*

I haven't cried in a long while,
not since I mostly got over Jack.
I pretty much thought my tear
machine was broken for good.
But no. I can barely choke out,
"I don't know. But I do know

I love you. See you in a little while."
I can't get her off my mind as I drive
to the address Lydia gave me. I feel
awful. Feel wonderful. And for
the first time in a long time, I feel
hopeful. A few more dates, a couple

of big wins, I'll get out of this
business for good. I'll find a real
job. Put money away. Help Mom
somehow. Stay in school, work my
ass off and get into college. Oh, there's
the motel. First things first.

I'm a Little Late

Usually Misty waits for me and we
go in together. Guess she didn't want
the guy to think we weren't coming.
I check the room number. Twice.
One time I knocked on the wrong
door. Was that guy ever surprised!

This time when I knock, Misty calls,
Come on in, baby. I do, find her
already mostly naked. The guy,
who's a totally forgettable middle-aged
nothing, is completely naked.
Jeez, man. I'm only five minutes late.

The dude, who isn't much down
there either, despite it being at full
mast, turns his attention away from
from Misty, focuses on me. *What
are you waiting for? Time is money,
you know.* Like it's going to take him

much time at all. But whatever. It *is*
his money. And less time is better.
Misty distracts him with her yummy
boobs and I start to pull my T-shirt over
my head. Suddenly the door explodes
behind me. What the . . . ?

Something—bear or bulldozer—
knocks me face forward to the floor,
forcing my breath into the carpet.
                    Misty screams and Nothing Man
                              yells, *What the fuck,* as my right
kidney takes two massive punches.

My shirt is still over my head and
I can't see a damn thing as I fight
for air. But I hear *crack-crack-crack.*
And the room goes silent, except
for strained breathing, right above
me. And then I hear . . . sobbing.

                    You fucking whore. It is Chris's voice.
                    You promised . . . no more . . . you
                    said . . . and you . . . he means me.
                    His boot takes out two ribs. Oh
                    my God. Is he going to kill me?
                    Jack! Didn't mean it. Don't want . . .

Snap! Lightning? White-hot. Electric.
Shattering. My back. Pieces. Bone.
Dark. Darker. Cut through the black,
blinding light. What? Buzzing. What?
Suck air. Where? Can't . . . No, please.
Ronnie? Sorry. So sorry. Ron . . .

Light Floats

Just beyond my eyelids. I want
to open them, see the light, but
the darkness is comforting. Not
much here. Beyond the nothing
(nothing? Nothing. Nothing Man?),
something. A hum. A whisper.

Wake up. Can you wake up for me?
Motion. All around me, movement.
Pressure. Wrapping me. Pressure.
Air. Saccharine air, pumping
into my lungs, through . . . plastic.
Plastic? My eyelids stutter. Light!

Sunlight. I am outside. Can't move.
Tied? Strapped. Strapped to a gurney.
Parking lot. Red and blue lights.
Oh my God. I remember. I roll my head,
see another gurney. "Misty?" A cloth
covers her face. "No." It is a whisper.

Best I can do. A second gurney
carries another still figure. Nothing
Man. Gone. Both of them gone.
But I am still here. "Thank you, Jack."
A paramedic asks what I said. "Phone,"
I tell him. "Call Mom. And Ronnie."

A Poem by Eden Streit
Still Here

At least I think so,
what's left of who
I used to be

        a shadow

on the sidewalk.
I look up, try to find
a rainbow, but the only
thing there is

        a lone cloud,

stretching thin
and thinner, clear
to almost not
there, across

        an upside-down sea.

I lower my gaze into
a puddle, close my
eyes at what I see.
Don't want to believe

        that ghost is me.

Eden
I Am Less Than a Ghost

I am a corpse, sleepwalking the streets
of Las Vegas. Sometimes I think

I should just head on out into the desert,
lay down on a soft mattress of sand,

close my eyes against the diamond sun
and circling black wings. And wait.

It might be preferable to this cement bed
behind a 7-Eleven Dumpster.

> There are lots of us living on the street.
> They say Vegas is easier than Reno. *Warmer.*

> *There are shelters,* I've been told, *where
> you can eat free. Shower sometimes. Sleep.*

But I'm afraid of the questions. Too many
questions. So when my stomach offers up

its acid, when I can't stand the hollowness
for another second, I sell one more slice

of my soul. One slice, twenty dollars. I've been
here three weeks. Not much left of my soul.

As for My Body

It's battered, scraped, bruised. The Tears
of Zion shift looks about a hundred years old.

I did spend a few bucks at the Salvation Army.
Bought a used skirt, two tank tops. Underwear.

I hate to think who used them, or why they gave
them away. But they only cost a dime apiece.

I stink, too. I've managed four or five showers,
when the man of the hour wanted to spring for

a motel room. More often, it's the seat of his car.
Quick and easy, five minutes or less. No emotion.

No pain. And the weirdest thing is, I'm not
the least bit embarrassed about doing it anymore.

That's the worst part. That, and when my brain
insists on remembering Andrew. Thinking

about how he held me, rained his love down
all around me, brings devouring pain.

So I'll think instead about the coming night, where
I might peddle the remaining tatters of my soul.

Rush Hour

The freeways are bumper to bumper,
so surface streets jam with commuters.

A few of the pushier girls go straight
up to them at traffic lights, knock on

        their windows. *How about a date?*
        Most of the guys shake their heads.

Some of them look close to panic. Afraid
they might catch something through the glass?

But every now and again, one of them
opens the passenger door and the girl slips

inside. The car takes off, and minutes
later, comes back around, business done.

I watch a girl get out of an older Cadillac.
At least they had plenty of leg room.

        She steps to the curb, stares me down
        with steel eyes. *What are you looking at?*

For some crazy reason, I shatter.
"N-nothing. I m-m-mean I d-don't know."

        Her gaze softens. *New to the biz, huh?*
        Well, sweetheart, this is a real bad place

for tears. *Those guys are freaking sharks.*
If they smell blood, they'll chew you up.

"I know. I'm sorry. It's just that you're
the first person who's even talked to me

since I got here. I mean except to tell
me to suck harder, or . . ."

She cracks up, and so do I. *Yeah, well,*
I know exactly what you mean. Uh, don't

get me wrong, okay? Her nose scrunches
up. *But you could really use soap and water.*

"That bad, huh?" My face actually heats.
Doing disgusting things with gross men

doesn't embarrass me, but her observation,
no doubt deserved, does? "I'm on the street."

She reaches into a pocket on her skirt,
pulls out a thin fold of bills. *Here's fifty*

dollars. Get a room and some food.
And listen, from the looks of you, this

isn't the right business. Get smart. Call
home. You don't belong on the street.

I shake my head. "You worked for that,
and I know what you had to do for it."

Everything about her hardens. *I told*
you to get smart. Take the money.

I don't know what you ran from,
but living like this can't be better.

Funny, but my girlfriend, Ginger, keeps
telling me the same thing. I never wanted

to listen before. Maybe now I'd better.
Her nose wrinkles again. *Call home.*

But shower first. She turns abruptly.
Later, she snorts over her shoulder.

Good Samaritan

The words pop into my head. That
is the second time someone I didn't

know and will likely never see again
handed me money they couldn't afford

to give away. I don't understand. Why
me? Other words surface from a place

of deep indoctrination: *Whatever they
do for the least of my children, they do*

for me. . . . I wander along the overbaked
cement, sucked into a cerebral vortex.

When it finally spits me out again, I am
on the sidewalk in front of a church. Guardian

Angel Cathedral. Catholic. I am struck
by the beauty of the angular architecture,

and by the amazing artwork above my head—
Jesus, hands extended in welcome, to one and all.

I've never once walked beyond the doors
of a Catholic church. But I am drawn inside

this one. I enter, a stranger to the faith.
To the God of this faith and every other.

Friday evening, no worshippers, I find cool
solace inside. I slide into a seat at the rear,

fold my hands. Close my eyes. Do I remember
how to pray? "God, you know I have done

terrible things. I don't want to do them anymore,
and ask for your forgiveness. I am so sorry. . . ."

My voice catches in my throat. Was I speaking
out loud? Just a little more. "Thank you

for good Samaritans. And please, God, please,
if it's your will, show me the way out."

> A sense of peace blankets me, and a gentle
> voice whispers, *How can I help you?*

God? No. There is shallow breathing, too.
I open my eyes. A priest sits beside me.

He reminds me of Andrew—handsome,
and fresh, with compassion in his eyes.

"I don't know how, Father, but I do need help."
Need his help, and God's help, to be saved.

A Poem by Seth Parnell
No Way to Be Saved

No way to hit reverse,
turn around,
go back home.

                        No

chance at forgiveness.
The shale cliffs of

                        redemption

have crumbled,
surrendered to the sea.
How do you look

                        for

miracles when you
deny belief? How can

                        someone

formed of bone and sin
trust his weight to wings?
How does a man

                        like me

find innocence again?

I Don't Remember Innocence

Not, I guess, that I need to.
        Nothing innocent about
        how I live now. Nothing
        naive about being a toy.
That's what I am now. A toy.

But, hey, what are my options?
        I thought about trying to go
        home. Once I even swallowed
        every ounce of pride, put
in a phone call to Dad.

        His raspy voice lifted
            memories, good and not so.
            Hello? Hello? Who the hell
            is this? Then he thought
        a sec. *Seth? Is that you, boy?*

Don't know if it was the "boy,"
        or just remembering his words
        the night he sent me away,
        but I couldn't say a damn
thing. I slammed down

the receiver, retreated into
        a murky cave of depression.
        It's a place I've visited
        more and more lately.
The only thing that seems

to yank me away from there
        is working out. Sweating
        poisons of body and soul.
        Having Jared around to help
me sweat isn't so bad either.

        In the few weeks since he
                started helping me, I can
                see a vast improvement.
                He agrees. *Much better form.*
        Both your lifting, and your body.

He is really close, and the smell
        of his sweat beneath his leathery
        fragrances reminds me of a tack
        room. For some reason, it is
desperately turning me on.

Despite my ballooning
        attraction, I have yet to overtly
        put any sort of moves on Jared.
        He might be taken. And I am
under ongoing ownership.

But no way can I lie back
            on this weight bench without
            that traitorous part of my body
            totally giving me away.
I inhale like I can't find air.

            You okay? he asks. His own
                        breath falls hot on my neck,
                        and the stable smell becomes
                        almost overpowering. Tack.
            Sweat. I remember something.

I was little. Playing at Grandma
            Laura's. Hiding in the tack room.
            Hiding with my cousin, Clay.
            He touched me. There. And it
felt good. So good. So . . . "Oh."

I turn to Jared. What the hell?
            "I'm okay. Except . . ." God!
            "I totally want you." There.
            Said it. He can laugh at me now.
But he doesn't. He kisses me.

We Are Alone

In here. The workout room
        is always deserted midday.
        Still, I might hesitate, but
        Jared is in total control.
    Come on. He leads me into

the sauna, but doesn't turn
        it on. Now our sweat scents
        mingle and the combination
        is heady. There is no need
for words as our bodies link.

He is strong. The first strong
        man I've ever been with, and
        this time I don't give. It is new.
        Frightening. Exhilarating.
But somehow I trust it to be

all right. And it is more than
        that. A piece of my puzzle
        falls into place, a piece I didn't
        know was missing. Fifteen
minutes to Seth, reinvented.

I'm Still Trying

To sort it all out in my head
        when Carl gets home. Early
        for once, and with no company.
        "Oh. Didn't expect you so soon.
I'll start dinner right now."

        Don't bother. He goes into
           the living room, pours himself
        a drink. Does not pour one
        for me. *So tell me. What
did you do today?* The look on

his face explains way too much.
        Something nasty bubbles up
        in my belly. But I'm not
        ready to confess—not yet.
"I read. Swam. Worked out."

        Sounds like a pretty easy day.
           You have it easy here, don't
           you, Seth? He doesn't wait
        for my reply. *So why in the hell
did you want to go and blow it?*

Okay, he knows. But how?
        And what does that mean
        to me? And how much,
        exactly, does he know?
"What are you talking about?"

He advances, sipping his drink
        like he doesn't have a care.
        You know exactly what I'm
        talking about. Did I give you
permission to pick up some

guy in the workout room? Slip
        into the sauna for, shall we
        say, an afternoon quickie?
        Did you think I wouldn't keep
tabs on you? All you young fags

are alike. Simon's philandering
        taught me a lesson—never trust
        a boy toy. And here in Vegas,
        there is no shortage of pretty
faggots, willing to do just about

anything to earn an extra dime.
        That includes acting as bait.
        I didn't expect Jared to follow
        through and actually do you,
but whatever. I start to protest.

Carl holds up a hand. *Shut*
        your mouth. You have twenty-four
        hours to pack up and get
        the hell out of here. Be gone
when I get home tomorrow.

He Will Not Allow

Explanations or arguments.
        He's had his say and I am
        to leave. He doesn't give a damn
        where or how. Won't even front
a few bucks to send me on my way.

I wander into my room, turn on
        my computer—the computer.
        It belongs to Carl. I've got
        less than a day and zero capital
to start completely over.

I have exactly one resource—
        a better, buffer body than when
        I arrived. I'll have to barter
        it more carefully. It's the only
one I have, after all. I go to

Craigslist, Las Vegas Personals.
        Click on Men 4 Men, scan the ads.
        Here's a Help Wanted ad for Have Ur
        Cake Escorts. Just in case, I jot
down the number. But what I'm

really looking for is another Carl.
        There are a few possibilities.
        Can't be too picky. I send
        out several e-mail intros, wait
less than patiently for a response.

A Poem by Whitney Lang
Less Than Patiently

The Lady waits. Pretty
China White demands
I listen, and hold her in

        my arms.

She is my only friend,
my one ally against
the low, throbbing

        ache

inside my brain,
against the loneliness
my heart was not
prepared

        to hold.

Will it break beneath
the obscene weight of

        him

not loving me? How
is it possible I could
have been so very wrong

        again?

Whitney
No Love

In this world for me. No hope.
No future. Nothing but plodding
through each day, not quite
surviving. I am not alive

except when I'm fresh off a plunge,
that first rush after a hot shot.
Then, for scant minutes, life
rages through my veins, a river.

Bryn comes later and later each
day, if he comes at all. Sometimes
I wait, barely hanging on,
wondering if he's back in Santa

Cruz, combing the mall for a new
Whitney. Then I get mad. Not only
because my body is twisted with spasms
of need, but also because I should

be there. Not him. I belong there—
used to belong there. Don't belong
there or anywhere like this. Waiting
for maintenance. And so, I've come up

with a plan. Bryn isn't the only supplier
in Vegas. Sometimes they hang out
at strip clubs. And, I suspect, I can find
one who might be up for a trade.

I watch from a distance as a car
pulls up against the sidewalk, a block
down the street from Skin Tight.
Don't know if the deal was set up before

or if this is a regular haunt for the guy
who goes to the window, collects
some cash, and tosses something at
the passenger. The deal is down in less

than thirty seconds. I can't be sure it
was H without a little scamming of
my own. The guy, who is pretty much
a stereotypical Latino deal-meister,

turns back toward Skin Tight. I sidle
up, flash some thigh. "Hey, honey.
You looking for a little fun?" Already
broke one of Bryn's rules. But this guy

def isn't the heat. He is high himself,
but not on junk. His pupils shout "crystal."
My heart sinks. I start to back away.
More reasons than one for rules, I guess.

The guy grabs my wrist, pulls me
into him. *Hey, now. Where you going?*
You ain't a whore and *a tease, are*
you? 'Cause that might make me mad.

I've gotten a whole lot better at reading
guys since my little choking incident.
This is not a guy I want to make mad.
"No, baby. Just a whore, and a good

one." Might as well play the game
for money if the Lady isn't on the line.
But I'm not giving up on that yet.
"I was just hoping maybe you had

a little something in your pocket."
I run my knee up over his bulging
groin. "Something besides that, I mean,
and something to take me down."

His turn to assess my eyes, looking
for lies. What he finds is a junkie.
He shakes his head. *Don't got no bonita,*
baby. But I could maybe get some.

That's the crystal talking. He wants to
get off, not an easy thing, high on meth.
I hate doing guys on meth. Takes too
long. But hey, this was my deal.

We Agree on a Time

To meet, and a corner three blocks
from my apartment, just in case
Lorenzo can't score. Not having
some crazed meth fiend thinking

he's getting laid with nothing
coming back the other way. After
Mr. Omaha, it was days before I'd
let a john come through my door.

> Bryn was patient. For maybe one day.
> After that he was all, *Get over it already.*
> *Odds are you'll meet up with a creep*
> *once in a while. You had your once.*

He promised to check in more often,
to keep a better eye on me. But it hasn't
happened that way. Ginger has showed
more concern, and I don't even know her.

> She knocks on my door at least
> every other day. *Just making sure*
> *you're still breathing,* she says.
> Doesn't come in very often.

But that's okay. Not like we're best
friends or anything. Girls in the business
don't really have friends. Our lives
are all about acquaintances.

I'm Supposed to Meet

My latest acquaintance soon. Don't
know if I can make it three blocks
without a little help. Please, Lorenzo,
score! I'm getting so low. It's only

been a few hours since my last visit
with the Lady, but I'm shaking like
it was yesterday. Just a small fix for
now. If Lorenzo doesn't come through,

maybe Bryn will show. I only know
I've got to stop the knotting in my belly.
Ah! Better. Have to go while my brain
can still tell my feet to walk. Three blocks.

Lorenzo! Right on time. Fine quality
in a dealer, right? Sexy. Look sexy.
Forget the schoolgirl part. This guy
isn't shopping for innocence. "Hey, doll.

Find what I'm looking for?" He smiles,
takes my hand, slides it down into his
pocket. Not one bag. Two. And,
farther down, something else.

No problem. It's part of the deal.
My guy says dis stuff is pretty good.
You wanna pay for one and fuck
for one, or what? We start to walk.

I have a little cash stashed. Don't tell
Bryn about my "extra" deals. A little
extra cash for a little extra service.
"Sounds good." Meth or no meth,

though, we have to go quick. I'm on
Bryn's clock already. "Before we start,
show me the stuff." He does. It isn't
white or even brown. "What's this?"

> You never seen black tar? Baby,
> it's the best. Believe me, those boys
> in Mexico know their shit. Now come
> over here. Take a taste of this.

I've heard of black tar Mexican.
Never tried it, but guess I'm gonna.
Ol' Lorenzo gets a ride around the world.
Doesn't take as long as I thought.

By the Time He Leaves

The Lady is singing a siren song
to me. Might as well try the black,
see if Lorenzo's acquaintanceship
is worthy of long-term cultivation.

Two bags stashed, might as well take
a real rocket ride. I cook a massive
spoon. Don't even bother to look for
a vein more concealed than on my arm.

Five. Four. Three . . . Whoosh!
Incredible. Lorenzo, I love you, baby.
Rush! Waves of pleasure flood my brain.
It's a regular cerebral orgasm.

Wait. No. Too much. Down I go.
And oh, the noise. The noise inside
my head. Pounding. Blowing.
Exploding like a hurricane.

Close my eyes against the wind.
Spinning in my brain. Air. Need air.
Suck it in. Thick. Can't breathe it in.
Damn stinking carpet. Again. Slow.

Slow. Slow. Heart. Beats. Slow.
Wind. Spins. Inside my head.
Don't like this. Bad wind. Hurricane.
Slow. Sleep. Slow. Sleep . . .

A Poem by Ginger Cordell

Wind

Shuffles autumn feet
across November sand,
stirring grit like

ice

chips. Crystal white.
It blows along
deserted sidewalks,

crusts

lonely avenues. Where
has she gone? Panicked,
I search for

her

in familiar places.
Restaurants. Theaters.
Alleyways adjacent the

heart

of the city. I call out
her name. It returns,
hollow, an echo.

Ginger
Late Night Last Night

Three outcalls, one post-midnight.
        It was a good night for tips, so Alex
and I celebrated with fine Italian

dining and people watching on
        the strip. I slept in this morning,
lay in our bed, still perfumed

with our lovemaking. We don't
        do that so much now. I've missed
it. But more and more, Alex flinches

when I touch her. Not just me,
        I think. But anyone. Everyone.
It took twenty minutes of gentle

kissing and easy massage to arouse
        her even slightly. And while she had
no problem pleasing me, nothing

I did could bring her all the way.
        Sex for Alex is nothing but a job.
It isn't in my power to fix that.

It's strange, really. Strange
        and sad. When we first got here,
it was me who shrank from touch.

Alex taught me the joy of skin
          against my own skin. She showed
me how to feel without fear.

Now she's the one afraid to feel.
          I wish that I could change that.
But she's built a fortress around

her. A sand castle. It's bound
          to crumble. And when the sea
rushes in, I'm afraid she'll drown.

It's Almost Noon

By the time I yank myself out
        of bed. "Alex?" I call, but my
intuition tells me I'm alone.

I check the bathroom, wander
        into the living room. No Alex.
Damn, damn, damn. She can't be

out turning tricks already! What
        is wrong with her? We don't need
the extra money. I don't get it.

I want to find her, drag her
        off the street or out of whatever
car she has gotten into. But Vegas

is a big city. Alex could be
        anywhere. Still, she has a few
favorite places. I clean up,

get dressed, call a cab, head
        out the door. Damn. What's
going on across the parking

lot? Looks like a garage sale.
        Oh. Whitney. An ambulance
took her away a few days ago.

Guess the landlord decided
          she's not coming back and neither
is her sleazy pimp boyfriend.

A small knot of people stand
          around watching the landlord
haul her stuff out of the place.

Sounds like the creep is taking
          offers. I go up to an older lady.
"Everything for sale, huh?"

          The woman barely looks at
                    me. Too busy checking out
          bargains. She shrugs. *Guess so.*

Poor Whitney. How far
          did you run this time?
"Why? Did she . . . is she . . . ?"

          The lady shrugs again. *Don't*
                    know. But hey, those junkies
          are the walking dead, anyway.

Junkies and Whores

Whitney and Alex. No life
       force left behind the lenses.
The walking dead. Spot-on.

      My cab arrives. Not a driver
            I know. *Where to?* he demands,
      tapping the steering wheel like

      he's got somewhere better to
            be. When I hesitate, he drops
      the flag. *Where you want to go?*

I'm not in the mood for snippy
      cabbies. "Just drive down Las Vegas
Avenue. I'll tell you when to turn."

It's my dime. I'll spend it how
      I want to. I have him cruise in
circles, in an area known for

its strip clubs and accompanying
      activities. "Slow down. I might
want you to stop." Feels good to be

the one giving orders for a change.
      I see several working girls. A few
guys. One or two in the "not sure"

category. There. That's her.
        Right there in the plain light
of day, hustling. "Stop here!"

        He pulls to the curb, and I hand
                him two twenties for a thirty-two-dollar
        fare. He looks at me. *Change?*

"Goddamn straight." No tips
        for smart-assed cabbies. Off
he drives in a huff. Good.

Alex doesn't notice me right
        away. Too busy working a guy
in ugly purple Bermuda shorts.

I tap her shoulder. "What's up,
        girlfriend? You're not thinking
about doing this guy, are you?"

        Alex jumps. *Ginger! What
                the hell?* She looks at Bermuda,
        who is seriously checking me out.

        He licks his lips. *Well, hello.
                You're not really her "girlfriend,"
        are you?* Meaning, are you two,

like, lezbos? "Actually, I am
        her girlfriend. Why, you want
to watch?" You effing pervert.

I can't believe how pissed
        I am, or how submissive
Alex is acting. I expected more

            of a reaction. Bermuda reacts
                    for both of them. *Hell yeah!*
            How much to do the two of you?

        Don't say anything, Ginger!
                Alex warns. Who the hell
        died and made her boss?

If she can hustle guys, so can
        I. This one won't get off cheap.
"Three hundred for all you can eat."

            Right on. Bermuda reaches into
                    his back pocket. But it isn't money
            he shows. *Vegas vice.* He flashes

            a badge. *You're under arrest for
                    solicitation.* Then, an afterthought.
            How old are you, anyway?

A Poem by Cody Bennett
Afterthoughts

Why can't an afterthought
be forethought?
Where does

> hindsight

take you if you're
focusing behind you?
What important

> is gained

when the lesson
defies recollection?
When Alice stepped

> through

the looking glass,
did she see herself
backwards, or did
the whole rabbit hole

> experience

simply make her
close her eyes?

Cody
Don't Want to Open My Eyes

If I do, it will mean I admit I'm still
alive. Right now, I think, I could
choose to let go, say a silent good-bye,
and join Jack on the Other Side.
Do I want to do that? Don't think so.
But what if it's better? Until I decide,

I lie here, churning in an anesthetic
sea, inhaling antiseptic air. I'm on
my stomach, and want to turn over,
but something won't let me. And when
whatever painkiller it is they've got
me on starts to wear off, my back catches

fire. While I wait for more, praying
they hurry, a tide of voices rushes in.
    Whoosh: . . . *he should have*
regained consciousness by now. . . .
    Whoosh: . . . *suspect was the girl's*
boyfriend . . . haven't found him yet. . . .

    Whoosh: . . . *know what the boy*
was doing there or his relationship . . .
    Whoosh: . . . *leave me, Cody. Don't*
you dare make me lose you, too.
    Whoosh: . . . *Colts, fourteen; Chiefs, ten.*
Figures. Goddamn loser Chiefs.

Eventually the Tide Recedes

One voice remains. Even if she wasn't
talking, a steady, downstream flow,
I'd know it was Mom by the hills
of her hands. They stroke my face,
gentle my hair from my forehead.
Carry me back to when I was little.

> *I don't know what you've gotten*
> *yourself into, Cody boy . . .* just
> like when I was little . . . *but you*
> *can work your way out of it . . .*
> just like when . . . *I don't know*
> *if I can help you, but I'll try. . . .*

Work my way out. But it's such
a long way out. I don't know if
I'm strong enough. Not even with
your help, Mama. Easier to just say
good-bye. Your hands feel good,
though. I love your hands. . . .

> There's a weird noise. A loud hum.
> *No! Cody!* Footsteps. Running. *Cody,*
> *you come back here right now!*
> More hands. Motion. I am on my back.
> Shit! That hurts. Different hands.
> Pressure. Something covers my nose.

Air. Sweet. Why is it sweet?
In and out of my lungs. Breathing
for me. The hum changes to a steady
blip . . . blip . . . blip . . . Hey, just
like in the TV shows. *Blip . . . blip . . .*
I know what that means. I'm still here.

Mama? Don't cry, Mama. Rub my hair
again. I'll stay for a while. Promise.
Goddamn! My back's on fire again.
But I can't say so. Can't open my eyes.
Can't promise I'll stay. That would
be lying. And I'm so, so tired of lies.

> Voices. Decisions. Voices. I'm okay
> for now. One voice I haven't heard.
> Ronnie, I understand. Hope you know
> I'm sorry. You . . . are . . . are . . .
> Mama's voice again. *His pillow is wet.*
> *Doctor, is he crying? Doesn't that mean . . .*

Yes, Mama. For now. Don't know
how long I'll stay. If I come back,
I'll try my best to change. Mostly change.
Feels good when you rub my head,
Mama. *Blip . . . blip . . .* Odds are good
I'll come back to you, Mama. . . .

A Poem by Eden Streit
If I Come Back

If I come back to you now,
can we be what we were

before

life's uncertain rhythms
tore us so far apart? If

I return

today, will your arms
gather me in, or will

I

be wrenched away,
snatched by a riptide I

have

no power to resist?
If I find my way

to

you, one man standing
in a crowd, will I even

know

who you are?

Eden
Off the Streets

Safely sheltered by the kind people here
at Walk Straight, thanks to Father Gregory.

What is it with me and good Samaritans?
I never believed so many really existed,

never guessed that any of them would ever
reach out and yank me away from hell.

That's where I was. Hell isn't some fiery
pit "down there." It's right here on Earth,

in every dirty city, every yawning town.
Every glittery resort and every naked stretch

of desert where someone's life somersaults
out of control. Satan—Evil—doesn't have

horns or poke you with a pitchfork. His power
doesn't come from full moon sacrifices, and he

doesn't go out looking for new recruits. He
doesn't have to. All he has to do is wait.

Walk Straight

Is an amazing place, a rescue for teen
prostitutes who want to turn their lives

around. All they have to do is ask. I didn't
know to ask, but Father Gregory did.

> *It's run by an exceptional woman,*
> he told me, *an ex-prostitute herself.*
>
> *When she got out, she wanted to help*
> *other young people get off the streets.*
>
> *You'll have a place to live, an education.*
> *They'll help you decide how to shape*
>
> *your future. If you have a pimp, they'll*
> *encourage you to testify against him,*
>
> *and they'll go to court with you so you*
> *don't have to be afraid to put him away.*

When I got here, they cleaned me up,
fed me, had a doctor run some tests.

I'm not pregnant, didn't catch some
horrible disease. I was a little anemic,

but that will change with good nutrition.
I didn't eat nearly so well at Tears of Zion.

My Caseworker

Is named Sarah. She's really nice, but
she does ask a lot of questions, some

of which I'm not prepared to answer.
Sarah: *Where is your home, Ruthie?*

Okay, so I haven't been completely
honest with them. I'm afraid if I give

them my real name, they'll find some
kind of all points bulletin out for me.

So I used my middle name—Ruth. Sarah
added the "ie" to make it "feel friendlier."

I didn't exactly lie when I answered,
"Las Vegas has been my home for a while."

Sarah: *Okay, then. Can you tell me
how you ended up in "the business"?*

More mostly truth. "I never wanted to.
I just didn't know any other way to survive."

Sarah: *I understand. And what about
your parents? Will you tell me about them?*

"They're dead." That was not a lie.
My parents *are* dead. To me.

Boise, Idaho

Is a bittersweet memory, and Tears of Zion
is a wake-up-shivering nightmare. My parents

are zombies, death-walking through both.
I would die before I'd go back, and I'll have

to tell Sarah all of that very soon. Because I did
find a way to get hold of Andrew. His mom is still

a professor at Boise State. And, duh, professors
have e-mail addresses. We have computer access

here at Walk Straight. I e-mailed her two days
ago. She got back to me yesterday.

> *Eden! Thank God you're okay. We've been*
> *so worried! Andrew has searched and*
>
> *searched for you. He pestered your parents*
> *so much, I thought they'd have him arrested*
>
> *again. . . .* She gives a long story about
> the first time they had him arrested, and how
>
> they and some of Papa's congregation
> harassed Andrew until he had to have
>
> his phone number changed. *He'll be so*
> *relieved. How can he reach you?*

I Insisted on E-mail

A phone call would mean somebody
knows and cares I'm here. I'm not

ready to confess that yet, not ready
to think about talking to Pastor Streit

and his not-nearly-as-sweet-as-she-seems
right-hand woman. She will never be Mama

again. I don't know how much I will ever
be able to tell Andrew about the past few

months. I'm changed, and he'll know
that. But does he have to know why?

If he finds out I'm here, I guess he'll figure
out why. I go to the resource room,

> open my Gmail. Oh my God. It's here.
> *Eden,* he writes. *I can't believe it's you.*
>
> *Every prayer answered. When can
> I see you? When are you coming home?*

To the point. All Andrew, in cyberspace.
I type a to-the-point reply: "Not sure

when I'll come home. Lots to talk about.
Just know, now and always, I love you."

A Poem by Seth Parnell
Home

Simple word. Four letters,
two consonants, two vowels,
one of them silent.

Home.

You wish you could walk
through a familiar
door, shout out

the word,

in a simple two-word
sentence: "I'm home!"
But that door

has

been closed to you,
slammed shut in
your face, and

no

amount of pleading
will open it again. Two
consonants, two vowels.
One word without

meaning

when you don't have
a home.

Seth
Always Believed

There would be a way back
        home eventually. Figured
        sooner or later, Dad would
        come around, accept me
for how I was born. Part Mom,

        part him. But no. I did finally talk
                to him on the phone. For all
                of three minutes. *You come
                to your senses? Asked
        the Lord for forgiveness?*

"That's between him and me,
        Dad. And anyway, I never had
        much sense to begin with. I'm
        still who I am, though, no more,
no less. Want you to know I love you."

He didn't budge. Didn't
        say okay, son, come on
        home. Didn't say I'm good
        with you, just how you are.
Didn't tell me he loves me.

I Also Messaged Loren

Found him on Facebook.
        Seems everyone has one of
        those now. "Moved to Las Vegas
        with a friend," I wrote. "Things
didn't work out, so I'm looking

for another place." I hoped, of
        course, that he'd write back,
        confess how much he misses
        me, ask me if maybe I'd like
to give upstate New York a try.

I didn't hear back for quite
        some time. So long, in fact, that
        I was beginning to think he
        was going to ignore me completely.
Finally, though, I got a reply.

Seth. Great to hear from you.
         Glad to know you wound up
         somewhere cosmopolitan.
         I've got some news of my
own. Hope you'll be happy for

me when I tell you I hooked
         up with someone really
         special. You'd like him,
         I think. In fact, he reminds
me a whole lot of you. . . .

Don't Know Where

I'll wind up in the future.
       I have no way to leave Vegas.
       Not for a while. So for now,
       I'll stay here, living with David.
Met him through a friend of a chat

buddy, and so far, so good.
       He choreographs major shows,
       and with over thirty years in
       the business, is something of
a Sin City icon. His house has

ten bedrooms. You could call
       the decor garish, with marble
       statues and white furniture.
       Paparazzi hang around outside
his parties, which are regular.

I have no more with David
              than I had with Carl, except
              for amenities. My life is still
              not my own. But it may never
be. One thing I did take away

from Carl is to try and earn
              a little money of my own,
              save up a small nest egg. Have Ur
              Cake Escorts is my way of doing
that. When David isn't looking.

A Poem by Whitney Lang
When You Weren't Looking

The child became a woman,
though she wasn't ready
to. Don't ask how or

> *why.*

Those questions are not
the important ones.

> *Can't you*

see you didn't

> *care*

enough to notice?
How will you feel
if we have no

> *more*

time together? I wonder
if you're sorry now

> *about*

the way you locked your
heart, access denied to
the beggar at your door.
She's nobody, only

> *me.*

Whitney
Almost Died

That's what they told me. Ninety
percent of me wishes they would
have let me go. Easier than battling
the vicious onslaught of withdrawal.

Easier than coming to terms with who
I was when I almost died. I don't even
know that girl. She's an esoteric
someone, like a movie character

you can't quite recognize. Even
with my head just about straight,
she seems like a caricature—a cartoon
rendition of one of the living dead.

Throughout a week of intensive care,
I drifted in and out of the almost corpse,
not quite warmed by hospital flannel.
Then there were several more days, mostly

conscious as they pumped sustenance
into my veins. Sustenance and heroin
substitutes. Easing me off the Lady.
Pretending they didn't want me to hurt.

I Can't Tell You

Exactly how many days I hovered
somewhere between this world
and another, or which was the scariest.
But the first face I saw, when I decided

I might as well open my eyes, didn't
belong to a doctor or a cop. Or Bryn.
I can't remember ever seeing it so full
of compassion. Who was this woman?

> *Oh, Whitney,* she said. I expected
> a *How could you?* but instead I heard,
> *Thank God you've come back to me.*
> To her? Did I come back to her?

Did I come back at all, and if I did,
would I stay? The jury was still out.
Still is today, a month later. No matter.
That day, her concern surprised me.

Pleased me. Overwhelmed me, though
I'd never admit it in a trillion years.
I pretended indifference. "Nice to see
you, Mother, I guess. Why are you here?"

> My snotty tone should have drawn
> a barb. But no. She came over to
> the bed, took my hand. *I'm so sorry.*
> *If I would have lost you forever,*

I don't know what I would have done.
Please, Whitney, whatever your reasons
for leaving, for . . . for . . . She actually
started to cry. *We can work through this.*

Daddy came in later. Angry.
And Kyra, on semester break.
She was upset that I might have
damaged her reputation. Whatever.

But it has been Mom chipping away
at me, trying to convince me we can
maybe—maybe—become a family
again. I don't know if I want that.

First I have to make it through rehab.
It's a pricey place, with a pretty staff
and lots of mindless activities. The shrinks
even pretend to be nice while they're

picking at my brain. I tell them just
enough to make them believe
they're fixing me. I'm probably
unfixable. But hey, you never know.

A Poem by Ginger Cordell
You Never Know

When a passing cloud
might meet another,
and together unleash

lightning

on thirsting ground.
One insignificant spark

strikes

bone-brittle tinder.
Buoyed by the quiet
breeze, an ember

smolders until

evening wind blows,
carries smoking wisps
upon its wings into

the forest,

sighs into crackling
summer leaves until
the canopy

burns.

So take note of every
passing cloud, because
you never know.

Ginger
Don't Know If It's the Same

Everywhere, but Vegas has
        its very own teen prostitution
court, complete with a special

judge who says he believes
        that underage hookers (my
term, not his) are the victims

of this particular crime. After
        watching him deal with a long
lineup of young tramps (my term

again), I think up to a point,
        he's right. Pimps and johns
are most definitely the criminals

here. The problem is that most of
        the girls in the courtroom, including
Alex and me, were willing victims.

Whatever. We are damn lucky to
        have a judge who cares even a little
about what happens to any of us.

His choices for what to do with
          us are limited. Juvie. Group homes.
Treatment programs, for those

who need them. Hard-core
          repeat offenders spend time in
Caliente, a lockup in mid-nowhere,

Nevada. And for the few
          lucky ones with families
who still care and will take

them, the chance to go home.
          Turned out for once in my
life, I was one of the few.

When I called Gram, she
          freaked. Good freaked,
I mean. All the bad of what

          I've done started spewing
                    from my mouth. She shut me
          up right away. *We can talk*

about that later. Right now,
        tell me what I have to do
to bring you home. She didn't

yell. Didn't cry. Not until
        she told me about Iris. *She's*
dying, Ginger. Advanced HIV.

Gram and the Kids

Really need me now. Iris, too.
            She's wasting away. Docs
say she's got maybe a year.

I tried to get Alex to come
            back to Barstow with me.
She's not budging an inch

from the group home her social
            worker assigned her to. A group
home for pregnant teens. She said,

            *Me and the baby will be just
                        fine. The program will find
            me a job, help me learn how*

            to be a mom. She vows to be
                        a better mother than her own.
            I just hope she's better than mine.

I'll miss her, of course. She's
            been the biggest part of me for
a very long time. But truth is,

the biggest part of me should
            be me. Just have to find her.
Maybe she's even a writer.

A Poem by Cody Bennett
Have to Find

The courage to leap
the brink, let myself fall
beyond the precipice
most people call

life.

I've grown tired of
stumbling, skinning
my knees. If flight

is

possible without
the sting of growing
wings, let me fly

a-

way, above the madness,
to a place where
there is nothing to

gamble

but another go-round.
And, win or lose, there
is a chance at something

after

the penultimate decision.
Because life, and maybe
death, will always be
a gamble after

all.

Author's Note

I am often asked how I decide to write about a certain topic. This one was inspired by a statistic I came across. Did you know that the average age of a female prostitute in the United States is twelve years old? This book doesn't explore the base reason for that statistic—young children are imported into this country from places like Thailand and Africa to serve as child prostitutes. Other books do address that issue, and I may too, one day. But for the purposes of this book, the statistic piqued my interest in teen prostitution. *Tricks* looks at a handful of reasons that might drive a young adult to sell his or her body. Here, and in real life, almost always you can distill the reason to survival.

Prostitution is not a glamorous profession. Even high-priced call girls often end up addicted, abused, or worse. No one deserves the kind of mistreatment often perpetrated by "johns" and pimps. Whatever the reasons for resorting to prostitution, whatever has happened in someone's past, the future is theirs to shape. The first step is to find a way out.

If you or someone you know have reached that place, and are under the age of eighteen, there is help. A wonderful organization called Children of the Night will take you off the street and help you start over. All you have to do is ask. Their hotline number is 800-551-1300. But if you can't remember that, dial 911. Local law enforcement can put you in touch with them.

What is *perfect*?

Keep reading for a glimpse of Ellen Hopkins's new
novel about four teens searching for perfection.

What would YOU give up to be perfect?

Cara Sierra Sykes
Perfect?

How

       do you define a word without
       concrete meaning? To each
       his own, the saying goes, so

why

       push to attain an ideal
       state of being that no two
       random people will agree is

where

       you want to be? Faultless.
       Finished. Incomparable. People
       can never be these, and anyway,

when

       did creating a flawless facade
       become a more vital goal
       than learning to love the person

who

       lives inside your skin?
       The outside belongs to others.
       Only you should decide for you—

what

       is perfect.

Perfection

I've lived with the pretense
of perfection for seventeen
years. Give my room a cursory
inspection, you'd think I have OCD.

But it's only habit and not
obsession that keeps it all orderly.
Of course, I don't want to give
the impression that it's all up to me.

Most of the heavy labor is done by
our housekeeper, Gwen. She's an
imposing woman, not at all the type
that most men would find attractive.

Not even Conner, which is the point.
My twin has a taste for older
women. Before he got himself
locked away, he chased after more

than one. I should have told sooner
about the one he caught, the one
I happened to overhear him with,
having a little afternoon fun.

Okay, I know a psychologist
would say, strictly speaking,
he was prey, not predator.
And in a way, I can't really

blame him. Emily is simply
stunning. Conner wasn't the only
one who used to watch her go
running by our house every

morning. But, hello, she was
his *teacher*. That fact alone
should have been enough warning
that things would not turn out well.

I never would have expected
Conner to attempt the coward's way
out, though. Some consider suicide
an act of honor. I seriously don't agree.

But even if it were, you'd have to
actually die. All Conner did was
stain Mom's new white Berber
carpet. They're replacing it now.

Mom Stands There Watching

The men work, laying mint
green carpeting over clean beige
padding. Thick. Lush. Camouflage.
I sit on the top stair, unseen.

Invisible. Silent. I might as well
not even be here at all. And
that's all right. At least I don't
have to worry that she will focus

> her anger on me. Instead she blasts
> it toward the carpet guys. *Idiots!*
> *You're scratching the patina!*
> Her hiss is like a cobra's spit.

> *I might want to expose that wood*
> *one day. I can't if it's marred.*
> But she never will. That oak
> has been irreparably scarred

by gunpowder-tainted
blood. And even more by
the intent behind the bullet.
Sprawled on the floor,

Conner wanted to die.
Mom and Dad don't think
so. In fact, for once they agree
on something besides how bad

their stock portfolios looked
last year. Both of them believe
Conner only wanted attention.
But he was way past hoping

for that, at least the positive
kind. No, Conner was tired
of the pressure. Sick of trying
to find the equation that would

lighten the weight of expectations
not his own. Listening to Mom
tell skilled laborers how to do
their job is almost enough to make

me empathize. The more she goes
on, the more I'm sure the carpet
guys understand. There is no
possible way to satisfy our mother.

I Guess In A Way

I have to give Conner a little
credit. I mean, by putting the gun
to his chest, he made an overt,
if obscene, statement—

> *I will no longer force myself
> inside your prefab boxes. I'd much
> rather check out of here than let
> you decide the rest of my life.*

"You," meaning Mom and Dad.
The pressure they exert individually
is immense. As a team, it's almost
impossible to measure up

to their elevated criteria. I have done
my best, pushed myself to the limit.
To get into Stanford, I have had to
ace every test, stand out as a leader

(junior class pres, student council),
excel in sports, serve as a mentor,
take command of extracurricular
pursuits—cheerleading, honor choir,

theater. All around dating Sean.
Sometimes I just want a solo vacation.
Hanging out on a beach, submitting
to the temptation of sand, sun, salt

water, sans UV protection. Who
cares what damage they might
inflict on my skin? Nice dream.
But what would my mother say?

> I can hear her now. *Don't be
> ridiculous. Who in their right
> mind would invite melanoma
> and premature aging?*

When I look at her, I have
to admit her beauty regime
is working. It's as if by sheer
force of will she won't permit

wrinkles to etch her suede
complexion. But I know, deep
down, she is afraid of time. Once
in a while, I see fear in her eyes.

That Fear Isn't Something

Most people notice. Not Dad,
who's hardly ever home, and even
when he is, doesn't really look
at Mom. Or me. Not Conner,

because if he had even once seen
that chink in her fourteen-carat
armor, he'd have capitalized on it.
Not her friends. (I think the term

misrepresents the relationship,
at least if loyalty figures into
what it means to be a friend.)
Book club. Bridge club. Gym

spinners. She maintains a flock
of them. That's what they remind
me of. Beautiful, pampered birds,
plumage-proud, but blind

to what they drop their shit on.
And the scary thing is, I'm
on a fast track to that same
aviary. Unless I find my wings.

I Won't Fly Today

Too much to do, despite the snow,
which made all local schools close
their doors. What a winter! Usually,
I love watching the white stuff fall.

But after a month with only short
respites, I keep hoping for a critical
blue sky. Instead, amazing waves
of silvery clouds sweep over the crest

of the Sierra, open their obese
bellies, and release foot upon foot
of crisp new powder. The ski
resorts would be happy, except

the roads are so hard to travel
that people are staying home.
So it kind of boggles the mind
that three guys are laying carpet

in the living room. Just goes to
show the power of money. In less
than an hour, the stain Conner left
on the hardwood will be a ghost.

The Stain

That Conner left on our lives will
not vanish as easily. I don't care
about Mom and her birds.
Their estimation of my brother

doesn't bother me at all. Neither
do I worry about Dad and
what his lobbyist buddies think.
His political clout has not diminished.

As twins go, Conner and I don't share
a deep affection, but we do have
a nine-months-in-the-same-womb
connection. Not to mention

a crowd of mutual friends. God,
I'll never forget going to school
the day after that ugly scene.
The plan was to sever the gossip

grapevine from the start with
an obvious explanation—
accident. Mom's orders were
clear. Conner's reputation

was to be protected at all costs.
When I arrived, the rumors
had already started, thanks
to our neighbor, Bobby Duvall.

> *Conner Sykes got hurt.*
> *Conner Sykes was shot.*
> *Conner Sykes is in the hospital.*
> *Is Conner Sykes, like, dead?*

I fielded every single question
with the agreed fabrication.
But eventually, I was forced to
concede that, though his wounds

would heal, he was not coming
back to school right away.
Conner Sykes wasn't dead.
But he wasn't exactly "okay."

When People Ask

How he's doing now, I have
no idea what to say except for,
"Better." I don't know if that's
true, or what goes on in a place

like Aspen Springs, not that anyone knows he's there, thank God.
He has dropped off most people's
radar, although that's kind of odd.

Before he took this unbelievable
turn, Conner was top rung on our
social ladder. But with his crash
and burn no longer news of the day,

all but a gossipy few have quit
trying to fill in the blanks.
One exception is Kendra, who
for some idiotic reason still

loves him and keeps asking about
him, despite the horrible way he
dumped her. Kendra may be pretty,
but she's not especially bright.

Kendra Melody Mathieson

Pretty

That's what I am, I guess.
I mean, people have been telling
me that's what I am since
I was two. Maybe younger.

                                        Pretty

as a picture. (Who wants
to be a cliché?) Pretty as
an angel. (Can you see them?)
Pretty as a butterfly. (But

                                        isn't

that really just a glam bug?)
Cliché, invisible, or insectlike,
I grew up knowing I was
pretty and believing everything

                                        good

about me had to do with how
I looked. The mirror was my best
friend. Until it started telling
me I wasn't really pretty

                                        enough.

Pale Beauty

That's what my mom calls the gift
        she gave me, through genetics.

We are Scandinavian willows,
        with vanilla hair and glacier blue

eyes and bone china skin. Two
        hours in the sun turns me the color

of ripe watermelon. When I lead
        cheers at football games, it is wearing

SPF 60 sunblock. Gross. Basketball
        season is better, but I'll be glad

when it's over. Between dance lessons
        and vocal training and helping out

at the food bank (all grooming for Miss
        Teen Nevada), I barely have time for

homework, let alone fun. At least
        staying busy mostly keeps my mind

off Conner. I wish I could forget
　　　　about him, but that's not possible.

I tumbled hard for that guy. Gave him
　　　　all of me. I thought we had something

special. He even let me see the scared
　　　　little boy inside him, the one not many

other people ever catch a glimpse of.
　　　　Did he show that boy to the ambulance

drivers who took him to the hospital, or
　　　　to the doctors and nurses who dug the bullet

out of his chest? Sewed him up. Saved
　　　　his life. I want to see him, but Cara says Saint

Mary's won't allow visitors. Bet he doesn't
　　　　want them—scared he might look helpless.

What He Doesn't Get

Is that everyone gets scared. I used
        to get sick to my stomach every day

before school. Reading, writing,
        and arithmetic? Not my best things.

I just knew some genius bully
        was going to make major fun of me.

Then I figured out Rule Number One
        of the Popularity Game—looks trump

brains every time. While it might be
        nice to have both, I'll settle for what

I've got. College isn't a major goal.
        Don't need it to model. Everyone says

I have what it takes to do runway.
        I don't think I do yet. But I will.